FIRE TEAM

A MASON SHARPE THRILLER

LOGAN RYLES

INKUBATOR
BOOKS

To my Advance Team...
For years for feedback, support, and enthusiasm. You rock.

Published by Inkubator Books
www.inkubatorbooks.com

ISBN (eBook): 978-1-83756-261-9
ISBN (Paperback): 978-1-83756-262-6
ISBN (Hardback): 978-1-83756-263-3

1

"Ladies and gentlemen, this is a robbery!"

The front door of the bank blew open, followed immediately by a string of rapid rifle shots cracking like firecrackers inside the sprawling building. I spun around in the office chair, my vision snapping toward the main entrance.

Two men, both dressed in all black from head to toe, faces obscured by ski masks. The first held a shortened AR-15–style rifle pressed into his shoulder, the muzzle sweeping the lobby. The second dangled a similar weapon from a one-point sling, an oversized backpack riding his shoulders while he bolted the doors. People lined up at the teller counter screamed and ducked for cover behind the credenza. The banker sitting across from me choked and dropped the phone pinned against his ear, fumbling beneath his desk for the silent alarm.

But it was much too late for that.

"Stay calm," I hissed, my own heart accelerating as the

second man in black finished with the doors and brandished his own rifle.

"Everybody on the floor!" Number One said. "Hands up, cell phones out. Let's move!"

"You hit the alarm?" I asked.

The banker nodded like a bobblehead, his face chalk white. I held up a hand to calm him while I tracked the two men toward the credenza. Number One kept his rifle at the ready while Number Two corralled the bank customers into the lobby—maybe ten of them, now all lying facedown on the dingy carpet, hands and legs splayed. Cell phones spinning into a pile.

I kept my voice low. "They're not here to hurt you, they're just here for the money. Don't panic."

The banker might have nodded again, I wasn't looking. Number One saw us through the glass panel of the recessed office and pointed his rifle at my face.

"You two! Out of the office. *Move!*"

We complied, stepping through the open door with hands raised.

"On the floor. Join the others. Hustle, fat ass!"

The last comment was directed at the banker. He stumbled, tears streaking his jiggling cheeks as he reached the pile of hostages. I dropped to my knees and lowered myself slowly onto the floor, measuring my breaths. Recalling SERE training in the Army.

A special hell of a school, dedicated to teaching soldiers how to survive capture by the enemy. Easily my least favorite portion of my entire stint in the military, but the lessons it taught came flooding back. Lessons about remaining calm. Humanizing yourself to the enemy. About not doing anything stupid.

I hit the carpet as Number One stood over me with his rifle, his companion clearing the other offices and the teller line in short order, driving the bank staff to join us on the lobby floor. The pile of cell phones grew rapidly, and the bank manager mumbled a plea for the safety of her staff.

A brave woman, but speaking at the wrong time. She caught a backhand across the face, not all that hard, but sudden enough to earn a gasp from the knot of people on the floor.

"On your stomach, sister!" Number One ordered. "Keep your mouth shut."

The manager went down with the rest, and the two men circled. I twisted my face toward the main door, looking beyond panels of glass, past a bank of elevators, to another row of glass doors that faced out over the parking lot and the street beyond. The bank was situated on the first floor of a fifteen-story building, the other floors presumably still accessible by elevator.

If the silent alarm hadn't worked, an office worker exiting the elevators would see us soon enough. This wasn't a well-conceived robbery.

I remained loose.

"All right! Here's how it's gonna go down," Number One shouted through his ski mask. I noted an East Coast accent. Definitely American by birth. Not New England. His tone sounded more central, but still carried that snap and pop of big-city energy. "Anybody who's caught with a phone gets my boot in their face, so if you held one out, you'd better toss it now. We're not here to hurt you. We just want the money. Am I clear?"

No answer, just a murmur of panic, followed by another string of blaring gunshots directed at the ceiling. Three of them, not automatic, but pressed together by the rapid use of a trigger finger. Brass rained across the carpet, and a woman shrieked.

"When I ask a question, you answer. *Am I clear?*"

This time a murmur of agreement rose from the crowd. I kept my mouth shut, focusing on what I could see of the men. Just black boots and black pants, joined by an oversized black bag I hadn't noticed before.

"Okay." The leader spoke again. "That's better. Now work with me, and we'll be out of your hair in time for lunch. Where's the head teller?"

Another hesitation. A foot landed hard on the carpet, right between my nose and the nose of a young woman with raven black hair. She faced me, her cheek pressed into the floor, one panicked eye visible over the toe of the boot. Late twenties or early thirties, maybe. Aging another five at present.

"Stay calm," I mouthed.

"*Where is the head teller?*"

"R-right here!" somebody choked. "That's me!"

"Great. On your feet. You too, Wonder Woman."

The bank manager was dragged to her feet alongside the head teller—a skinny Hispanic guy. They both looked ready to faint, but they had nothing to worry about. I figured the vault worked in halves, like the missile codes on a nuclear submarine. The captain and the executive officer were both needed for a launch to occur—or in this case, for the vault to open.

"Let's move!" Number Two took over. He propelled the two bank staff toward the vault while Number One kept the muzzle of his rifle sweeping the crowd. The faint smell of gunpowder still hung in the air, mixed with the infrequent moan or whimper of a strained voice choked by tears and panic.

I rolled my head an inch, just enough to stare up Number One's pants leg. He was shorter than his companion, but stood straight, holding his rifle at low ready, trigger finger stiff against the receiver. Shoulders loose. Eyes up and moving.

From the vault, Number Two snapped an unintelligible command, and something clanged. I pictured the bank manager and the head teller scooping cash out of the dual-access vault. Probably less of it than the gunman expected. I doubted banks carried all that much cash anymore. Why take the risk in a cashless society?

This wouldn't take long. With every passing second, the value of *just one more dollar* would be offset by the increased risk of being caught. They would take what they had and split for the white panel van parked under the portico outside, leaving the bank staff and patrons alike to clean out their pants. A terrifying but relatively harmless experience.

"Back to the lobby!" Number Two shouted from the vault room. The manager and head teller stumbled out of the vault room, back into the open lobby. They dragged a duffel bag between them, half full and not that heavy, dropping it as they reached the knot of bank staff and customers.

"Back on your face!" Number One ordered. The pair complied, returning to the floor. But I didn't see Number Two. Number One now looked toward the vault room.

Rotating my face in that direction, my view was blocked by a pair of desks resting in the middle of the expansive lobby. But in the momentary stillness, I thought I heard a sound. A dull scratch, followed by a whoosh. Vaguely familiar to me, but not in a firsthand way. Like a sound I had heard in a movie.

Number One's body remained loose, dark eyes perfectly calm behind the ski mask. Lifting his wrist to his mouth, he spoke a calm word into an invisible mic.

"Sitrep?"

Whatever reply he received must have been channeled through an earpiece. I didn't hear a voice, but I did hear an intensified whooshing from the vault. I remembered the oversized backpack Number Two wore, and suddenly the noise made sense.

A *blowtorch*. The guy was going for the safety-deposit boxes. Was he out of his mind?

I twisted my arm to look at my watch, guesstimating how much time had passed since the two men had burst into the building. Not less than six minutes. Maybe eight.

The police would be here in no time. They could be screaming this way even now. And that *wasn't* a good thing. The moment cops arrived, this would become a hostage situation. A standoff with no clear resolution. A potentially lethal predicament.

"You should go now," I said, keeping my voice calm. "Somebody on an upper floor will have heard the gunshots. The cops will be here soon. Take the cash and leave."

I braced myself for a boot to my exposed ribcage, but Number One didn't even flinch. He calmly checked his own watch and remained silent. I lifted my head an inch and surveyed the pileup of people gathered around me. It was a hodgepodge of humanity if ever I'd seen one. Young bank tellers in pants suits. A Hispanic guy in a dirty T-shirt with a landscape company logo, clutching a cross necklace with his eyes closed. A fat guy in a sweat-soaked white dress shirt, heaving and red-faced.

And the raven-haired woman next to me, clutching her purse for dear life, her face still streaked with drying tears.

"Hey, asshole! Head down!"

Number One toed me in the ribcage, and I dropped my face. The whooshing continued from the vault room, hissing now and again as the oxygen lever on the torch was depressed to make a white-hot cut.

And then I heard another sound. Distant at first, enough so that I hoped I had imagined it. But ten seconds later it was louder. Screaming toward us, wailing like a hurricane wind.

A police siren.

2

"Cops inbound." Number One spoke into his wrist mic again, his voice every bit as calm as before, but his dark eyes darting with nervous energy toward the front door. A man in a business suit had just stepped out of the elevator. He held a cell phone against one ear, his face washing pale as he looked into the bank. The gaping mouth of Number One's AR-15 spun toward him, and the guy ran.

"You should go *now*," I repeated. "Clear the parking lot before the cops get here."

Number One ignored me, bending to scoop up the cash bag. Another metallic clang rang from the vault room, and Number One peered in that direction. Ignoring the wrist mic, he shouted this time.

"We good?"

"Jackpot!" a shout returned from the vault room, followed by pounding boots. "Let's roll!"

Number Two appeared with the backpack slung over his left shoulder, his right hand now gripping his rifle. From the vault room the smell of burnt metal and soot drifted into the lobby, followed a split second later by the shriek of a fire alarm. I rotated my head toward the ceiling just in time to see the sprinklers spin to life, unleashing a deluge of cold, over-chlorinated water.

I was instantly soaked, but even through the scream of the fire alarm, I heard the police sirens racing in. I saw blue lights blaze from the parking lot. A black and white Ford Taurus flashed beyond the parked panel van. My stomach tightened as the two men in black hesitated over the bank staff and patrons, momentary indecision dragging the seconds into slow motion.

Don't do it. Please don't do it.

"We're blocked," Number Two snapped. "Pick two. Let's go!"

Number One turned, and his rifle rose. Those dark eyes swept the crowd, skipping over me and surveying the other water-saturated bodies. He paused briefly on the landscaping guy, then stopped at the overweight man in the now drenched dress shirt.

"Him," he said. "And the woman."

Number One's rifle pointed to the woman lying next to me—the one with raven hair, still clinging to her handbag. He grabbed her by the shoulder and hauled her up.

"On your feet, honey! Time to take a ride."

My stomach tightened, but I didn't move. There was nothing to be done now. As much as I wanted to step in, doing so would dramatically increase the odds that somebody would wind up shot.

Number Two advanced to the man in the dress shirt, grabbing him by his soaked collar. "Let's go, doughboy!"

The guy's flushed face washed pale. He choked and staggered to his feet, wheezing hard. Something spilled out of his hand and spun on the carpet as torrents of water streamed down his chest.

It was an asthma inhaler. My gaze snapped upward again, and I noted bloodshot eyes rolling back in his head. His body went limp, and then he stumbled sideways.

"Hey! *Wake up!*" Number Two shook him, but it was too late. The guy fell like a tree, collapsing on the saturated carpet.

"He's having an asthma attack!" I said, lifting my head. "It's okay. Take me! I'll go."

I rose to my knees, water streaming from my face. Number Two looked to the floor, noting the inhaler. Then he cast a glance toward his companion. It was a brief moment, a hesitation. Indecision.

"He'll do," Number One said.

Number Two jammed his rifle's muzzle toward me, and I rose without complaint. Both hands up, my light sweater clinging to my chest. I didn't even feel the cold. My heart beat in steady rhythm, calmed by systematic breathing that kept natural panic at bay, even as the rifle rammed into my ribcage.

"Okay, Superman. You asked for it. Let's move!"

I fell in next to Raven—her dark hair now sodden and dripping. The four of us marched to the main doors. Outside, the flash of blue lights had doubled—two cars now, with more screaming toward us from not far away. The first sat just beyond the panel van, the driver's door slung open, a blue and gold shield emblazoned across white paint:

Office of Sheriff, Jacksonville Police.

A cop in a blue uniform knelt beyond the engine bay, his arms extended over the hood, pointing a Glock handgun dead at us.

Not good.

Number Two twisted the door lock, holding Raven at gunpoint, the muzzle of his rifle pressed into her ribcage.

"Okay, hotshot," Number One said to me. "You'll go first, hands up. Try anything smart, and the chick gets it. You got me?"

I nodded. "Got it."

The lock snapped open, and Number Two pushed on the glass. Then a commotion erupted behind us. Muted cries, and somebody shouting, "*Don't!*"

I looked over my shoulder in time to see one of the patrons rising from the floor. An old guy, maybe seventy, with white hair protruding from beneath a dripping *Vietnam Veteran* ball cap. His right hand rose from his hip, polished steel dripping with water, a gaping muzzle swinging toward the door.

"*No!*" I shouted.

It was too late. The bank rang with the harsh snap of the 1911's safety disengaging, followed almost instantly by the crack of gunfire. Orange flame was matched by shattering glass as a heavy .45-caliber bullet zipped past my face and broke through the door. I hurtled forward, shoving the door open as the two bank robbers followed. Neither one pivoted to return fire. They shoved Raven ahead as the 1911 continued to thunder; then Number One grunted in pain. Raven stumbled and almost fell. Outside, cops shouted and ducked for cover. I rammed through the second door with both hands up, screaming over the parking lot.

"Don't shoot! Armed civilian firing from inside!"

A heavy hand ripped me sideways. I staggered toward the van. Number Two yanked the rolling back door open while Number One hurled himself through the passenger door. Blood streamed from his shoulder, his left hand clamped over the wound while his shortened AR-15 rode from its sling. The next thing I knew, I was falling into the empty rear of the van, my elbows biting metal. The black duffel bag hit the floor next to me, and Raven piled in, still clutching her handbag like some bizarre kind of shield. The door rammed shut behind us, and Number One shouted from the passenger seat.

"Go! Go! Go!"

3

Number Two took the wheel. The van fired up, but I didn't hear shots from the cops or the Vietnam veteran. Tires screamed, and both myself and Raven tumbled in the empty back, slamming against metal walls as the vehicle hurtled forward. Sirens screamed someplace outside, and Number Two yanked his ski mask off, exposing tangled blond hair and panicked eyes. I propped myself against the wall and grabbed Raven's shoulder just in time to stop her from face-planting into hard steel.

"Left! Make for the bridge!"

Number One shouted directions, his ski mask also removed. Brown hair, cut close above his ears. Dark eyes and one hand still clamped over his shoulder. The other held the shortened AR, the muzzle bouncing and swaying erratically, but pointed generally into the back of the van.

"You two try something and you both get it!" Number One shouted.

I wasn't in any position to try something. The floor beneath me erupted upward, sending both me and Raven hurtling toward the ceiling as a speed bump passed beneath the tires. We hit the floor again in a tangled heap, immediately sliding toward the wall as Number Two hung a hard left through an intersection. Horns blared, and tires screamed. I was conscious of sirens behind us and caught a glimpse of a red traffic light through the windshield.

The van didn't slow. Not even a little. The tall gray towers of downtown Jacksonville faded into a blur as we gained speed. The van lunged as it hit a curb, then bounced onto a sidewalk. Human screams joined the police sirens, and Number Two laid on the horn.

"Out of the way! Move it!"

I fought my way into a seated position, clinging to the rear wheel well and looking for Raven. Before I could locate her, we spun through another intersection, the top of the van swaying to the point I thought we might roll, two tires hopping, the other two screaming. Another blast of horns and a crunch of metal as a passing vehicle clipped the van's back bumper.

We didn't roll. We leveled out instead as Number Two planted his foot on the accelerator.

"Bridge coming up!" he shouted. Then, glancing sideways for the first time at Number One, "You good?"

"Right shoulder," Number One said. "Arm is gone. Working on blood flow."

"Copy. Hang tight."

The van hit another bump, softer this time. A change in pavement, maybe. Asphalt to concrete. Road to bridge. I looked through the windshield to see the dull blue of a bridge superstructure rising ahead of us—one of the several bridges that crossed the St. John's River in downtown Jacksonville, from the south bank to the north. Number Two accelerated again.

A small hand closed around my arm. Raven had clawed her way next to me, still clutching her handbag as though her life depended on it. Eyes wide, mascara running down her cheeks, hair disheveled. One shoulder of her blouse torn and dropping over her arm. I could see the panic in her face, her chest heaving.

"Stay calm," I said. "We're gonna be okay. Give me your hand."

I reached out for her hand as the tone of the tires changed from a hum to a high-pitched whir. We had crossed onto metal—maybe a section of drawbridge somewhere near the middle of the faded blue superstructure. Number Two laid on the brakes as red taillights blocked our path ahead. He hit the horn and shouted.

Raven's gaze darted, moving from the swaying muzzle of Number One's AR to the windshield.

And then to the rolling side door.

I knew what she was about to do before it happened, but I moved a microsecond too late. Raven lunged for the door, wrenching the handle open. Metal shrieked, and the door slid open. Number One shouted from the front seat, wheeling around and dropping his AR.

"Stop!"

He shot his good arm around the seat back, grabbing Raven by her shoulder and jerking. The van swerved, and she twisted, arms flailing as she lost her balance. The handbag flew through the open door, and I caught the back of her bra strap just in time to prevent her from tumbling face-first into rushing concrete. She slipped, and her knees hit the metal floor. Number Two tapped the brakes, and the rolling door rushed forward, ready to smash her skull in the door jamb.

I yanked on the bra strap, hauling her backward. The door crashed shut.

Then Number One was on top of us, exploding out of his seat and into the back of the van. The AR was back in his good hand, the muzzle driving Raven away from the door.

"Are you out of your mind? Get on the floor!"

I released Raven and pushed her aside, placing myself in front of the erratically swinging rifle muzzle. The muzzle brake clipped my lip, and I tasted blood. The van hit another bump, and I almost fell, catching myself on the back side of the passenger seat in time to keep my body pressed between Number One and Raven.

"Back off!" I shouted.

The floor was now slick from our saturated clothes, but a streak of red joined the sprinkler water. Blood, from my lip or from Number One's gunshot wound. I wasn't sure, but when I looked up the swaying barrel of the AR into his strained face, I saw the color leaving his cheeks. He kept his left hand clamped over the gunshot wound to his right arm, his right hand barely clinging to the weapon.

He'd lost blood. Maybe a lot of it. Much more, and he'd pass out.

"Put the gun down, and I'll help you," I said calmly. "I'm battlefield medicine trained. I can stop the blood."

Number One staggered back against the wall, putting some distance between us. He cast a nervous glance toward the rearview mirror, meeting Number Two's gaze. For the first time I saw real uncertainty in his eyes.

"I was in the Army!" I snapped. "I can patch you up. Stop fooling around, or you're gonna bleed out."

From the driver's seat, Number Two nodded. Number One pressed his back against the wall of the van and slumped into a seated position. The vehicle lurched again as we left the far end of the bridge, now entering Jacksonville's north shore. I ignored the flashing buildings as Number One pointed the AR toward my gut, propping the weapon up on his thigh.

"Do it." He spoke through gritted teeth, still clutching his arm.

"Gun down," I demanded. "I don't care if you bleed out."

Another hesitation. Then he flicked the selector switch to *SAFE* and held his finger against the receiver. He didn't lower the weapon.

I rolled my eyes and reached into my pocket, my fingers closing around the Victorinox Locksmith I always carry. An oversized Swiss Army knife with a locking, three-inch blade. That blade snapped open, and momentary panic flashed across Number One's face. But I wasn't going for his throat. I rammed the blade through my sweater, cutting a strip off the bottom. Two feet long, four inches wide.

I dropped the knife on the floor. "Give me your arm."

He released his arm reluctantly, exposing the wound. The .45 slug had been a round-nosed target round. Not a mushrooming hollow point. That much was clear, because he still had most of his arm. The slug had torn through the inside of his bicep, missing the bone, but taking a chunk of muscle with it and leaving a wicked exit wound.

Blood rushed out the moment he moved his hand, and I rammed a wad of the sweater strip into the exit wound. Then I wrapped a strip around the bicep, just above the entry wound, and cinched down hard.

"You got a pen?" I directed the question at Raven,

steadying myself as the van lurched around another corner. The sirens were constant now, screaming just behind us. The cash bag slid, slamming into my feet. Raven clung to the vehicle's wall, wide eyes gazing vacantly at me.

"A pen," I repeated. "Something stiff, straight, and strong?"

"In the bag," Number One wheezed. "There's a screwdriver."

"Get it." I jerked my head to the bag, and Raven finally moved. She unzipped the lid and dug through it, dumping out banded stacks of cash and a mess of grandma's jewelry.

Proceeds from a safety-deposit box, no doubt.

I met Number One's gaze as Raven passed me the screwdriver. A good part of me wanted to ram it straight through his eye, but with Number Two driving, it wasn't worth the risk. I couldn't count on Raven to protect herself if we went hurtling into an office building.

Sticking the shaft of the screwdriver through the folds of the sweater strip, I twisted, rotating again and again. Cinching that strip down until the veins and arteries were cut off, then binding the handle in place with the tail end of the sweater strip.

"You good?" Number Two shouted from the driver's seat as the engine roared again.

"All good," Number One hissed, flicking the selector switch back to *FIRE* just as I released the screwdriver. The muzzle of the weapon pressed into my gut.

"Secure them," Number Two said. "We're about to hit the highway."

4

Number One jabbed me with the AR. The thrust was shaky, his body no doubt weakened by the loss of blood. But I figured his trigger finger was still good, and at three inches, the velocity of a 5.56 NATO round would be enough to eviscerate my chest cavity.

"Get against the wall," Number One growled. I inched back, resting my shoulder blades against the interior of the rolling door.

"In the bag," Number One continued, addressing Raven now. "Get the zip ties. Tie his hands."

She complied, her face still a mask of streaking black mascara and pale skin. She found the zip ties buried beneath another stack of cash. I kept my shoulders loose and my hands in my lap as the first one closed around my wrists, the plastic tick of the locking mechanism tightening until it almost cut off the blood flow to my fingers.

They weren't the cheap, flimsy zip ties you buy at Walmart. These were the heavy, wide kind you find at a hardware store. Almost industrial quality. Number One growled at Raven until she had fixed my hands with three of them, and my ankles with two more. I watched my Victorinox spinning across the sheet metal floor of the van as Number Two swerved around a truck on the highway, and I mentally kicked myself for not taking my chances with the screwdriver.

It might have resulted in a wreck, but at least it would have been a low-speed wreck. My initial strategy had been to buy time and calm the guy with the AR down, but every passing minute seemed to worsen our predicament by an order of magnitude.

"Now you." Number One addressed Raven again, jabbing at her with the AR. "Sit down and hold out your wrists."

Raven swallowed hard. She descended into a seated position along the opposing wall near the rear of the van, and Number One knelt sideways on the floor with the rifle resting on his knees, pointed at my face. It took him a moment to zip-tie her wrists, and I contemplated making a lunge for his weapon. With my hands tied, it would be difficult to use. Maybe not impossible, but there was also a chance he got off a shot first. Inside an all-metal vehicle, even a miss could be deadly.

I remained still, and Number One finished with Raven's wrists. Then he retrieved my fallen Victorinox and fought to get the blade closed. It disappeared into his pocket, and he staggered backward toward the front passenger seat, the muzzle of the AR still sweeping between Raven and me.

"Another stunt from either one of you, and you both get it. You hear me?"

Raven nodded. I just stared.

Number One's lip twitched, and his face remained pale,

but something in his eyes felt...wrong. He didn't look panicked. He didn't even look afraid.

He looked as cold and collected as an elite quarterback stepping onto the gridiron with a two-score lead.

"How we looking?" Number One called toward the driver's seat.

"Six cars on our ass!" Number Two answered. "I think I hear a chopper."

Number One spat across the floor, and I joined him, discharging blood from my busted lip. Our gazes met, and I narrowed my eyes.

"Thank you for your service," Number One said, sarcasm tainting his tone. I didn't answer, and he staggered back to the cabin. Sitting sideways in the passenger seat where he could keep the AR pointed into the back, he fumbled a cell phone with his bad hand, struggling before finally dialing 911.

I kept my mouth shut, watching his every move. Noting a rippling scar poking from beneath his sleeve. Measuring that same elite quarterback glint in Number Two's eyes whenever he glanced into the rearview mirror.

And feeling very confused. Because none of what I observed in either man aligned with their actions.

The emergency operator picked up, and Number One went straight to barking at her, not giving her time to question.

"I'm calling from the van headed west on I-10. We have two hostages, and we'll kill them both if the cops don't *back off!*"

He hung up and deposited the phone into the cup holder. I listened to the wail of sirens behind us, a full orchestra of them, sounding a little like a bad high school band. Maybe a dozen cops, with more on the way. The van vibrated a little as a hurricane-force wind passed briefly overhead, joined by a chopping sound, and I thought about a police helicopter.

A narrow highway. Headed in one direction. Aerial surveillance crushing down from ahead, the hounds on our heels.

We weren't escaping. Not one chance in hell.

I leaned against the van wall, noting Number Two's frequent glances into his sideview mirrors as he relaxed the van to an easy fifty-five miles per hour. The cops behind us relaxed also, not closing or surpassing. Biding their time as the temporary stalemate continued.

The whole bizarre scenario reminded me of OJ Simpson in his white Ford Bronco, rolling slowly down a California highway with an army of cops on his heels and helicopters beating overhead. A gun held to his own skull. An imperfect standoff with only one possible ending.

My heart rate calmed, and I turned to check on Raven. She lay curled up next to the wall, bound hands pressed protectively over her chest. The raccoon makeup on her face gave her a wild and crazed look, but she was no longer shaking or crying. She kept her gaze glued to the muzzle of the AR pointed randomly into the back of the van.

"We'll be okay," I whispered.

She caught my eye, but I wasn't sure if she had heard me. I didn't risk speaking twice. I thought instead about SERE training. About negotiating with my captors. There was a fine line between keeping an open dialog and provoking rash action, but the energy in the cabin had cooled considerably. Both men relaxed in their seats now, monitoring the mirrors and the open lanes ahead. I didn't see many cars, and I wondered if the police were clearing the highway. Trying to prevent additional casualties when things inevitably escalated.

"You should pull over," I said. "There's no chance you'll escape now. Let's work together and come up with a story. I'll do what I can for you."

No reply from the cabin, but I felt Raven's eyes on me. Number Two flicked the van's console open and retrieved bottles of water. The two men guzzled, still monitoring their mirrors as though their prisoners and the pile of cash behind them had ceased to exist.

"You ever read about OJ?" I prompted. "There's only one way this ends. The longer you keep it going, the more chance they place a sniper on the next overpass."

Still no response. Not even a blink. I narrowed my eyes, glancing once to Raven.

"Shut up," she mouthed. Her eyes were wide again, the panic returning. The raccoon makeup now glistened with sweat.

I leaned against the wall, adjusting my bound hands as the lack of blood flow made my fingers burn. Now that the adrenaline had begun to fade from my body, frustration was taking over. Frustration...and more confusion.

The phone in the console buzzed, and Number One snatched it up. To my surprise, he placed the device on speaker as he answered with only one word: "Speak."

"This is Special Agent Ron Whitmer with the FBI." The voice was calm and collected, speaking with just a hint of authority, but not overbearing. A hostage negotiator, I thought. Probably from the Jacksonville field office.

"What do you want, Agent?" Number One demanded.

"I want what you want—to find a way out of this mess."

It was a nice line, but neither Number One nor Number Two seemed the least bit intrigued.

"I received your request for police presence to back off," Whitmer continued. "I'm working on that now, but you have to meet me halfway. I need to know that the hostages are alive and unharmed."

Number One didn't answer. Number Two remained fixated on the road. It was as though they hadn't heard the comment. Whitmer waited ten seconds, then pressed ahead.

"What's your name? Who am I speaking with?"

No answer. Number One tilted his water bottle back and drained it, then bent his neck to peer into the sky.

"Are you still with me?" Whitmer said.

Number One pointed, marking what I thought to be the location of the chopper. Number Two nodded.

"Let's work together, here," Whitmer said. "Tell me what you need, and—"

"How about this?" Number One snapped. "Lose the chopper, or I waste the woman and dump her body out a window. You have thirty seconds."

Then Number One hung up.

5

The chopper pulled off immediately, but I still saw flashing lights in the driver's side rearview mirror. Number Two accelerated again, bringing the van up another twenty miles per hour until the floor vibrated and the engine howled.

The cops kept pace, their sirens a little more distant, but still audible. Still right on our heels.

The status quo unchanged.

With nothing else to do, I relaxed against the wall and focused on calming Raven. I shot her a reassuring smile and shrugged as though our predicament were nothing more than a daily aggravation. She looked less sure, still fixated on the AR even though the muzzle now pointed toward the van's floor. Number One clutched his arm again, wiping away a trail of blood that had oozed through my makeshift bandage. I could see the pain on his face—more than pain, pure agony. I couldn't blame him. The bullet wound and resulting blood loss should have taken him out of the fight.

And yet it hadn't. He'd barely grunted when he was hit, simply gritting his teeth. And he hadn't returned fire.

"Am I missing something, here?" I said.

Number Two glanced into the rearview mirror, our gazes meeting for just a minute. He had quick eyes. A cutting glance. But he didn't answer.

"You guys know how this ends," I said. "They're going to force you off the road. Lay out a spike strip. Come in with the helicopter and drop tactical monkeys on our roof. It's only a matter of time."

No answer. I suddenly felt irritated, more by my own confusion than by either man's refusal to acknowledge me. I decided to poke the bear.

"Are you hearing me? You need to make a play while you still hold some cards. You're going to jail regardless."

That got Number One. He spun in the seat, snatching up the AR. The muzzle of the weapon centered over my chest, the selector switch still set to FIRE.

But he didn't fire, and I didn't blink. Number One glared, suppressed agony ripping across his face. Sweat dripping from his nose and chin. Lips trembling even as he clamped them together.

Like a cornered animal.

"Not as long as we have *you*," he snarled. "Now *shut up*."

The AR dropped slowly, and I shut up like he asked. Tires hummed, the distant wail of the sirens persisted behind us, and from time to time the buzz of the chopper passed overhead. But it didn't descend. It didn't deploy an army of tactical monkeys onto the roof of the van.

And Number Two didn't stop.

So I sat against the wall while an hour dripped by in slow motion, and then we closed on two. I thought about the

Florida road atlas folded up in the glove box of my '67 GMC pickup, back at the bank. The same road atlas I had used to navigate from the beaches of the Emerald Coast to Jacksonville in the first place, taking the same highway we now blazed down.

There wasn't a lot to see along that route. Only three cities, really. Tallahassee. Then Lake City. Then Jacksonville. Taking the route in reverse, I was confident we had already passed Lake City, but I-10 runs well north of downtown, and I assumed the police would have cleared any local traffic anyway.

Tallahassee was a different story. The interstate connected with the northern part of the metropolitan sprawl. I didn't remember a lot about the city, but I did recall passing a lot of exits. A lot of neighborhoods, shopping districts, gas stations and churches, all sitting directly off the highway amid a weaving myriad of streets overhung by live oak trees.

And a lot of people.

Number One was correct in his assumption that the cops wouldn't force a play so long as he held hostages, but the moment we rolled into Florida's capital, that math would change. The army of highway patrol who now trailed us had no way of knowing that this van wasn't loaded with a fertilizer bomb, or maybe stacked with ammo cans filled with thirty-round magazines for Number One and Number Two's AR rifles.

The loss of two hostages would be tragic. The commission of mass carnage in a major city would be unthinkable. Whitmer and his team would have to make a play before we reached Tallahassee.

As if on cue, Number One's phone rang again, buzzing in

the cheap plastic of the cupholder. He ignored it the first time, twitching in his seat and still clutching his arm. But the phone rang again, and on the fourth chime of the default tone, Number One snatched it up and placed it on speaker as before.

"*What?*"

"This is Special Agent Whitmer again, FBI. Who am I speaking with?"

"You're speaking with *me*, jackass. What do you want?"

"We need to talk about what happens next," Whitmer said. His tone had changed. It was still calm, but less open. Less optional. He sounded more like a parent or a teacher now. Not lecturing but laying down the law.

"What happens next is imma blow both these jerks' heads—"

"You're not going to do that," Whitmer said calmly. "You're not that person."

"You don't know who I am."

"I know you didn't hurt anyone at the bank. I also know you're wounded. Somebody shot you on your way out. I imagine you've lost some blood. We can get you medical care."

"I don't want medical care. I want you *off my ass*."

A slight pause. Whitmer was measuring his beats.

"I'm sorry, but that can't happen. We're just men with a job to do. You have to understand that."

"I understand that I've got two people in the back of this van who aren't walking away unless you *back off*."

Another pause.

"Let me speak to the hostages."

"Not happening."

"If I can't speak to them, I have no way of knowing

they're still alive. And if they're not alive, I have no reason to back off. Be logical."

Number One licked his sweaty lips. Then he bent around the seat and held the phone toward my face.

"Speak," he said.

"Agent Whitmer, this is one of the hostages," I said, keeping my voice just as calm.

"What's your name, brother?" Whitmer asked.

"Mason." I left my last name out. Whitmer didn't need it, and I didn't want him googling me. For my own reasons.

"Are you safe, Mason? Have they hurt you? How about your friend?"

"I'm fine," I said. "So is she. They haven't hurt us."

Number One pulled the phone back. "That ain't gonna be true much longer if you don't clear out."

I cocked my head, watching Number One as he delivered the ultimatum. Something was wrong. I could feel it in my gut. Something about the way Number One sat. About the way Number Two drove. They were both *acting* desperate, but maybe that was the problem. They were acting. And it didn't feel sincere. Certainly, they had every reason to be legitimately desperate. But I didn't buy it. Aside from the reckless outbursts Number One projected into the phone, both men appeared completely collected.

Ice cold.

"What do you want?" Whitmer said after a pause. "If you have an ask, now is the time."

"I want a plane on an airstrip with clearances for Mexico," Number One said. A little sarcasm crept into his voice, but I knew Whitmer would indulge the request, or at least pretend to. He had two innocent lives at stake.

"That may take some time," Whitmer said. "In the meantime, how do you feel about slowing down? There's no need to risk a wreck."

"I'll give you until Tallahassee," Number One said. "Put a plane on the tarmac, fueled and ready to go. And you'll back the hell off when we get there, or I swear the chick gets it. You hear me?"

Again with the projected tone. Number One shouted into the phone, but his shoulders were loose. He looked at Number Two while he spoke.

"Okay," Whitmer said. "My people are making calls. Let's just stay on the line and discuss—"

Number One hung up. This time he didn't drop the phone. He gripped his wounded arm.

"You good?" Number Two said quietly.

Number One closed his eyes. Breathed slowly. Nodded once. And then he said the words that sent a chill down my spine.

"Tallahassee. We'll do it there."

6

Whitmer called back, and Number One bumped him. I no longer thought about the two men in the front seat, or the mismatch of body language that left my head spinning. I wasn't thinking about Whitmer and his team, either. I wasn't even thinking about the army of cops following us.

I was only thinking about myself and about Raven. Because whatever was happening, there was nothing those cops would be able to do for us.

Edging slowly toward the rear of the van, I moved my hips a couple of inches at a time, keeping my back pressed against the metal wall until I sat directly across from Raven. Number One and Number Two were now heavily invested in watching for the helicopter, gazes snapping between windows and mirrors, holding a whispered conference. When Number Two looked into the rearview and saw my position had shifted by a yard, he seemed unconcerned, turning his attention back to the highway and keeping his foot on the gas.

"Hey," I whispered, just loud enough for my voice to carry across the narrow space.

Raven's eyes were now rimmed with red. She looked almost comedic, as though the streaked mascara had been intentionally applied by a makeup artist on the set of a B-rated horror movie. Her bound hands were still pressed over her chest, her knees curled up into a protective ball. Like an upright fetal position.

I thought about shifting across the van to join her, then decided against it. Number One still had his AR. I didn't want to draw his attention until I was ready to make a checkmate move.

"What's your name?" I whispered.

Raven's lip trembled, and she ran her tongue across it. She glanced nervously toward the cabin, then risked a reply.

"Brooke."

"Hi, Brooke. I'm Mason. Are you okay?"

Brooke blinked rapidly and shook her head. "They're gonna kill us!"

"They're not going to kill us, Brooke; we're too valuable. Without hostages there's nothing to stop the police from gunning them down."

"They don't need both of us. One hostage is just as good."

"Fair enough. So if they start shooting, I'll make sure they shoot me first."

Her eyes widened. "Are you crazy?"

I offered a quick grin. "Not crazy, just Superman. Remember?"

That brought on a smile. It didn't last, but it looked good on her. She had straight white teeth, and even through the streaked makeup, I noted matching dimples.

"We're gonna make it out of this," I said. "Just stay loose, okay? When the time comes, follow my lead."

"Why should I do that?"

I hesitated. Then shrugged. "Because, believe it or not, this isn't the first time I've been kidnapped."

Her lips parted, primed with another question, but then the van lurched hard to one side. I looked forward to see Number Two slamming on the brakes and jerking us to the left. I kicked out with both feet, catching myself against the opposing wheel well as I almost spun into the far wall. A chorus of curses exploded from the front seats; then Number One answered his buzzing phone. Speaker again.

"You trying to get cute with me, Whitmer?"

"It was an honest mistake, I promise," Whitmer said. "We asked the construction crew to leave the highway. They must have pulled the traffic cones with them. I didn't know about the pothole."

"I hope you break your jaw on it," Number One snapped. "Or I guess you're probably in the chopper, aren't you?"

"Actually, I'm not. I'm not even in Florida. I'm in Atlanta."

It was extraneous information, probably designed to perpetuate the conversation. Whitmer giving a little and hoping to receive a little in return.

No dice with Number One.

"Where are we with the plane?"

"We've found one," Whitmer said. I figured it was a lie, but something told me Number One knew that also.

"Can you fly a King Air?" Whitmer continued.

"You let me worry about that," Number One said. "Have it fueled and ready on the strip. We'll drive right to it. You stand back. We're taking the hostages with us."

"I can't agree to that. I got you the plane. I'm going to need you to leave the hostages in the van."

Number One snorted an angry laugh. "Yeah, so you can send the Air Force to blow us out of the sky? No thanks."

"Nobody's sending the Air Force. You're American citizens. You have rights."

"You don't know who we are."

"I guess that's true. Why don't we start with a first name?"

I expected Number One to hang up again. Instead, he spoke calmly into the phone. "My name is Matthew David Pearson."

The van went quiet. Whitmer didn't answer. I wasn't sure if he was taken off guard, or if he was having an assistant run the name through a database. Surely Whitmer wasn't the only person on the call.

"Okay, Matt. Mind if I call you Matt?"

"Sure." Number One's voice dropped suddenly. It sounded...tired. And defeated.

"Great. You can call me Ron. Now, Matt..."

Whitmer broke off. A weak smile crept across Number One's face, but it wasn't a happy smile. Not even a satisfied one. Just a pained one.

"Yes," he said. "The *same* Matthew David Pearson."

Long pause.

"You're going to have to help me understand," Whitmer said. "I can't believe the file I'm looking at is the same person who would endanger so many lives."

I knew they were calculated words. Whatever Whitmer had seen in Number One's file, he was playing up the shock. Pretending to be genuinely confused, even though I knew he couldn't be. I'd been in law enforcement myself just long enough to kill any surprise I might feel at the depravity of mankind. To learn that pretty much anybody was capable of pretty much anything.

"There's only one thing you need to understand," Number One said, voice turning cold again. "I'm ten miles from that airport, and if there isn't a King Air sitting on that tarmac, fueled and ready to go, I'm gonna put two in the chest and one in the head of both hostages. And you know I know how."

Then he hung up again.

7

Number Two dropped the hammer immediately after the call ended, and I knew that whatever bizarre game we were caught up in was driving rapidly toward a terminus. Number Two swerved aggressively as he changed lanes, and I noted the whine of the sirens behind us growing louder. Maybe closing a little distance.

I thought back to my atlas of Florida and pinched my eyes closed, struggling to visualize Tallahassee. I knew that I-10 ran north of downtown, connecting with a bypass. Was the airport north of town also, or south?

It mattered, because if this crazy chase was about to pass through a highly populated area, the cops would make a move first. There was zero chance any King Air waited on that strip, or that Whitmer had any intentions of allowing an escape. He'd want to take the van out of commission someplace rural, without many people or buildings to crash into. Off the highway, at a lower speed.

But not in the city.

I focused on my memory of the map, but any precise layout I conjured up simply looked like a morphed version of Phoenix, my hometown and the only major city I was really familiar with.

I decided it didn't matter, in the end. Whether the airport was north, south, or in a separate county, Whitmer and his people would move soon after the van left the highway. Probably as soon as it slowed down. Maybe hit it with a spike strip, and have local sheriff department SUVs equipped with brush guards on standby to drive it off the road.

That meant a tumble. And I wasn't wearing a seatbelt.

"Exit!" Number One called.

Number Two swerved right, and I used the sudden shift as an excuse to roll toward the other side of the van, aligning myself alongside Brooke. My hands were completely numb now, my fingers puffy and beet red. My hips ached with the constant pounding of the hard floor, and my head smacked against a metal bracket as Number Two swerved again.

The van had left the highway. I could tell by a change in the tone of the tires, now spinning over some new type of pavement. Fresh asphalt, it sounded like. But Number Two wasn't slowing down. I thought I felt us descending a slight grade, and I pictured an intersection at the bottom. A stop-light, and maybe cars rushing by. The cops should have cleared it by now, but if they hadn't...

"Listen," I hissed. "We're gonna wreck, okay? I need you to hold your head away from the wall and try to grab onto something. You don't want to tumble."

Brooke's eyes widened. "What do you mean, *wreck*?"

"The cops will force us off the road before we reach a populated area. They can't risk further casualties."

"How do you know?"

"Because I was a cop! Don't worry about that now. Grab hold—"

The breath left my lungs as Number Two slammed on the brakes and yanked the wheel. The back end of the van swung wide, skipping over asphalt. My spine slammed into the wall, and my head snapped back. A horn blared; then the van's engine roared. We were off again, rear tires screaming next to me, evergreen trees flashing past the windshield on either side of a narrow road. Brooke bit back a scream, shoulders smacking against sheet metal.

"Slow down!" I shouted. "You're gonna kill us all."

"Tell it to the cops!" Number One said. "We're not the ones picking the tempo."

I fought my way back into a seated position, pressing my numb hands against the wheel well. Brooke pulled herself upright, her lip bleeding now. The sleeve of her blouse had caught on a cargo bracket, and as Number Two hauled us through another stiff curve, the sleeve tore away. Brooke yelped, and her feet slipped free. I dove, catching her with my bound arms.

Her neck pressed against my face. I smelled sweat and perfume, and as I fought to sit up again, my eyes fell across her now exposed shoulder.

There was a tattoo. Thick black ink. Simple lines. An eagle with its wings stretched, a pair of DOD-style dog tags dangling from its talons.

A single tear slipping from its left eye.

"Hey! You two grab hold of something!" Number One's voice jarred my attention back to the present crisis. I turned toward the passenger's seat, but he wasn't looking at me. He was looking at Brooke.

"Hold on," he said again, like that would do either of us any good.

Number Two executed another crazy maneuver. He laid on the horn, and I hit the wall again. Brooke spun away from me. The van lurched, hopped, then crashed back onto the asphalt with a rapid, flapping sound. Blown front tires, followed immediately by rear ones. The back end fishtailed, and my feet scraped across the metal floor. Brooke shrieked, and a heavy V8 engine thundered behind us.

"Impact!" Number One shouted. He looked over his shoulder, again meeting Brooke's gaze. "Hang tight!"

Then I felt the tap. Not a hard one, but hard enough, and completely unnecessary after the spike strip. Some overenthused deputy in a brand-new sheriff's department Tahoe, I thought. Eager to make his name by derailing what was now certain to be a nationally televised car chase.

The Tahoe's brush guard collided with our rear corner, and the van spun completely out of control. Shrieking metal scraped over asphalt. The back end fishtailed again, and this time it failed to self-correct. Shouts from the front seats were joined by an AR rifle spinning past me in midair. A crunch of dirt was followed by a terrible, wrenching sound of twisting metal and shattering glass.

Then we were rolling. I made myself into a ball and forgot about Brooke. There was nothing more I could do for her. The van hit its side and then tumbled onto its roof, me sliding down the cargo walls with my back scraping metal. I hit the upturned roof a millisecond before the vehicle toppled three more times, eventually landing on its side again, leaving me resting in the bottom with a spinning head and an aching back.

My vision blurred, and my ears rang. Someplace outside

the van, voices shouted, and boots pounded the dirt. Everything smelled like gasoline and burning rubber.

Then the back doors were wrenched open, all shrieking metal and groaning hinges. Bright sunlight streamed in, almost blinding me. A flurry of figures filled the open space, and the black mouths of a trio of handguns pointed straight for my chest.

"This is the police! Hands up!"

8

The next half hour was like any after a major police operation involving heavy participation from multiple law enforcement departments—organized chaos. Cops rushed around. A helicopter landed on the road, and some FBI agents spilled out. Ambulances crowded in around the scene, backing in to provide paramedical services while red lights flashed.

And nobody would shut up.

Our bonds were cut away; then Brooke and I were hauled into separate ambulances and placed on stretchers. My mind still spun, and my ears rang, but other than heavy bruising and slight lacerations on my back and wrists, I was pretty much okay.

I wasn't so sure about Brooke. She had tumbled pretty bad as the van rolled. I worried about broken bones, or at the very least a bad concussion.

But that was out of my control now. I was simply grateful the van had come to a stop without killing either of us. For icing on the cake, both Number One and Number Two had been taken into custody. Not a single shot fired.

One hell of a Monday morning.

The ambulance doors slammed shut, and the vehicle whined toward a hospital, a paramedic busy poking needles into my arms and taking my vitals. He was a chatty guy, with a lot of questions. He wanted to know everything about the robbery, the chase, the crash.

I said nothing, flatly ignoring him as I stared at the ceiling. When we reached the hospital, I was wheeled into triage, quickly cleared, then deployed to an ER room, where X-rays were taken, my back was stitched up, and I was mercifully granted a paper cup loaded with a heavy painkiller.

An hour later, I was starting to feel like myself again. Certainly not thrilled to be sitting in a hospital dressed in a skimpy gown. But at least I was alive.

I'd only just begun to review the events of the morning when a nurse poked her head in, asking how I felt. There was something loaded about her question, and I thought I knew what it was. I couldn't help but be annoyed, while also admitting that if the shoe were on the other foot, I would be doing exactly the same thing.

In fact, I had. Many times.

"Send them in," I said simply.

She disappeared, and thirty seconds later the curtain pulled back to expose two men in uniform and two men in suits. The men in uniform were both patrol cops, both from Leon County according to the patches on their arms. They were here to fill out reports about the accident, I guessed. I assumed the other two would be from the FBI field office in Jacksonville. Guys from the helicopter.

"You all right, buddy?"

The older of the two uniformed cops spoke first. He looked to be in his late forties, hair graying at the temples, relaxed and confident. The tape on his chest read *Mullins*.

"I'm alive," I said. "So yeah. I guess I'm all right."

Mullins nodded. "Wild way to start the day, huh? I'm Sergeant Mullins with the Leon County Sheriff's Department. This is Officer Cook, Special Agent Carver with the FBI, and Mr. Holder. We just have a few questions about what happened."

I surveyed the small knot, stopping at the last man in the line. The man in a plain black suit. No badge or department-identifying uniform. *Mr. Holder.* He was tall, handsome, and had a sort of debonair look about him. As if he thought he owned every room he set foot in.

I didn't like that.

"Who are you?" I said flatly.

"John Holder," he said. "So sorry about your experience."

"I know your name. I'm asking who you *are*. What agency are you with?"

Holder hesitated. Special Agent Carver stepped in.

"Mr. Holder is a consultant. He's here in an advisory capacity."

I locked gazes with Holder. I didn't believe Carver. Not for a second. *Consultant* is a vague enough title to conceal any number of wicked little occupations, and I'd had just enough experience with three-letter agencies to trust none of them.

Then again, my painkillers were kicking in, my body was starting to relax, and I decided I didn't care who Holder was. The sooner I resolved this conversation, the sooner I was out of here.

"You want a statement, Sergeant?" I addressed the question to Mullins.

"If you don't mind."

Officer Cook produced a clipboard. Then the questions began. I could have rattled off answers in sequence without needing to be asked, but I chose to play along. Whatever kind of pill the nurse had put in that plastic cup had left me in a magnanimous mood.

"Name?" Cook asked.

"Mason Lewis Sharpe. ID is in my wallet." I jabbed a thumb toward the pile of clothes resting on a table next to me. Cook wrote my name down without bothering to retrieve the wallet.

"Address?"

I hesitated. Sucked my teeth, then shrugged. "No fixed abode."

Cook looked up. "What does that mean?"

It was a self-explanatory term, but I knew what he was really asking. I'd had this conversation before with law enforcement, several times since leaving Phoenix. I was slowly learning how to answer it without inviting further discussion.

"I travel around," I said. "I'm transient."

"Oh, cool." Cook grinned. "Like van life?"

I thought of my '67 GMC pickup still parked in front of the bank back in Jacksonville. It was fit with a white camper shell over the bed. Just a metal roof with some dusty windows that rattled when it stormed. Inside was an air mattress. A camp stove. A few water-damaged paperbacks and a duffel bag with two changes of clothes.

And not much else.

"Something like that," I said.

Cook made another note, and I glanced to Holder and Special Agent Carver. Neither man said anything. They just stood, hands in their pockets. Listening.

"Why don't you tell us what happened, Mr. Sharpe?" Sergeant Mullins said. "In your own words."

So I did. I began with the explosion of two armed men barreling through the bank's front door. The screams. The gunshots. The threats.

It all happened very quickly. Like combat—*bang, bang, bang.* And then over. But I estimated the whole thing actually lasted around ten or twelve minutes, entry to exit. It couldn't have been longer than that. We were downtown. Fifteen minutes would be a disastrous response time for local cops.

"Tell us about the car chase," Special Agent Carver said. "What did the two men say?"

I searched my mind to recall every exchange. Every terse word, every random comment. Most of it would be recorded on the phone calls between Number One and Special Agent Whitmer, the hostage negotiator. Only one statement stuck out of the pile, like a shiny piece of glass glimmering in the mud.

"He said, '*We'll do it there.*' With *there* being Tallahassee."

"Do what?" Carver asked.

I shrugged. "I don't know."

"Arrange the plane," Mullins grunted. "It's a quiet airport close to the gulf. Makes sense."

I thought about that a moment, then shook my head. "I don't think so."

"Don't think what?" Carver asked.

"I don't think it was about the plane. I think they were talking about something else."

"What?" Carver pressed.

I unpacked the car chase again in my mind, replaying it all in slow motion. The painkillers were heavy. I was feeling a bit loose and loopy. The men around me stood motionless, but seemed to waver a little. Like distant figures across the Arizona desert, shimmering through the heat waves.

"I don't know," I said at last.

"Mind telling us why you were at the bank this morning, Mr. Sharpe?"

It was the first question from Holder. I rotated toward him, squinting. Feeling vaguely irritated by both his question and his presence.

"Banking," I said simply.

"Personal banking?"

"No. Actually I was making a deposit for the cartel. Laundering drug money. I do it every Monday."

The words left my mouth before I could stop them, my sarcasm unleashed by the drugs. I regretted them instantly, but to my surprise Holder smiled. Just a little.

"Why that bank?" Carver asked.

I ran a hand over my face. My lips felt vaguely numb, but the warm relaxation coursing through my body was nearly perfect. Opioids, I guessed. Dangerous cocktails. I was beginning to regret taking them.

"I'm from Phoenix," I said. "I had some banking to take care of. Some *personal* banking."

The last comment was addressed to Holder. He said nothing.

"I've been staying on the coast," I continued. "Destin. Pensacola. Panama City. I needed to go to my bank, and Jacksonville was the nearest city with a branch. It's a west coast bank."

Holder nodded slowly. Cook was still taking notes. Mullins and Carver joined together to ask another two dozen questions about the robbery, the car chase, and the crash, most of which I couldn't answer, but I did my best. Already the fog of war was blurring my memory. Or maybe that was the opioids.

At last Cook stopped writing. Mullins wished me well. Upon request, I gave them the phone number to the burner phone I kept in a backpack for emergency use. Truth be told, I almost never powered the thing on, and I probably wouldn't take their calls anyway. As soon as I completed my banking, I would be moving on.

Because ever since Phoenix, that's what I do.

"I hope you start to feel better, Mr. Sharpe," Carver said. "We appreciate your cooperation. I think that's all my questions for now."

I nodded. Carver turned to Holder, as if passing him the mic. Giving him the floor.

"Just one other thing," Holder said. "Can you recall what exactly the men took from the bank?"

I paused. Thought back to the open duffel bag spilling stacks of bloody cash across the van's metal floor.

"Lots of cash," I said. "I think I saw some jewelry. Like I said before, they broke into some safety-deposit boxes."

"Anything else?" Holder asked.

I chewed my buzzing lip, playing back the memories in my mind. Focusing on the details. Thinking took effort, like slogging through waist-high water. A slow and meticulous process.

I couldn't remember anything else. Just cash and junky old jewelry.

"That's all," I said. "Why?"

Holder shrugged. Shot me another casual smile. "The bank will ask. You know how it is. Insurance claims to file."

He pushed the curtain open, looking back over one shoulder. "You rest up, Mr. Sharpe. You're a lucky guy."

Then the four men disappeared, leaving me floating someplace between the bed and the ceiling. Head spinning.

9

I've never been a drug user. As a kid, I smoked my share of marijuana alongside my delinquent friends, trolling the backstreets of Phoenix and looking for trouble. Once as an adult I took cocaine.

But drugs have never been a habit. I don't like being high. It makes me feel detached and out of control. Vulnerable and uneasy to a point verging on paranoia. The opioid painkillers in my system were hitting me harder than I thought they should, and I resolved to exit the hospital and find other methods to soothe my bruised and battered body.

A bottle of whiskey, maybe. And some music.

I called for the nurse and asked for a discharge. She returned with a billing specialist who had a lot of questions about how I would cover the ninety-eight-hundred-dollar tab I had generated in barely four hours. The ambulance ride had come compliments of the fire department, so the county would pick up the bill for that.

But the X-rays, tests, medication, and doctor's consultation had added up quickly. I didn't have medical insurance.

Hadn't had it since I abandoned my job at the Phoenix Police department almost...

No, not almost. Exactly three hundred and sixty-one days prior. Something I didn't want to think about.

I signed the hospital document, declaring my intention to pay cash when billed, and gave my burner phone number and my old Phoenix address. I would send the hospital what I could when and if I could, but I had no intention of paying nearly ten grand for some X-rays and painkillers I wished I hadn't swallowed. That kind of robbery rivaled the bank heist in Jacksonville.

After re-dressing, I floated down the hall to the hospital's front door. Nothing hurt. I wasn't even stiff. The floor felt as though it were made of clouds, the beeps and buzzes of hospital machinery distant and unimportant.

I stepped back into the early November breeze and stood for a moment with my face pointed toward the sun, savoring the beautiful Florida weather. And thinking.

The feeling had first bubbled up in the back of my mind when the four men stepped into my ER room. Two cops, one federal agent, and one *consultant*.

It wasn't the number of people, or even the unexplained presence of Holder that bothered me. It was something vague bouncing around in my skull, stirred and further provoked by my recounting of the bizarre events at the bank. I couldn't put my finger on it, but as my mind slowly cleared and I detached myself from the three-hour hurricane of madness, something felt very wrong.

Like I was missing the forest for the trees.

I closed my eyes in the warmth of the sun and thought again about the day's events, played in reverse. I thought about the van ride and about Brooke. I wondered if she was okay, and figured she had her own astronomical medical bill to worry about. I rewound past the crash to the car chase, then back to Jacksonville. All the way to the moment those front doors burst open, and Number One and Number Two exploded inside.

Ladies and gentlemen, this is a robbery.

Who says that?

I opened my eyes and ran my tongue gently across the inside of my busted lip. Playing and replaying the memories. Fishing deep for what was bothering me.

Then I wondered if there was actually nothing bothering me. Maybe I was just high.

High...and looking for something to fixate on. Something other than what I had been doing in that bank in the first place.

I took two steps out from under the ER portico and scanned the parking lot. Ten yards ahead a bench sat in the sunlight, painted green, a little grimy. On that bench sat Brooke. She wore the same clothes she'd worn during the robbery. Black jeans, black running shoes, and that white blouse, now with the left sleeve torn off. Her raven black hair was pulled back in a bun—a tight little knob smaller than my fist. A hairstyle I've seen a few thousand times.

But never on a civilian.

Pocketing my hands, I noted the absence of my Victorinox and figured the cops had taken it off Matthew David Pearson—Number One. I breathed an irate curse and covered the ten yards to the bench, stopping when my shadow fell over her face.

"Mind if I sit?"

Brooke looked up quickly. Her eyes were still wide and a little strained, but the raccoon makeup was gone. I noted fresh lacerations around her wrists, compliments of the zip ties. A developing bruise on her neck. But despite the complete lack of makeup and all the battle scars, I couldn't help noticing what I hadn't before. Smooth, clear skin. High cheekbones and a delicate mouth. Strong but elegant shoulders. And deep, dark eyes with an ocean-sized soul behind them.

She was gorgeous in a very natural, casual way. The kind of woman who could roll out of bed and land a date with whomever she wanted.

"Sure," she said, shifting over to give me room on the bench. Her shoulder flexed as she moved. Taut muscles rippled beneath the tattoo.

I settled onto the bench and relaxed, still basking in the sunshine. Florida had been insufferably hot barely six weeks prior, but now I couldn't think of any place I'd rather be.

"You check out okay?" I asked.

"Yeah," she said. "Just some bumps and bruises. You?"

"No worse than a rough day in basic." I met her gaze as I said it, and she didn't look away. I saw something swirling in that dark ocean. Conflicted thoughts, and extended nervousness. A completely natural reaction for somebody who had just been subjected to automatic gunfire before being kidnapped, then tumbled around in the back of a crashing vehicle like a marble in a soup can.

But I already knew Brooke wasn't just *somebody*. And I had a growing gut feeling that this wasn't the first time she'd experienced automatic gunfire or faced death.

"Are you a sir or a grunt?" Brooke asked.

I propped both elbows atop the bench's back and stretched, choosing to enjoy the floaty feeling the best I could before the pain returned.

"Neither," I said. "Not anymore. Once upon a time I was a sergeant. And you?"

A long pause. Brooke picked at a loose thread in her jeans with one hand, staring at the concrete. Maybe evaluating. It told me I was right about what I already suspected. The military heritage was clear.

As was the signature of trauma.

"Army," she said at last. "Corporal. Infantry."

"Thank you for your service," I said.

"Likewise."

She continued to pick at the loose thread, but now she looked across the parking lot and toward the road. Then she checked her watch.

"Waiting for somebody?" I asked.

"They called me a cab. I'm headed to the bus station."

"Back to Jacksonville?"

"Right. I...have to get back to work."

"What do you do?"

She opened her mouth again. Then she faced me. "I don't think I caught your last name."

"Sharpe. Mason Sharpe. And you?"

"Brooke Oswilder."

"Nice name."

"Thanks."

She looked for the cab again. I didn't. I continued to watch her as the toes of her shoes scraped the concrete. She looked edgy and unsure. Maybe dealing with waves of anxiety unleashed by the experience in the bank. God knew, it was one of the closest experiences to the Middle East I had experienced since returning to the States. Never a good thing.

But I didn't share in the anxiety. Not because I was

immune to the stress, but perhaps because the opioids were doing their magic, and certainly because much more painful trauma had long since superseded the horrors I experienced hunting terrorists.

"You gonna talk to the media?"

Brooke's next question took me by surprise. She turned suddenly to face me, and I cocked my head.

"Why would I do that?"

"They wanted to talk to me. I...I don't want to talk. But I thought you might."

"Why would you think that?"

"I don't know. They might pay you."

"Pay me?" I attempted a weak laugh. "Do I look like I need the money?"

She blushed. "I just mean...they want the story."

"What story?"

She squinted. "You don't know?"

"Know what?"

"About Pearson."

I frowned, thinking of Number One again. Of the phone call with Whitmer. Of what Number One had said.

Yes. The same *Matthew David Pearson.*

"Who is he?" I asked.

Brooke looked surprised again. "Wow, you must live under a rock."

"Eh. They gave me some heavy pills. You have two heads right now."

It was an exaggeration, but it made Brooke smile. I saw a flash of the dimples again, and the lightness in my head was joined by a brief rush of warmth to my chest. The sensation took me off guard, and I looked away.

"He famous or something?" I asked.

"He's the son of a congressman," Brooke said. "Glenn David Pearson, from Pennsylvania's 11th district. Matthew is a war hero, apparently. An ex-Army Ranger."

The warmth in my chest vanished at her last line. I faced her again, lifting my chin.

"He was seventy-fifth?" I asked.

There's some difference between a Ranger and a *Ranger* in the Army. Almost anyone can apply to participate in the US Army's famed Ranger School, where they are tortured, starved, overworked, harassed, and taught how to lead. It's a brutal experience and a phenomenal accomplishment to earn a Ranger patch. But that by itself doesn't make you a combat Ranger. It doesn't grant you admittance into the Army's 75th Ranger Regiment, where Rangers lead the way.

Where I served.

"Yeah..." Brooke said softly. "He was. I saw it on the news, in the ER."

I thought again about Whitmer on the phone. The long pause after Matthew Pearson had disclosed his identity.

Whitmer hadn't been looking at a criminal record at all. He'd been looking at a DOD file.

"I can't believe the file I'm looking at is the same person who would endanger so many lives."

Whitmer had sounded genuinely confused. Suddenly, so was I. My mind swept back to years prior, serving alongside other proud members of the 75th, parachuting and door kicking and hiking long miles over hostile Afghan mountains.

Men at my shoulder who were every bit as tough, determined, and dedicated as I. Hard men. But good ones. Honest ones. Men I trusted my life to without a second thought... and they trusted me.

I pictured the scene at the bank again and replaced the ski-masked bulk of Number One with one of the faces of the men I served with. The image wouldn't compute. I couldn't force it. It was like imagining a new color or picturing the sky without air. It simply wasn't possible.

I turned back to Brooke, another question on my lips. But just then a car rolled up in front of us. It was jet black, a Chevrolet Impala. Late model, with heavily tinted windows. A bug-splattered Virginia plate mounted to the front bumper.

It wasn't a taxicab. Seated behind the front wheel, I recognized the bulky frame and debonair face of John Holder—the *consultant*.

He pulled even with us and lowered the passenger window. Dark sunglasses concealed his gaze, but I felt his eyes pass over me as he twisted his head to face Brooke, chewing gum slowly. Then he spoke.

"You two okay?"

Brooke nodded once but didn't answer. I had the feeling that she was familiar with Holder. He had interviewed her also.

"Waiting for somebody?" he prompted.

"Just my ride," Brooke said. "Thank you."

"Where you headed?"

No answer. Holder shifted into park with a sigh, then swung slowly out of the car. He stretched in the sun, then removed his glasses as he approached us.

"I'm really sorry about...everything. I can only imagine what it must have been like."

I looked above his rotating jaw, past two days' worth of razor stubble into dark gray eyes. Squinted in the sun but calm somehow. Relaxed.

"Look," Holder said. "I'm headed back to Jax. You're welcome to ride with me, if you like. Save you the bus ticket."

"Who are you?" I asked, voice calm.

Holder laughed. "Man, you're really hung up on that, aren't you?"

I said nothing.

Holder slid his glasses back on. Popped his gum and faced me. Then he shrugged. "You're both military people. You know how the government works. Some of us...don't have titles."

"Oh, I'm familiar with that," I said, hoping the tone of my voice communicated the fact that I was also unimpressed by it. "I'm just wondering why such a titleless person is interested in a bank robbery."

Holder worked the gum in his mouth, a little slower now. Then he grunted. "She tell you who Pearson is?"

I nodded.

"Well, that should answer your question."

He rounded the nose of the Impala, then turned back to look over the roofline.

"Seriously, guys. Free ride. Nice tunes. And the guy next to you won't be tweaking on crack. That beats the bus."

I glanced sideways at Brooke. She seemed undecided, but I wasn't. I stood, feeling that floating sensation fade into the back of my head.

"Mind if I take shotgun?"

10

Brooke hesitated outside the Impala, but when I shot her a smile and a confident nod, she climbed in behind Holder.

Not behind me. Not in the middle of the back seat. Behind the driver.

I thought it was an interesting choice and reflected a hint of defensiveness. Maybe she felt safer behind the driver, assuming that Holder would protect his side of the vehicle first in the event of an accident. But I didn't think so. I had the feeling Brooke had her own reasons for selecting the one seat where she was most sheltered from Holder's rearview mirror.

Just like I had my own reasons for selecting the seat beside him. Where I could see his face.

Holder shifted into drive, and we passed Brooke's taxi on the way to the highway. I squinted, missing the sunglasses I had left in my truck. Thankfully, it was now midafternoon, meaning that once we reached I-10 and turned east for Jacksonville, the sun would no longer be a problem.

In the meantime, I wasn't thinking about the glare. I was thinking about the bank. And the robbery. And the car chase. And every little thing every person had said, from the moment that door blew open to the moment I climbed into Holder's car. Because now that the opioids were fading, my mind was returning. And with it came the overwhelming conviction that the opioids hadn't been the problem. Something, somewhere, was legitimately off. Call it intuition or instinct or a mental skill set honed by years of hunting terrorists in Afghanistan followed by homicidal maniacs in Phoenix.

Whatever the source of the voice in my head, I'd learned to trust it.

"So, Holder, were you military?"

Holder pressed a fresh stick of gum between his teeth, looking and sounding a little like a cow chewing its cud. He glanced into his rearview mirror, maybe looking for Brooke's face. Maybe checking traffic.

"Once upon a time," he said vacantly.

"Army?"

"Right."

"Hooah, brother." I broke into an overbearing smile I didn't quite feel. Holder matched it with a tight smirk.

"So how did you find yourself in the consulting business?"

A long hesitation. Holder fiddled with the climate control settings, and I wondered if he was regretting picking us up.

At last he said, "How does a decorated Army Ranger become a homeless vagrant?"

There was no hostility in his tone, but a definite challenge. I saw Brooke look up abruptly, those dark ocean eyes snapping toward me. I hadn't told her I was a Ranger. I had only said I was a sergeant. I hadn't told Holder either, for that matter. Apparently, he had looked me up.

I wondered what else he had discovered. Whether he had investigated my tenure as a Phoenix police detective... and how it ended.

I decided to ignore his question and change tack.

"So this Pearson guy. He was a service member also."

"Yep." Holder nodded. "A war hero."

"Hard to imagine a guy like that robbing a bank."

"Isn't it, though?" Holder cocked his head. "Kinda makes you wonder..."

"About what?"

"About why."

I shrugged. "Why else? Money, right?"

Holder's gaze flicked toward me again, a split second come and gone before he refocused on the highway. Behind me I knew Brooke could feel the tension, and I wondered if she was as lost as I was about *why* there was tension. I felt like I was blindfolded, bumbling across a football field in the middle of the Super Bowl. Conscious of the noises and the play calls and the pound of feat on the gridiron.

But still lost as to *what* exactly was happening.

Holder set the cruise control at eighty-five, racing down the fast lane and flashing his lights anytime a slower car failed to yield. He didn't seem to be concerned about a speeding ticket, and I wondered if he had some kind of *consultant* ID in his wallet. A get-out-of-jail-free card. Or maybe he was just an ass being an ass.

"Where did you serve?" I addressed the question over my left shoulder. Brooke twitched nervously, her gaze sliding left as she answered.

"Kentucky," she said.

"Never deployed?"

"No." The answer was quick. "I was a reservist. Kentucky National Guard."

"Is that right?"

Brooke didn't answer, and the voice in the back of my mind grew just a little louder, its warnings now clearly audible.

They were lying to me. Both of them, right through their teeth, and for no apparent reason. I felt caught in the middle of some kind of game, like the third wheel of a friend trio, where two friends were both dating and fighting, and the third guy knew nothing about it.

It made me want to light a stick of dynamite and chuck it into the murky depths. See what blew to the surface.

"So this Pearson guy. His father is a congressman?"

"That's right," Holder said. "Pennsylvania. Eleventh district."

"How about that," I said. "That's crazy. Don't you think, Brooke?"

Brooke met my gaze, her face now set in hard lines, those ocean black eyes blaring a silent message that I couldn't interpret and didn't really want to.

"Crazy," she said.

I leaned back in my seat, relaxing a little. The fog of the painkillers was gone, but they were still doing their job as far as my body was concerned. I felt terrific.

"So, Brooke," I said, "you're from Kentucky?"

"Yep."

"What part?"

"Louisville."

"Louisville! Never been there."

"You should check it out," Brooke said, her tone relaxing a little. "It's pretty great."

"I'll bet it is. Hey, quick question." I sat up, twisting around in the seat. "What congressional district is Louisville in?"

Both Brooke and Holder stiffened. The interior of the car felt suddenly cold, the sound of the tires the only noise to break the tension. But I felt no tension. Only focus. I slid casually back into my seat, choosing not to press Brooke for an answer. Her silence was all the answer I needed. Instead I allowed the car to fall silent for the next two hours while I basked in the warmth of the afternoon sun shining through the back glass, and ran through the events of the robbery one last time.

Slowly. Each picture. Every scene. Every word.

By the time Jacksonville rose out of the horizon to fill the windshield, my list of questions had doubled in size, but several of the most critical details had finally been resolved.

Details like the ceiling in the bank, the moment the sprinklers kicked on. And what had been wrong with it.

Details like the moment the van crossed the bridge, and Brooke flung the door open. And what was missing when she was yanked back inside.

And perhaps the biggest detail of all...details about the person who had lied the most. And was still lying.

Holder remained silent as he crossed another of Jacksonville's downtown bridges, returning to the south bank. I looked over the expanse of the St. John's River, my gaze focusing on a spot just beneath the blue mass of the drawbridge. And I smiled. Not in humor, and not even in satisfaction.

Just in a moment of respect.

The Impala rolled to a stop outside the line of yellow crime scene tape blocking off the entrance of the bank. A black FBI van was parked under the portico now. Cops and agents in dark blue windbreakers rushed in and out of the tower, shouting after one another as salty wind swept their hair and bright Florida sunshine faded into the west.

Holder shifted into park.

"Is this okay?"

"Perfect," I said. I reached for the door. Holder caught my arm.

"Say, Sharpe." He extended his hand, a white card pressed between two fingers. "If you think of something."

I took the card, not bothering to thank him for the ride as I stepped onto the smooth concrete. My truck sat fifty yards away, across the street from the bank in a small parking lot. Dusty green paint framed by a white cab and a white camper shell.

It looked strangely like home, but I didn't head for the truck. I turned for Brooke instead, waiting until Holder had rolled away. She stood awkwardly, seeming to hesitate and looking twice over her shoulder to trace the Impala out of sight. Then she turned back.

"Good luck, Sharpe."

And that was the nail in the coffin.

Brooke walked away, hands in her pockets, taking the sidewalk alongside the bank that led between a tight cluster of buildings to the south bank river walk beyond. She kept her head low, almost jogging. As soon as she was out of sight, I followed.

Around the corner. Down a narrow concrete sidewalk sheltered by the bulk of the bank tower. Past a steakhouse and through a parking garage.

Then she stepped out onto the river walk, moving straight to the edge. She leaned against the railing, both hands clasped around the top rail, and peered toward the drawbridge.

I accelerated, reaching the river walk and keeping my steps soft until I had closed to within five yards. Then I broke the silence, because it was time to break something.

"Nice job, Corporal."

Brooke flinched and spun, facing me as I stopped at the far edge of the river walk. A sad but knowing smile on my face.

I said, "You almost had me."

11

Brooke turned her back to the river, those ocean eyes glancing quickly over my shoulder. I already knew there was nobody behind me. Not Holder. Not one of the cops working the crime scene. Not even a jogger pushing a stroller.

Just the two of us.

"I don't know what you're talking about," she said, a little too quickly.

"I think you do," I said. "I never would have seen it at the bank. Probably never would have seen it at all, but you tipped your hand. All those details about Pearson? How could you know that? You said you saw it on the TV, but there was a TV broadcasting near my ER room, and I heard nothing about a congressman's son. You don't even know what congressional district you were born in, yet you know that Pearson represents Pennsylvania's eleventh."

Brooke's lips twitched just a little. But she didn't break eye contact. I pressed ahead.

"Then you lied about being in the National Guard. I've

never known a service member who was never deployed to get a memorial tattoo, but calling me by my last name was the real giveaway. National Guardsmen are part-time people. More civilians than soldiers. They don't address people they've just met by their last name. That's an active-duty thing."

Again with the lip twitch. Then her little chin rose, her mouth pressed into a hard line. "What's your point, Sharpe?"

"My point is you've been lying to me. And Holder is lying, also. And nothing that happened in that bank makes a damn bit of sense. If Matthew Pearson really was a Ranger, he's the stupidest Ranger I've ever met. Kicking a bank door down halfway through the morning rush, storming in guns blazing. Who robs a bank like that? Especially in the heart of a big city? Your chances of escape are nearly zero. Subzero, once you start messing with safety-deposit boxes. They barely gave the cash a second glance once they reached the van, and the first thing Holder asked me in my interview was: *What did they take?* He didn't care about the money or that junky jewelry. He was looking for something else. And all that leads me to ask...*what was in the box?*"

Brooke's lips turned pale. She looked again over my shoulder, and this time she seemed to make eye contact with somebody.

"I don't know what you're talking about," she said again. Then she turned and began to fast-walk down the river walk, away from the bank, toward the base of the drawbridge. The river walk ducked down there, a retaining wall holding back the river as the walkway passed beneath the bridge.

A flash of heat rushed to my face, and I turned after her. Maybe I was pissed about being lied to. Maybe opioids make me obsessive.

Regardless, I wasn't finished with my interrogation. I wasn't about to let her walk.

"They fired half a dozen rounds into the ceiling," I said. "But when the sprinklers kicked on and I looked up, there were no bullet holes. They were firing blanks."

Brooke accelerated. I matched her pace, my long legs easily keeping up with her trot. She glanced over her shoulder again, and this time I looked behind also. There was nobody. The river walk was empty.

"When I volunteered to be taken hostage, Pearson and his buddy had to think about it. Then Pearson said, '*He'll do.*' They had to think about something again when we neared Tallahassee; then Pearson said, '*We'll do it there.*' Escape was never part of their plan, was it? Tell me what I'm missing, Brooke."

Brooke vanished into the darkness beneath the bridge. I accelerated from a fast walk to a jog, dropping in after her. Ahead, I noticed yellow lights pinned underneath the bridge, barely bright enough to illuminate the concrete path. Cars rushed overhead, and then a semitruck. Concrete groaned, and metal clapped. The path bent to the left, circling back toward the south bank. I followed it, rounding the corner, squinting as the yellow light broke across my face.

And then I saw the fist rocketing toward me, thick and meaty, the size of a baseball mitt. I hurled my body to the left, barely missing it as fat fingers and a muscled forearm raced across my shoulder. I saw the face behind it, nearly a yard away. A huge guy, easily dwarfing my six-foot-two frame. Broad shoulders and a gnarled face twisted into a horrible sneer. He swung with his left fist, but a moment after he missed, he was already following up with a right hook.

I couldn't dodge that one. His second blow struck me in the stomach, knocking the air clean out of me. I staggered back and nearly fell, overwhelmed by the raw power. I'd been hit before—many times. But this felt like being struck by an oncoming car. I staggered against the wall and heaved.

The big guy didn't advance. He stood in the shadows like an oak tree, his muscled arms hanging at his sides, a chest the size of a dump truck barely rising beneath an olive-drab T-shirt that was at least two sizes too small.

He looked like a caricature. The cartoon of a supervillain.

"Go away," he growled. His voice gurgled and rasped, not sounding quite human. I met his gaze as he stepped into the light.

I nearly puked. The entire left side of his face was something out of a horror movie. Twisted and distorted flesh, capped by a stretched eyelid that exposed too much of his right eye. Closely cropped hair was burned away on the left side of his skull, and burn marks rippled down his neck and beneath his shirt. I saw more on his left forearm, and for the first time I noticed that his left hand was crooked and twisted, two fingers missing.

He favored his left leg as he took a step forward. The breath whistled between his lips, and I now saw that the sneer was permanent. Part of his upper lip was simply missing, exposing teeth far too straight and clean to be natural.

"You follow her, I'll kill you," the big guy gurgled.

Then he turned away, limping a little on that twisted left leg. I watched him go, saliva dripping from my lips.

Then something molten hot erupted in my stomach.

Like a volcano spewing angry lava through my guts and into my chest. Outrage mixed with frustration and the irrefutable feeling that I had been used. I wasn't sure how. I wasn't sure what sort of bizarre game I had fallen headlong into the middle of.

I was only sure that I was now being discarded, and that was unacceptable.

Leaving the wall, I jogged after the oak-tree guy, shoulders loose. Hands at my sides. I saw Brooke at the end of the tunnel, turning back in the daylight. Pointing toward the monster and me, a warning ready on her lips.

The big guy didn't need the warning. He heard my steps and twisted toward me, cocking back a fist the way big guys always do. Ready to deliver overwhelming force and absolute devastation, like a battleship from naval conflicts of yesteryear.

But battleships are slow. And I'm not.

The third blow rocketed toward me, that fist the size of a Volkswagen whistling easily past my face as I twisted and ducked. Then came the follow-up right hook, as before. This time rising upward toward my jaw.

Another easy shot to miss as I swung right and moved lightly on my feet. The big guy leaned forward, overcome by his own momentum.

I went straight for his injured leg, kicking out and down, putting all of my body weight behind it. My foot made impact, and agony broke across his twisted face. He lost his balance, and long before he could regain it, I was on him. A right hook to his jaw, followed by a snapping kick to his chin. I ignored his chest and stomach. I might break my fingers on those steel abs. I went for the weak places instead—the injuries and his groin. Fighting dirty because I was fighting to win.

The big guy struggled to return fire, but like a battleship caught by a submarine, he couldn't get his guns on me. I was too close, moving too fast. He fell against the wall, and I delivered two more rabbit punches to his nose, hard and fast enough to send blood spraying across the concrete. He staggered, and I snapped my left shin into his crotch.

Then I cocked my right arm, ready to drive his skull straight into the concrete retaining wall.

"No!" Brooke's shriek caught me from the end of the tunnel, small feet pounding the pavement. "Don't hurt him, please!"

12

Something about the sincerity of her cry got through to me. The red mist closing in on the edges of my vision, supercharging my body and blocking out the surrounding world, began to fade. I caught myself, arm still cocked, and looked down at the slumped man between my legs.

Blood gushed from his nose. Agony clouded his eyes. His breath came in ragged gasps, whistling through those fake teeth.

And the scars. White and swollen, running down his neck and beneath the skin-tight olive drab shirt. All of the monster I'd seen only moments ago faded in an instant. Now he just looked...broken.

A shell of a man.

I lowered my fist as Brooke reached me, grabbing my arm and hauling me back.

"What's wrong with you?" She sobbed, tears running down her cheeks. "He's *one of us!*"

I shook her off, still catching my breath. Brooke knelt

next to the big guy, grabbing his arm. He made no effort to rise, sliding into a seated position and leaning against the wall instead. Breathing hard through that distorted mouth with the permanent sneer.

He spat blood and shook his head.

"I always hated Rangers." His voice gurgled as before, almost like a baby struggling with complex words. His vocal cords sounded shot, his lips unable to properly pronounce. I briefly wondered how he knew I was a Ranger, but it wasn't all that difficult a riddle. Brooke must have told him—probably when she texted him to come jump me.

I clenched and unclenched my fist, looking down to regard swollen fingers and busted knuckles. Abs or no abs, I'd hurt myself about as much as I'd hurt him.

I looked back to Brooke as her face pivoted toward me. I saw rage in her eyes, bottled deep behind that stormy ocean. But even as she directed that rage at me, I didn't really think I had caused it. The anger was too deep. The darkness too real.

I wiped my mouth with the back of one hand, then lowered myself against the retaining wall. It fell short of the underside of the bridge, and eight inches behind me, the river lapped against concrete. Cars continued overhead, a constant rush. The jogger I had imagined earlier appeared, pushing a baby stroller and clinging to a dog leash. She entered the tunnel and looked suddenly alarmed, her gaze darting from me to the big guy.

Then she turned around and pushed the stroller the other way, jogging faster now.

I turned back to my newfound companions.

"Now that we've got that out of our systems, which one of you is going to start telling the truth?"

No answer. The tears dried from Brooke's face while the anger remained. For his part, the big guy glared hellfire at me, saliva mingling with the blood from his nosebleed as both ran down his chin. He looked like an oversized kid, freshly pounded on the playground, confused and hurt.

I gave them a full minute; then I hauled myself to my feet with a pained grunt. The opioids were all but gone now. My violent Monday was catching up with me.

"All right," I said. "Have it your way. I'll just ring up Holder and ask him instead. Should be a fascinating conversation. Peace, out."

I started back the way I had come. I figured I'd make it half a dozen strides.

Brooke gave me only four.

"Wait."

I turned back. Brooke was standing now. She held her chin up, toned arms hanging at her sides, that memorial tattoo glistening in the yellow light. She looked at the big guy, and the big guy shook his head.

I lifted my shoulders in a "*Well?*" shrug. Brooke started toward me, and the big guy got up.

"Brooke," he gurgled, the word coming out more like "book".

She ignored him, meeting me halfway through the tunnel right where the traffic was loudest. Stopping, she lifted her head to make eye contact.

I waited, now confident in my position of leverage.

"Can I trust you?" Brooke asked. Her voice was strong, but I could hear the strain in it. Exhaustion, maybe. Or deep stress.

"Corporal," I said, restraining a laugh, "you don't have a choice."

Her ocean eyes flashed, and I regretted the condescension. I remembered what she had said about the big guy only moments before. *He's one of us.*

A service member. Or an ex-service member. A family of brother- and sisterhood not shared by most of the world. Good people, ready and willing to put their lives on the line for millions who may not be nearly so good.

Us.

"Yes," I said, killing the arrogant undertone. "You can trust me."

Brooke looked back to the big guy. He stood twenty feet behind her now, glaring death at me. I couldn't say that I blamed him.

Again he shook his head, but I knew he wasn't in charge. Whether by circumstance or necessity, Brooke was in charge.

She squared her shoulders. Then she turned around and headed for the tunnel's exit.

"Follow me."

13

I waited for the big guy to step in behind Brooke, unwilling to let him out of my sight. The two of us trailed her out of the far side of the tunnel, back onto the south bank with the bulk of downtown Jacksonville clustered along the far side of the river to our right. The sun was beginning to set behind the skyscrapers now. A cool breeze blew off the St. John's River, making me miss my jacket.

My muscles were stiffening now. Tomorrow morning would be hell.

Brooke left the river walk two hundred yards later, turning in past a two-story building labeled *The Museum of Science and History* before stopping in the adjacent parking lot alongside a dark blue Honda Civic. Three or four years old. Kentucky license plates.

She dug keys out of her pocket and hit the locks, gesturing for us both to climb in.

"You're kidding, right?" I raised both eyebrows, surveying the big guy. In the daylight I managed a better estimation of his height. Six feet six, at the least. Three hundred pounds, most of it raw muscle.

"Stop whining, Sharpe," Brooke said. She took the driver's seat, and I piled in behind her. I figured there would be more room behind the driver's seat than behind her passenger.

The big guy crammed himself through the door, comically landing in the passenger seat with his knees rising nearly to his chin, his neck bent over sideways to avoid collision with the roof. He looked ridiculous, but I had even less room to talk than I had room for my own legs. Packed into the back seat, I felt the roof riding the back of my skull on its way to the trunk.

Brooke slammed her door and started the little engine. Then we were off, rolling away from the river walk and headed east. Brooke said nothing as she drove, but I noticed her dark eyes flicking to the mirror every few seconds. Checking her six, and checking every sidewalk we passed.

She was paranoid. Wired.

"Do I get your name?" I addressed the big guy, just to break the silence. He rotated a little in the seat, exposing the mutilated left side of his face. Spiderweb scars crept up his neck and around his ear, which was also distorted and curled in on itself. I hadn't given the nature of his injuries much thought while he was pounding me, but now the origin was crystal clear.

A bomb blast—probably an IED—and a bad one, at that.

He looked away again without comment, and Brooke sighed.

"His name is Clay Dufort. And in case you couldn't tell, he's the life of the party."

"A pleasure," I said. And I meant it. If he swung at me

again, I would break his arm. But so long as we could remain civil, I had nothing against the guy.

Dufort wiped drying blood from beneath his nose and spat. A ball of snot and saliva landed on the dash.

"Dammit, Dufort. Clean that up! Napkins in the glove box."

Dufort snorted. "Can't get it open," he warbled. He was right. His big knees completely blocked the glove box, leaving the snot and saliva to slowly drip onto the floorboard.

Brooke shook her head, muttering more curses. Downtown Jacksonville was well behind us now, but I noted a gas station passing on our left that I had seen before. The digital fuel price sign flickered beneath a busted oil company logo. Brooke was driving in circles and still surveying the space around us.

She was running an SDR, I realized. A surveillance detection route—a tactic designed to expose tails prior to reaching your destination.

What?

I almost questioned her, then decided against it. Brooke was going to do what Brooke was going to do, that much was clear. I decided to bide my time and was eventually rewarded as we pulled into the parking lot of a dingy chain hotel. Battered pickup trucks and work vans sat all around us—a working-class joint, with a cheap nightly rate. I knew all about those. Prior to arranging my sleeping situation in the bed of my pickup, I'd spent a lot of time in discount hotels like this.

Brooke parked in a compact spot near the front entrance. Dufort and I unfolded ourselves from the car, and two minutes later we stepped into a hotel room on the second floor of the building, the window overlooking the front parking lot. Brooke walked straight to it and peeled the curtain back, surveying the lot for a long moment before eventually dropping her shoulders in an exhausted sigh.

I glanced over the room. It was messy, with an open suitcase resting on the floor, women's clothes scattered at random over the unmade bed. There was a laptop on the desk, and Styrofoam takeout cartons piled in the corner.

I remembered the *Do Not Disturb* sign on the door as we entered and wondered how long Brooke had been staying here.

She left the window and sat on the bed, unwinding the regulation hair bun. Long black hair fell over her shoulders, looking dirty and sticking with dried sweat. She ran her fingers through it as Dufort advanced to the corner and folded his arms.

He looked like a gargoyle, standing so still he almost appeared to be made of stone.

"Okay," I said. "So now you start talking."

Brooke's dirty face looked suddenly exhausted. I wondered how old she was. My initial estimate had been somewhere around my age. Right about thirty years old. Now I wondered if she was much younger but had aged prematurely.

"Why don't we order some food," Brooke said. "You can tell us about yourself."

"No dice," I said. "You've stalled long enough. Talk now, or I'll talk to Holder."

Brooke looked to Dufort. He shook his head again, but again I knew he wouldn't stop her.

She faced me. "What do you know?"

"What do you mean, *what do I know*?"

"I mean...what do you *think* happened?"

I replayed the events of that day one more time, focusing on the highlights. Reviewing my mental notes. Looking to Dufort, and adding him to the puzzle. Then looking back to Brooke.

"I think you're one of them," I said flatly. "I think you were in on this from the start. And I don't think it was about money. There was something in one of those safety-deposit boxes that you wanted badly. So Pearson and his buddy planned this thing and staged you in the bank as a hostage. I'm not sure why. But they never really planned on escaping, and they certainly didn't plan on hurting anybody. Hence the blanks."

Brooke didn't blink as I spoke, and Dufort didn't move from the wall.

"Let's say you're right," Brooke said slowly. "Does that make us the good guys?"

I thought about that. Using blanks and planning to be caught didn't make anyone a good guy. A robbery was still a robbery. Pearson and his buddy had still terrorized a few dozen people and ruined my day.

On the other hand, I'd participated in enough military and police operations to appreciate the gray void that exists between black and white. It's a dangerous place, mired by human corruption. But there's goodness there, also. Diamonds of truth buried in the mud.

"It depends on what was in the box," I said, at last.

Another long pause from Brooke. Another distrusting shake of his head from Dufort. Then Brooke stood.

"Okay. No more games. I want to know everything about you. Service history. Retirement history. The music you like and whether you wear boxers or briefs. Right now."

"Aren't you going to buy me dinner first?" I quipped.

"No. I'm not. And I'm not laughing, either, because this isn't a joke. So you either get serious and give me a reason to trust you, or Dufort is going to stuff your body in my trunk, and that will be the end of you. Those are my terms."

I looked to Dufort, gauging the big man's intentions. Noticing for the first time how closely he stood to the dresser, one hand resting near the top of an open drawer.

A handgun lay inside, I figured. An unfair advantage. But it didn't really concern me because the fact that Brooke and Dufort had brought me here at all told me they weren't holding all the cards. So I leaned against the wall and gave Brooke what she wanted.

I began in Phoenix. The story of an orphaned kid on the wrong side of the tracks. Busted for motorcycle theft, which was kind of a joke, because I'd done much worse and gotten away with it. I talked about the judge who gave me the opportunity to repay my debt to society via the Army. I talked about bootcamp and Ranger School and Afghanistan. I hit the highlights right up to the end of my military service, at which point I returned to Phoenix. Became a beat cop. Then a detective.

And then I stopped telling my story, because the next chapter was the worst of my life. The most painful memory, the most horrific agony I'd ever experienced. Like Dufort and his IED.

Three hundred sixty-one days prior.

"Why did you leave the Phoenix police?" Brooke asked.

"Reasons," I said.

"What reasons?"

"Reasons I'm not going to discuss. The bottom line is I'm not a cop anymore. I'm not anything. I live in my truck, and I wander around. Which isn't a crime, so stop acting like I'm the one with something to hide. I've met your conditions. It's your turn to sing."

I waited. Brooke looked again to Dufort. He grunted and shook his head one more time. Glaring death and mistrust at me.

But I knew Brooke would talk. And right on cue, she did.

"You ever been to Yemen, Sharpe?"

14

I relaxed while Brooke stared at her feet and told the story.

It wasn't a new story. It wasn't an original story. It wasn't even a special story. It was only one more in ten thousand tales of heartbreak, tragedy, and loss in the war against terror. A different landscape with bullets flying under a different flag, but from the outset, what Brooke described in Yemen was a mirror image of a thousand similar missions in Afghanistan.

Until it wasn't.

"Are you familiar with the civil war in Yemen?" Brooke asked.

I shook my head.

"It began a while ago," Brooke said. "Some new government was installed, and half the country didn't want to go along with it, so they started shooting. I'm not an expert on the specifics. I only know that sometime around 2014, the Saudis got involved. They supported the installed government and wanted to suppress the rebels. Houthis, they're called. I guess the Saudis were worried about Iran using the conflict to gain a foothold in the region. I don't know. Regardless, Saudi Arabia invaded, and then they formed an international coalition to help squash the Houthis and bring the war to a close. That coalition included the United States."

I glanced across the room to Dufort. He still faced me, not so much as twitching.

"You went?" I asked.

Brooke nodded. "In late 2014. I was part of an Army detachment stationed at Al Anad Air Base, tasked with providing security for US shipments of arms and munitions. It was supposed to be guardhouse duty. Stand in the sun, and don't sweat to death. Direct US action was supposedly restricted to drone strikes and logistics support. We weren't supposed to be shooting."

"But you did," I said.

"Not directly, no. I mean, I was just infantry. But there was this segment of the air base where we weren't allowed to go. I used to see Americans coming in and out of metal buildings over there. Big guys, long beards. Dark sunglasses. You know."

"SOCOM," I said. "Spec ops."

"Right," Brooke said. "I guess the Pentagon never misses a trick. Any installation of US troops is an excuse to deploy SOCOM to hunt terrorists. And there are plenty of terrorists in Yemen. Matthew Pearson was there, along with the other guy from the bank—Tyler Spraggins. Both Army Rangers. There were maybe a dozen of them, and there were SEALs, also. Another dozen."

I glanced to Dufort. The big man still hadn't taken his eyes off me. I raised both eyebrows, and Brooke nodded.

"Yeah. Dufort was a SEAL."

"What happened?" I said.

Brooke inhaled deeply. "One day we got orders to go out on patrol. That wasn't unusual. We would escort convoys of ordnance in from the coast, sometimes, to resupply the coalition. So at first, I thought that's what this was. I was told to drive the lead Humvee, and then there were a couple of trucks, then another Humvee. Matthew Pearson was in command of the convoy. He was a captain. Just before we left the airbase, I noticed some of the SOCOM guys loading into one of the trucks. Heavy camo, thick beards. Dufort was with them."

She tilted her head toward the big guy without looking up. I waited patiently.

"Not long after leaving the base, I was ordered to turn north—away from the coast. Pearson rode next to me. Next thing I know, we're in the mountains, and I knew this wasn't a security op. We were too heavily loaded. There were too many spec ops guys. In hindsight, I think it was probably a kill op. The CIA got wind of some high-value target in the mountains somewhere, and the SOCOM deployed the SEALs to deal with it. Maybe they wanted us to bring some people back with us. Hence all the trucks. Whatever the reason, I wasn't worried about it at the time. I was just driving. Staying focused."

Brooke began to cry. She didn't sob. Her breathing didn't change. A lone tear rolled down her cheek, spilling out of her ocean eye.

It hit me harder than I thought it would, sending a hot knife straight through my gut. Maybe it was the raw honesty. Maybe it was simply a primal reaction to seeing a woman in pain. Whatever the cause, I bottled it up. And waited.

"We reached the mountains and were moving between two ridges on some busted road," Brooke said. "I knew we were getting close. Pearson was super tense and kept checking in with everybody. We made it halfway between the two ridges, and then...it happened."

"Ambush?" I asked. I pictured two rocky ridges overlooking a roadbed, and wondered who thought it was a good idea to drive through it. Afghan mountains were full of such places, and the Rangers had learned the hard way to stay out of them.

But Brooke shook her head.

"No. Not an ambush. An explosion. I felt it behind us, and then it was like a semitruck hit my rear bumper. We spun and slammed into the ditch. I couldn't see anything. It was all smoke and chaos and Pearson shouting into his radio. There was some gunfire, but it died out quickly. Pearson told us to bail and take cover, and I fought my way out. There was so much smoke I couldn't see. I couldn't breathe. I almost passed out right there on the spot. I guess I hit my head. But...I saw the damage."

Brooke looked up, twin tear trails running down her face. "Both SEAL trucks were lying on their sides. One was burning. The other was barely recognizable. All blown to hell. I found Dufort lying in the ditch, one whole side of his body nearly blown away. He...he was burning. I did what I could. The whole place was horrifying."

She stopped, and I looked to Dufort. The big man was crying also, his blue eyes still wide, still fixed on me. But no longer blazing hatred. Now I saw only pain. Deep, agonizing pain.

It hit me in my gut and wrenched, hard. I'd seen people die before. I'd held my fingers in a guy's neck one time, attempting to block a severed artery only to watch him bleed out anyway. I'd lost buddies and fellow Rangers. I'd seen human beings commit unspeakable acts against each other —on both sides.

I knew the pain Dufort and Brooke felt, and I knew it wasn't merely physical. But I had also learned through long experience and difficult practice that I couldn't open that box. Keeping the lid on my memories and the way they made me feel was the only way to manage the outrage they unleashed.

In this context, that meant I had to keep the conversation moving. For all three of our sakes.

"I'm sorry about everything," I said. "But I fail to see what any of this has to do with robbing a bank and terrorizing two dozen people."

Brooke wiped her eyes, apparently unoffended that I had pushed her narrative along.

"The blast was ruled to be an IED. A big one...but still an IED. There was a crater in the hillside, not far from the trucks. We snapped some pictures while we waited for the medevacs...and then we were out of there. We got back to base, and the casualties were counted. Three SEALs and two Rangers dead. Half a dozen more badly wounded. Dufort was the worst of those. He...well, you can see."

I held Dufort's gaze and nodded once. A signal of respect, but not sympathy. A warrior like him would be offended by sympathy.

"What happened next?" I pressed.

"Some guys came down. You know the types. Pentagon people. They made it clear that our mission was technically illegal, and therefore we could never talk about it. We were all guaranteed cushy medical retirements or promotions...

and that was that. Everybody went home. The families were told their loved ones died in training accidents. Because of course they did. In March of 2015, Al Anad Air Base was evacuated and fell to the Houthis. We all went home. My enlistment expired, and I got out. We all went our separate ways, and that was it. Until..."

I raised both eyebrows. Waited.

"Until six weeks ago, when I heard from Matthew Pearson. He sent me an email and asked me to drive to Atlanta. He said we were having some kind of reunion. My therapist thought it would be a good idea. So I went. I met Pearson at a hotel downtown, where only two others showed. Dufort and Spraggins."

"And it wasn't a reunion," I guessed.

"No. It wasn't."

Brooke stopped again. Squared her shoulders. "This is the part where I have to trust you, Sharpe. Completely. I have to know you can handle a secret."

"I've handled plenty before," I said.

"Yeah, but this is the kind of secret that can get you killed."

"My favorite kind."

Brooke and Dufort locked eyes again, and this time I saw a question in her eyes.

And this time, for the first time, Dufort nodded.

Brooke turned back.

"Are you familiar with Agon Defense?"

"It rings a bell," I said.

"They manufacture air strike technology. Drones, mostly."

"Okay."

"Ten weeks ago one of their IT guys at their corporate

office here in Jacksonville found something. An old mission file. Something that was meant to be destroyed. That file contained the exact specifics of our mission in Yemen...and confirmation of an air strike gone bad."

My blood ran cold. I stood up from the wall. "Are you saying..."

"I'm saying those three SEALs and two Rangers were murdered by our own government," Brooke said. "And the truth was buried."

15

"Where's the proof?" I said.

It was a clinical question. A very direct one. But after two careful minutes of analyzing the claims Brooke had just lobbed at me like artillery shells, it was by far the most rational.

I could believe that a friendly-fire accident had occurred. Friendly fire had been such a problem in the early years of the war against terror that a name was developed for it: blue on blue. Every soldier's worst nightmare. And as for the Pentagon covering things up...it would require a nuclear level of naiveté to deny that possibility.

But drone strikes and IED blasts are two very different things, and the men and women in that convoy should have been familiar with the appearance of each. It was a stretch for me to believe that, even in the chaos and smoke, somebody hadn't snapped a picture or observed a blast signature that exposed the truth.

"The whistleblower had the proof," Brooke said. "He just didn't know what to do with it, and he was scared. Understandably. He did enough research to find Pearson's name, and learned that he was the son of a congressman. So he contacted him and told him what he had. According to the whistleblower, the bad strike was more than an accident. It was the direct result of malpractice. Apparently Agon had been experimenting with targeting systems powered by an early form of artificial intelligence. A sort of automated thing, like a security robot. The drone was flying overwatch, automated to respond immediately to perceived threats. That's something not authorized by the military, of course, for obvious reasons. The drone fired on the wrong target."

"And that looked like an IED to you?" I pressed.

"That's the thing," Brooke said. "I'd never seen an IED blast before. Neither had several of the other drivers. But Pearson said he had. And he said the blast marks were consistent. So he didn't believe this guy at first. But the guy had pictures taken by the drone, showing the blast...*as it was happening.*"

Again, a chill rippled up my spine, and I stepped across the room to fish a bottle of water out of a grocery sack on the TV stand. Dufort kept his back to the wall and his eyes on me while I drank, processing what I'd been told and again matching it against everything I'd most recently experienced.

I thought I saw the connection. But I needed to hear it from Brooke.

"What next?" I said, turning back.

"I think you know," Brooke said. "Pearson told the whistleblower to secure the evidence and dig up anything further that he could. Then Pearson flew to DC to meet with his father...Congressmen Pearson."

"And?"

"And they were assembling an investigation. Pearson was working quietly to avoid being sabotaged. But somehow it got out. The whistleblower was found in his apartment, overdosed on heroin. Stone dead."

"Hell of a coincidence," I said.

"Matthew Pearson thought so," Brooke said. "His father was unsure. Pearson spent the next month trying to push the investigation forward, but he got nowhere. Nobody would believe him."

"Not even the congressman?" I raised both eyebrows.

Brooke shrugged. "I guess Matthew's father was waiting for hard proof. And then there wasn't any."

"Where did the bank come in?" I pressed.

"Right. The bank. That was when Pearson called for the reunion. He needed help. We met in Atlanta, and he outlined everything that had happened. He was strung out. Apparently, just before the whistleblower died, he told Pearson that he had the evidence secured in his safety-deposit box."

"And instead of taking that to his father, he decided to rob the joint?" I challenged.

"He did take it to his father, but at this point the congressman wouldn't bite. I got the feeling they weren't on the best of terms. Some bad blood. Pearson turned to the FBI next, but that went nowhere. There wasn't enough probable cause to justify an investigation."

"There were drone pictures..."

"Of a mission that *didn't happen*," Brooke said. "Aren't you listening? They covered the mission up from day one. They covered everything up. Destroyed all documentation. There are no records of the convoy. No fuel receipts. No weapons fired. Nothing."

"So why didn't Pearson turn to the media?"

"The whistleblower already tried, before he ever contacted Matt. It went nowhere. Again...not enough evidence."

I ran the data through my mind and reconfigured it half a dozen different ways. It didn't take long for me to compute a mission brief that aligned with my experiences that morning.

"So Pearson decided to rob the bank," I said. "But not very well. Pearson should have known enough to hit it at night, or at least some other time of day. Early morning, with witnesses and cops, it's like setting off fireworks."

"Exactly," Brooke said. "Exactly like setting off fireworks."

I opened my mouth, then stopped. Thought again about the bank. The swinging doors, the brash shouts. *Ladies and gentlemen, this is a robbery!*

Then the gunfire. The blanks fired into the ceiling. The mad car chase out of the city. All the needless theatrics.

"You *wanted* the attention," I said.

Brooke nodded. "Pearson was ready to go to jail for this. So was Spraggins. Pearson saved his life on an earlier op, so the two were kinda tied at the hip. They had stayed in contact and everything. The plan was to bust the bank, grab the box, then flee the city. Generate a story the media couldn't ignore. National attention. A crazy, bizarre car chase. The son of a *congressman*."

"Who fell on his sword," I finished.

"Yes." Brooke nodded.

"And that explains the hostages," I said. "You wanted me to witness everything. To talk to the media."

Brooke shrugged. "That was Spraggins's idea. We didn't bet on kidnapping another Ranger in the building. I was placed in the bank to scope things out. Make sure there were no armed guards or anything before Pearson and Spraggins burst in."

"I guess you missed the old guy with the 1911," I said.

Brooke shrugged. "It's Florida. It was a calculated risk. Lots of people carry guns."

I conceded the point and gestured for her to continue.

"The plan was for me to be taken hostage and manage the other hostage. Make sure they perceived the right things and would talk afterwards. But...well, I got *you*. Not an easy person to manage."

I reviewed the car chase again, picturing it through this new lens, and I couldn't help but be impressed. It was brash. Some might say even stupid. Definitely theatric. Definitely doomed to end in failure.

But for a small group of soldiers hell-bent on exposing the truth, reality is a malleable concept.

Exposing the truth.

"What was in the box?" I said.

"A hard drive," Brooke said. "Nothing else."

"Pearson didn't take it?" I said.

"Of course he took it."

"But it wasn't found by the cops," I said.

"That's because it left the van," Brooke said, indulging in the briefest flash of a smile. The expression exposed her dimples, and I cocked my head.

Thinking again. And then I grinned.

"Your purse."

Brooke nodded. "Yep."

"It flew out the door when you faked an escape attempt."

"Yep."

"But it went into the river..."

I turned to Dufort. The SEAL pursed his mutilated lips, took a step to the dresser, and pulled a drawer open. He removed a watertight bag made of plastic. Transparent and crinkling. He tossed it onto the bed, and I saw the drive.

Just a rectangular hunk of plastic, barely larger than a deck of playing cards, with a USB cable wrapped around it.

Leave it to the SEALs, I thought.

"We put a tracking beacon on it prior to dumping it," Brooke said. "Dufort was waiting in the water."

"Nice job," I said, addressing the last comment to Dufort. He merely grunted.

"So what's on it?" I asked.

Brooke's shoulders dropped. "We don't know. It's encrypted."

"You hooked it up?"

"I did," Dufort garbled. His voice whistled a little in the quiet hotel room, and it made me wince. I recalled pounding him in the tunnel, and suddenly I wasn't so impressed with myself.

Dufort had seen hell. In another universe, a time when he wasn't half burned up and was on top of his game, he would have wiped the floor with me.

Then again, he had already tried. Maybe we were even.

"Can I see the drive?"

Brooke dropped off the edge of the bed and retrieved a laptop from the desk. She unwrapped the drive from the bag, handling it with the care of Indiana Jones and his latest invaluable artifact. The USB cable slid into place, and she opened her file manager.

As soon as she clicked on the drive, the screen went black. A chain of numbers and letters played across the field of darkness, and then a dialog box popped up with only three words printed across the top:

INPUT DATA KEY.

"What's a data key?" I asked.

"Dufort googled it. It's the password to a variable code. Like a constantly changing puzzle. You need it to encrypt and decrypt stuff."

"And you don't have it," I guessed.

"No." Brooke's voice dropped in defeat, and I stared at the screen.

I thought about her story. The blast. The fire. The horrid stench of burning flesh.

War movies focus a lot on the visual—on the screams and the blood. But what they miss is the *smell*. It's impossible to describe, and gut wrenching to the core. Once you smell it, you never forget it, and I'd smelled it plenty of times.

It's the smell of death. Of humanity at its absolute worst. I pictured American soldiers strewn across that valley floor, dead and slowly dying. And then I pictured some fat cat at the Pentagon. Some pencil-pushing mass of biological waste making a call and giving an order.

Covering it all up. Forever. Writing off those lives as numbers on a spreadsheet, and then simply erasing those numbers. Like they never existed.

The heat in my gut redoubled into subdued rage. A cocktail that I fully acknowledged probably had as much to do with my own recent heartache as what I felt for Brooke, Dufort, and their convoy. But logic doesn't play a factor in anger. It's an irrational thing, masquerading as the most rational thing on the planet.

"Tangos," Dufort gargled. "Parking lot."

I looked up to see the big SEAL standing at the window, peeling the curtain back just far enough to expose a slit of light. Moving quickly alongside him, I followed his fat finger to a black car sitting parallel to the entrance. Some kind of sedan—a Ford Taurus, I thought, with heavily tinted windows. I couldn't see a full plate, but what I caught bolted to the front bumper looked white, with blue letters. It was a design I'd seen quite recently—Virginia.

Holder.

I thought about the "consultant" and his question —*What else did they take?*

And then I believed Brooke. I believed Pearson. I bought the whole enchilada.

"Time to move," I said. "Follow me."

16

Brooke shoveled her things into a backpack, placing the drive at the bottom beneath a bundle of clothes. Then we left the hotel room, taking the stairs, not the elevator. I took point, speaking quickly as I fast-walked down the steps.

"When we reach the bottom, we head straight for your car. They won't confront us here. Too many witnesses. If they give chase, we'll take it as it comes. Brooke, you drive."

She nodded as she flipped the hotel keys into a fishbowl at the reception desk, then the automatic glass doors hissed open, and a wash of early evening Florida warmth rushed across my face.

I saw the sedan—a Taurus, as I thought—parked just outside the pavilion, the driver's side window facing the hotel entrance. The glass was tinted dark enough to shield the occupants, but I stared right through it anyway. Daring the driver to make a move.

He didn't. We circled the car and found Brooke's Civic right where we left it. Dufort took shotgun again, and I folded myself into the back seat. Brooke tucked the backpack between her legs and started the little engine.

Across the lot I saw the reverse lights of the Taurus flash, just once. The driver had shifted into gear. I patted Brooke on the arm—the soldier's go-ahead. She hit the gas, and we spun toward the street.

"Which way?"

There was no strain in Brooke's voice, but I could detect the focus. She was slipping into old patterns, beaten into the fabric of her identity by months of brutal training. She was a driver, after all. That was what she had been doing in Yemen.

It was her job to remain cool under pressure.

"Left," I said, only because I knew left would take us farther from downtown. I'd been in Jacksonville only about an hour at the time of the robbery, and it was my first visit to Atlantic Florida. I knew nothing about the city, but I knew I didn't want to be downtown. Not if I had to escalate this confrontation.

The Civic bounced out of the parking lot and hit the four-lane. A horn blared, but Brooke ignored it. She planted her foot on the gas, and the engine whined. I looked over my shoulder and saw the Taurus stall at the exit of the hotel, blocked by traffic.

"Ease up a little," I said.

Brooke met my gaze in the rearview mirror. "What?"

"Slow down. Let them catch up."

"Are you crazy?"

"The game has changed," I said. "Hiding only worked as long as they didn't know who you were or what you have. We can assume that advantage is forfeit at this point. Now we need to know who *they* are."

"You're going to..."

"Me and Dufort, yes."

Dufort's perpetual sneer twitched, and he caught my gaze over his shoulder. I saw something dark in his eyes—violent satisfaction. He nodded once, and Brooke eased up, taking the right-hand lane and dropping ten miles per hour.

I looked back to see the Taurus half a dozen cars behind, driving aggressively. Closing the gap quickly. I could see two men behind the windshield—both bulky, square-jawed types in black suits and dark glasses. They were obviously not concerned with concealing their presence, which only further reinforced the two points I had already outlined to Brooke.

Her cover was blown. And we *needed* to know who these people were.

"Hang a right at the next light," I said, voice calm. "You got a gun?"

Brooke shook her head. "I...I don't keep guns anymore."

She trailed off, and I held up a hand. "I understand. Dufort?"

"I flew here," the big guy gargled. I thought of the open drawer in the hotel room and couldn't resist a derisive shake of my head. Dufort had faked me out.

I twisted in the confined space and felt along the carpeted deck behind the back seats and beneath the back glass. I found what I was looking for in a little latch situated behind the right-hand rear seat. It popped when I pulled it, and the seat back leaned forward, exposing the trunk.

I ducked in as Brooke made the turn, taking us off the four-lane. In the darkened interior I found another suitcase, a jacket, and a mess of female traveling paraphernalia. The smell of cosmetics and hair products billowed into my lungs and made my stomach twist.

It reminded me of another small car. Another crowded trunk space.

Another woman.

I shoved the luggage aside and found the pull handle of the floor panel. I managed to wriggle my arm in and felt past a spare tire and a jack, my fingers jabbing blindly in the dark until I touched what I was looking for—the lug wrench. A fourteen-inch metal bar with a crooked wrench head on one end.

It had become a favorite implement of mine over the last year. I'd used it once in North Carolina. Again in Alabama. In the right hands, it could break glass and bone alike, and every car has one.

Returning to the Honda's cabin, I checked the Taurus. In the darkness of post-sunset the bright LED headlights gleamed like beacons. We were off the main drag now, navigating through a quiet and dated residential district. All the houses were split-levels and California A-frames. 1970s architecture, part of that boom era when everybody was building unique houses that somehow all looked the same. The streets were quiet, but not empty. I saw occasional children bouncing balls in driveways—adults perched on front porches, smoking cigarettes.

"Not here," I said. "Quieter. Hit the gas."

Brooke punched it, and the Taurus hurried to follow. The maze of homes continued for another two miles. Then we were back on a city street—but this one was more desolate than the first. More of a service avenue for the industrial side of town. I saw no houses and no retail. Only heavy equipment rentals, storage units, and a semitruck dealership marked by high-powered security lights.

"This will do," I said. "Ease up a touch."

Brooke complied. The Taurus drew in another ten yards. I couldn't see the meatheads behind the windshield anymore. It was too dark, their own headlights too bright.

"You ready, big guy?" I kept my gaze fixated on the back glass.

"Ready," Dufort said. "And don't call me big guy."

"My mistake. Brooke, when I say, stomp the brakes."

"Huh?"

"Now! Hit the brakes."

Brooke hit the brakes. The Civic nose-dived, dropping from forty miles per hour to a full stop amid a scream of tires on asphalt. The Taurus hit the brakes also, unable to swerve around us as an oncoming semitruck rushed by on our left.

The timing was perfect. I rolled left and threw the door open the moment the semi was gone. My feet hit the asphalt, and the lug wrench swung along with me. I saw Dufort on my left, his massive frame swinging easily toward the Taurus. Three seconds after the Civic stopped, we were alongside the black car. I readied the lug wrench, prepared to smash in the driver's side glass. But I didn't think I'd need to.

I was right. The driver chose to confront the threat instead of fleeing from it. An arrogant, foolhardy mistake.

The driver's door popped open, and the square-headed suit stepped out, fumbling with a gun in a shoulder holster. The angles were all wrong for him—his own door blocked his draw—and I was much too fast anyway.

Long before the weapon cleared the holster, my lug wrench made impact with the base of his neck, right where it met his shoulder. It's a vulnerable spot, mostly flesh and sinew, with not much to break. But a direct strike from a lug wrench hurts like hell and makes you forget about silly things like handguns.

He shouted and fell back, dropping the pistol and automatically raising his arm to deflect the next blow. But the next blow wasn't headed for his face, it was headed for his stomach. A lightning jab that sent searing pain ripping up his spine and triggered an order from his brain to protect his vital organs.

His body followed orders, and both arms dropped to shield his gut. *Then* I went for the head.

He hit the ground in an unconscious heap, barely two seconds having passed since my wrench made contact with his neck. His pistol skittered across the asphalt, and I ducked to retrieve it—a Glock 19, chambered in 9mm. I press-checked it before tucking the weapon into my waistband. On the far side of the car, the second guy struck the asphalt, Dufort's distorted breathing not the least bit accelerated.

"Wallets!" I called.

Sifting through the driver's pockets, I found a regular wallet and an ID case and pocketed them both without checking either. Then I turned back for the Civic and sprinted for the back door. Tires hummed on the highway from someplace behind. Heavy tires—probably another semi.

We didn't need somebody identifying Brooke's license plate at the scene of a beatdown.

Dufort dropped into the passenger seat, and Brooke punched the gas. The little wheels spun, and she swerved right at the next turn. I checked my watch, heart thumping as I leaned back into the cramped seat.

Thirty seconds, brakes to accelerator. Then we were once again lost amid the darkening mass of Jacksonville.

17

"What now?"

The stress level had spiked in Brooke's tone when she next spoke. We were off the two-lane now, on more back roads leading behind sprawling industrial complexes. It was quiet, with no sign of cops or unmarked black sedans, but we couldn't stay for long. The cops would turn up as soon as somebody reported the two unconscious meatheads next to the stalled Taurus.

"Find another hotel," I said. "Someplace near the first one."

"Near the first one?" Brooke squinted into the rearview.

"They won't think to look for you there," I said. "We need some time to think."

I opened the wallet over my lap and shook it, dispensing a small pile of cash, credit cards, folded receipts, and one driver's license. Maryland. John Daniel Moss, age thirty-six. He looked just as meatheaded and ugly in the ID photo as he did in person, minus the bruised neck and the lump on his head.

"What have you got?" I asked Dufort.

The ex-SEAL was busy conducting a similar inspection of the passenger's wallet. He flicked me a driver's license without comment.

Jeremy Robert Falk. Virginia. Age thirty-two.

I inspected the IDs and ran my thumb over the corners of each, checking for the imprinted state seals. They appeared to be perfectly legitimate, but it wasn't what I saw that raised my suspicion. It was what I *didn't* see.

No concealed-carry permits, not for Moss or Falk, and that was wrong. Not because both men were carrying guns. As Brooke had stated previously, plenty of people carry guns in Florida, and they don't need a permit to do so. Florida is a permitless carry state. But while I wasn't sure about Maryland and Virginia, I knew the odds were that one or both states required a permit, not to mention any number of states the two men had driven through to reach Jacksonville.

Yet I hadn't found a permit, which technically meant both firearms were being transported illegally. That could be indicative of careless disregard as much as malicious intent, but regardless it certainly wasn't a vote in either man's favor.

Leaning back in my seat, I rotated Moss's ID in my right hand and gazed out the window at the passing cityscape. Brooke was taking a wide circle back to the hotel district, driving just under the speed limit and signaling at every turn. She was smart.

I tuned out the hum of the tires and thought again about Brooke's story. About everything she had said. About the robbery and the van chase and the two men we had just pounded into the pavement.

It had all happened so fast that I hadn't really considered

what I was doing or how quickly I had become a willing accomplice of Brooke and Dufort's campaign. Looking back over the past year, I couldn't deny that I was developing a habit of acting first and thinking later. Moving on instinct. Then again, maybe that wasn't a new thing. Maybe I'd always been that way, ever since I was an orphaned kid in Phoenix.

Maybe now that I was no longer a Ranger and no longer a cop, I was simply off the leash. Regardless, the wave of exhaustion closing over the back of my mind was now irrefutable. It had been a meat grinder of a day, and I knew my mental faculties were taking a toll. I needed to think. And I needed to know *for sure* that I wasn't being lied to.

"Did you bring your computer?" I asked.

Brooke nodded.

"When we get to the hotel, you check in," I said. "Two rooms, adjoining. One night."

Brooke exchanged a glance with Dufort. I knew what she was thinking. *Who put you in charge?* I had assumed the position almost by default as we fled the last hotel, which wasn't exactly intentional. But now that I had a chance to think about it, I was ready to make it intentional.

"If you want my help, I'm going to call some shots," I said. "Otherwise you can drop me at the corner and be on your way. I certainly don't need any more problems in life."

Brooke met my gaze in the mirror. She licked her lips. "Look. It's not like we're ungrateful. But we barely know you. How do we know anything you've said is true?"

I snorted. "Pretty sure I take the gold on most believable story."

A long pause. We sat at a stoplight. I noticed Dufort

sweeping the sidewalks and the cars, his narrow eyes inspecting every face, the captured G19 riding between his thigh and the door. Ready. Once a SEAL, always a SEAL.

"I guess that's fair," Brooke said at last. "But unless you can hack computer drives, I don't know if you can help us anyway."

I thought about the missing data key necessary to access the files on that hard drive. It was a perplexing problem, but ironically, it wasn't the first time I'd been faced with a password-encoded computer drive concealing critical evidence. As a homicide detective with the Phoenix PD, I'd encountered plenty of secure computers, phones, and hard drives, any number of them containing crucial breadcrumbs in a bloody investigation.

There was a procedure for cracking such devices. It involved an expert—an expensive one, usually. Not somebody employed directly by the city, but a contractor. Some nerdy guy with long, unwashed hair and smudged glasses who commanded a six-figure salary but dressed like a homeless person. As a recently retired member of the PPD, I no longer had access to those contractors, of course.

But I still had friends. One friend, in particular. Somebody who could help.

Maybe.

I said nothing as Brooke pulled into another cheap chain hotel, parking in the back this time. She switched off the car and looked into the rearview.

"Well?"

"I may have something," I said. "An old contact."

"Somebody in Jacksonville?"

"No. But that may not matter."

Long pause. Brooke was playing hard to get, but I knew she'd take the bait. She didn't have much of a choice.

"Check into the hotel and wait for me," I said. "I need your phone."

18

TWO YEARS PRIOR

"On your left! Top floor!"

Jacquie's voice exploded from my shoulder-mounted radio, and I looked to the top of the three-story apartment building. A fire escape was built along the outside, rusted metal baking under a blazing Phoenix sun. A metal door exploded open, and a skinny guy lunged out—long black hair and a Hispanic complexion.

My man.

Hurtling around the corner, my duty weapon cleared the holster as I sprinted down the alley. Jacquie called through the radio again, and police sirens screamed as she raced to close off the far end of the alley. It was another fifty yards to the base of the fire escape, and my suspect was already dropping off the final level and smacking the ground. I expected him to turn for the open end, running headlong into the side of the police cruiser as Jacquie rushed in. Just like the movies.

I was wrong. The perp turned toward me, lunging ahead as I raised my service Glock.

"Police! On the ground, *now!*"

I might as well have shouted gibberish. He hurtled on, eyes wild and crazy, saliva dripping down his chin, white slurry smeared across his nose. Hyped up on enough Colombian cocaine to overwhelm any better judgment.

I placed a finger on the trigger and called again for him to stop. I didn't see a weapon. I knew if I shot him, the case would collapse. We'd have a dead body, and I'd go under investigation...but the victim's family would never know.

Not for sure.

"*Stop!*"

He ignored me. I released the trigger and raised the pistol, sidestepping left to bring the butt of the Glock over the back of his head.

The cocaine in his brain must have kicked his perception up a notch. He saw what was coming and leapt like a jungle cat, landing right on top of me. His body mass sent me stumbling backward, and I flailed. The gun flew from my hand, and I hit the concrete. He lay on top of me, jagged nails biting my flesh as his fingers closed around my throat. My right hand dropped automatically to my belt for my combat knife, ready to ram it up to the hilt into his rib cage.

The knife wasn't there, because I wasn't a Ranger. Not anymore. I felt a duty light instead and attempted to yank it free, but I couldn't get it out of its holster. I flailed for the Taser affixed to the appendix section of my belt but couldn't get my fingers around it.

He rammed my head against the concrete and clamped his fingers around my throat, squeezing and crushing, saliva spraying my face. Those wild animal eyes crazed with bloodlust.

"Die, pig!"

I choked. My vision blurred.

And then the gunshots rained in. One, two, three, four. His head exploded, and his body toppled over sideways as a fifth and sixth shot tore through him. I lay on the concrete, heaving, staring up at that blazing Phoenix sun until curly black hair and chocolate eyes blocked it out.

"Mason! *Mason*, you dumbass. Can you hear me?"

I coughed and blinked. The fear in Jacquie's eyes faded quickly to anger, and she kicked me in the ribs.

"Why didn't you shoot him?"

I took Jacquie's hand and fought my way into a seated position as more sirens screamed in the distance. *Backup.* Just a little too late, as always.

My vision cleared, and I looked to the perforated body of our suspect, lying in a pool of drug-laced blood. Jacquie's petite shoulders rose and fell as she heaved a little, but there was no regret in her face. She dropped the magazine on her Glock, cleared the chamber and pinned the slide back, then deposited the weapon on the ground. Ready for the internal investigators.

"Nice shooting," I wheezed.

Jacquie cocked her head, half blocking the sun. White teeth flashed in a quick smile.

"You gotta marry that girl, dude. You're gonna get us both killed."

"What if I told you I was working on it?"

"Then I'd say *work faster.*"

She smacked my shoulder and shot me a wink, then walked coolly toward the incoming cops. As collected as ever. I watched her go, still catching my breath and massaging my bruised throat. Then I called after her.

"Hey, Jac!"

Jacquie looked over one shoulder, squinting in the sun.

"Thank you," I said simply.

Jacquie nodded softly, the grin subduing into a gentle smile. "I got your back, Mason. I always will."

———————

I STOOD OUTSIDE THE HOTEL, cradling Brooke's cell phone and gazing at the screen. The background was a cat. Some big orange and white thing curled up in Brooke's lap while Brooke grinned into the camera. She didn't wear any makeup. Her raven black hair fell around her shoulders, her bronze skin glistening from a recent shower.

She looked...not happy. No. I was far too familiar with the traces of PTSD and encroaching depression to ignore their fingerprints in her eyes. But I could tell she was trying. Really hard.

I knew what that felt like, also.

Tapping the web browser application, I ran a quick Google search. Located a phone number. Tapped it and directed the phone to dial. Then I leaned against the hotel wall and listened to the digital ring.

It had been months. Almost a year. I hadn't dialed this number or spoken to the person on the other end since North Carolina. There had been phone calls, probably. But I had changed numbers. There were emails also, I knew. But I had ignored them.

Not because I resented or was afraid of the person on the other end. Simply because I didn't know what to say. I didn't want to answer the questions. I didn't want to explain the person I had become since losing Mia.

"Phoenix Police Department, front desk. How may I direct your call?"

"Detective Richardson, please," I said.

Brief pause.

"Detective Richardson is unavailable. Would you like to leave a message?"

"Yes, please."

Another pause was followed by a brief voicemail recording. I recognized the clipped Arkansas drawl, heavily suppressed but not yet eliminated. The voice sounded a little duller than I remembered. Maybe a little more tired.

I waited for the beep, then drew a breath.

"Jacquie...it's Mason. Call this number when you get my message. I need your help."

19

I turned the phone's ringer on and found my way to the fourth floor, where Brooke had rented adjoining rooms for the night. She admitted me without question, not asking for her phone as I stepped into the cramped room. It was old and dingy, much like the first hotel. I made a mental note of that and wondered if Brooke was light on cash.

A large pizza lay on the bed, the lid open, two slices missing. Dufort sat in the corner with another large pizza in his lap, most of it already missing as he folded a greasy slice into a taco shape and shoveled it in. With every bite he smacked and slurped, his twisted lips leaking marinara sauce. Watching him reminded me of this ugly old pug one of my foster mothers owned. I hated that dog from the day I met it, partially because I knew that no matter what happened, my foster mom would always prefer the dog over me.

But also because it ate like Dufort was eating now. All smacking and slurping nastiness. At least Dufort had a good excuse.

I ignored the pizza and found Brooke at the little desk next to the TV, poring over her laptop. She looked up as I approached, and I noted renewed strain creasing her face. Pivoting my attention to the screen, I immediately understood why.

It was a news report about Matthew Pearson. Squatting next to the desk, I surveyed the headline and the attached pictures of both Pearson and Spraggins. They were both in state custody while investigations into the robbery, chase, and crash unfolded. Pearson, it was noted, had sustained a gunshot wound while fleeing the bank. He was now undergoing medical care before joining Spraggins at the Leon County jail.

"It's all over the news," Brooke said. "National, local... everybody is talking about it."

I studied the mugshot of Spraggins. There was no shot of Pearson yet. Probably due to his surgery. But the picture of Spraggins matched the guy I remembered from the robbery. He looked cold and perfectly calm. Standing upright with his shoulders square, glaring dead ahead.

A military stance, which was highlighted by the article, along with a brief summary of his military record. It was fast journalism, but not difficult journalism. As soon as Spraggins's name was published, the next logical step would be to check his background. Somebody called the DOD's information office. A favor was exchanged.

And there you had it.

"I'm worried about them," Brooke whispered. "They're sitting ducks in jail."

"They won't stay at county," I said. "The feds will extradite them, or the state will move them."

"Isn't that worse?"

I didn't answer. I found a bottle of water on the TV stand, and Brooke followed me through the door into the adjoining room, leaving Dufort to demolish the last of the pizza. I folded my arms and faced her. But I didn't say anything.

"Did you reach your contact?" Brooke asked.

"I left a message."

She nodded a couple of times, chewing her lip. Looking strung out as hell, as though she hadn't slept in days. I thought maybe she hadn't. This woman had nerves of steel —that much was obvious in the way she'd handled the van chase, then our flight from the hotel. Most of the crying and panic during the robbery had been faked for my benefit. She had been calculating the entire time.

But I also knew I wasn't looking at a whole person. Not even a healthy person. Despite her fit body and confident stance, the marks of depression were obvious. The signs of anxiety as evident as fireworks. Inside, someplace deep beneath the strong exterior and calculated production of raccoon makeup tears, I saw the carnage.

I saw it because I'd felt it.

"I've never liked bullies," I said. "I like liars even less, and I like bureaucrats least of all. The world would be a better place without all three."

Brooke didn't answer. She waited.

"I'm going to help you decrypt this drive," I continued. "When my contact calls back, we'll arrange somebody to have a look at it. I want to see whatever is inside. And then, if it is what you say it is, I'm going to go back to my life and let you do your thing. Let the truth do what it does."

Another reserved nod. Her head tilted ever so slightly. Elegant chin rising in just the hint of a question. Because she wasn't stupid.

"But?" Brooke asked.

I selected the nearest of a pair of queen-sized beds and settled onto the end, resting palms against my thighs. I breathed out slowly, suddenly so tired I could barely hold my head up.

One hell of a Monday.

"There is no but," I said. "I just want to be sure that there isn't a punchline."

"A punchline?" The tilt in her head magnified.

"A twist," I said. "A plot hole. Something you're not telling me that changes the right and wrong of this situation. Before I start leaving fingerprints, I need to know, one soldier to another, that you're telling me the truth. The *whole* truth."

I waited. Brooke didn't answer. She kept her head cocked, looking very tired and battle worn, but not uncertain. Then settled onto the end of the bed next to me.

"You're asking if you can trust me?" she said.

"Yes. That's exactly what I'm asking you."

Brooke nodded. Just once. "You can trust me. One soldier to another. I wouldn't lie about this."

I measured her words, reviewing her story again in my mind. Fully aware that the very nature of her story made it unverifiable—all the business about Yemen and an unauthorized op and a bad strike. Dufort's presence was some proof, as were the military histories of Spraggins and Pearson. But in reality, she could have made everything else up. I could be blindly entangling myself in the web of a mastermind, becoming an accomplice to a laundry list of felonies.

In the end, I had to make a decision. It was that simple. Go, or no go. Trust, or don't trust.

And I chose to trust. Not because the story was especially

airtight, or because any evidence I had seen to date had won me over. I trusted her because of the storm I saw brewing inside her. Deep and tumultuous...and all too familiar.

I extended a hand, and Brooke clasped it. Her grip was firm, but not overbearing. I shook her hand once.

"All right, Corporal. Consider me on your team."

20

We turned in for the night shortly thereafter. Until Jacquie called, there wasn't much more we could do, and all three of us were dog-tired. Dufort and I took the room with two beds, offering Brooke a little privacy for the night, and the ex-SEAL crashed without so much as a "good night", falling asleep almost instantly.

And snoring like a chainsaw. The sound was guttural and irregular. Hissing and wheezing, snorting and choking. It was a wet, snotty, rumbling sound. Like my foster mother's pug, curled up on the couch, sawing logs until the wee hours of the morning.

I rolled my back toward Dufort and faced the window, clamping my eyes closed and longing for my air mattress in the back of my old GMC. I never thought I'd miss such a primitive arrangement, but right now a sticky night spent under the stars with the rusting suspension of the old truck groaning at my every turn sounded like paradise.

In hindsight, the last twelve months looked like something of a personal spiral. A year ago I had been a decorated detective. I'd had a mortgage. A pension plan. A beautiful, loving fiancée.

And now I lived out of a truck. I wandered around. I spent money out of my pocket with no thought of a credit score or a retirement account. I just...existed.

I thought at first the change was a temporary one. Just a way to clear my head before eventually facing the personal carnage and rebuilding my life. But the longer I slept in the bed of that truck, my head resting on the tailgate, staring up at the stars...the less I cared about pension plans and addresses. The less I cared about anything. Having a home and a stable job had once felt like security. Something I'd longed for since childhood.

Without Mia, that life now felt like a prison.

Dufort gurgled on for another twenty minutes, sometimes going silent for as long as ten seconds before heaving like a free diver returning to the surface. I was just beginning to contemplate the rental of my own hotel room when Brooke's phone rang. I'd set it on the nightstand next to my bed, the picture of her and the orange cat flashing quickly across the screen before an unknown number replaced it—area code 480. East Phoenix.

I lunged out of bed and scooped the phone up, but I didn't answer. I exited the room instead, leaving Dufort's gurgling behind as I glanced both ways down the hallway.

The hotel was quiet.

I selected a quiet nook near a window that overlooked the hotel pool. The phone was vibrating for the fourth time before I hit the answer button.

"Hello?"

"Mason?"

The voice on the other end was tired. A little strained. A lot concerned. And very familiar.

Just hearing Jacquie speak for the first time in nearly a year sent a flash of heat through my chest. I found myself suddenly tongue-tied and dry-mouthed. I swallowed hard and cleared my throat.

"Hey, Jacquie."

Long, long pause. I waited, ready for tears or a profane outburst. I probably deserved both. I received neither.

"How...how are you?" Jacquie said slowly. I detected a hitch in her voice, but she held it together well.

"I'm good," I said. I wasn't really sure how to answer her question. Most people would probably say, based on casual observation, that I was very much *not* good. But you can't measure internal peace from external instability.

"Where are you?" she asked. A logical next question. She probably assumed I was moving around.

"Florida," I said. "Jacksonville."

"I hear it's nice there."

It was an absurd comment. Such a trite, trivial, small-talk thing to say for two people who were so close. Or used to be.

"It is," I said. Because I could think of nothing else to say.

"What can I do for you, Mason?"

The next question was almost flat. I felt the barb in the undertone and knew I deserved it. I briefly debated whether I should address the elephant in the room; then I decided I couldn't even if I wanted to. It was too much to unpack. I would clear the air with Jacquie once this mess with Brooke was ironed out.

"I'm in a situation," I said. "Some old Army buddies of mine need help. I could use some backup."

The pretext of my request danced the line between truth and lie, but I didn't have time to explain myself in full detail.

"What do you need?" Another flat question. I plowed ahead.

"We've got an encrypted computer drive we need to unlock. I need a specialist to take a look at it. I thought... maybe you could call one of the department contractors."

I waited, half convinced that she'd shoot me down cold. Maybe I deserved that.

Instead, Jacquie simply grunted. "I'll make a call."

"He'll need to fly to Jacksonville," I said. "We need this done in person."

"That will be expensive."

"Right." My mind clicked into gear, quickly estimating the value of the cash in my wallet and the captured cash I'd taken from Moss and Falk. Not enough.

But I had their credit cards, also. A little credit card fraud wouldn't kill anybody.

"I'll cover it," I said.

"I'll see what I can do. Anything else?"

"Yes. I've got a couple of IDs...I'll text you pictures. Anything you can find would be helpful."

No answer. I leaned against the wall and closed my eyes, waiting for the storm. Jacquie was famous for her temper. Heaven knew I deserved it, but she said nothing. The silence was somehow worse.

"Jacquie..."

"It's no problem, Mason." She cut me off, that hot undertone creeping into her voice. "I'll make some calls. Text me the pictures."

And then she hung up. I stared at the picture of Brooke and the orange cat, a little stunned, but mostly just numb.

Digging the captured IDs from my pocket, I snapped pictures of each and texted them to the number Jacquie had called from. I also texted her the name *John Holder*, suggesting that he was probably ex-military and asking her to find anything she could on him. Then I pocketed the phone and took the stairs to the first floor. The late-night desk clerk was chugging Mountain Dew and watching Netflix on an iPad. She yanked headphones out as I approached, shooting me a perfunctory smile.

"How can I help you, sir?"

"I'd like another room, please." I dug into my pocket, producing Moss's credit card and sliding it across the counter. "As far from the fourth floor as possible."

21

I rose at seven a.m. and checked out of my first-floor room, stopping by the lobby long enough to grab a handful of stale bagels from the "continental breakfast" bar. Then I took the stairs back to the fourth floor and knocked on Brooke's door.

She answered in a T-shirt and shorts, a towel wrapped around her head, cheeks glistening with shower steam. She glanced sideways toward Dufort's room, then grunted knowingly.

"Snoring?" she asked.

"Like a tank with a bad transmission. Have a bagel."

She accepted the bagel with a flash of a smile, and I saw the dimples again. Even without a hint of makeup on, there was a rosy warmth to her cheeks that brought color to her dark eyes. I felt a flush of warmth in my chest again, followed almost instantly by a much colder wash of guilt.

I thought of Mia curled up on our living room couch with a book. Wearing a turtleneck sweater and peeking at me over the top of the pages. It was one of the few images I could still clearly picture. I clung to it like gold.

"Sharpe?" Brooke cocked her head, the dimples fading. I realized I had been standing at the door, staring at her dumbly while holding the bagels. I blinked.

"Sorry...didn't sleep much."

On my way to the dresser to deposit the bagels, Brooke's phone buzzed in my pocket. There was a message waiting from Jacquie, as abrupt as ever.

> IT contractor based in Atlanta agreed to help. Will fly to Jax today. Fee is $1,500, plus expenses. Will text you travel itinerary.

I shot back a quick reply.

> Sounds good. IDs?

> Will run them today. Stand by.

I hovered over the keyboard, hesitated, then punched out one more quick message.

> Thanks, Jacquie.

I waited three minutes, but saw no response. Pocketing the phone, I looked up in time to see Dufort stumble in. He also gleamed with shower steam, but unlike Brooke, he was shirtless. As he reached for a bagel, his left side twisted toward me, and the breath left my lungs.

His torso looked even worse than his face—like a horror sketch for a graphic novel. His entire left side was swollen and distorted, twisted by fire and the force of the blast wave, with bulging white scars running up his rib cage and down the length of his arm like coiled snakes.

I'd seen plenty of gore before, but this turned my stomach. I couldn't help but look away.

Dufort laughed, cold and humorless. "Pain is weakness leaving the body, Army man."

I grunted. "You must have been weak as hell."

It was a bad joke, and for a moment I thought it would fall flat. Then Dufort guffawed like it was the funniest thing he'd ever heard, throwing his head back and gurgling toward the ceiling. I was reminded of that stupid pug again, but I couldn't resist joining him with a dull smile.

"Put a shirt on, Dufort," Brooke snapped, pushing him toward his room. "I'm trying to eat."

Dufort continued to laugh as he migrated back to his room, mumbling the joke back to himself in that gurgling, distorted voice. "Weak as hell...that's a good one."

I met Brooke at the bed, where her laptop was already propped up. She was scanning the news sites again, skipping from one source to the next. All of them carried headlines about the robbery and subsequent car chase. It was a national sensation, just like Brooke said it would be.

Robbery Suspects Refuse to Talk. Demand Lawyers.

Congressman Pearson in Shock: "That's not the Matty I know."

Robbery Victims Describe Pure Terror; Bank Security Footage Leaked.

Brooke looked up from the laptop. "It's working."

"For now," I said. "News cycles are short. We'll need to feed the beast if we want to keep it alive."

Brooke looked back to the computer, scanning mugshots of Spraggins and Pearson.

"I never actually thought...you know. They'd go to jail."

"They were ready for it," I said. "That was their job. Our job is to decrypt that drive and clear their names. My contact in Phoenix arranged an IT specialist from Atlanta. He's flying in this morning. But...somebody has to pick up the tab."

Brooke grimaced. "How much?"

"Fifteen hundred, plus expenses. Call it two grand or more, total."

A long pause. "Is he good?"

"I've never used him before, but I trust my contact. I'd say he's good."

"Okay. I can help, but...I can't cover that by myself."

I pondered a moment, considering the stolen credit cards and how long it would be before they were cut off.

Not long, I thought. And they couldn't be used to write a check to the IT guy, anyway.

"I've got maybe a grand on me," I said. "My own cash, plus what we took from Moss and Falk. We'll pool our resources and figure it out."

I offered Brooke a confident nod I didn't quite feel, and she smiled. Just a hint, a flash of dimples. The warmth returned to my chest, and I was grateful for the distracting buzz of Brooke's cell phone. Another message from Jacquie.

Specialist landing at JAX, 10 AM EST.

My old partner had moved quickly—so quickly we might

have to hustle. I checked my watch and was relieved to find that it was just past eight, leaving us a little under two hours to reach the airport. Plenty of time.

And then it wasn't. Dufort's gurgled voice boomed from the adjoining room. "Tangos in the parking lot."

I turned automatically for the window. Pushing back the blinds, I peered into the front lot beyond.

They were tangos, all right. Another jet-black car sat near the front entrance—a Ford Taurus, with half of a blue and white Virginia license plate visible above the rear bumper. Two men sat behind the windshield while a third stood next to Brooke's car, snapping pictures with a cell phone.

Black suits. Chiseled jaws. Dark sunglasses.

More meatheads.

"How did they find us?" Brooke's breathing quickened, but she didn't panic.

"Doesn't matter," I said. "They did."

I shut the blinds and thought quickly as Dufort entered the room. He wore a shirt now—thank God—and he looked to me. Mouth closed. Shoulders squared.

Ready for orders.

"We can't rough them up twice," I said. "They'll be ready this time. We've got to outthink them."

"How?" Brooke said.

I thought about her dark blue Civic with Kentucky plates. A possible liability at this point. We needed to switch it up.

I tossed Brooke her phone back. "Call a rental company and have a car delivered someplace nearby. A big parking lot would be best. A Walmart or something. Use Moss's credit card if you need to. Then pack your stuff and go downstairs. Wait in the lobby for my signal."

"Where are you going?" Brooke said, uncertainty creeping into her tone.

I gestured for Dufort to follow me. The big SEAL fell in without question, Falk's Glock barely visible beneath the tail of his shirt. I grabbed Moss's Glock from the bedside table.

"I'm going to cheat," I said.

ufort followed me down the steps, taking them two at a time all the way to the bottom. We exited via the side entrance, stepping into bright Florida sunshine and creeping slowly around the end of the building.

Kneeling at the corner, I watched as the meathead with the cell phone completed his inspection of Brooke's Civic, then returned to the Taurus. A conference was held at the car's windshield. The driver appeared to be in charge, but he also seemed unsure what action to take next. There was some debate, with hands gesturing toward the hotel, then back toward the car.

I slipped a hand into my pocket, fishing for my Victorinox Swiss Army knife. My fingers met loose change and a toothpick, and I breathed a curse. The knife was still someplace in Tallahassee.

"Dufort, you got a blade on you?"

A sharp snapping sound answered my question, and

Dufort dropped a Benchmade Infidel into my outstretched hand, the double-edged blade already extended.

Perfect.

"Call Brooke," I said.

Dufort dialed and passed me the phone. Brooke answered on the second ring.

"All good with the rental?" I asked.

"They're working on it now. They said they can deliver in about an hour."

"That'll work. Go down to the front desk and complain about something. Try to make a scene. When the two guys come in, take the hallway to the end of the building and exit out the side entrance. We'll be waiting."

"Okay."

Brooke hung up, and we waited. I rolled the Infidel in my hand, feeling the weight and testing the balance. Measuring in my mind the amount of force I would need to apply.

Two minutes passed. The meatheads at the Taurus waited; one leaned against the hood, the other sitting behind the wheel. Apparently content to wait us out.

Brooke didn't leave them hanging. I couldn't see into the lobby, but I marked the moment Brooke appeared at the front desk. The guy leaning on the hood straightened, jabbing his chin inside. His companion held up a hand, urging him to wait.

I imagined Brooke at the desk, arguing with the clerk. Causing a scene.

It wasn't enough. These guys were smarter than I estimated—unwilling to venture into uncharted territory.

I held out my hand, and Dufort passed me the phone again. I texted Brooke.

Look to your left. Make eye contact, then run.

It was a transparent ploy, but I figured these guys had their limits. They were hounds, not hunters. Trained to react to the scent of their prey, moving on instinct, not wit.

At least, I hoped that was true.

I sent the text and waited. Ten slow seconds passed. Then the guy next to the hood broke for the sliding glass doors, and the guy behind the wheel threw his door open and hurried to follow, all flopping legs and flailing arms.

"Now," I hissed. "Get the car!"

I tossed Dufort Brooke's keys, only then wondering whether the big guy could fit behind the steering wheel. It was too late to worry about that detail. Dufort caught the keys and jogged toward the Civic. I dashed for the Taurus.

Both men were gone now. I moved to the driver's side rear tire and brought the Infidel down hard. Steel bit rubber, and compressed air exploded out. The front left tire met a similar fate; then I rendezvoused with Dufort at the opposite end of the parking lot. He slid to a stop in the little blue car, packed behind the wheel with his head dropped low to see beneath the roofline, his knees and elbows almost touching. I hood-slid to the passenger side and jumped in.

"End of the building! Go!"

Dufort smashed the gas, and the little engine whined. Tires spun, and we rocketed around the back of the hotel. My shoulder slammed into the right-hand window, and I grabbed the armrest to steady myself. Dufort drove like a maniac, yanking the wheel and punching the accelerator liked it owed him money. Every move was abrupt and severe, brakes screaming as we slid to a stop near the end of the hotel, right where we'd crouched only a minute prior.

Brooke exploded through the door, the two meatheads visible ten yards behind.

"Get in!" I shouted.

Brooke tore the rear door open and threw herself in behind Dufort. The four cylinder raced again, and tires burned. The lead meathead reached the glass, his right hand dropping to his hip.

Then we were gone. Through the parking lot, past the disabled Taurus, and onto the road. Dufort hung a hard left, the back end of the Civic sliding and screaming. Brooke joined the shriek, and the rear door slammed shut under the force of inertia. Traffic closed around us, and a horn blared.

Dufort relaxed off the accelerator, and I caught my breath. Everything had happened so quickly it all felt like a blur.

But I remembered the pop and hiss of the Infidel blowing out the Taurus's tires. Those guys were going nowhere.

"Rental?" I asked, craning my neck around the seat.

Brooke looked up from the back, her raven hair a clouded tangle around her face, ocean eyes alive with adrenaline.

"Walmart," she gasped. "Shops Lane."

23

We arrived at the Walmart with twenty minutes to spare before the car was delivered, giving me time to replenish my essentials. All of my clothes, toiletries, and personal items were still in my pickup parked at the bank. Or, at least, I hoped it was still parked at the bank. It might have been towed by now.

Problems for another day. For the time being I bought a toothbrush, deodorant, and a change of clothes. People make fun of Walmart clothes, but after a year of living on the road, I had become quite fond of them. They're cheap, generally durable, and I could always find my size. I changed right there in the Walmart bathroom, trashing my old clothes for lack of a place to store them.

Back in the parking lot, I rendezvoused with the others near the garden center just in time for the arrival of Brooke's rental: a baby blue hatchback about the size of my left shoe.

"Are you freaking kidding me?" I snapped, not even trying to hide my irritation.

"What?" Brooke shrugged. "We're balling on a budget. I did what I could."

"We're balling on a stolen credit card," I corrected. "You should have rented an SUV."

Brooke ignored me, signing the clipboard the rental guy handed her while I surveyed the parking lot. I was pretty sure I knew how the meatheads had found us a second time —they had simply put people on patrol, looking for a dark blue Civic with Kentucky plates in the parking lot of a hotel. There had to be dozens of hotels surrounding Jacksonville, but even so, it was a simple process of elimination.

After blowing out their tires and changing vehicles, I was confident we had bought ourselves a buffer. Hopefully, a significant one. But I still felt an edgy uncertainty creeping at the back of my mind.

"Let's move," I said. "The IT guy should be landing soon."

Brooke loaded her limited luggage into the abbreviated cargo space at the rear of the hatchback, then moved for the driver's door. I waved her off.

"I'll drive."

"Excuse me?" Brooke's eyebrows arched upwards.

"I'm not letting that fool drive again," I said, jabbing my chin toward Dufort. "And thanks to your microscopic selection of conveyance, I can't fit in the back seat. So I drive."

She still looked pissed, but Brooke couldn't argue. She folded her petite body into the cramped back seat, and I folded my much larger body into an only slightly more spacious driver's compartment. I felt like a clown.

The motor started with a soft rumble, and Dufort packed in next to me, his shoulder jammed against mine. Then we were off, following directions on Dufort's phone for the airport. It lay on the north side of the city, thirty-five minutes' drive along the bypass. That put us arriving just after ten a.m., when Jacquie's IT guy would land. I thought about calling her for further details, but just then Brooke poked her arm between the front seats, pressing her phone into my hand.

"Arizona number?"

The area code was 480. I took the phone and swiped to answer before I could overthink it.

"Hello?"

"Mason, it's Jacquie. You got a minute?"

Jacquie's tone was all business. It reminded me of her investigator voice, back when we were partners. It was a happy memory.

"Go ahead," I said.

"I ran those IDs you sent me. Jeremy Falk and John Moss."

"Right."

"Clean records. Both military. Falk was a Marine, Moss was Army. They both got out within the past two years. I have residential records that match the addresses on their IDs. Falk lives in an apartment complex, but Moss purchased a home last year. I ran down the mortgage application and found an employer listed as Bridgewater Security, Chantilly, Virginia. It's just outside DC."

I listened quietly as Jacquie rattled along, impressed as always with her results. She had been thorough, a quality I had always admired about her. It wasn't lost on me that she had likely bent some rules to assemble her report. Documents such as mortgage applications weren't easy to come by and usually required a warrant.

Jacquie was doing me a favor. One I didn't deserve.

"Is Falk employed by Bridgewater?" I asked.

"I don't know. I couldn't find his employer, but I did check into Bridgewater. Or I tried to, anyway. No website. No phone number. The address listed on his mortgage application corresponds to an office building in an industrial park. Like someplace you'd find carpet cleaners and plumbers, but I couldn't find any other documents listing Bridgewater as a tenant there."

"Could be a fake," I said. "Something he manufactured to justify illicit income."

"Could be, but probably not," Jacquie said, still all business. "Since the housing crash, these mortgage companies are under stringent regulation. They verify and reverify everything. Especially income. You know that."

Her last comment carried a barb, and I thought it probably had nothing to do with my ignorant suggestion. I decided to bypass it, at least for now.

"What about John Holder?"

"Nothing yet. I'm still checking."

"Thanks for the help, Jacquie. I'll let you know how it goes with the IT guy."

"Mason."

I held the phone near my ear and waited. Unsure what was coming, but ready for a barrage of almost anything.

"I watch the news," Jacquie said. "They say there was another hostage taken during that bank heist. An Army vet."

I let her comments hang. Acknowledging without acknowledging.

Jacquie sighed. "Whatever you're doing...be careful. And whenever you're finished...*call me back*. Do you understand?"

"I will, Jacquie. I promise."

She hung up, and I rested the phone against my leg.

Through the corner of my eye, I noted Brooke watching me in the rearview mirror, raven hair held tight in another regulation bun. Looking very strained, but calm. Like she had been trained to be.

"Old friend?" Brooke asked.

"Something like that," I said. "She said Moss worked for a security firm outside of DC. No records on Falk, but we can assume he did, also. They're both ex-military. The firm is off the radar, big time. No website, no phone number."

"Contractors," Dufort gurgled, his lip lifting in a slight sneer that was exaggerated by his wounds. "Hired guns."

I nodded. "Yeah. I thought so, too."

I'd encountered them before, in the Middle East. All us special ops guys had. Ex-soldiers now employed by "security" firms in the United States, masquerading as guards while serving a much deadlier and more direct role—that of mercenary. Hired guns, like Dufort said. America employed thousands of them during the war on terror, and active-duty guys generally disliked them. We all did the same job, but while the military worked with crappy gear, enjoyed crappy food, and was paid a crappy salary, the mercenaries enjoyed only the best gear. The best food.

And six-figure salaries, tax-free.

Of course, many of the same troops who looked down their noses at the aforementioned mercenaries quickly put in applications after returning home to find their wives living with other men, and almost no jobs matching their specialized skill sets. In hindsight, I didn't blame them, but I wasn't in denial about the ugly underbelly of the contractor world, either.

Sometimes America hired "private security contractors" to perform functions the military weren't allowed to perform, and for good reason. Sometimes the contractors became little better than outlaws, riding deep in the gray area of warfare, slipping slowly into the black.

With enough money on the line, morality had a way of becoming optional.

"The Pentagon wouldn't hire contractors to operate on American soil," Brooke said. "It's far too dangerous. Imagine the scandal."

"They might if they were protecting a bigger scandal," Dufort said.

"It doesn't matter who they're working for," I said. "It'll all come to light once we unlock this drive. Brooke, you got your computer?"

"Roger. In my backpack."

"Great. We'll put this guy straight to work. With any luck, this will all be over by sunset."

24

Jacksonville International Airport was sprawling—
just like the rest of the city. It sat north of downtown,
sleek white jets streaking in and out of the clouds as
we navigated toward the pickup zone.

I texted with Jacquie on the way, learning that the techni-
cian's name was Ronald, and that he'd be wearing a red T-
shirt. Easy enough.

I spotted the guy halfway down the curb, and I almost
punched Brooke in the face. He was *huge*. Not tall. Not
muscular. Just magnificently obese—wrapped in a tight red
T-shirt with video game characters printed on the front, the
sleeves constricting around his arms. He wore headphones
and pecked at a cell phone, oblivious to the world around
him as I stopped the baby blue hatchback ten yards away
and sat fuming.

"Mistakes were made," Brooke said softly.

"You think?" I snapped.

I extracted myself from the sub-subcompact. Ronald was

still lost in the cell phone, a backpack slung over one shoulder. Looking as blissful as a newborn colt.

But four times as large.

"Ronald?" I called his name twice before he pulled the earbuds out, flabby cheeks rising in a smile.

"Wassup, dude? You must be Mason."

"That's right."

He extended a sweaty palm, and I clasped it briefly. Then Ronald leaned off the sidewalk, lowering his voice to a raspy whisper.

"Dude, I've never worked with the agency before. Super stoked."

"The what?" I questioned.

Ronald laughed. "*Riiiiight*. My bad."

I glanced back to the car. Dufort glared knives from the front seat, and I couldn't see Brooke. I figured she was already packing herself into a cup holder to make room.

"Where's your wheels, dude?" Ronald asked, adjusting the backpack. I gestured to the hatchback.

"For real?" he said.

I hesitated, wondering what the hell Jacquie had told him. Clearly, she had pulled some strings. Maybe implied some things. I might as well lean into that.

"Covert," I said. "Nobody expects it."

"Duuuuude." Ronald's flabby cheeks spread into a grin. "Legit!"

I motioned him toward the back seat, catching a whiff of body odor as he lumbered along. The red shirt clung to his skin, sticky with sweat. I'd need to crank the little car's AC up.

I slid the driver's seat forward two notches to allow Brooke more room to cram in behind me. Then Ronald packed in, heaving and wheezing, but not complaining as he jammed his bulk into the micro seat and slammed the door. His backpack bulged from his lap, but I could still see his eyes over the top, flashing bright and happy beneath tangled dark hair.

"No joke," he said. "Coolest job I've had all year. Sweet tickets, too. First time I've flown first class!"

"Say what?" Brooke choked. Already the interior of the car smelled like a gym bag.

"Yeah! Jacquie said all the agency contractors get first class. It's better than the movies!"

Brooke shot me a look in the rearview, and I knew what she was thinking. *Fifteen hundred dollars...plus expenses.*

Thanks, Jacquie.

I shifted into gear. Already horns blared behind me, urging the little car forward. I imagined our wheels bent inward beneath the wheel wells, tires scrubbing as we gained speed, and prayed that the whole contraption wouldn't fly to pieces the moment we hit the highway.

"Brooke, get the drive," I said.

Brooke fumbled for her backpack. The car groaned and swayed, and Dufort breathed curses under his breath. His knees were nearly touching his chin, his own seat run forward to allow room for Ronald's thick knees.

I cranked the AC up.

"Here," Brooke said, jabbing the drive toward the tech. "This is what we need unlocked. It said something about a data key."

Ronald accepted the drive. It was housed in a protective foam case, zippered on the outside, dangling a lanyard.

"Now?" Ronald asked.

"As quick as you like," I said. "We're on a tight schedule."

"Oh...well, sure, sure. No problem."

Ronald heaved and hissed as he unfolded a laptop from his bag before unzipping the drive's case. A cable dangled out, and he poked it into the side of his computer. Not unlike I had done.

I hoped his expertise moving forward would be a step above.

"So," Ronald said. "What do we know about the drive?"

Nobody answered. Ronald looked up.

"What do you mean?" I said, smashing the gas to allow the hatchback to gain speed on the bypass. The little motor wound up to sixty miles per hour, then seemed to give out. I set the cruise.

"Like...who owns it, what kind of person they are, what do you know about them?"

I looked to Brooke in the mirror. She turned to Ronald.

"I'm not sure how that's relevant," she said. "We just want the drive unlocked. We'll take it from there."

Ronald breathed a raspy little chuckle, grinning over the top of the laptop. The grin faded as he met each of our gazes, and nobody reciprocated.

"Oh, you're serious," he said. "Wow. Okay."

He wiped a trickle of sweat off his forehead, scanning the screen. I could only imagine it displayed the same image I'd seen before. A black field with a data box asking for a key.

"I assumed you were familiar with data keys," Ronald said. "Has anyone here ever worked with one?"

No response. Another nervous chuckle. "And you people are agency? Wow! You must be way out in the sticks, huh? I mean, this is elementary stuff. You're telling me you never—"

"Assume we haven't," Brooke snapped, frustration

creeping into her voice. She was still jammed up against the door, her legs half folded beneath her.

"Right," Ronald said, nodding quickly. "Okay. So you're familiar with a password, right? Like on your email or your Netflix account?"

"Yes," Brooke said.

"A password is like a door key. You input the code, and the door opens, and all your data is housed inside. You use the same passcode every time, just like you'd use the same key for your house. Door locked or unlocked. Really simple, right?"

He wiped another trickle of sweat. "But the thing is, this drive isn't asking for a password. It's asking for a *data key*. That's a completely different thing. We're talking about encryption here, not just a locked door."

"I don't understand the difference," Brooke said.

"Okay. Imagine a house again. Encryption is like...if every piece of the house were disassembled, then scrambled in a box. You'd need detailed instructions to know how to assemble it, right? Like a blueprint."

"Right..."

"That's what a data key is. The contents of this drive are disassembled and scrambled. Every piece of data has been assigned a code name—like, a letter or a number. Something like that. Then everything is blended up. The only possible way to read the data is to input the data key. The data key is like a blueprint that tells the computer all the code names for all the individual pieces of data. Almost like translating a foreign language, except much more complicated. With a data key my computer could decrypt the drive in mere seconds. But without it..."

"You didn't fly all the way here to tell us we need what we don't have," I said.

Ronald grinned. "Of course not. You're working with the best, dude! There are ways to crack this sucker. But it's helpful to know as much as possible about the person who encrypted it, so I have someplace to start. I mean, if they used a simple 256-bit encryption, that's hard enough. I'll just need some time. Maybe a lot of time. But if they tried something personal, something *custom*...that's a whole other kettle of fish. We could be talking, like...a lot longer to decode it."

"How long?" I demanded.

Ronald exhaled through thick lips, then rocked his head. "Maybe...a week? Two, tops."

"*A week?*" Brooke's voice cracked in frustration. A rush of heat reached my face, and I tore my gaze away from the highway, twisting toward the back seat.

"Look, buddy. We haven't *got* a week. We were told you—"

"Tangos, five o'clock."

Dufort's gurgling voice cut me off, and my heart rate spiked. I followed his gaze to the right-hand mirror and spied a jet-black Chevy Impala closing fast, one lane over. The front bumper was fit with a blue and white Virginia plate, and I made out two men sitting behind the windshield.

Dark sunglasses. Square jaws. More meatheads.

"Another on our ass," Dufort said. One of our captured Glocks appeared in his right hand as if by magic, resting across his thigh. I glanced into the rearview mirror and saw it. A Ford Taurus. More Virginia plates. More meatheads.

"How did they find us?" Brooke's voice was a little less

calm than Dufort's. I flicked the cruise control off and smashed the gas, sending the little tachometer spiking toward the redline. The engine howled, but the speedometer barely moved.

"Doesn't matter," I said. "We've gotta get off the highway. They'll run us dead in this piece of crap."

Ronald's face washed pale, his neck craning as he looked toward the back glass. The Impala was only fifty yards back, and the Taurus rode our bumper.

"Hold on, big guy," I said. "It's about to get bumpy."

25

I yanked the hatchback right, cutting the Impala off with only inches to spare. The Chevy nose-dived as the driver slammed on the brake, and I caught his face in the rearview.

It was Holder. The *consultant*.

"Dufort! Track a course off the highway. We need someplace where we can lose these guys. No chance we outrun them."

Dufort dug his phone out and went to work on the maps application, his dark eyes snapping regularly to the rearview mirror. Ronald panted from the back seat like a winded dog, his sweaty face twisted over his shoulder to catch sight of our pursuers.

"Are they Russians?" he wheezed.

I swerved left again, nearly knocking the Taurus's bumper loose as I cut the driver off from passing us.

"*Now*, Dufort!"

"Next exit," Dufort gurgled. "Hard right. Industrial park."

Good enough.

I saw the exit sign a quarter mile ahead just as the Impala pulled alongside us. Holder sat behind the wheel, dark sunglasses reflecting Florida sunshine. He motioned to the side of the road with two fingers, like a fighter pilot ordering an airliner to land.

Dufort raised his flame-seared left fist and shot back a different kind of signal. The Taurus went left, riding the checkered line between the middle and far left lanes, and gaining speed again.

These fools were going to *bump us.*

I beat them to the punch and hit the brake. Brooke screamed, and Ronald slammed into the back of Dufort's seat. The hatchback squealed, and the Impala raced by. The Taurus braked hard, then yanked left into the fast lane, raking past our driver's side taillight as it passed. The hatchback jolted, and the wheel snatched in my hands. Horns blared all around us, but I didn't wait to look.

I hit the turn signal and yanked the wheel to the right. The little engine howled, and the transmission jolted. The Taurus raced to follow us as Holder's Impala blazed past the exit.

Then the hatchback caught the off-ramp, blasting across the striped white lines, my left-hand mirror torn off by the exit sign. I pulled the wheel left again and leaned hard into the driver's door as the little car hopped and leaned against its right-hand tires. Burned rubber and engine heat flooded the cabin. We were doing barely forty miles per hour, but it felt like eighty. Brooke clung to the back of my seat, and Dufort pivoted his head to peer through the back glass.

"Nice work," he said. "You lost the Impala. Still got the Taurus."

"Hit me with the turns," I said, not even braking as we raced toward a stoplight at the bottom of the ramp.

"Hard right," Dufort said. "Everybody lean together!"

It was a good judgment call. Even as the four of us leaned into the turn, the passenger side tires skipped across the pavement as I yanked the wheel. A horn blared, and a pickup truck swerved around us, close enough to take off my side-view mirror if it had still been there. Brooke gasped but didn't scream. I smelled an acrid ammonia stench, and as I looked into the rearview mirror, I noted Ronald pressing his legs together, wide eyes framed by chalky pale cheeks.

"Did you piss?" Dufort barked.

It was a moot point. I hit the window switches, rolling all four windows down as I mashed the gas back to the floor. We were on a two-lane now. Nice and wide with a gentle shoulder, but still a two-lane. The Taurus closed behind us but couldn't pass thanks to a steady stream of semitrucks chugging along the oncoming lane, headed for the highway.

"What next?" I shouted over the beat of the wind through the narrow cabin. Dufort fumbled with his phone, nearly dropping it as his chunky fingers traced the screen.

Behind us an engine roared. I looked into the rearview and saw the Taurus—closing now. Sixty yards back and gobbling up the gap quickly. Whatever micro motor was housed beneath the hatchback's hood, it was no match for the Ford. Even with my foot jammed against the floor, the speedometer couldn't reach sixty. The two-lane ran along dipping and curving roads, each incline killing what little power the engine could muster.

"They're gonna ram us, Dufort!" I said. "I need a turn."

"Right—one hundred yards!"

Dufort pointed, and I saw the turn. A stop sign gleamed

alongside a tangle of Florida undergrowth, another two-lane road connecting with our path of travel and leading up another hill. I didn't like the idea of the hill any better than I liked the idea of being rammed, but at this point I had to change the status quo. The Taurus was barely ten yards back and closing by the second.

I tapped the brakes hard, hoping the meathead behind me would flinch. He did flinch, but not as badly as I needed him to. The Taurus slowed, but he guessed my intention. Just as I swung wide to make the turn, he followed suit. The hatchback hurtled past the sign, tires chirping. Then we hit the hill, and I planted my foot onto the accelerator.

A red light blinked from the dash—an engine temperature warning. Power bled off from the motor as we topped the hill and turned down again. The car was apparently programed to limit RPMs while overheating—a perfectly reasonable function under normal circumstances, but completely unacceptable now.

"We need a play," I said.

Dufort ducked beneath the roofline to look ahead. Beyond the trees, a few hundred yards away, two warehouses rested amid the greenery. The left-hand one was marked with the familiar logo of a popular food services brand, with a fence surrounding it and a row of semitruck trailers backed up to a loading dock. A very public place where we might hope to outmaneuver our pursuers and obtain help from the security staff.

But then the police would be called. There would be questions to answer. And with the drive still encrypted, we weren't ready for that. Not to mention the fact that if things turned violent, innocent third parties would be caught in the crossfire.

I switched my gaze to the second warehouse and found an abandoned structure surrounded by a broken fence and a field of high weeds. A busted concrete drive led to a brick building with a vacant loading dock, multiple rolling doors suspended half open with empty blackness stretching beyond.

"Right hand, brace for impact!"

I pulled into the turn and left the smooth asphalt, smacking hard into the concrete drive. Dufort's head struck the ceiling, and I was sure it dented the flimsy metal. The red light on the gauge cluster flashed again, and power evaporated. I mashed the gas and felt no acceleration in response. The engine was either dead or dying, overworked and now shutting down in a last-ditch effort of self-preservation.

Behind us the Taurus turned off the two-lane, fifty yards back and slowing. No longer hugging our bumper.

"We gotta get inside," I said. "Take cover and set up an ambush."

Dufort nodded, and I hit the brakes. The hatchback died completely as it ground to a halt, gravel popping from beneath burned tires. I threw the door open and rolled out, leading with my captured Glock. The Taurus was now stopped fifty yards away, turned sideways, both meatheads invisible behind tinted glass.

"Go!" I hissed.

Brooke rolled out with her bag on her back. She circled to help pry Ronald out of the back seat. I watched the Taurus, sheltering behind the smashed rear corner of the hatchback. Waiting.

The tangos didn't move.

"To the warehouse!" Dufort called.

I followed, the four of us reaching the end of the loading

dock and racing up the steps. The first of the rolling doors stood half open, thick shadows beyond. I smelled grease and abandoned hydraulic fluid. Ronald, Dufort, and Brooke raced by.

I looked across the grassy field, back toward the two-lane, and then I saw it. A sleek black sedan with a Chevy bowtie affixed to the grille.

Holder had arrived.

26

I followed the others into the warehouse. Dufort snapped a flashlight on, casting a bright glow across a sprawling room. A thousand feet long and three hundred wide, most of the building was completely empty, dust covering the concrete floor while random beams of sunlight cut in through holes in the roof. Against the far wall a number of shipping pallets rested in a stack. In one corner a trash compactor sat, rusting slowly away, still half full of rotting cardboard. Forgotten machinery and a pile of shipping timbers were all else that occupied the massive room.

Not much to hide behind.

I returned to the door, leaning out just far enough to catch a glimpse of the yard. Holder's Impala sat next to the Taurus, and all four men had exited the vehicles. They stood behind open trunks. Moving slowly. Laughing while they unpacked their gear.

Taking their time.

The hope drained out of me when I saw the first rifle. It

was a shortened AR-15, similar to what Pearson and Spraggins had hit the bank with. Even from sixty yards out, I detected the presence of a red dot optic. Then I saw another rifle. A third. The guys replaced suit jackets with body armor, drawing charging handles and turning toward the building with all the casualness of old friends headed out on a turkey shoot.

They're gonna exterminate us, I thought.

"We're screwed," Dufort gurgled. I saw raw hatred burning in his narrowed eyes. Pure rage, and I thought I knew why.

It's all a brotherhood in the military. Whether by nature or nurture, being shot at brings men together. You trust the guy next to you, maybe because you have no other choice. You depend on them. You have their backs. You stand together.

But not everybody honored that brotherhood outside the uniform. And clearly, these guys couldn't care less.

A quick mental inventory of our weapons and situation produced only one obvious play in my mind. With only two handguns amongst the four of us, only two of us could actively engage the enemy, and only three of us were qualified to do so, anyway. The thought of putting Brooke into the fight ignited a sudden, unexpected tightness in my chest. I saw blood—I saw a woman slumped against a wall, with a shotgun leveled over her stomach.

I shoved the thoughts away and planted myself back into the moment.

"We'll have Brooke and Ronald hide," I said. "Then we wait until we can get the jump on them. Aim for the head; shoot fast. It's our best play."

Dufort press-checked his Glock. He met my gaze, and I saw something searching in his gnarled features and twisted, swollen face. An open question.

I nodded once. "I got your back."

Dufort turned away without comment. We both jogged to where Ronald and Brooke waited in the darkness. Ronald looked ready to pass out, still clutching his laptop and the attached drive to his chest, breathing like a cow in labor.

"I saw guns!" Ronald gasped. "I didn't sign on for this."

"Shut up," I snapped, kneeling in the dust and motioning everybody in like a quarterback about to call a play. "Listen closely. I can only say this once. You'll both find cover and remain concealed no matter what happens. Understood? You *do not engage*. Dufort and I will spread out and pick them off."

"P-pick them off?" Ronald choked.

"Did I freaking stutter?" I said, smacking him lightly across the face. "Do what I say, and you'll be fine. You hear me?"

Ronald licked his lips. Brooke nodded once, ocean eyes alive with strain, but focused. I could see the training clicking in, taking over her brain. Silencing the panic.

She knew what to do.

"Break," I hissed.

Ronald and Brooke scrambled for cover, the computer tech crouching behind a stack of pallets while Brooke selected the trash compactor. I waved Dufort to the left, deploying him to protect the end of the building closest to the two-lane while I backed into cover behind the broken half of a conveyor belt assembly. With the tangos caught in our crossfire, we risked shooting at each other. But I trusted a Navy SEAL's marksmanship enough to embrace the advantage of descending on our enemy from both flanks.

With a little luck, there would be momentary disorientation. A flickering second of hesitation as gunshots clapped.

Just two headshots each. Thirty-yard shots. Not easy...but doable.

I descended into a crouch. From outside the metal walls of the building, footsteps thumped on concrete. Leather dress shoes ascended the steps in unison. There was no clink of weaponry. No meaningless *click, click, click* of weapons being shouldered, like you hear in the movies.

The men approached in near perfect silence, their weapons already shouldered. Already chambered. Ready to fire.

And unlike Pearson and Spraggins, they wouldn't be firing blanks.

I kept my breathing low, the Glock held in a two-hand grip with my trigger finger pressed against the slide. There were sixteen rounds in the weapons—fifteen in the mag, one in the pipe. But I'd never fire them all before being taken out by a rifle round to the chest. I'd get two, maybe three shots before diving for cover.

I needed those shots to count.

A shadow fell across the sunny section of concrete just inside a rolling door. I lifted the gun and waited.

"Sharpe!"

It was Holder's voice. I recognized it from the long car ride back to Jacksonville. That snake.

"I know you're in there, Sharpe. You too, Miss Oswilder. You should come on out, and we can talk about this."

I didn't answer. Neither did Dufort or Brooke. I looked to

the pallets where Ronald was concealed and prayed that he wouldn't melt down and start sobbing.

"I don't know what they told you, Sharpe," Holden continued. "But I know they can't prove it. You guys come on out, and nobody will get hurt. We can iron this out and move on with our lives."

Sure we can, I thought. Holden was right. Brooke and Dufort hadn't proven any of their claims about Yemen or the bad strike or the coverup. But rolling out this way, heavily armed and ready to kill, Holden was adding credence to their story. And I'd seen Dufort's scars. I'd seen Pearson's and Spraggins's records. I'd seen how willingly Brooke was willing to risk her own life to obtain the encrypted drive.

The drive. I breathed a silent curse, remembered that Ronald still held it. I'd have felt better if Brooke had taken it back.

"We're coming in," Holden shouted. "You start shooting, and I promise you'll regret it."

The shadow across the sunny section of concrete lengthened. I saw the outline of a man holding a rifle. Then one of the meatheads ducked through, falling into a crouch with his rifle rising automatically to his shoulder, sweeping the warehouse.

I could have taken him out with a quick flick of my trigger finger. He was twenty yards away, the right side of his head fully visible. But there were still three other men outside, and the sheet metal wall at my back was useless to deflect their gunfire.

Come on. Step on in, all four of you.

I waited. Another shadow fell across the concrete, but with it I heard rapid footsteps thumping the loading dock behind me. I turned toward the wall, hesitating. Listening as the footsteps rushed to the end of the dock where another rolling metal door stood closed. In the inky shadows beyond, I couldn't make out another opening.

But then metal screeched on metal, and the door rose six inches. Bright light spilled in. I breathed another curse. The door rose two feet, and a rifle barrel poked inside.

They were on both sides of me now. The broken bulk of the conveyor system provided substantial concealment, but imperfect cover. If I engaged either target, I would draw immediate fire from the second man.

Holder was smart, and so were his guys. They knew how to take a building.

Turning to Dufort's end of the warehouse, I saw more light break across the concrete as a regular door swung open. It groaned a little, betraying the intruder's position, but he wasn't trying to sneak.

We were pinned in now. One guy behind me, one guy behind Dufort, and one guy in the middle, plus Holder. It was like they *knew* where we were positioned. I couldn't budge now without drawing fire.

How the hell?

Then Holder appeared. He stepped through the door, wearing a bulletproof vest, but carrying no rifle. Instead, a G19 hung from his right hand, identical to the one I gripped.

He walked casually into the warehouse, shoulders loose, and spoke to the darkness.

"I know there are four of you. You picked up somebody at the airport, right? Some big guy."

Only echoes of his own voice answered from the expansive room. Holder took another two steps, the pistol swinging easily at his side. Almost as though he were walking across the lawn to check the mail.

"I'm going to make this easy for you, big guy. Step out now, and hand over the drive. Then you get to live. Make me find you, and I'll blow your brains out."

Long pause. My heart thumped in my chest, cortisol levels spiking as I fixated on the pallets where Ronald was hiding.

Don't do it. Don't you dare do it.

"This is a limited-time offer," Holder said, scanning the room, arms held out like some kind of preacher making an altar call. I looked over my shoulder to calculate the distance to the man behind me. Thirty yards, maybe. I could only see the dim outline of his rifle barrel, leaving me to guess where his head would be. I couldn't shoot for the chest—he wore body armor. And unless I hit him on the first shot, the guy crouching just inside the first rolling door would gun me down. Dufort's predicament was identical, and I was sure he had completed similar combat math. For the moment, we were hamstrung.

But this wasn't checkmate. It wasn't even a stalemate. So long as we all remained hidden, Holder would eventually be forced to deploy his men into the building to run us out, like cats chasing mice. And then we would pounce.

"I'll give you ten seconds," Holder said. "Then I'm gonna light this place up like freaking Ramadi. You get that refer-ence, big guy? It's a city in Iraq. Kind of a hellhole, if you ask me. I should know...I was there."

I gritted my teeth. Holder began to count, starting with ten and dropping one number every two seconds. Slow and easy. Like a teacher threatening a third grader. Holder's teeth flashed in the darkness. The grin widened. As he dropped below five, he brought the Glock in close to his chest, two-handed, finger on the trigger.

"Two...one..."

"Wait!" Ronald's voice broke from the far side of the room, echoing against the walls. My heart leapt, and I leaned out around the conveyor system just far enough to look.

"Wait! Don't shoot...p-please...don't shoot."

Ronald appeared from behind the pallets, clutching the computer in one hand. The drive inside its zippered pouch in the other. His face pale. Eyes wide. Flabby cheeks trembling.

"Don't shoot!" he repeated, raising both hands.

No, no, no! Don't do it, you dumb—

My freight train of enraged thoughts were cut short by Holder's voice.

"Now there's a smart guy! Step on up. You got the drive?"

Ronald swallowed hard. "It's right here."

He took another two steps forward. I looked over my shoulder. The guy with the rifle was still in place, as were the other two. Any move now would be suicide.

I watched as Ronald reached the midpoint of the warehouse, and Holder met him there, lowering his gun. He held out his free hand.

"Let's see it."

Ronald cast a glance around the building, shaking so hard he looked ready to drop.

Don't look at me, fool!

Holder snapped his fingers. "Now, big guy."

Ronald complied. He handed the case over. Holder used his teeth to open the zipper and peer inside. He pocketed the case and raised the gun.

"You copy anything off of it?" he demanded.

"N-no! It's all encrypted. We couldn't get in."

"Is that right?"

"That's right, I swear."

"Okey-dokey, then," Holder said. "I guess that's all we need."

Then he pointed the Glock at Ronald's forehead and pressed the trigger.

27

The gunshot thundered across the warehouse, echoing off the walls and reverberating for what felt like an eternity. Ronald hit the concrete, blood streaming from a hole drilled right in the middle of his forehead, the back side of his skull blown out.

I thought I heard Brooke shriek amid the gunshot, but Holder didn't seem to notice. He holstered the weapon with a casual flip of his suit jacket, inspected the drive case for a moment, then turned for the door.

I raised the Glock, momentary indecision clouding my mind as my tactical awareness reminded me that I was pinned in. I wouldn't get more than a shot off before exposing my position and catching a three-round burst to the back.

Holder moved toward the door, the drive swinging casually by his side, his shoulders as loose as before. Like a stoned teenager strolling through a park—not a care in the world.

He reached the door, then stopped. His entire left side

was fully exposed to my field of fire. One flick of my trigger finger, and he'd crumple just like Ronald had crumpled, his brains sprayed across the floor just like Ronald's were.

I raised the weapon. Hesitated.

Then Holder turned his head and looked dead at me. I couldn't see his eyes behind the dark sunglasses he still wore, but I knew the moment when our gazes met. Holder grinned. Just a little, exposing straight white teeth.

"Watch your six, Sharpe."

I flinched, then detected a shift of rubber on concrete. I glanced over my shoulder to see Holder's man pivoting into the building, his muzzle fixed on my back.

I looked back to Holder, blood surging. Face flushing. Ready to rip his throat out with my bare hands.

But I lowered the pistol. I had no other option.

"That's a good boy," Holder said. "Say hello to the cops for me. Good luck explaining jumbo over there."

Holder shot me a two-finger salute, sloppy and dismissive. Then he ducked through the door, and I heard the sirens—a now familiar wail of a police car racing over those same winding and ducking roads we had hurtled down only moments prior. Perhaps summoned by workers at the food services warehouse across the street after they heard the shot.

But no. The response time was far too immediate. Holder had called them before entering the building. This had been the plan all along.

Rubber ground on the concrete, and I looked over my shoulder again to see the man behind me vanish. I lunged to my feet and snapped my sights in line with the door, pivoting to follow Holder. Ready to fire.

And then stopping, because the sound of sirens was closing, fast. Barely a mile away. Holder and his crew were rushing back to their cars, ready to flee. By the time I cracked off three shots and rained brass over the warehouse floor, it would be too late to evade the incoming cops. It wouldn't matter that the ballistic marks of the bullet in Ronald's skull didn't match my gun. The caliber matched, and cameras at the airport would mark the moment he stuffed himself into the baby blue hatchback. I wouldn't be able to find witnesses from the road who could verify Holder's presence. They'd left no evidence.

The entire situation was a crap sandwich, and Holder had just smashed it right into my face.

"Come on!" I shouted, jamming the gun into my waistband. "We've got to move!"

Dufort appeared from the shadows, eyes blazing, probably having just completed the same mental trigonometry I had. And feeling just as enraged by it.

"What about..."

Brooke stood from behind the trash compactor, red-rimmed eyes fixed on the body.

"No time now. *Move!*"

The edge in my voice got through to her. Brooke snapped out of it, training kicking in again, and the three of us raced for the door.

Holder and his goons were long gone, someplace over the hill and streaking for freedom, far out of reach of the dinky hatchback and its rubber-band engine. I dashed for the car anyway, throwing myself into the driver's seat and scrambling with the keys. Dufort crushed in beside me, his face twisted to survey the incoming cops.

"Three cars," he gurgled. "Move your ass."

I twisted the key. The engine whined and coughed, but

started. I didn't see the engine heat light. Brooke slammed her door, and I punched the gas. The front tires spun, and we shot across the parking lot, dust exploding in a cloud around us as I snatched a quick left around the rear corner of the building.

The sirens behind me sounded right on our heels. My head slammed into the ceiling of the little car as we rocketed behind the warehouse, sliding and hoping, the engine temperature light flashing back to life.

"Are they on us?" I demanded.

"I don't see them," Brooke called from the back seat.

I made for the road, marking a secondary drive connecting with the parking lot behind the abandoned warehouse. It was blocked by one of those pole gates—a single galvanized steel bar, chained to a post. I figured there was a fifty-fifty chance that the chain would break or the hatchback would crumple, but I hit it anyway, foot jammed onto the accelerator.

The chain broke—and the hatchback crumpled. The hood buckled upward, leaving only the top ten inches of the windshield for me to drive by. Power bled off as the engine heat management system kicked in again, governing our RPMs. I cursed Brooke for her choice in rentals and yanked a hard right onto the road.

"Where are they?" I said.

"Still don't see them," Brooke said. "I think they stopped in front of the warehouse...I don't think they saw us."

The hatchback clacked and grumbled, the entire cab shaking as the speedometer dropped to twenty, but mercifully stopped there. Smoke rose from the engine bay, clouding around the crumpled hood. I kept driving, checking the mirror every few seconds as I topped two hills, then made a right-hand turn onto another street, this one framed by trees on one side and a garbage dump on the other.

The hatchback coughed once, then rolled to a stop and died right there on the side of the road, still steaming. I twisted the key, but the engine wouldn't start. It didn't even click. The ignition engaged, and then multiple red and orange lights flashed from the dash.

It was done.

I dumped the keys on the floorboard and ran both hands through my hair. For a moment I wanted to put my hand through the windshield, just to break something. I forced myself to remain still and breathe evenly, slowly regaining control.

Then Brooke said the words we were all thinking.

"We're screwed."

28

I kicked the door open and fought my way out of the POS hatchback. The ditch outside was packed with tall grass bending gently under a crisp breeze. Dufort extracted himself, and Brooke dug her backpack out before meeting the two of us at the nose of the car. I gave only momentary inspection to the engine bay before confirming what I already knew—the hatchback was finished. The radiator was ruptured, the cooling fan shattered, and the engine seriously over-heated. Not like it had been much of a vehicle in the first place.

"What now?" Brooke asked. Nervous strain laced her voice, as though sobs were only moments from breaking through. I wiped sweat from my forehead and looked up the road. I didn't see cops. I didn't hear sirens.

But we couldn't have traveled far. Three, maybe four miles at the absolute most. The cops obviously hadn't detected us fleeing the scene, or they would have given chase. But it wouldn't be long. They would identify the victim. Maybe find an airport receipt in his pocket and proceed to check the cameras.

Soon enough they would identify the baby blue hatchback, and even if none of the airport cameras got a clear look at any of our faces—which was likely, given how close my head rode to the ceiling—they would have at least recorded the vehicle's license plate.

Then there would be an APB. A county-wide search. Interdepartmental cooperation. A drag net.

I ran my hands through my hair again, clenching my fists and clamping my eyes closed.

Brooke was right. We were screwed.

"We gotta ditch this car," Dufort said.

I opened my eyes. Nodded once.

Without comment, the three of us worked together to push the car off the road and into the trees. High grass tore at the undercarriage, and the wheels sank up to the rims in the muddy ditch, but the flimsy thing couldn't weigh more than a couple of thousand pounds. A tin can on wheels.

Once we had it behind a row of bushes, Dufort threw some fallen limbs over the roof, and Brooke went to work on the interior, wiping down every surface to clear away our fingerprints. Ideally, we would torch the car, but under present circumstances that would only attract attention. Better to simply abandon it.

Back on the road, I looked both ways for traffic. I hadn't seen a car since leaving the warehouse. Someplace beyond the fence surrounding the dump, a grind of heavy machinery rippled through the air, but I couldn't see anyone.

"What now?" Brooke said. She seemed to be the queen of that question. It was starting to annoy.

"Call a car," I said.

"Another rental?"

"Hell no. Call a cab. Or Uber. Whatever."

Brooke punched at her phone for a moment; then her finger stopped over the screen.

"Where to?"

I hesitated. "Where are we?"

"Northwest of the city. Kinda in the middle of nowhere."

"Take us downtown," I said.

Brooke exchanged a glance with Dufort. The big man wrinkled his nose at me.

"You bailing on us, Army man?"

"I'd be smart to, wouldn't I?" I snapped. "Order the car."

Brooke's shoulders drooped, but she ordered the car. Then the three of us stood behind the tree line, just in case any cops passed by, and waited. A cop did pass, five minutes later. Driving slowly and leaning low to peer through the windshield.

He glided right past the concealed hatchback without so much as pausing. Then he was gone.

"What—" Brooke began.

I shot her a glare, and that froze the voice in her throat. Arms folded, I faced the road while barely containing the boiling rage surging beneath my chest. I saw Holder gunning down Ronald, wide and terrified eyes flashing only moments before the slug turned those lights out forever.

Then I saw the grin on Holder's face. The slight lift of his lip. That condescending sneer.

He *knew*. Somehow, he knew right where I was. Right where Dufort was, too. From the start. Before he even entered the building. How the hell could he know that? How could he have found us in the baby blue hatchback? For that matter, how had he found us at the second hotel?

Well, the hotel could have been luck. Or the simple result of patient, systematic searching. The airport could have been further luck. But the positioning at the warehouse? No chance. He had no way of knowing we would head that way. He didn't know we would take that exit.

And regardless of how he knew, it didn't matter. That wasn't what ignited the boiling frustration growing into a bonfire in my stomach. What fueled *that* fire was my own lack of control. From the moment those bank doors hurtled open until now, I had never obtained the initiative. I'd been playing from behind, short on information and even shorter on influence, the victim of circumstance and bad luck. At the mercy of my enemy, even before I knew I had one.

It was a situation no self-respecting Ranger could tolerate. Not for a microsecond. Being a Ranger was all about leadership. About finding a way.

About taking control.

Brooke's car arrived—an SUV, thank God. We got in without a word and ignored the chatty driver during the thirty-minute cruise back to downtown. He dropped us at the south bank river walk, just a stone's throw from the bank tower where this entire mess had begun, and I passed him a ten-dollar tip before stepping back into the Florida sunshine.

Ignoring Dufort and Brooke, I walked straight for the river. Sweat gathered on my scalp before I reached the rail, placing both hands around the top and gripping until my knuckles turned white. I clamped my eyes closed and saw Holder again, grinning at me, perfectly at ease. Because he knew he had me cornered. He knew he had bested me. Long before the confrontation even began, I had been boxed in. I hadn't even realized it. The man was more than tactically aware—he was flawless.

I remembered what he had said to Ronald about Ramadi, and wondered what branch he had served in. Army? Marines? A Navy SEAL, maybe?

Whatever the case, that life was long behind him. All that heritage, all that pride, all that commitment to brotherhood and country had been pissed away like so much bad coffee. He was an affront to the uniform. An affront to the entire nation. A murdering scumbag who had traded honor for money and somehow believed himself to be a better man for it.

I knew because I had encountered his type before. I'd seen what happens when values are cashed in. Oaths are forgotten. It's a moral spiral that never ends, one violation building on another until the *only* thing that matters is the payday.

There's only one way to deal with it. Like an exterminator eradicating cockroaches—swift and merciless justice.

"Sharpe..." Brooke trailed off. I opened my eyes but didn't face her. She stood at my elbow, hands resting on the fence, Dufort somewhere behind. I could hear him breathing.

"We have to get it back," Brooke said, her voice almost pleading. "We *need it*."

The drive.

I'd already forgotten about it. Not because it didn't matter, but because Ronald's death was so fresh in my mind. So absolutely pointless. A normal guy working a normal job, erased from this world in a heartbeat.

And it was my fault. It was absolutely my fault.

"Mason?" Brooke pressed.

"He's already gone," I said. "You'll never find that thing. You may as well proceed to plan B."

"We haven't *got* a plan B," Dufort gurgled, voice laced with anger.

I gazed across the river, clenching the rail. From our position on the river walk, I could see the bulk of downtown Jacksonville, a portion of the skyline barricaded by the faded blue arc of the same drawbridge I had hurtled across the day prior. Rolling around in that stupid van, fighting for my life. At the mercy of the enemy.

I saw myself pinned against the wall, formulating an escape plan to get myself and Brooke out of that van...

Out of that van.

In a flash I remembered Brooke standing up. Rushing to the door. Pretending to flee as her purse hurtled through the open door, over the edge of the bridge, into the river...

"The tracker," I snapped, turning on them.

"Huh?" Brooke looked up.

"You put a tracking beacon on the drive, remember? So Dufort could find it in the river. Was it in the case? Is it still active?"

Brooke and Dufort exchanged a glance. Momentary hope flashed across their faces. They both ran to the nearest bench, and Brooke dug her laptop out of her backpack. I circled behind them while Brooke piggybacked off her phone's hotspot to allow her laptop access to the internet.

Dufort squatted next to her, his facial scars dripping sweat as he fixated on the screen. I folded my arms and waited. Brooke called up some kind of map inside her web browser. She clicked and typed again. Input a password. Waited. Typed once more.

Then a green dot appeared on a gray map. I saw an

outline of Jacksonville nearby. The green dot marked a place north and east of the city, near the coast, not far from the Georgia state line.

"That's it!" Dufort said.

Brooke bit her lip, ocean eyes unblinking as she double-tapped on the dot. Then her shoulders slumped.

"It went offline twenty minutes ago. They must have found the beacon."

The laptop slumped. Dufort slammed his open palm into the railing before stomping off, quivering like an angry bull.

I squatted in the grass behind the bench, studying the dot. And then what lay around it.

"It didn't go offline," I said. "It lost signal."

Brooke looked up. "Huh?"

I pointed. "Look. Right there. Due south of the marker. What do you see?"

Brooke squinted. Adjusted the zoom.

"An...airport?"

"An *executive* airport. Where you might land a small plane. They didn't find that beacon, they just took off. Above a few thousand feet, the beacon lost signal."

Dufort returned to the bench. I stood up, my mind spinning again. Still angry, but now focused. Leaning into my training. Thinking about solutions—refusing to acknowledge defeat.

"How does that help us?" Dufort said. "We still can't track them."

"Not right now," I said. "But they have to land eventually. When they do, the signal will return. It'll lead us right to them."

"By then they might destroy the drive," Brooke said. "There's no reason for them to keep it."

"Sure there is," I said. "They can't destroy that drive until they know exactly what's on it. Every word. Every file. It's a wide-open liability. They won't scrap it before they decrypt it...and like Ronald said, that could take days."

"But they might have the data key," Brooke pressed.

"The data key was set by the whistleblower," I said. "No chance they have it. Even if they've got somebody faster than Ronald, we've still got a window."

I turned for the street, my back to the river walk. Headed for my truck.

"Where are you going?" Brooke said.

"To get my things. And then to find a rental car I can actually fit in."

The laptop smacked shut. Brooke and Dufort hurried to follow.

"You're going after it?" Brooke said.

"You're damn right I'm going after it." I stopped, facing the two of them. "We can do it together if you want. But from now on, we do it my way. We rent the cars I say to rent. We make the plays I say we make. We do this professionally, like we were trained. We execute the mission. No more mistakes."

Brooke looked to Dufort, like she had when he and I first met. But this time, he didn't shake his head. He didn't even hesitate. He just nodded.

I turned for my truck again. Dufort's voice stopped me.

"And Holder?"

I looked over my shoulder.

"He's the enemy," I said simply. "We kill the enemy."

29

We split from the river walk after exchanging phone numbers. Brooke and Dufort retreated to a nearby coffee shop to monitor the tracker and order another rental car using Falk's credit card—a *real* rental car this time, I told them. A large SUV with a chase-worthy engine, ideally.

I returned to find my truck still sitting in the short-term parking lot across from the bank. The '67 GMC was dusty, looking dull in the midafternoon sun. Two parking tickets and a tow notice were pinned beneath the left-hand windshield wiper—the only windshield wiper, actually.

I tore them loose and crumpled them into a ball before unlocking the door and sliding onto the sagging bench seat.

The cab was as dirty as the exterior, but it smelled like home. My backpack lay on the passenger-side floorboard alongside my violin case, both battered but well loved. A quick glance through the narrow rear window into the camper-shell-covered bed confirmed that my air mattress and bins of camping gear were present and accounted for.

The inline six coughed and gurgled like Dufort snoring when I twisted the key. While I waited for the engine to warm, I lifted the backpack into my lap and unzipped the main compartment, digging for my cell phone. It was a burner device—some prepaid thing I'd picked up in a drugstore outside of Pensacola. I'd learned to live without a phone and was greatly enjoying the change, but headed into action, I would need some communication.

My fingers scraped the bottom of the bag, but I still didn't find the phone. Instead I touched soft plastic, and I stopped as a sudden wash of overwhelming loneliness passed over me like a wave. I pulled the sandwich bag out—a makeshift water barrier to protect the precious, leather-bound book within.

It had been nearly a week since I'd held the Bible. Almost two since I'd taken it out of the bag and flipped the cover open to view the single photograph I kept there. As the days dragged by, and those weeks morphed into months, I needed that photo more than I ever imagined. Time was having its way with me despite my most desperate attempts to turn back the clock.

Memories were starting to fade. To turn gray and colorless, slowly losing their warmth even as I fought to keep them alive. Sometimes I would wake up in the morning, and for a split second I couldn't remember at all.

I couldn't remember her face. The brightness of her smile. The touch of her skin on mine, or the electricity it ignited.

I would race to that sandwich bag—race to the Bible. Pull out the picture and lose myself in it.

Or I would try, anyway. It was getting harder. The picture itself seemed to be losing color. To be less and less a portal, and more just...an image. A piece of cold paper. Lifeless.

And that terrified me.

I swallowed hard, rubbing my thumb across the plastic, and I thought about the date. No longer Monday. Now it was Tuesday.

Three hundred sixty-two days.

I felt the thought dragging on me, pulling me down. Like a mental black hole, eager to consume me. I pushed away instead, tucking the Bible into my backpack again and finally locating the phone. Powering it on, I focused on the task at hand, using it like a barricade against the clutching darkness. I found the navigation app and used it to locate a parking garage which offered multi-day parking. It was only a few blocks away, and the rates were printed in bold letters on a sign posted near the gate. Twenty bucks a night. Not ideal, but at least my truck would be safe until I returned.

Whenever that might be.

Parking a couple of floors off the ground, I took the backpack and sheltered my violin case beneath a coat. Then I locked the doors and texted Brooke.

She arrived half an hour later, driving a dark gray Ford Edge. Not the Tahoe I had envisioned, but worlds better than the baby blue hatchback. She rolled up beside me and started to climb out, but I willingly took the back seat, tossing my bag in ahead of me. I noted that she and Dufort must have already visited her parked Civic. Their suitcases lay in the back.

"Just the one bag?" Brooke asked.

"Yeah."

She twisted in the seat. Her smooth cheeks were still a little flushed by that day's chaos—or maybe that was the

Florida sunshine doing its work. She was already tan, but I couldn't help but think that she'd look even better after a couple of weeks lying on the beach.

The thought conjured up an image of Brooke in a dark bikini that complemented her ocean eyes—a picture that was somehow more vibrant and real than the image of my fiancée. It made me want to grind a boot into my own eye. Two months ago, I might have done just that.

Now I was too tired.

"You okay, Sharpe?" Brooke said softly.

"Fine," I said, arranging my backpack on the seat next to me. "We should get going."

Short pause. "Where? The tracker still hasn't come online yet."

I looked up to see Brooke's laptop propped up in Dufort's lap. The big guy was leaned over it like a giant playing with a dollhouse. It might have been comical were I in a more amiable mood.

I pinched my lips together, grateful for something to focus on, but I didn't have to think long.

"North," I said. "First Savannah. Then if we still don't have them, we'll head toward DC."

"Why DC?"

"Because the airstrip they took off from ran east to west, but the beacon was north of the airport when it went offline. Meaning they had turned north deliberately. Also, Bridge-water Security is headquartered just outside DC, and they might be headed to base."

I leaned back into my seat, rocking my head back and closing my eyes. Trying to picture Mia. Only seeing Brooke on the beach.

"But mostly," I said, "because these guys are scumbags.

And DC is scumbag headquarters."

30

I had Brooke and Dufort replace their phones with burners before we left the city, and we all exchanged numbers again. I didn't really think that was how Holder and his men were tracking us—obtaining access to cell phone location data is tricky without advanced software and/or a warrant. But it was still the most logical weak point, and it didn't hurt to be careful. We could obtain replacement phones at almost any retail store.

Once on the highway, I took over the laptop while Dufort settled back into his seat to glare at the open road like it had raped his sister. He didn't wear sunglasses, and he didn't even squint into the afternoon sun blazing through the windshield.

He just stared, and Brooke drove, and I worked the internet connection hosted by my burner phone.

I had questions. A lot of them, beginning with the two men who had kidnapped me from the bank. A quick Google search produced columns of news stories, most of which focused on the robbery, but a few delved into Spraggins's and Pearson's service records. DOD files had been obtained, and a particularly thorough piece by the *Washington Signal* painted a vivid history of the two men.

Spraggins—that being Tyler J. Spraggins, of Montpelier, Vermont— had served eight years in the United States Armed Forces, all with the Army. He had been a proud member of the Army's 75th Ranger Regiment, just as Brooke claimed. *Sue Sponte*—of his own accord. Enlisted, not commissioned. First Battalion, Bravo Company. Hunter Army Airfield, Georgia. The article claimed six combat deployments, but made no mention of Yemen.

That didn't surprise me. That deployment could be classified...or erased.

Spraggins was a good soldier, praised by his superiors and awarded a Bronze Star for heroism in a combat zone. The *Signal* didn't have details of that heroism, either, but focused heavily on the medal while expressing their own consternation that such a man could become an armed bank robber.

Matthew David Pearson's story was more extensive—and a lot more colorful. Born in Harrisburg, Pennsylvania, he was the first and only son of Glenn David Pearson. Now *Congressman* Glenn David Pearson, but at the time a mere councilman for Harrisburg. Matthew's mother had died of cancer when he was only five, leaving Glenn to raise him amid the turmoil of a growing political career. Glenn ascended from city council to state representative, and Matthew went to boarding school. Glenn ran for congress, and Matthew made West Point.

By the time Matthew graduated with honors and

completed Ranger School, Glenn was an established member of the House of Representatives. A mover and a shaker, touted for his relentless dedication to the military and his passionate campaigns to bolster the defense budget. "I'm anti-war," one quote read. "But if we must fight, don't give our boys the Honda. Give them the Rolls-Royce, and let's get it done!"

It was gaudy rhetoric on a good day. Exactly the kind of inauthentic nonsense I'd expect from a guy who'd spent his life chasing votes. Certainly, I'd never enjoyed any helmet or socks during my years of service which I would classify as the *Rolls-Royce* of helmets or socks, but maybe that was why the rhetoric had worked out for Pearson. He was now a leading member of the congressional appropriations committee, responsible for managing the purse strings of an entire nation.

I scrolled past the diversion into the father and returned to details of the son. Matthew Pearson had served nine years in the Army, all of them as a member of the 75th. Seven combat tours, one more than Spraggins, but again the *Signal* made no mention of Yemen.

They did mention his Silver Star. Awarded for gallantry in action, but as before, there were no details of that action.

I pinched my eyebrows together, puzzling a little as the Ford rumbled along I-95. It wasn't unusual for good soldiers who served that many combat deployments to be awarded a medal. But the Silver Star was a big deal, ranking only two levels beneath the Medal of Honor. I would have expected a merit of such significance to be accompanied by some documentation about how it was earned, but the article reported very little on Pearson's service history. The only note of interest beyond the Silver Star came at the conclusion of his military career. According to the *Signal*, Pearson had been medically retired in 2017.

Not simply discharged with honors or even handed a general discharge. *Medically* retired.

I looked up from the computer, chewing the inside of one cheek. And thinking. Something about Pearson's story felt wrong to me. I couldn't put a finger on it, but it was as though I were holding a film negative over the developed copy, and the two images wouldn't quite match.

Like I was missing something.

"Brooke," I said.

"Yeah?"

"Was Pearson injured in Yemen?"

"No. Not that I remember. Why?"

"It says here that he was medically retired. I didn't notice any disabilities when he was manhandling me out of the bank."

Long pause. I looked into the driver's seat to see Brooke fixating on her mirror as she changed lanes. We passed a truck. She changed lanes again and reset the cruise control.

"I don't know," she said. "You know there's all kinds of things you can be MDed for. Could have been...like a lung thing. Or hearing loss."

Hearing loss. Right.

I returned to the laptop and switched fire—turning my attention from Pearson and Spraggins to the supposed object of their campaign. Agon Defense.

But if details of the two Rangers' service histories were difficult to come by, details of Agon Defense were almost impossible to trace. The company owned no website. No mailing address. No public contact details at all.

Just like Bridgewater Security.

The best I could find were some public records relating to the Department of Defense's annual budget, including notations about contracts granted to Agon for various "research and development projects". Those contracts valued in the nine-figure range, all of them. A hundred million or more, listed down to the penny for proper accountability.

It was enough to prove that Agon existed, and they were certainly some kind of major player in the defense realm, but it offered me no leads as to their true identity, or *what* exactly they had been researching and developing. I was sure I could find an inquiry box someplace. A form I could fill out requesting public information regarding the company, which I would be entitled to as a taxpaying citizen.

But that would take weeks, at best, and I already knew what the response would be. Some things would be classified, and Agon itself would probably be a subsidiary of another, larger corporation. Hence the lack of address.

The ambiguity of it all made me think again of John Holder, the consultant. It was Special Agent Carver with the FBI who had defended Holder when I challenged him at the hospital. Carver had said that Holder was present in a "consulting capacity", shutting down my challenges about his identity.

Did that mean Carver was dirty also? That the FBI was in on this?

Maybe. But probably not. It more likely meant that Holder—whoever he was—had serious connections. Connections sufficient to have an FBI agent not only grant him access to a bedside interview in a hospital, but also to shill for him when the interviewee challenged his credentials. And that could only mean that this mess was far more insidious than I first imagined.

I closed the laptop and watched the highway streak by. We'd been on the road for a little over an hour, and it was full dark. Brooke complained about her eyes and pulled over at a gas station for Dufort to take the wheel. I wasn't happy about it, but I wasn't interested in driving either. The exhaustion of the last thirty-six hours was striking home, and I was starting to think about a nap myself.

Brooke bought bottled water at the gas station, but when she returned to the Ford, I was surprised to find her skipping the front passenger seat and sliding in next to me instead. She plopped the water between us and offered me the flash of a smile, her dimples playing peek-a-boo on tanned cheeks. I felt that flash of confusing warmth in my chest again and looked away.

"You good?" Brooke asked.

"Yeah." I settled into the seat, propping my head against the door pillar. "Just tired."

Dufort stomped the gas, lunging back into traffic and finding the fast lane. I couldn't see the speedometer beyond his bulging biceps, but I knew we were moving well in excess of the speed limit. I decided not to say anything, closing my eyes and embracing the hum of tires on asphalt. It was a rhythmic, soothing sound, and I let my body relax.

Shutting out the stress of the questions swirling in my mind, I went to my quiet place instead. That sacred mental room I only allowed myself to enter at the end of the day. A battered Chevy K-10 parked out in the Arizona desert, the howl of distant coyotes the only sound to break the stillness.

A billion stars twinkling in the sky. The kiss of a summer breeze washing over my face. A camp pillow under my head.

And Mia in my arms.

I savored every detail of the memory, focusing on each one until the picture felt real. As though it were happening all over again, right around me. Imagining the rough texture of the K-10's bed, countered by the smooth press of Mia's cheek against my arm. The slight creak of the suspension. The howl of that coyote, building into a song. Her lips on mine. Her body pressed close. My shirt sliding off...

"Oh my God." Brooke's voice cut through the vision like an artillery shell, and my eyes snapped open. She sat next to me, her laptop propped across her knees. "Mason! Look."

She pivoted the screen. It displayed another news story, this time from CNN. A headline about Pearson and Spraggins.

"What is it?" Dufort gurgled.

I scooped up the laptop and read the headline out loud.

"Bank-robbing duo assaulted in prison riot at Florida detention facility. Pearson and Spraggins transferred to secure ICU to undergo immediate surgery."

My voice trailed off, and I scanned the body of the text, but I didn't need any further details. The story was blatantly clear at face value.

"Holder," Dufort snarled.

"Seriously?" Brooke said. "There's no way."

"They're tying up loose ends," I said, handing the laptop back. "No witnesses, no story."

"What does that mean?" Brooke said.

"It means they have something to hide," I said. "And it also means we're running out of time. Dufort, let's step on it."

Dufort was already stepping on it, but the Ford's engine howled a little louder, and the traffic outside blurred like stars flashing by a spaceship. I leaned back into my seat, but I no longer thought of Mia or that starry night in the desert.

I thought of Holder, and my hands around his throat.

The Ford hurtled on.

31

The beacon came back online forty-five minutes later. I had relieved Dufort of his driving responsibilities after his frequent and violent lane changes erased any hope of getting any sleep. He sat next to me with Brooke's laptop propped across his knees, his gurgling voice cracking a little just as we raced across the South Carolina state line.

"I've got it!"

I glanced at the screen. Dufort was zooming in, and sure enough, the little green blip marking the location of the drive had returned to the map.

"Where?" I asked.

"Northern Virginia. Not far from DC...let me get a satellite image."

I glanced over my shoulder to see if Brooke had woken. She was still curled up with her head pressed against a door post, snoring softly. Altogether unlike Dufort's raucous diesel gasp, Brooke's snores were gentle and uniform—somehow vaguely calming. I decided to let her sleep as

Dufort called up Google Earth on the laptop and input coordinates from the tracking software. He pinched his lips together and waited. The image loaded slowly under crappy cellular service.

"What is it?" I asked.

Dufort tilted his chin toward the emergency lane. I pulled the Ford over and shifted into park. Brooke snored on as I leaned across the console. Dufort rotated the laptop.

It was a building—a *very* large building. Surrounded by thick green trees with a sprawling parking lot populated by a couple of hundred cars, and a long, narrow airstrip stretching the length of the structure on the back side. It was some manner of compound.

The location of the drive pinged from a much smaller building situated on the front side of its bigger brother. An office building, I thought. The coordinates were no more precise than that.

I settled back into my seat and scratched one cheek. Dufort zoomed out, exposing miles of dense forest with fields speckled among them. The nearest municipality was someplace called Culpeper—a midsized town situated seventy or eighty miles southwest of Washington.

"Any name on the building?"

Dufort shook his head. "There's a fence circling the compound with a guard shack near the road. Trees overhanging it. If there's a sign, I can't see it."

"And Google?"

"No details. It's just a spot on a map."

I shifted back into drive and piloted onto the highway. Dufort used the GPS built into the Ford's dash to plot a course to the nameless structure. We were still five hours out, assuming no traffic. Time enough for me to calculate an arrival strategy, I decided. Still no need to wake Brooke.

Twenty miles hummed beneath the tires of the Ford while I considered our options. With such little information, it was difficult to determine a path forward.

"We need to recon." Dufort's voice cut through my thoughts as though he knew what I was thinking. I glanced sideways at him and suddenly wondered how many missions like this he'd executed during his time with the SEALs. How many deployments.

How many seek and destroy operations.

SEALs are good at making plans, in my experience. In fact, making plans is forty percent of what they do for a living—another fifty percent being split between training and the consumption of vast amounts of booze, and the final ten percent being spent on actual military action. Planning, boozing, fighting machines like no other.

"I agree," I said. "Once we reach Culpeper, we'll put a plan together. I have to assume that structure is an Agon facility—maybe *the* Agon facility—but we won't know until our boots are on the ground."

Dufort grunted in answer, still fixated on the laptop. He flicked the mouse across the screen, zooming and panning around, searching out the smallest details. Google's satellite imagery was good, but it paled in comparison to the high-powered lens of a surveillance drone, flying high out of sight, capturing live feed.

At last he looked up from the computer and peered over his shoulder, checking Brooke in the back seat. Then he faced me, his twisted lip suspended half an inch over its twin. Exposing teeth. Making him look nasty.

Like my foster mother's pug.

"I'm putting a lot of trust in you," he said softly.

"No, you're not."

He twitched. "Excuse me?"

"You could have killed me any number of times by now. You've only followed me after discussing our plans ahead of time. You've only told me what Brooke is willing to divulge, and it seems that you trust her implicitly. I'd say you're putting a lot of *calculation* into me."

Dufort thought about that, then grunted. "Like you're any different."

"I never claimed to be, and I'm not shaming you. I'd do the same in your shoes. But now that we're having a heart-to-heart, I've got a few things of my own to say."

Dufort waited. I settled into the seat.

"I just want to be sure we're on the same page about what sort of operation this is. I'm helping you for two reasons. First, because we're all military, and that means something. Maybe not for Holder and his thugs, but it means something to me. I've never understood this arbitrary mindset that we're all one thing overseas and something else when we come home. That's stupid. It's the same world, and it shouldn't matter what part of it we find ourselves in. If you and I were overseas, you'd have my back, and I'd have yours. So the fact that we met in Florida means nothing to me. I've got your back. You've got mine. And we honor our oaths to this country, just as we would in Iraq or Afghanistan. We defend our people against all enemies, be they foreign or domestic. I think you agree."

Another grunt from Dufort. A little less aggressive this time. More like a grunt of agreement.

"And the second reason?" Dufort said.

A weight descended over my shoulders as my mind

switched to the second reason. It was a weight I had fought back all day long and couldn't ignore any longer. A weight of responsibility and maybe guilt.

"The second reason is Ronald. I didn't pull the trigger, but he's still dead because of me. I've got to make that right. Which is why I need to be clear about what my intentions are with Holder, and where those intentions end. I'm going to bring him to justice, but this isn't a revenge spree. Whatever Agon is up to, it's clearly a systemic issue, which means you could never kill enough people to stop it. The solution here is to expose them. Turn the country against them. Then trust the system. All right? I see how angry you are, and I don't blame you. But I need to know you're going to control yourself."

Another long pause. Dufort squinted. I thought he might object, but instead I saw a glint of respect in his pale eyes. He looked away.

"You'd have been a good officer."

I snorted. "No such thing."

That brought on a smile from Dufort, and we relaxed into silence. I counted the flashing mile markers, checking the GPS now and again to measure our progress. We'd arrive at the compound in northern Virginia just after sunrise.

First thing in the morning. Bright and early. A good time to slink in and set up a stakeout. It was a blend of my Ranger skills and my cop skills, all mixed together into some kind of bizarre cocktail. Calculation and raw warrior spirit, all at once.

A deadly mix.

I was just contemplating turning on the radio when the burner phone resting in the console next to me buzzed, and I checked the screen. Incoming call, area code 480.

I flicked the answer button and held it to my ear. "Jacquie?"

"Mason, what the hell are you mixed up in?"

Jacquie's voice was clipped and direct. Right to the point.

"What are you talking about?"

"I'm talking about *John Holder*."

A chill ran down my spine. I sat up. "What about him?"

"I just got an email back from my contact at the Department of Defense. It took us a while to locate him. It seems John is a middle name. Full name, Aaron John Holder, of Augusta, Georgia, originally."

"He was military?" I asked. I already knew he was.

"I'd say so." Jacquie snorted. "He was seventy-fifth."

My blood ran cold. "*What?*"

"Captain Aaron John Holder, a graduate of the United States Military Academy, West Point." Jacquie was reading from her notes now. I could tell by the cadence of her voice. It was a familiar rhythm. "He earned a bachelor's degree in chemical engineering—graduated summa cum laude. A smart cookie, by anybody's measure, but a total savage. He opted for Ranger School and crushed it. Immediate admittance in the Seventy-Fifth Ranger Regiment, First Battalion, Alpha Company. Hunter Army Airfield, Georgia. Two deployments to the Middle East. Multiple commendations. He was awarded a freaking Legion of Merit, no less."

"And then?" I could feel the punchline coming. My stomach twisted tight. The bombshell still detonated with the force of a broadside from an Abrams tank.

"And then he gang-raped a trio of Iraqi teens," Jacquie quipped, her voice quivering with suppressed rage.

I shifted the phone to my other ear. My blood was hot now. I saw Holder's confident smile in the rearview mirror of his car during that long drive from Tallahassee back to Jacksonville. The way he'd flicked his business card at me, in case I "thought of anything". I still had the card in my pocket.

"Why is he still breathing?" I demanded. From the back seat Brooke sat up and rubbed her eyes. Jacquie plowed ahead.

"Your guess is as good as mine. My contact at the DOD indicated that Holder made himself a sweetheart deal with the prosecution. Apparently, he had a reputation for being a dirt peddler—he knew all kinds of things about all kinds of people. He ratted his fellow rapists out, then he ratted out a couple of superior officers who were in possession of kiddie porn...and that was that. He faced a court-martial and a dishonorable discharge for conduct unbecoming an officer of the United States Army, but never saw a day of jail time. Game, set, match."

And now he's a freaking hired gun, I thought. *Walking the streets, a free man. An American traitor.*

It was all I could do to focus on the road ahead. My blood boiled. Not just because Holder was a swine of the very most sordid sort. Not just because he was a rapist, a backstabber, and a dog.

Because he was—or because he *had been*—a Ranger. A member of the esteemed 75th. A sworn defender of every virtue the Land of the Free ever claimed.

He was one of *us.*

"Thanks, Jacquie," I said. My voice was just as clipped now.

"Mason, you're messing with some hardcore people," Jacquie said. "I can't help you if you won't talk."

"I can't talk now," I said. "I'll call soon."

I hung up before the boiling rage got the best of me. The phone found its place in the bottom of a cup holder. My fingers tightened around the steering wheel.

I saw red. An open highway of it.

"Holder?" Dufort asked, his voice a low growl.

"Seventy-fifth," I said simply.

Dufort's teeth ground. Brooke's voice was soft from the back seat.

"Not anymore."

No, I thought. *Not anymore.*

Now he was the enemy.

And I had been trained to kill the enemy.

32

The beacon went offline at four a.m., which only served to confirm what I already suspected. Wherever we were headed, it was the heart of the hornet's nest. The operations center. The headquarters where Holder and his meatheads would turn the drive over to the brainiacs who would go to work on it.

Those brainiacs would have then unpackaged the drive. Removed it from its zippered case and discovered the tracking beacon Pearson had installed at the bank. They would have immediately disabled it, then cursed out the meatheads.

But the drive wouldn't move again, because this was the heart of the hornet's nest. A safe, secure place. What could a washed-up Army Ranger, a PTSD-stricken Humvee driver, and a mutilated SEAL do, anyway?

A good question.

An hour from our destination, I stopped to top off the Ford's tank, stock up on bottled water and dry foods, and shotgun two energy drinks. I wasn't sleepy—any fatigue was now subdued under a deluge of nervous pre-deployment energy. Feelings I was familiar with. But the sugar and caffeine would sharpen my mind and keep me alert. I had a vague feeling I would need to be on the top of my game for whatever came next.

The last big city we passed through was Fredericksburg, just beginning to wake as predawn light turned the sky from black to gray. The GPS led us up Highway 3 toward Culpeper, rising and falling amid sweeping Virginia country-side picturesque enough to serve as calendar material. I watched it roll by and marveled for a moment at how accus-tomed to changing scenery I had become. Landscapes and vistas have always attracted me. Traveling in the Army, I learned to enjoy new scenery and embrace the beautiful, even when it was found in a war zone. Maybe especially when it was found in a war zone.

I never thought I'd learn to love it like this, though. It was like a strange kind of very mild drug. Barely noticeable, but potent enough to quicken my heart rate as brand-new views spilled across my windshield.

Virginia suited me just fine.

As we neared Culpeper, Dufort took control of our navi-gation, using the laptop to scope out a route and calling the turns as burbling commands. I complied without complaint, pulling the Ford to the shoulder of a two-lane farming road just as the sun crested the horizon through the passenger-side windows.

Dufort peered through the windows into the brightening west. Across the road lay a dormant field planted thick with some kind of bright green cover crop. Beyond that stood a tree line, followed by a steep hill covered over by dense hardwoods.

"There," Dufort said. "Far side of the ridge."

"Range?"

"Half a klick. Give or take."

I unbuckled and reached for my backpack. The three of us bailed in unison, not speaking as we locked the SUV and jogged across the two-lane. I hadn't seen another car since leaving Highway 3, but that could change as the sun rose. Without any good place to hide the Ford, our time would be limited before somebody called in an abandoned vehicle.

Traipsing through the cover crop, I noted that Brooke and Dufort had fallen automatically into a triangular formation, each fanning out to my four and seven o'clock positions. Allowing me to take point while they crab-walked semi-sideways, providing constant surveillance over our rear and our flanks. I didn't think the strategy had been prearranged, and something about the default nature of our movements brought a warm confidence to my gut.

Old habits die hard.

We entered the trees and started up a long, sloping hill. It wasn't steep, but it felt like it went on forever, thick brambles and sharp thorns dragging at my jeans. By the time we reached the top, all three of us were breathing hard, sweat dripping from my forehead despite the chilly Virginia air.

I raised a fist, and the three of us stopped, catching our breath before I lowered my body into the brush. Stiff branches and more thorns tore into my arms and shoulders, snagging on my jacket. I ignored them and pressed forward, army-crawling now with Brooke pressing in close to my side and Dufort hanging back to cover our six.

The warmth of the rising sun spilled over my back, and I slowed to barely a creep as the trees cresting the top of the hill began to thin. When I reached a sheltered spot next to a towering oak, I stopped to fish my binoculars out of my backpack. Brooke settled in next to me, head lowered. Ocean eyes gleamed with a blend of excitement and trepidation as she parted the brush. I lifted the binoculars.

The valley below looked just like the one we had climbed out of. A wide, two-lane highway ripped right down the middle, with a sprawling field planted in a cover crop filling the space between the bottom of the ridge and the blacktop. But beyond the blacktop, in place of a third field, lay the compound.

I adjusted the binoculars and settled onto the ground. Brooke pushed the brush back a little farther, expanding my field of view. But I could already see most of what I needed to.

The bulk of the compound consisted of a single massive building completely encircled by dense forest that sheltered it from view of the highway. I could see the facility only by virtue of our elevation. The primary building was all metal in construction, maybe a thousand yards long and a couple of hundred wide. In front of that complex sat a six-story office tower, looking like an upturned brick encased in white metal and black glass, an immense American flag flapping in the breeze from its top. There was also a parking lot, obscured by treetops but packed with personally owned vehicles and utility vans that glimmered in the morning sun.

And beyond the parking lot, the office tower, and the industrial complex, I saw something else. A streak of dark gray ripping across the valley floor, twice as long as the complex, but much narrower. Lined on one end by little white dots that looked no bigger than children's playhouses from this distance.

It was the airstrip we had observed using Google Maps,

joined by fully enclosed hangars, their doors rolled shut. Their contents perfectly sheltered.

On the far side of the airstrip, the forest closed in again, and the ground lifted into another ridge that completely sheltered the compound from that angle. A cozy little dot on the map, hidden in plain sight.

I scanned the airstrip once, then moved back across the compound and through the forest belt to the highway. The entrance to the entire facility was clearly marked by an over-sized guardhouse pinned between two massive steel gates—an entrance and an exit, both painted jet black and fully eight feet high. They were connected to a twelve or maybe fourteen-foot-high chain-link fence topped by razor wire.

The guardhouse sat in the middle of a split where incoming and outgoing traffic could be inspected as they came and went. I noted three men inside, but they didn't look like security guards. They looked like full paramilitary, dressed in all black with bulletproof vests and bulky sidearms. One of them even carried an M4-style assault rifle, suspended by a one-point sling over his chest rig.

"What have we stumbled into?" I breathed.

I moved the binoculars back to the end of the entrance drive where it connected to the two-lane, and found my answer on a small concrete sign planted alongside the ditch, almost like an afterthought. So understated that a delivery driver might have missed it on the first pass.

A white sign. A blue shield logo, typed with blocky letters.

Agon Defense — Protect the Homeland.

33

I passed the binoculars off to Brooke. She took her time conducting her own inspection, muttering curses when she noted the fence and the gate and then the guys with guns. I wasn't sure what path her mind was hurtling down, but I knew she would reach the same conclusion I had. An inevitable, crushing reality.

There was no chance in hell we were getting inside this place.

Brooke lowered the binoculars and turned to me, a question in her eyes. Dufort appeared from the trees and snapped his fingers, reaching out a hand. Brooke passed him the binoculars but said nothing. I allowed him time to conduct a third sweep before I gave voice to what we all knew.

"We're not getting in there."

Dufort hocked up snot and spat it into the leaves by way of answer. Brooke twitched beside me.

"Just...hold on. Let's think about this. There's got to be a way."

I shook my head. "There isn't. Not with the resources we have, and the personnel they have. This isn't just some research lab tucked into an office building. This is some kind of major manufacturing facility, and whatever they're cooking up in there, it's clearly very sensitive. See those guys at the gates? I'd bet good money there's a dozen more patrolling those woods. Another dozen inside the buildings, along with cameras. Secure access doors. Checkpoints. All kinds of twenty-four-hour surveillance. It would be like infiltrating the Pentagon. Actually, probably worse than that, because the Pentagon receives regular visitors. This place is an invite-only sort of establishment."

"Holder and his boys got in there," Dufort snarled.

I pointed to the guardhouse. "And that's how."

Brooke frowned. "What do you mean?"

"Look at those guards. They look like mall cops to you? More paramilitary."

"Contractors," Dufort gurgled.

"Yep. Bridgewater Security. Which gives us our link between Holder and whatever this place is. I tried to look up Agon Defense and got nowhere. The name is probably a DBA—a *doing business as*. A subsidiary of a larger corporation, which might itself be a subsidiary of another, larger corporation, like Russian nesting dolls. You'd need a good corporate lawyer and access to all kinds of public filing docs to unweave the mess and determine who owns what. Which is exactly the point."

"What point?" Brooke said.

"The point about Bridgewater. I couldn't find an address or website for them, which is probably because they aren't an actual security firm searching for clients. They have only one client—Agon. Because they're owned by Agon, with a few corporate smoke screens standing in between, of course. A way for a big company to *literally* own a private army without anybody being the wiser."

"Why would a corporation need a private army?" Brooke said.

"A great question," I muttered. But I already knew it didn't matter *why*, only that the army was there. And I didn't have one to match it.

Rising to my feet, I dusted off the leaves and turned down the hill.

"Sharpe!" Dufort called. "Where are you going?"

"To find breakfast," I snapped. "I can't think on an empty stomach."

THE THREE OF us packed into a table at the back of a Waffle House twenty minutes later. The place was mostly empty, the hour as yet too early for most sane people to want food. I ordered black coffee and an All Star Special—my go-to meal while working graveyard shift with Jacquie. She used to roll her eyes when I requested chocolate chips on my waffle, prophesying heart failure in my near future.

The memory might have brought a smile to my face, but the building frustration in the back of my mind smothered any joy into silence. Dufort was jammed into the far side of the booth, his bulky frame curled over the table while Brooke used the restroom. He grunted "same" at the waitress after I ordered, guzzling piping hot coffee as though it were ice cold. I noticed the waitress casting quick, horrified glances at Dufort's disfigured face, and I glanced around the restaurant to find patrons and cooks doing the same. Looking, but not looking. Pretending they didn't notice.

Dufort, meanwhile, focused on his coffee—pretending not to notice them like they pretended not to notice him. I saw the pain in his eyes, and my gut twisted.

Neither of us spoke as Brooke returned from the bathroom, her face glistening with traces of cold water. She swept raven hair behind her ears and slid automatically next to me. Her thigh brushed mine, and an electric bolt shot up my spine. I twitched and shifted toward the wall, placing a narrow gap between us.

"What are you having, honey?"

Brooke passed the menu to the waitress. "Two egg special, bacon and hash browns. Sweet tea to drink."

"For breakfast?" Dufort gurgled.

Brooke shrugged. "I'm from Kentucky. Sweet tea goes with every meal."

I rotated the coffee mug in one hand, enjoying the warmth against my palm as I studied the Ford parked just outside. It was dusty with road grime, chrome trim gleaming in the rising sun. I thought about the ten-odd hours we'd spent burning a trail from Jacksonville to Culpeper, and wondered if it had all been a wild-goose chase.

I'd kicked some doors in my time. More than a few of them *after* I left the Army. I knew something about forcing entry, clearing rooms, detaining suspects. All while avoiding enemy fire or avoiding detection altogether. Some call it a science; others call it an art form. Whatever the case, it's a skill you can learn, practice, and master. But like every skill, door kicking has its limits, and I was pretty certain that the Agon compound lay well beyond those limits.

Solid steel gates. Cameras, trip wires, and roving

surveillance. Heavily armed security. Key card access doors protected by yet more cameras. Winding hallways and legions of uniformed staff who would pick out an intruder like blood in the snow.

This wasn't door kicking. This was something closer to an espionage target—CIA territory.

"What if we ask for a tour?" Brooke said. The waitress returned with her tea, and Brooke unwrapped a plastic straw. "We could say we work for some media agency or something. Public access. Right?"

Dufort snorted. "They're not giving tours. Better off kidnapping somebody."

"We're not kidnapping anyone, Dufort," Brooke said. "Get your head out of your ass."

"Better idea than posing as a fifth-grade field trip," he retorted, staring into his coffee.

"Okay. So what if we pose as regulators, then? They have to open the door for regulators. Like...EPA or something. An environmental concern. Rare tree frogs, endangered. We could sneak in; then one of us splits off and finds the drive."

"No dice," I said. "Holder knows who we are, remember? We're not getting inside that facility, and we're not getting that drive back. We may as well accept that. The moment it entered that compound, it was out of our reach. By now they've got it hooked up to some supercomputer. They may have cracked the data key or simply decided to incinerate it."

Brooke's mouth fell open half an inch, indignation flashing across her face. "Are you kidding me? We just drove—"

"Eleven hours. I know. I did most of the driving. That doesn't change the reality of the situation. This place is far more fortified than it looked on Google, and even assuming we *could* find a way inside, how do you propose we find the drive? You're talking about two or three *million* square feet of industrial space. That drive is barely bigger than a deck of cards. Worse than a needle in a haystack. More like a needle in the Grand Canyon."

Brooke's shoulders squared. Her nostrils flared. She set the tea down hard enough to send droplets of it raining across the table.

"So what? You're just *giving up*?"

I sighed laboriously, snatching a napkin out of the dispenser to wipe my tea-splattered arm.

"Not for a minute," I said. "But I know when to take a step back and recalculate. Calm down."

The food came, and Dufort and I dug in while Brooke sat with her arms folded, pouting like a teenager. I didn't think she meant it to be cute, but I couldn't help thinking it was. With her bottom lip poked out just a little, stormy eyes clouded with indignation—

I cut the train of thought short, fork hovering over my eggs. That same flash of heat had returned to my chest, and for the first time since I met Brooke, I didn't deny it. I questioned it instead.

What was I feeling? Attraction? Lust? Or was my lonely mind simply latching onto a warm body and a beautiful face?

Dufort's fork slammed into his plate, jarring me out of my thoughts. He was attempting to cut bacon, but the bacon was seriously undercooked and rubbery. The fork wouldn't slice through, and he ground down on it. For the first time since leaving the compound, I noticed his flushed cheeks, breath whistling between his mutilated lips. He pressed on the fork again, cranking his arm down like a chef slicing an onion.

The bacon cut, and the plate cracked. Dufort's arm slammed into the table, and his jaw clenched. He threw the fork down and shoved the broken plate away, sliding out of the booth in a rush. Next thing I knew, he was barreling out the door, into the parking lot. Disappearing around the corner.

I sat with my fork halfway to my lips, raising an eyebrow. Brooke wiped her mouth and pushed out of the booth.

"It's okay. He struggles to manage his moods...something about the blast. I'll talk to him."

I looked to the shattered plate and almost told her to leave him be. Then I figured she knew what she was doing, and returned to my eggs. Brooke left the Waffle House, and I promised to pay the indignant waitress for the busted plate before requesting another order of bacon—well done, this time.

As I wrapped up my meal, I felt no closer to an answer than I'd been lying on that hilltop, staring down at Agon. I wasn't ready to admit defeat, but I knew we'd need to hit this thing at a completely different angle if we hoped to gain a foothold.

The drive was gone. Which meant the whistleblower's evidence was gone. Unless...

My pocket buzzed, and I fished for the phone as I leaned toward the window to look for Brooke and Dufort. I saw them standing thirty yards away at the end of the building, Dufort sucking on a cigarette, Brooke rubbing his back gently. Calming him. Talking softly. Sunlight playing across dark hair, flashing on her teeth as she smiled.

I checked the phone: 480. I answered.

"Yeah?"

"Are you alone?"

I squinted. Jacquie had never asked that before. I glanced around the room, but the restaurant was still mostly empty.

"I'm good. What's up?"

Long pause. I waited.

"Look," Jacquie said. "Maybe I shouldn't have, but...I had a look into Pearson and Spraggins."

"The bank robbers?" I feigned ignorance. Jacquie snorted.

"Give me a break, jackass. I know you were the Army guy they kidnapped. I know what this is about."

I seriously doubted Jacquie knew *exactly* what it was about, but I was interested in her theory.

"So what did you find?" I prompted.

"Not much on Spraggins. Dude kinda fell off the map after service. But Pearson...the man is off the reservation. In a big way. I was able to pull his DOD files and uncover some medical records. He was medically retired in 2017...for mental health."

"What?" My voice snapped a little.

"I don't know the details, but his DOD file is covered with psychiatric reviews. The discharge was honorable, but I don't think it was optional. His forwarding address after discharge is a psychiatric hospital in Philadelphia. Of course, I couldn't get those records without a warrant, but..."

"We can guess," I finished.

"Yeah," Jacquie said. "He's not okay, and...I thought you should know. Just in case...you're trying to help him."

Trying to help him.

Suddenly, I understood. Jacquie wasn't guessing about military coverups, missing hard drives, or staged bank robberies. She was simply assuming that I'd been kidnapped by a crazed service member, and after having a run-in with some feds—people I'm known to dislike—I had decided to take matters into my own hands and help Pearson out. One soldier to another.

Just like Jacquie was helping me out. One cop to another.

"Thanks for letting me know," I said. "That actually does help."

The door swung open, and Brooke stepped back in, leading stormy Dufort behind her. The big guy walked with his head down, shoulders bulging. Eyes flashing fire.

"I gotta go," I said. "I'll call soon."

I hung up, and Brooke and Dufort slid back into their seats as though nothing had happened. A fresh plate of bacon waited for the SEAL. This time he ate it with his fingers.

I watched Brooke sip tea, then raise a butter knife and delicately go to work on her toast. Smearing jam with precise flicks of the blade.

She caught me staring and stopped. "What?"

I kept staring, not blinking. Not answering.

Brooke set the knife down, looking suddenly irritated. "*What?*"

"You lied to me," I said.

"hat are you talking about?" Brooke played it cool, but I detected a twitch of her lip, and Dufort grew still.

So they both know.

"Pearson," I said. "I asked you why he was medically retired. You said you didn't know. But you do. And it matters."

Brooke laid the toast down. I waited.

"You didn't ask me why he retired," she said. "You asked me if he was injured in Yemen."

"Wasn't he?" I pressed.

Brooke hesitated. Her eyes rimmed red. "Not...physically."

I drained my coffee. Half of me wanted to shove out of the booth and help myself to the Ford. Leave them right here in this Waffle House. Drive eleven hours to get my truck, finish my banking—

"Look." Brooke faced me, and this time I saw a tear

bubbling in one eye. She blinked it away. "I didn't tell you because...we needed your help. And I knew if I told you..."

"I'd write this whole thing off," I said. "Just like the media. Just like *his own father*. Am I right?"

Brooke looked to Dufort. Dufort gritted his teeth and glared at the window. I was suddenly glad neither of us were a plate.

"Start talking," I said. "Or I walk."

Brooke guzzled tea. It dripped down her chin, and she wiped it with the back of one hand. Swallowed. Breathed.

"Let's go," I snapped. "I haven't got all day."

"Okay, okay." She held up a hand. "I just...it's personal. All right? For Pearson."

"Yeah, well, it's getting pretty personal for me, also. And my friend in Phoenix. And *Ronald*. So stop screwing around, or—"

"Matt has psychological problems," Brooke said, voice soft. "Something...snapped with him. In Yemen. I guess it was the trauma. What he saw. Being in command of that column. It just...he couldn't take it. He started drinking a lot. Just kinda...fell apart."

I glanced to Dufort to confirm Brooke's story. The big SEAL avoided me, fixated on his now empty plate. But I could see red rimming his eyes, just like Brooke's.

"There's so much stigma around PTSD," Brooke said. "So much...you know. Machismo. Matt was a Ranger. A West Pointer. A congressman's son. He wouldn't get help, and it just kept spiraling. We were in touch back then. We were... well, for a short time we dated."

The admission should have been a bombshell, but I somehow wasn't surprised. Dufort's motivation for assisting Pearson's crazy bank heist plan was obvious—it was written all over his burned and mutilated skin. Brooke's motivation was less apparent. She was just a driver, after all. Army infantry. Not bound by any direct bond to the special ops soldiers killed that day.

Unless she had been, at some point in time. And still carried a flame.

My stomach twisted a little at the thought, suddenly understanding the storm behind those ocean eyes. But that didn't clear the problem at hand.

"How many hospitals?" I asked.

Brooke shrugged. Lip trembling.

"How many?" I repeated.

"Maybe...like...five."

Five.

I ran a hand over my face, clenching my knuckles amid my hair. Waiting for a minute. Then peeling out my wallet and flicking two twenties across the table.

"What are you doing?" Brooke said.

"I'm going back to Florida," I said.

"No, wait. You can't do that."

"Really?" I snorted. "Because you just admitted that this *entire goose chase* is predicated on the word of a mentally wrecked war vet. A guy who's so messed up he's being forcibly checked into mental facilities. So messed up his own father doesn't believe him."

"No." Brooke shook her head. "No, you can't say that. You don't understand. He's not some crazy person—"

"Oh, no," I snapped. "I *do* understand. I understand more than you understand. You watch a bomb go off and see people get blown to hell. You run to the sound of the guns and arrive too late. You get shot up yourself, and you keep pulling the trigger while she bleeds out on the floor..."

I stopped, suddenly choked up. Tears bubbling up before I could resist them. Hands trembling against the edge of the table. Suddenly very aware that half the restaurant was staring dead at me.

I'd said too much. But it was too late to backpedal now. It was time to leave.

"You go through hell, and you want a justification," I muttered. "But sometimes there isn't one. Sometimes life is just hell. I wish Pearson all the best. I'm not burning the world down based on his crazy hunch."

I headed for the door, ignoring the staring patrons. Scrubbing my face as I stepped outside into a blast of chilly Virginia air. I stopped on the sidewalk and looked up at the sun, shutting my eyes and breathing slowly. Forcing myself to calm.

The images had rushed in like a tidal wave. All at once. Dominating my mind in a split second.

But I was used to that by now. It had been three hundred and sixty-three days. The pain didn't leave. I just learned how to manage it.

The door groaned behind me. I opened my eyes but didn't turn around. I knew who was there. Digging the keys out of my pocket, I unlocked the Ford and went for my backpack. The rental was in Falk's name. Brooke and Dufort could keep it. I'd hitchhiked plenty of times before.

"Mason," Brooke said.

I slung the backpack on, suddenly wishing I'd brought a coat. Maybe there was a Walmart nearby. I like Walmart clothes.

Turning for the street, I started off. Brooke's voice cracked like a bullwhip.

"*Stop*, soldier!"

I did stop. Not because she said to, but because the sudden command and anger in her voice surprised me. Gravel crunched as Brooke marched toward me. Fists clenched, chin down. Ocean eyes blazing as the wind tore at her raven hair.

She looked a little like a cartoon. A really pretty cartoon.

"Don't you move another inch," she snarled. "You grimy coward."

I sucked my teeth. Twisted slowly until I was facing her, one arm still clenched around the backpack strap. And then I waited.

"Matt may be wounded," Brooke began, voice faltering. She swallowed, then started again. "He may have some bad mental health problems. But that *doesn't make him crazy*. And it doesn't make him wrong."

I waited, sun on my face. Listening. Brooke inhaled slowly.

"You saw the drive. You saw Holder and his goons come after us. The whistleblower was a real person, and he's dead. All of that is *fact*."

"Right," I said. "Fact. But not evidence. Did you see any *evidence*? Firsthand? Any *proof*? Because otherwise this is all on Pearson. And as much as you may want to believe it, it could be nothing more than psycho trauma on steroids."

Brooke hesitated. Looked back to Dufort. The big guy stood ten feet back with his arms folded like a granite statue.

"No," Brooke said softly. "Pearson was the only one to talk to the whistleblower before he died."

I nodded. I wasn't happy to be right. I didn't *want* to be right. Being right only meant that Ronald's death was that much more pointless. That Holder was just a crazy psychopath. That Pearson was just a very sick, very abandoned war hero who—

"There were emails," Dufort gurgled.

My gaze snapped toward him. "What?"

"The whistleblower had emails," Dufort repeated. "It's what led him to start digging."

Brooke looked up, eyes flashing. "Yes! *Yes!* I forgot about those. There were emails. Internal communications from inside Agon. Requests for mission logs to be scrubbed, with dates corresponding to the bad strike in Yemen. The whistleblower stumbled over them while conducting routine IT work."

"Where are they?" I asked.

Brooke hesitated. "Matt had them."

"Did you read them?"

"I read them," Dufort said. "They didn't prove anything. But they convinced Pearson the whistleblower was legit. And that convinced me."

Dufort closed the gap between us in two short strides, glaring down at me. His permanent snarl accentuated. Eyelids stretched. Fake teeth bared. He also looked like something out of a cartoon—a really ugly cartoon.

"It convinced *us*," he said. "Because *we* aren't spineless cowards who walk away from our brothers-in-arms. Because we trust each other. So if Pearson says it happened, then it *happened*."

I held his gaze, reading the anger and the challenge, but not threatened by it. Wondering how many screws were loose inside his flash-cooked brain, and if he was just as broken as Pearson.

I wouldn't judge him if he were. I wouldn't judge anyone.

There's no shame in a battle wound. Only in running from the battle.

I inhaled deeply. Held it. Breathed out. Then I looked to Brooke.

"If the whistleblower had emails—and then he had a drive full of hard evidence—he shouldn't have gone to Pearson. He should have gone to the cops. Or even the media."

"He tried," Brooke said. "I told you before. Nobody would believe him, even with the mission logs on the drive. And then he got spooked. I guess somebody at Agon caught on to what he was up to. That's when he locked the drive in the safety-deposit box and contacted Pearson."

"Right," I said. "But he *tried*. So that means he talked to somebody else, right?"

Sudden understanding flashed across Brooke's face. She looked to Dufort hopefully. Dufort screwed his swollen eyebrows together.

"Some...some reporter..." He trailed off.

"Think, Clay," Brooke urged. "Focus. What did Pearson say?"

"It was..." Dufort ground his teeth. "Somebody with the *Washington Signal*, I think. A woman. K...Karen...no. Maybe. Kelly..."

"Kelly Davis," I said.

"Huh?" Brooke said.

"Her name is Kelly Davis," I repeated. "And she just wrote a beautiful piece about Pearson and Spraggins...with some details she shouldn't have had. Like how Pearson was medically retired in 2017."

Brooke's eyes widened, turning suddenly triumphant. She snapped her fingers. "She talked to the whistleblower!"

I held out my hand to Dufort.

"Keys," I said.

"Why?" Dufort snarled. Defiant again.

I lifted my chin to meet his gaze. "Because I don't walk away from a brother-in-arms, either. So let's go talk to this Kelly Davis."

35

K elly Davis wasn't difficult to find. She was a reporter, after all. A syndicated columnist with a long and complex bio full of acronyms and accolades I couldn't possibly care less about. Her office was located in downtown Washington, on K Street, only a few blocks from the White House. It was the headquarters of the *Signal*, although her floor wasn't listed. I figured there would be a directory, and we hit the road. I took the wheel, not trusting Dufort in his recently enflamed mercuriality. The last thing we needed was a speeding ticket or a traffic accident.

Brooke worked her laptop while gorgeous north Virginia countryside rolled by like a circulating screensaver. Everything was dead now, with auburn and amber leaves having long ago reached the ground and turned deep brown. Even so, the smooth hills and hardwood forests specked with two-hundred-year-old barns and split-rail fences took me back to a simpler time. A time I'd never actually experienced, but somehow felt connected to.

It wasn't difficult to see why people loved Virginia. I could only imagine it in spring.

"No update on Matt," Brooke said quietly. "Last report, he's still in critical condition."

"Spraggins?" I asked.

"No word."

Dufort's teeth clicked, and I glanced sideways to see him grinding them as he glowered out the window. The sound suddenly annoyed me, like nails on a chalkboard, but I knew it was his demeanor that was getting under my skin.

"Are you always this annoying?" I asked.

Dufort snorted. "Are you always a crybaby?"

"I am when I look at you."

Dufort froze, and I waited. His lip twitched, and Brooke's eyes went wide in the rearview mirror. Then the lip twitch was accompanied by a deep, throaty, gurgling sound. Dufort's shoulders rose, and the gurgling became a wet laugh. He shook his head and ran the back of one hand over his twisted nose.

"Good one," he said. "I got nothing."

The traffic hit us twenty minutes later, and what should have been an hour-and-a-half drive quickly stretched beyond two hours. I'd been to DC only once before, briefly, while in the Army. I didn't recall a lot about that visit other than the traffic, but my memory served me well. It sucked. We crawled along the freeway at barely twenty miles per hour, the gorgeous Virginia countryside now replaced by the urban sprawl of Arlington. By the time we crossed the Potomac, I was ready to be almost anywhere else.

But then we hit Constitution Avenue, and the Washington Mall stretched out to our right. First, the Lincoln Memorial, sheltered by trees but still visible as a white marble monolith, impossible to miss. Then came the White House to our left, and the Washington Monument to our right. I watched in the mirror while Brooke stared in transparent fascination, leaning low to peer out the rental's window, her small mouth hanging half open.

Dufort glowered straight ahead, angry eyes fixed on the rear bumper of the Toyota riding in front of us. I thought I understood why, but I liked Brooke's reaction better. There was something to be said for remaining awed by the magic of it all—the grand experiment. The Free World. Democracy, as history had never seen it.

Even if dark, sinister truths might swirl just beneath the surface of those polished, marble facades.

I parked the Ford on the street across from the *Washington Signal* and peered up the face of the multistory building. American flags flapped in the breeze just outside, and the *Signal*'s name was proudly emblazoned in bold letters. Not a subtle place, by any means. But the First Amendment isn't subtle.

"How are we gonna play this?" Brooke said. "Is she just gonna...talk to us?"

Not a chance, I thought. *Not when she sees Dufort or learns who we are.*

If the whistleblower really had approached Kelly Davis about Agon, there would have been a reason she refused to pursue the story. Maybe because it was absurd or unfounded. Maybe because she was a reporter and a columnist, not an investigative journalist.

Or maybe because, somewhere along the line, Holder had paid her a visit. Maybe an anonymous piece of mail had arrived in her inbox, scaring her silent with the promise of a car bomb or a gas leak.

Whatever the reason, Davis hadn't chased the story before, and she would require some convincing before she discussed the subject again. To open the door for that conversation, we'd need a pretext. A pretext...and an unthreatening face.

"You go," I said, addressing Brooke. "Tell her you're one of the kidnap victims from the bank robbery, and you'd like to share your story. Get her to buy you lunch someplace quiet. We'll meet you there."

"Why me?" Brooke protested, a little indignant. I figured that meant she already knew why.

"Because I cry," I said.

"And I make people cry," Dufort said.

Brooke snorted. "It's because I'm a woman. Because people aren't threatened by women."

I shrugged. "It might be sexist. It's still true."

Brooke rolled her eyes and leaned between the front seats to straighten her hair in the rearview mirror. I smelled something like flowers and clean water as she brushed past me. That warm feeling returned, and this time I didn't over-think it. I just looked away.

"Okay, jackasses," Brooke said. "Hang tight."

Brooke dropped out of the Ford and smacked the door closed. She jogged quickly across the street, and I watched her go. The black jeans she'd worn since leaving Jacksonville clung close to her curves.

They looked good.

I turned away from the window, the warmth in my chest fading quickly to a cold knot in my stomach. My gaze flicked across the dash, where the Ford displayed the date next to the clock. It was the last thing I wanted to see.

"Tread carefully, crybaby," Dufort said. He sat with his

head resting against the seat, eyes closed. Warm sunshine played across his disfigured face.

"Huh?"

"You pump and dump her, and I'll break your knees," Dufort gurgled.

"Excuse me?"

He opened one eye. Stared me down. Closed the eye. "I can smell the interest."

I sat back. The knot in my stomach was gone, but had morphed into a lump into my throat. I shook my head.

"I don't know what you think you saw. I'm not in the market."

Dufort snorted.

"What?" I said.

Long silence.

"*What?*"

"I never said the interest came from you."

I twitched, my face rushing hot. Before I could answer, the back door popped open, and Brooke reappeared out of nowhere, sliding into the seat.

"She's not there," Brooke said.

"What do you mean?" I avoided the mirror.

"The receptionist said she was working from home. I got the feeling she was under the weather."

"Did you get a home address?" Dufort asked.

"Sure I did." Brooke rolled her eyes. "I just said, 'Can you get me her home address?' and they handed it right over, no problem. Here you go."

Dufort glowered. "I was just asking."

Brooke folded her arms and sat back in the seat. "What now?"

I looked down the street, tapping the steering wheel.

Thinking. Cars rolled slowly past the *Signal* building, a mix of jet-black government sedans, POVs, and taxi cabs. Street vendors sold hot dogs and submarine sandwiches. One guy had a cart loaded down with bouquets of flowers.

I reached for the door. "Wait here."

Jogging across the street, I reached the flower vendor and purchased a bouquet of tulips—bright yellow and white, altogether foreign amid the crisp fall air. I paid in cash, using three twenties from Falk's supply, and had the guy wrap up the flower stems in emerald green plastic. Then I headed for the *Signal*.

The first floor was surprisingly calm for the headquarters of a busy newspaper. The custodian directed me to the third floor for *Signal* reporters, and I took the elevator. At the top I pushed through twin glass doors into the sort of media-frenzied bullpen I expected—a field of cubicles, glass offices, whirring copy machines, clacking keyboards, and buzzing voices. Organized chaos, not so different from the bullpen of the Phoenix PD.

Maybe a little less smelly.

I approached the receptionist and offered a smile. "Good morning. Delivery for Ms. Kelly Davis?"

The receptionist was young, probably an intern from one of the local liberal arts colleges. Her eyes lit up at the sight of the bright flowers, barely glancing at my face.

"Oh, wow. So beautiful! Let me guess...from Rick, right?"

I shrugged innocently, as though such information was classified, but yes. She was right.

The receptionist blushed. "Ohmagawd, he is *such* a dreamboat. I freaking hate Kelly."

Okey-dokey, then.

I waited, and the girl seemed to snap out of it. She

blushed. "Right. Uh...actually, Kelly's working from home today. Did they not give you her home address?"

I shook my head. "No...the order was for her office. But if you have it handy—"

"Sadly, I can't. Confidentiality and all that. But I'm sure Rick has it."

I checked my watch, puffing out my cheeks and breathing hard. "Actually, we're pretty crunched today. Maybe I can just leave them on her desk?"

The girl's phone rang. She scooped it up automatically, rattling off a perfunctory greeting. I tilted my head toward the bullpen, and she peeled the phone away. "Number twenty-eight," she mouthed.

I winked and hurried down the row of corporate partitions, dodging incoming reporters and bustling research aides on my way to cubicle number twenty-eight. Kelly Davis's name was posted on the wall, just above that long list of complex credentials and certifications that I couldn't care less about.

I cast a quick glance over my shoulder before slipping inside. The flowers found their way next to her computer, and I made a show of arranging them while I scanned the desk. Notes, a cup of pens, a stack of books, a paper tray and...bingo.

I returned to the Ford, jogging across the street and sliding into the driver's seat. Brooke leaned forward expectantly, that wash of flowers and clean water rushing my nose again.

"Well, flower boy?"

I reached beneath my jacket and flicked out the document. A cable bill, already opened, displaying the *Signal*'s address on the outside. But on the inside, there was a service address. A home address.

Brooke grinned, dimples flashing. "Okay. That's impressive."

Dufort snatched the bill and punched the address into the GPS with a thick finger. "Yeah, yeah, we're all impressed. Let's roll."

36

Kelly Davis lived in Washington's Brightwood Park neighborhood, north of downtown, almost to the Maryland state line. The address was a townhome constructed of painted brown brick with other townhomes built directly against it, a sidewalk and lots of crepe myrtles sheltering a narrow front porch.

There wasn't a front yard to speak of. There wasn't a driveway. The neighborhood looked old—maybe a hundred years, but well maintained and updated by a deluge of multi-six-figure salaries and yuppie money from the West Coast.

Different city, same story. I'd seen it a thousand times.

I parked the Ford around the block and checked my cell phone for battery. The device still held half a charge.

"Dufort, you take overwatch," I said. "Brooke and I will go in."

Dufort snorted. "Better plan, I go in. One look, she craps her pants and spills her guts."

I rolled my eyes. "Stop flattering yourself, Dufort. You're not *that* ugly."

I tossed him the keys, and Brooke and I left the SUV. Dusting myself off and stretching, I was surprised by the sting of a sharp breeze whistling down the street. As early afternoon aged, the temperature was dropping. Living in Florida over the past four months had spoiled me.

"How are we gonna play this?" Brooke asked.

"Directly," I said. "I'm tired of beating around the bush."

"She might clam up," Brooke said.

"I'm very persuasive."

Brooke shot me a sideways glance. "I don't know if I like the sound of that..."

"Neither will she."

"What if she freaks? What if she pulls a gun?"

We approached the townhome, and I scanned the yard. Three political signs flexed on metal stakes in the light breeze. Two campaign signs for local elections, and a third that displayed a punch list of progressive political talking points like *tax the rich* and *the economy belongs to everyone.*

"She doesn't have a gun," I said.

I ascended the steps after completing a quick check for security and finding two cameras pointed down from the corners of the porch. I didn't see wires and figured they were powered by Wi-Fi. I made a mental note to look out for a cell phone. I didn't want her summoning any DC cops.

I raised my fist. Brooke stopped me.

"Sharpe?"

"What?"

"Be cool. She's not the enemy."

"Don't worry. I'm very aware who the enemy is."

I knocked. Waited. Knocked again and pressed the bell. I wasn't sure if it worked. They generally don't, especially on homes this old.

After a long pause I heard soft, padding steps on hardwood beyond. Somebody leaned against the door, and the peephole darkened.

Rookie mistake.

"Just leave it on the doorstep," a raspy voice called through the wood. "I tipped you on the app."

"Kelly Davis?" I called.

Long pause. "Who are you?"

"My name is Mason Sharpe. I'm working an investigation into Agon Defense. I'd like to speak with you."

It was direct—right to the point. I figured anything less might justify her pressing that electronic panic button on her phone. Summoning the cops via her Wi-Fi security system.

Davis didn't answer. The peephole remained dark. I heard a sniffing, sniveling sound. She really was sick, it seemed. Not just sleeping off a hangover.

The lock clicked, and the door swung open three inches, stopped by a brass chain. A blue eye rimmed in red appeared in the gap, tangled blonde hair falling over pale cheeks. It was Kelly Davis, all right. I recognized her from her bio page on the *Washington Signal*'s website.

"Who are you?" Davis's voice cut out any pretense of pleasantries. I could appreciate that.

"Mason Sharpe," I said again. "I'm working—"

"I know what your name is. I'm asking what your *title* is. Are you a cop?"

I hesitated. Then Brooke stepped in.

"Ms. Davis, my name is Brooke Oswilder. Sergeant Sharpe and I are from the Army. Department of internal investigations, Pentagon. We'd like to discuss your participation in an investigation into Agon Defense."

No, no, no...

My chest tightened, and I held my breath. Ordinarily I would have no problem lying about my credentials when necessity called for it, but the first thing a syndicated reporter would ask for was credentials.

Kelly Davis didn't ask for credentials. She withdrew from the door instead. "I don't know what you're talking about. Please leave."

The door began to close. Brooke stepped ahead, placing one fist against it and pressing it open against the chain.

"He's *dead*, Ms. Davis. Your whistleblower is dead. If you don't talk to us, we can't protect you."

I glanced sideways at Brooke. She met my gaze and shrugged.

Bold.

The door remained open, three inches. The brass chain taut. Kelly Davis didn't push it closed, and I wondered if even now she was working the Wi-Fi app on her phone. Summoning those cops.

I looked over my shoulder and down the street, suddenly remembering the Glock in my waistband. DC is the furthest thing from a gun-friendly city. Possession of the weapon alone would be enough to lock me up.

My train of thought was derailed as the door shoved shut abruptly. I reached for Brooke's shoulder, ready to retreat to the Ford and re-evaluate. Waiting for the door bolt to snap closed.

Instead, the chain rattled. The door swung wide, revealing Kelly Davis. She was a small woman, a lot smaller than she looked in her headshots. Not that headshots show much beyond a head. Wrapped tight in a bathrobe knotted at the waist. Blonde hair hanging in a mess over her shoulders, her cheeks puffy and pale. Her nose bright red and moist. She wiped it quickly as narrow eyes swept us both; then she stepped back and tilted her head. Granting us permission to enter.

We obliged, and Davis shut the door, blowing her nose loudly into a tissue. I cast a quick glance around the base floor of the townhouse. It was simple enough—pretty much what I'd expect from a hard-charging career woman who spent most of her time away from home. An elegant but unused living room with a small flat-screen TV. A kitchen with granite countertops, takeout containers and empty coffee cups spread across them. Dirty laundry on the table. A dead houseplant resting on a windowsill.

Davis cleared her throat, and we faced her. She folded both arms, and I suddenly understood why she had let us in. Why she hadn't pressed that digital panic button.

This woman was absolutely fearless. I could see it in her square shoulders and elevated chin. In her complete uncon-cern at facing two strangers in her living room, even while she wore a bathrobe and her nose ran like a faucet.

There was no reservation. No discomfort or hesitation. Kelly Davis was all business.

"Okay," she said. "I know you're not from the Pentagon, and I know you're not cops. I don't tolerate drama on a good day, and today isn't a good day. So start talking, or I'll have Metro PD down here before you can blink."

I noted her right hand tucked into the pocket of her bathrobe, and wondered if her finger was hovering over that panic button.

Probably.

I nodded to Brooke. My instincts told me she should take

point. Davis had caught her in the lie about the Pentagon. She should be the one to repair that bridge.

"Okay," Brooke said. "Fair enough. We aren't from the Pentagon, and we aren't cops. But we are Army. Or...we were."

"How did you know about Newton?"

"Who?" Brooke said.

Davis narrowed her eyes. "The *whistleblower*. How did you know?"

Brooke's lips parted, but she didn't speak. I could see what she was thinking in those ocean eyes. *Do I spill everything?*

I filled the silence. "May we sit?"

Davis shook her head. "No."

"Okay. Let me start here, then. Are you a good reporter, Ms. Davis?"

More narrowed eyes. Davis wiped her nose. "If I have to answer that, you really don't know who I am."

"Fair enough. So you appreciate a good story, then. You appreciate the truth. We have some truth for you."

37

I told Davis the story, as I knew it, start to finish. The bank robbery, the hard drive, the private army hired by Agon. I left out the details of Ronald's death, simply stating that the drive had been "recovered" by Agon's people and was now lost.

I wasn't ready to admit to being present when the big guy from Atlanta had been shot in the head like a cow. Without knowing whether I could trust Davis, I didn't want her to have any information she could use against me.

Davis listened without question, arms folded, only moving to blow her nose and answer the door when more takeout arrived. I could tell she was engaged, a flash of surprise passing across her face when I reached the part in my narrative about Spraggins and Pearson's true motives in robbing the bank in Jacksonville.

But for all that, the core of the story didn't seem like news to her. She'd heard it all before, which only confirmed our existing theory that prior to finding Pearson, the whistle-blower had visited Davis.

I finished my spiel, and Davis just stared. Unmoving. Expressionless. It occurred to me that she might be on some heavy meds for whatever sort of ailment was waylaying her, and I wondered if this entire exchange had been a magnificent waste of time.

It wasn't. Davis piloted around one of the wing-backed chairs in her living room and sat. She did not offer us a seat.

"I was afraid I hadn't heard the end of this," she said simply.

I waited, but she didn't elaborate. Brooke stepped in.

"We're hoping the whistleblower may have told you something. Something we can use."

Davis laughed dryly. "If he had, don't you think I would have reported on it?"

Fair point.

"We're actually wondering why you didn't report on it," I said. "Or even investigate."

"How do you know I didn't?"

I didn't know. But I figured any self-respecting, syndicated reporter would be vulnerable to a barb about incompetency. I was right.

"I'm a top twenty reporter on the East Coast, Mr. Sharpe. Do you have any concept of how impressive that is?"

Again, I said nothing. Davis smirked, almost as though she knew I was baiting her, and was deliberately choosing to fall for it.

"I'm a very good journalist," she said. "And any good journalist is an investigative journalist. That's the nature of the job. You have to find the truth. But *being* an investigator and having the *job* of an investigator are two different things. I report breaking news for a living. I fly places, and I talk to people, and I spend a lot of time on the phone. It's a lot of digging. But that's not the same as prying into people, events, and corporations that don't want to be pried into. Digging for dirt, in other words. Uncovering corruption."

"You're saying that's not your skill set," I said. It was another calculated barb. It earned me another knowing smirk.

"I'm saying it's not my *occupation*. I work eighty hours a week on a lazy week, even when I'm sick. I don't have a hell of a lot of time to invest into chasing rabbit trails, and believe me when I tell you, my life is *full* of potential rabbit trails. People send reporters like me 'leads' all the time." Davis made air quotes with her fingers. "My public inbox is so full of junk, I barely check it anymore."

"So why didn't you pass the whistleblower off to some-body else?" Brooke said, jumping on my bait wagon now. "Why didn't you hand the lead to an investigative colleague?"

Davis didn't answer right away. She sucked her teeth. Then she got up, walked to the kitchen, and filled the coffeepot.

"Because I believed him," she said, at last. "When you've done this as long as I have, you develop a sort of sixth sense. An ability to *feel* when a story has the ring of authenticity to it. When somebody is telling the truth."

Davis produced three coffee mugs from a cabinet. She flicked the pot on and folded her arms while it brewed, leaning against the refrigerator.

"So you looked into it," I said.

She nodded. "Yes. I looked into it."

"And?"

No answer. For the first time, Davis broke eye contact.

"Did they threaten you?" I asked.

Davis snorted. "I wish they had. I would have felt some justification to bend the rules, then. What they did, Mr. Sharpe, is lawyer up. Agon sent a cease and desist order to the *Signal* so fast it was like they had prepped it ahead of time. They threatened a lawsuit, and we knew they weren't kidding. My boss was on my ass, that quick. He wanted proof. Of course, I wanted proof also. Jim Newton—that's your whistleblower—didn't have any proof. He had some emails from C-suite requesting his department to scrub certain classified mission briefs. He showed them to me, but I never took possession, primarily because they were internal business documents and his right to copy them was dubious, at best. When I filed an interview request with Agon, that was when the cease and desist was triggered. I never told them that I was talking to one of their employees. Newton claimed he could get hard proof, but by that time my boss was all over me, wanting me to shut it down. Anything Newton obtained would be stolen intellectual property, meaning that if and when we reported on it, we would be subject to a lawsuit."

"Isn't that the very nature of being a national media outlet?" Brooke prodded. "Reporting the facts. Investigating. *Being sued.*"

Another derisive laugh. "The nature of being a national media outlet, Ms. Oswilder, is *picking your battles*. The *Signal* is a business, like any other. We make investments and take calculated risks. Writing an investigative piece on the shady business dealings of a corrupt politician is good business. He'll sue, but he'll likely lose, and even if the *Signal* has to pay a settlement, they'll make way more money off the circulation anyway. Attacking a billion-dollar defense contractor is something else entirely. We're talking about enough political power to shut us down. Permanently. Years and years of legal proceedings, burning through capital and choking out our business like an anaconda wrapping around our windpipe. It's not a matter of whether or not the *Signal* is in the right. It's a matter of whether or not the company can survive the proceedings."

"So you chickened out," Brooke said.

Davis didn't laugh this time. She lifted the coffeepot instead, slowly pouring three cups. Then sighing.

"No, Ms. Oswilder. I was shut down. And two weeks later, I learned of Jim Newton's tragic demise. Heroin overdose, but I'm sure you already knew that."

Davis set the pot down and carted two cups to the counter nearest Brooke and me.

"A tragedy," she said.

"And an *obvious* coverup," Brooke snapped, ignoring the coffee. "You can't tell me you actually believe—"

"You were in the Army, Ms. Oswilder?"

Brooke nodded.

"Were you ever in combat?"

Brooke's mouth hung half an inch open, momentary pain flashing across her face. She looked away.

"Yes."

"Did you ever see anyone die?" Davis pressed, lifting her own coffee mug and blowing on the surface to cool it.

"Yes," Brooke said.

"Then you know," Davis said, "at some point, you have to keep moving. People get shot. They die. There's nothing you can do. You know the enemy is still out there, and you know they got away with murder. But if you chase every insurgent with an AK into the hills, you'll never get anywhere. You'll never win the war."

"Is reporting the news war?" I said, not bothering to hide the edge in my tone.

"Yes, Mr. Sharpe. It is. It's the most important war of them all—the war of truth. The war of accountability. It's an endless, bloody grind. You watch stories bleed out right in front of you, *knowing* somebody got away with murder, and you've got two options. You can throw away your career chasing every possible lead, ramming your head against closed doors and drowning in lawsuits, or you can pick your battles. Play it smart. And win something."

Davis's voice turned very hard as she finished the spiel, red-rimmed eyes flashing. She tossed the coffee into the sink, tearing off a paper towel to blow her nose again. I couldn't tell if she was angry with us or herself or the inevitability of the realities she described. Maybe it didn't matter.

"I'm sorry I can't help you," Davis said. "I understand wanting to vindicate your friends. I really do. But I'm not a vigilante, and I'm frankly not interested in becoming a martyr."

Brooke flushed a little. I felt her anger reflected in my own chest, but before I could say anything, the phone in my pocket buzzed. I scooped it out while Brooke went to work on Davis, pressing for any details Newton might have disclosed that might be useful.

I unlocked the phone and found a message waiting from Dufort. My heart skipped.

Tangos inbound. Backup?

I raced to the front door, choosing the window instead of the peephole. Raising one blind louver a half inch and peering between the tangled crepe myrtles to the street.

A black Ford Taurus. Virginia plates. Two meatheads in black suits walking our way.

38

I dropped the blind louver and shot a quick response to Dufort. Three words.

Copy. Stay put.

Then I turned for the kitchen, snapping my fingers to arrest Brooke's attention.

"Tangos," I said. "More Bridgewater thugs."

Brooke's gaze snapped up, but it was Davis who panicked. She reached for her bathrobe pocket, no doubt ready to draw and brandish her home security panic button like a Mossberg shotgun.

Not like the two have anything in common.

"No, wait," I hissed, voice low as footsteps tapped across the porch. "Stay calm. They don't know we're here. We can defuse this."

"*Who?*" Davis said. "What are you talking about?"

A harsh knock rapped against the door, abrupt enough

to rattle the front windows in their century-old frames. I gestured for Brooke to hurry into the back of the house.

"They're people from Agon," I said, addressing Davis. "Private security. Not friendly. They're here to tie up loose ends. They know you were investigating, and they know we're investigating. Don't let them in, and *don't* tell them we're here. Got it?"

Heat flashed across Davis's face. Outrage, maybe. Or indignation.

I ignored her, pressing my hand against Brooke's shoulder and guiding her into the first-floor bathroom. It was little larger than a closet, with just a toilet and a sink. Brooke pressed against the wall, and I eased the door shut, keeping the light off.

Another harsh knock rang against the front door. Davis moved to answer it, and I lifted my shirttail, resting one hand around the grip of the Glock. Holding my breath.

"Hello?" Davis spoke first.

"Kelly Davis?" A booming, commanding voice. The guy sounded like a Marine. Maybe he had been, back in the day. Or, more likely, he was a washout. A wannabe who'd crapped out of Parris Island in the first week.

The lock twisted. The door creaked a little on its hinges, and the chain rattled. Davis was doing her routine again— looking through the chain gap, one hand concealed behind the door, her thumb hovering over the panic button. As a cop it always amused me how people do that. Relying on those flimsy chains as though a good kick from a mid-sized dude wouldn't tear the anchor screws right out of the door frame.

"Can I help you?" Davis's tone was all business. A little

cutting. Maybe she was running out of patience with demanding visitors.

"Hello, ma'am. I'm Special Agent O'Hare. This is Special Agent Gordon. We're just stopping by for a quick welfare check. Nothing serious. We have a few questions for you, if you don't mind."

"Special Agent with *who*?" Davis pressed.

A good reporter. Going straight for the credentials.

A soft laugh. "I doubt you would have heard of us, ma'am. We...work for the Pentagon. Sort of a consulting position. Special Agent is just a title."

Davis didn't answer. Cheap suit cloth rustled against itself. "Special Agent" O'Hare spoke again.

"We were just wondering, have you seen these people?"

Long pause. Davis spoke.

"No."

"Are you sure?"

Another pause. "Isn't that the woman from the bank robbery down in Florida? One of the hostages."

"That's right," O'Hare said. "How did you know?"

"I wrote a piece," Davis said, tone still cold. "I'm a reporter. I'm sorry, why are you here?"

Another rustle of the suit jacket. O'Hare, putting the photos away.

"We're lending a hand with the investigation. Helping out with some legwork. We just wanted to check and see if you'd spoken with any of these people, or if they had stopped by?"

"Aren't they in Florida?" Davis asked. "Why would they speak to me? And what does the Pentagon have to do with any of it?"

"Right," O'Hare said. "Well, the thing is, ma'am. Confidentially...I'm not supposed to say this. But it turns out several of the participants in that bank robbery were ex-military. You already know about Spraggins and Pearson. You wrote that piece on them. But the two hostages, Oswilder and Sharpe...they were ex-military, also. And we actually think they may have been participants in the robbery. We've had a look at their DOD records, and they aren't pretty. Oswilder has major PTSD. She's taking half a dozen different medications. And Sharpe...well, he actually just lost his fiancée. Brutal school shooting, about a year ago. He abandoned his job as a police officer and drove to Florida. We're not exactly sure what all the connections are, but it's safe to say both of them are...off the rails. Not safe people."

I felt Brooke's eyes on me, her body pressed close to mine in the darkened bathroom. So close I could feel the warmth of her skin on my arm, her breath a gentle current running past my neck. Carrying the smell of clean water and fresh flowers.

I didn't look at her. I remain fixated on the bathroom door as Davis shot down O'Hare again.

"I don't see what any of that has to do with me."

"That's the thing, ma'am. We have reason to believe that Sharpe, Oswilder, and perhaps a third unidentified accomplice may be launching some manner of vigilante effort. To get their buddies out of jail. They aren't rational people. It occurred to us, what with you writing the report on the robbery and all, that they might come after you. Make you a target for...your journalistic efforts."

What?

I held my breath. Listening.

"I haven't seen them," Davis said. "And I'd like you to leave now."

"Are you sure?"

"About not seeing them, or wanting you to leave? Yes to both."

A dry laugh. Another rustle of cheap suit fabric.

"Here's my card," O'Hare said. "Feel free to call me, day or night, if you hear from them. We're only looking out for you."

Footsteps on the porch. "Have a safe day, Ms. Davis."

The door closed, and the lock slid. I eased out of the bathroom, finding Davis standing behind the door, staring at a black business card in one hand. She snorted.

"*Consultant.* Yeah. Sure you are."

She pocketed the card and met our gazes. I saw a question in her eyes. Or maybe that was just her fighting back a sneeze.

"You believe us now?" I asked, listening as the Taurus whirred away.

"I believed you from the start," she said. "Just like I believed Newton. I simply can't help you."

I walked to the window, lifting the blinds to check the street for another car. A tail, left behind to wait for our exit. That would confirm that the meatheads knew more than they were letting on—that they had tracked us here.

But I saw no second car. Only a quiet street lined by expensive, century-old town houses.

"I would appreciate it if you left now," Davis said. "As you can see, I'm well under the weather. You can leave a card if you like. In case...well, something should change."

I detected an undertone of compassion in her voice. Maybe sympathy. It made me think she really did believe us, but belief alone was pretty near useless.

Brooke gave Davis her number. Davis did not reciprocate. Then we were back on the street, walking amid the crape myrtles, breathing crisp DC air.

"What now?" Brooke said. Her voice trembled a little, and I looked down to see red-rimmed eyes, turning moist at the corners. She avoided my gaze, pocketing her hands. Shivering a little in the breeze.

I remembered what O'Hare had said about her PTSD. About her pills. I wondered if it was true, and figured it probably was. He had spoken the truth about me, after all. Considering her condition now brought to mind her mention of a therapist. Her aversion to firearms.

Suddenly, I wanted to hold her. That warmth in my chest redoubled, and I wanted to pull her close. Wrap my arms around her shoulders and let her know she wasn't alone. That I *knew* what the pain felt like. Knew how the ghosts kept you awake at night. How the world felt like one giant, vague blur. Days running together. Nobody around who truly understood...

"We've got nothing," Brooke said, cutting my thoughts short. Her voice cracked a little, desperation seeping through. "*Less* than nothing. No evidence. No proof. No way to get any. That inside man was our only hope. Without that drive..."

She shook her head. I stopped on the sidewalk, twenty yards short of the Ford. Looking back toward Davis's townhouse, I squinted.

Inside man.

"They're tying up loose ends," Brooke said. "Davis will end up with an overdose of her own before this is over. Anybody they suspect. I've got to go home! They'll go after my family."

Brooke fast-walked to the Ford. I didn't move. I kept staring at Davis's place.

Tying up loose ends. Anybody they suspect.

Anybody.

Then I smiled, the warmth in my chest fueled by sudden, animalistic satisfaction. Like the elation a hunter feels as a deer turns broadside in front of his rifle.

Rushing to the Ford, I tore the door open and addressed Dufort first. "We got plenty of gas?"

He checked the gauge. "Quarter tank."

"Go and fill it up, then come right back here. Keep your phone handy. Brooke, you're with me. Let's roll."

"What?" She looked up from the back seat, a tear streaming down her cheek. "What are you talking about?"

I ignored her, shutting the door and starting back to Davis's house. Brooke followed, and Dufort spun off in the Ford.

"Sharpe! *What* are we doing? I've got to go home! My mom—"

"Your mom is fine," I said. "They won't touch her."

"How can you be sure? They killed Newton. They killed Ronald. They'll kill anybody who exposes them."

"Exactly," I said. "Especially an inside man."

"Huh?"

"Just follow me. I've got a plan."

39

D avis answered on the second knock—no chain
this time, but the look on her face told me she
might be reevaluating her politics on guns.

"I know how you can help us," I said before she could
stop me. I forced my way in, Brooke in tow, Davis glaring
through watery, sick eyes.

"I told you, Mr. Sharpe. I can't help you. Now get
out of—"

"There's something happening here, and you know it," I
said. "You said you believed us. So just listen. Those guys are
tying up loose ends. Patching leaks, which means there's
something at stake. Something to protect. Right?"

Davis said nothing, standing beside an open front door. I
pushed the door closed.

"There's zero chance we crack this thing open from the
outside. We need another leak—we need what we had on
that drive. But we're not going to get it. Not without an inside
man."

"Yeah, well, I'm not your inside man. And I don't know where to find one," Davis said.

"You don't," I said. "But *they* do."

Davis narrowed her eyes. Brooke looked to me, a question on her face. I pointed to Davis's pocket.

"You'll call them back," I said. "Tell them you were scared before, but you're ready to talk. Have them return. When they do, you'll tell them that we were here. That we were asking questions about Agon and a bad strike in Yemen. Tell them we have an inside man feeding us information. Somebody local, who works at the Culpeper facility. You don't know who it is, but maybe they should investigate. Then send them away."

"How does that—"

"We'll follow them," I said. "The first place they'll go is to stop the leak. Shut down the inside man."

"But you don't *have* an inside man," Davis said.

"We don't now, but we will. They're going to lead us right to him."

"I don't understand."

"Think about it. These guys are running a full emergency protocol. They showed up at your door because somebody made a list—a list of all weak points. Potential leaks. Somewhere on that list is the name of a person working inside that compound. A person they are already concerned about. We don't know who that is, but we don't have to. *They* know. And that's the first place they'll go—to plug the leak. We'll... intercede. And then we'll have our inside man. A man we already know is primed to blow a whistle."

Davis wrinkled her cherry red nose. She looked from me to Brooke. Then back to me.

"That's certifiably insane," she said.

"So certify me, then. And make the call."

"I can't. And neither can you. If anything you just said is true, I'd be triggering a murder. You realize that?"

"You'd be triggering an *attempted* murder. Trust me, it won't go that far."

"You can't be sure."

"Absolutely I can. Just watch."

"It's a good plan," Brooke said, nodding quickly. "It could work."

"It will work," I said. "But not without you."

Davis folded her arms. I couldn't tell whether she was primed to call the police, or if she was now vaguely amused. Maybe curious.

"You'd need to wait," she said.

"What do you mean?"

"You'd want me to call them this evening. That way your inside man will be home, not at work. If they lead you back to their corporate compound, you can't...'intercede'." She made air quotes again.

I checked my watch. "It's two thirty now. Five o'clock?"

"Six," Davis said, turning for the stairs. "Beer in the fridge. Hot Pockets in the freezer. Netflix on the TV. Keep the noise down."

I CALLED Dufort to fill him in on the plan, asking him to wait in the car for the next three and a half hours. It was a big ask, but he immediately understood. Davis was barely on our side. Brooke and I needed to remain in the house in case she got cold feet, but exposing her to the horror of Dufort and his brutal injuries might well derail the train. Plus, we still needed a sentry. Just in case the meatheads returned to ask more questions.

Brooke warmed the Hot Pockets, but I skipped the beer. Since landing in Florida three months prior, I'd done a lot of drinking. Usually whiskey. Usually straight out of the bottle. As the calendar slowly melted away, I blurred the dates together. Maybe in an effort to ignore them.

Whatever the case, it wasn't me. I've never been an alcoholic, and I didn't want to become one. I opted for water instead, leaving the Hot Pocket to cool on a plate. Somewhere upstairs a shower ran, and soft music played.

Davis—a confident woman. Not the least bit perturbed by strangers in her house. I was impressed.

Brooke sat across from me in one of the wing-backed chairs, taking little rabbit bites of her Hot Pocket. Raven hair fell over her ears, and she shifted uncomfortably in her chair.

"You wanna watch something?" she said after a minute.

I shrugged. "Sure."

She didn't reach for the remote. Neither did I.

"I..." She started and stopped, avoiding my gaze. Brushing hair out of her eyes. "What the guy said. At the door. About the meds..."

"You don't have to explain," I said. "It hits us all in different ways. I'm glad you're getting help."

She nodded softly. Picked at the Hot Pocket but didn't eat it. She looked up.

"And...you?"

I drank water, stalling for time. "What about me?"

I knew what she was asking. I knew I didn't want to talk about it. And yet, somehow, I couldn't make myself change the subject. There was something about the calm of those ocean eyes, her lips parted, complete openness in her face. It froze the words over in my throat before I could even form them.

"What was her name?" Brooke whispered.

I looked away. Rotated the water glass in one hand.

"Mia," I said, at last.

Brooke didn't answer, and after a while the silence became awkward. I looked up and was surprised to see her crying. Soft, slow tears slipping down smooth cheeks. Lips barely parted. Not blinking.

"I'm so sorry," she said.

I forced a smile, feeling my own eyes sting. Feeling that rush of warmth, also. Like some kind of invisible magnetic force.

Suddenly, I wanted Brooke next to me. I didn't want to talk. I didn't want to discuss, or delve into the past, or work things out with a friend. I just wanted to not be alone, but I didn't know how to say so.

I didn't have to say it. Brooke eased around the coffee table to the couch. Without asking, she leaned down, placing one hand on my shoulder. Her other tracing my cheek, then running down my neck. The warmth in my chest grew into raw heat as she neared. I smelled clean water and flowers. Her neck bent.

Then she kissed me. Long and slow and soft. Her tongue touched my teeth, and I tasted those flowers.

I put my hand behind her neck, and I kissed back.

40

Brooke and I spent the next three hours sitting across from each other, watching some eighties sitcom on the TV. Not talking. Not looking at each other. Not even laughing.

Just smiling from time to time at a good joke. And not being alone.

When Davis came back downstairs at six p.m. on the dot, she looked better than before. Her hair was pulled back in a ponytail. The bathrobe was replaced by sweatpants and a Yale sweatshirt. She looked very crisp and all business.

"I'll make the call," she said. "But I want assurances."

"Okay," I said, not rising from the couch.

"First, nobody gets hurt. I don't want any blood on my hands. Period."

I didn't answer.

"Second," she said. Then she stopped, folding her arms. Seeming suddenly awkward.

"You want the story," I finished.

Davis found her grit again and held her chin up. "Right. I want the story. I think that's fair."

I looked to Brooke, and she nodded.

"Okay," I said. "No innocents get hurt. You get the story. I can agree to that."

"No*body* gets hurt," Davis corrected. "You're not Batman. I don't tolerate vigilantism."

I stood and walked across the room. I picked Davis's cell phone off the counter and handed it to her.

"Why don't you just make the call."

DAVIS MADE THE CALL, and she sold it well. I was impressed. In a faltering voice she spun a story about two crazed veterans—a man and a woman—who visited her house. No, she didn't get their names, but she thought they matched the pictures the "special agents" had shared with her.

She wouldn't say anything more over the phone. She was scared. Couldn't the special agents come by her house? That would be great.

Davis hung up and shook her head. "These guys really aren't the brightest bulbs, are they?"

Brooke and I returned to the car. The Ford smelled of greasy fast food, and there was trash on the floorboard, but Dufort said nothing about being left outside. It was dark now and colder than before. I took the passenger seat with a clear view of Davis's house and waited.

The Taurus turned up exactly twenty minutes later, squealing in next to the curb. Two meatheads got out— O'Hare and Gordon, I guessed. Really bright bulbs. They met Davis at the door, and the exchange was quick, but theatric. She moved her hands a lot, and I noticed that she had disheveled her hair.

Don't lay it on too thick, Davis...

Two minutes passed; then the men were marching back to their car. Hard faces. Cold, angry eyes. Already zeroed in on their next target.

"It worked," I said, adjusting the Glock in my lap. "You know how to tail?"

Dufort snorted and put the Ford in gear. The Taurus raced by, and he swung in to follow. Within seconds we were turning south, out of DC. Back into Virginia. That made sense. If we were headed to confront some weak link in the Agon chain, it likely wouldn't be a senior executive. Maybe something more along the lines of middle management. Somebody with a comfortable six-figure salary, but not metro DC money. A suburbs guy.

Only, we didn't stop in the suburbs. Dufort hung fifty yards back, sometimes allowing a car or two to fill the gap between us, but never losing sight of the Taurus. Through Arlington, then Fairfax, then Centreville. We caught I-66, headed west and not getting off until Sudley Road, taking a left turn toward Manassas.

"You think they made us?" Dufort said.

I shook my head. "No. But they know exactly where they're going. They know their target."

Thick evening traffic closed around us amid the Manassas shopping district. The Taurus faded amid tail-lights. I lowered my window and pushed my head out just in time to spot the Taurus sliding into a turn lane.

"Left turn," I said.

Dufort slowed but didn't put on his turn signal. He waited until the Taurus completed the turn before he blazed through a yellow light, keeping the distance between us. Keeping the car and its blue and white Virginia plate in sight.

Retail stores and restaurants melted away, quickly replaced by sprawling subdivisions, but not the kind I expected. These weren't half-million-dollar soccer-mom homes with minivans and BMWs in the drive. No carefully manicured lawns, stone mailbox posts, or elegant, winding streets. These streets were chopping and straight, the houses small and mismatched. Two-hundred-thousand-dollar homes, maybe. Nice, but not fancy. Not ornate. The drive-ways were short, with plenty of cars parked directly on the streets.

It was a middle-class neighborhood. Not middle management. Lower management, or maybe line worker.

Brake lights flashed on ahead of us, and Dufort slowed. I press-checked the Glock, confirming the presence of a 9mm round in the chamber. I didn't plan to use it. This needed to be a stealth mission.

But I would be ready for anything.

The Taurus stopped in front of a split-level home with a faded Subaru in the driveway. Dufort pulled in behind a contractor's work truck, parking on the street with a clear view of the split level. He pressed-checked his own Glock, and Brooke leaned in between us.

"Wait," I said, holding up a fist.

The Taurus's taillights died, and both front doors opened. The meatheads stepped out, casting quick glances around the quiet street but failing to notice the parked Ford Edge they had passed in Brightwood Park. They unbuttoned their coats as they moved across the unkempt lawn toward the front door.

Then the guy on the left produced a pair of surgical gloves, snapping them on.

"They're gonna kill him!" Brooke gasped.

"Not before they find out what he told us," I said. "Just wait."

The meatheads reached the door. The gloved guy knocked. The second guy reached across his body and beneath his jacket—for a gun, no doubt. Meathead One knocked again.

The porch light flashed on. The door swung open. Both meatheads barreled through, overwhelming the man beyond and slamming the door behind them.

"Okay, let's move." I swung my door open, and Dufort and Brooke followed. As the three of us reached the driveway, I motioned Dufort to the left and Brooke to the right— to circle around back, cover our flanks, and enter from the rear.

They split without hesitation, and I ascended the porch. From inside the house I detected heavy thumps followed by muted cries. Something made of glass shattered, and a voice boomed.

"Start talking, you runt!"

I tried the knob. It was unlocked. *Rookie mistake.*

I eased the door open, my free hand grasping the Glock tucked into my waistband. Just in case.

A wood-floored foyer greeted me. Undecorated, faded with scuffed paint on the walls. Car keys hung on a rack. Shoes scattered next to the baseboards. The muted cries and thumps were louder now, coming from some kind of parlor or living room to my right.

I waited, looking down the foyer into a kitchen beyond with a sliding glass door. I saw a shadow outside—a very big, very ugly shadow. Another crash from the parlor was joined by a scream, and Dufort forced the glass door open, leaning against the handle and smashing the flimsy metal latch. It slid open with a growl, but the meatheads didn't hear. Brooke appeared behind Dufort, crossing the kitchen and reaching the far side of the parlor entrance.

I made eye contact and signaled to the left side of the parlor with two fingers. Dufort nodded. His lip was curled up again, accentuating that permanent snarl. He looked like something out of a nightmare.

I drew the Glock, rotating the weapon in my hand until my fingers clenched the slide like a hammer handle. I raised three fingers, listening as one of the meatheads wheezed and shouted obscenities at his victim. Cajoling him to talk. Threatening much more severe punishment if he didn't.

"What did you tell them?" he roared.

Not a thing. But he's about to.

I dropped the fingers quickly, one at a time. Then Dufort and I exploded around the corner, Glocks held like clubs, rushing into the small room.

The bloody-faced victim on the floor saw us first. He lay with his back against the wall, his feet splayed across hideous orange shag carpet. Blood streamed down his face. Eyes wide with terror.

Two bulky men stood over him.

Meathead One stood on the right—the guy with the gloves. The guy doing all the beating.

Meathead Two stood to the left—and he held a pistol. Another Glock 19, pointed dead at his hostage.

Dufort's heavy footfalls blew our cover, but by then it was far too late for anybody designated a target. Meathead One spun toward me, eyes widening just in time to catch the butt of my Glock squarely on the nose—hard enough to shatter bone and send shock waves ripping through his brain. He stumbled, throwing gloved hands up at random to block my next blow.

But I didn't swing again—this time I faked a kick to his right, and he stepped backward defensively. His full body weight descended on his left leg. I kicked again—for real this time. My foot plowed straight into his left knee with everything I had, slamming my foot into the joint from its unprotected side.

Something snapped, and he shrieked like a teenage girl in a slasher movie. His hands dropped, doubling over as he fell.

That was when I struck again with the Glock—right into the back of his skull. Full force. Overwhelming velocity.

Lights out.

Meathead One collapsed, unconscious, and I turned to see Dufort pinning Meathead Two against the wall, pummeling his unprotected face with the Glock, using the pistol like brass knuckles. Already the nose and cheekbones were caved in, torn flesh streaming with blood, body limp.

"Clay!" Brooke reached him first, wrapping hands around his left arm and dragging him back. "He's had enough—he's unconscious! Let him go."

Meathead Two wasn't unconscious. He was dead. Dufort's right arm froze, already cocked for another blow. Then he simply released the body. It hit the floor in a limp pile, and Dufort breathed through his mouth like a panting bull.

He turned toward me slowly. His scarred and mutilated face was sprayed with blood, his eyes dark. Lip quivering.

Like something out of a horror film.

"What the hell!" Brooke shouted. "We promised the reporter we wouldn't hurt anybody!"

"I promised we wouldn't hurt any *innocents*," I clarified, wiping sweat from my nose and surveying the two bodies. My guy had a busted knee and would wake up with a headache. Dufort's guy wouldn't wake up at all. In my gut I knew Brooke was right—we'd gone too far. But what was done was done.

I faced the third man on the floor—the one still conscious. He clawed his way back from the three of us. Fresh terror flooded his face, his back already against the wall. In the short period between when the meatheads made their entry and we arrived for the rescue, the guy had already been beaten badly. It made me regret my decision to wait, but it also assuaged any guilt for pummeling the guys. They had it coming.

Calmly rotating the Glock, I returned it to my waistband. Then I kicked aside Meathead One's limp legs and addressed the man on the floor.

"Who are you?"

41

His name was Adam Grieves, and it took some time to calm him down. While Dufort retreated to the front porch to smoke cigarettes and stand watch against meathead backup, Brooke and I guided Grieves to his kitchen table. Brooke fixed him a hot cup of coffee and spent a while talking softly to him, walking him through the events that had led to the violent invasion of his home, along with his subsequent beating and rescue.

Even then he seemed unable to speak. His hands shook. His lips parted, but no sound came out. He kept looking for the cordless phone Dufort had tossed into the trash on his way to the porch.

"The police aren't coming," I said, taking a seat across from him and accepting a cup of coffee from Brooke. She had already explained to Grieves on a high level who we were and what we wanted.

What we knew.

I wasn't sure if he understood us at all, or if Meatheads One and Two had selected a perfectly random target who truly knew nothing about his company's internal corruption. But I did know that Grieves worked for Agon. I found his wallet on the kitchen table, and beyond a Virginia driver's license, a credit card, and a membership ID to some kind of eccentric gaming club in Arlington, I found an Agon employee ID. A very fancy thing—it reminded me of a DOD Common Access Card, or CAC. They were issued to both military personnel and civilian contractors working on military bases, and featured a photo, full personal details, a barcode, and a little brass chip similar to a chip on a credit card, which provides access to on-base computer systems.

A very sophisticated form of identification, and Agon's employee ID was every bit as advanced. It included the same type of photo, personal information, and brass chip, all joined by that bold blue shield logo.

Protect the Homeland.

I dropped the employee ID on the table. Grieves looked at it. He shifted uncomfortably in the chair and looked away.

"Who are you people?" he muttered, not making eye contact.

I sighed, running a hand over my tired face. Then I ran through the high points Brooke had already hit, summarizing the Agon coverup and dead service members.

I told Grieves only as much as he needed to know, concluding with our generous efforts to save his life—I left out the part about us setting him up in the first place—before politely requesting that he lend us a hand in our investigation.

Grieves blinked a lot, shifting in his seat and biting his lip. He was a small, skinny, nervous-looking guy with unkempt black and gray hair. Late thirties, I imagined. Maybe early forties. No visible tattoos. He wore a button-down shirt with a pocket protector in the breast pocket, a pair of reading glasses and several pens jutting out. Worn khaki pants. An oversized digital watch.

There were no family photographs, sports or movie memorabilia, or even very many creature comforts scattered around the house. The furniture was old and mismatched, as though he had purchased it at a thrift store. The house was dated and worn, as though it hadn't been updated since whenever it was built. Probably the mid-seventies.

Grieves lived alone, it seemed. And while he had every reason to be terrified, I had the feeling he was awkward and uncomfortable with humanity on a good day.

I picked up the work ID and scanned his personal information again. There was a full name, an employee ID number, an access level—"A4", whatever that meant—and a job title. *Programmer Lev 3.*

"What do you program?" I asked.

Grieves glanced up at me—very quickly. A flick of his eyeballs. Then he looked away again and twitched.

"Hey." Brooke kept her voice low, sliding a hand across the table. Her fingertips brushed Grieves's arm, and he bolted like a startled cat. In a flash he was across the room, into the kitchen. I stood and reached for my Glock. Brooke held up a hand.

"No, wait!"

Grieves reached the kitchen and threw a cabinet open. Pill bottles fell out, and he shuffled through them, hands shaking, darting glances shooting toward us. He found a bottle and cracked it open. Two pills fell out, and he gulped them down dry. For a minute he just stood in front of the wall, blinking rapidly.

Then he breathed deep and looked at the floor.

"Xan-Xanax," he stuttered. "I...I'm not...people make me nervous."

I released the Glock. Brooke walked quietly across the kitchen and stood a few feet from Grieves. She extended a hand, palm up. A sort of sad smile on her face.

"Me too," she said.

Grieves's gaze rose slowly. He met hers. Licked his lips. Then he lifted the bottle and dropped a pill into her open palm. Brooke swallowed it; then the two of them made a pilgrimage to the sink to fill water glasses.

I observed the awkward ritual in silence, feeling a little like an intruder, somehow. Brooke returned to the table, but Grieves remained at the sink. Fifteen minutes passed, but every time I opened my mouth to speak, Brooke stopped me. Grieves leaned over the sink, just breathing. Sipping water. Wiping blood from his face.

Slowly calming.

At last he looked up, and when he rotated toward us, a strange calm had blanketed his body. Not relaxation or anything close to it. But the Xanax had kicked in and was working some magic.

"You think Agon is corrupt?" he said softly.

I said nothing. Brooke nodded slowly.

Grieves finished his water and dropped the glass into the sink. Then he snorted softly and shook his head.

"You have no idea."

42

G rieves returned to the table and introduced himself. He wouldn't make eye contact, and his voice never rose above a low mumble, but in short order he provided a little about his background and enough of his résumé for me to confirm what I already suspected.

He was a programmer—not a web developer or an IT guy. Grieves worked deep inside Agon's core business, which was, as he claimed, not weapons or ordnance, but software.

"They're a computer company masquerading as a defense contractor," Grieves said, running his words together as if it was painful to talk at all and easier to rush it. "Their end product is automated and remote-controlled aerial surveillance and strike technology. Drones, essentially. But most of their drone technology is pre-existing. They buy parts from third-party contractors and just assemble them at Culpeper. The true core of their business is the software that drives the drones. All the remote controls. The surveillance tech. The...targeting systems."

He licked his lips, shifting in the chair. His coffee was cold, but he drank it anyway.

"What did you mean when you said we had no idea?" I said. "Do you know about the Yemen strike?"

Grieves swallowed hard, one thumbnail scratching his coffee mug. "When was that, again?"

"Early twenty-fifteen," Brooke said.

Grieves nodded slowly. "Yeah. That's about when it started."

"When what started?" I pressed.

Grieves twitched, looking suddenly toward the front door. I heard it also—Dufort pacing on the porch. Grieves had seen his scars and mutilated face as Dufort pounded Meathead Two into the grave. I imagined that left an impression.

"Is he..." Grieves started. "I mean...was he..."

"Yes," Brooke said. "He was there, in Yemen. So was I."

"And you?" Grieves asked.

"I'm just a concerned citizen," I said.

Grieves finished his cold coffee. Sat up. Sat back again. Rotated the cup. Then he breathed deep.

"Are either of you familiar with AI?"

I squinted. "Artificial intelligence?"

"R-right."

"I know what it is. I don't know much about it."

Another series of rapid nods. "AI is...well, everywhere. And it has been for a long time. Your phone has AI. Your car probably does. Basic forms of AI are present anywhere you go, interpreting human needs and making artificial decisions to meet them. We're so used to it, we don't even notice. But... lately. Well, for a few years now. Things are really accelerating. Artificial intelligence is growing by leaps and bounds. It isn't sentient or anything. It's not...well, conscious. But advanced software is now solving problems at the fifth, tenth...twentieth level. At the snap of your fingers. Like, instantly. With all variables and possible inputs and human responses considered and compensated for."

Grieves's gaze widened, and he looked up briefly. He met blank faces.

"Think of it this way," he said. "You play chess?"

"Sure," I said.

"Imagine you're playing chess on a computer. On a basic computer, the game works off a program. You select moves, and the computer counters with preselected moves based on a set of established parameters. Like selecting a tool out of a toolbox. The computer isn't *thinking*. It's just reacting."

"Okay."

"AI is different. With AI, the computer simulates conceptual thought. It analyzes not just what moves it can make, but what moves *you* can make, and how those moves will change its moves, and so on. So the AI starts planning the game three and four moves ahead, recalculating and calibrating based on every decision you make. It's still not thinking...but it feels like it's thinking."

"Okay." I still had no idea where this was headed, but somewhere deep in my gut, a bad feeling had taken root.

"Now, *advanced* AI...what we're seeing today, it's completely different." Grieves swallowed, placed both hands on the table, then moved them to his lap. Then exhaled. "Advanced AI doesn't just guess your moves. It learns *you*. It sucks in every data point imaginable. How quickly you move. What pieces you favor. What portions of the board you're focusing on. It inputs all of that into advanced algorithms that estimate not only *what* you're likely to do, but how the AI can make moves that will *change* what you're likely to do. It's...like a mind game. On the most advanced level."

"That's not comforting," I said.

"I...I know. I mean. Objectively. It's *really cool*. But..."

"What does any of this have to do with Yemen?"

Brooke's tone was impatient now. Cutting straight to the point.

Grieves ratcheted himself back to the problem at hand. "Right. So...okay. What I do...my job, I mean. I write code. Advanced code. For...well, AI. Essentially I, uh...program the drones."

"With *AI*?" I didn't bother to conceal the disbelief in my tone. Grieves simply nodded.

"It's been happening for years. Agon has always led the way with it. Simple things, like adjusting landing procedures for the speed and direction of wind. Fine-tuning the performance of their hydrogen-fuel-cell engines for maximum efficiency. That kind of thing. But Agon always wants to push the limits. So for a few years now...they've been experimenting with fully autonomous, AI-driven drones."

Grieves stopped and finally looked up. Neither Brooke nor I answered, and he raised both eyebrows.

"Robot drones," he said.

"Are you telling me..." Brooke's voice faltered. "In Yemen..."

Grieves shook his head. "No. I mean, I don't know. That was before my time. But I do know they began experimenting with AI-based targeting systems as early as then. And it's only grown from there. Exponentially. The stuff they're playing with now...it's terrifying. It's off the rails. They have this new model called the X-40 that can fit in a backpack. It's equipped with machine guns and a camera that can read faces. Like the facial-recognition system in your phone. It's literally a killing machine—all automated. You give it a target and turn it loose."

"Why have I never heard of this?" I demanded. It was a somewhat rhetorical question. Military drones are predominantly managed by the Air Force and the Navy. I was Army. And anything as advanced as Grieves now described would be above my pay grade, anyway.

"It's all classified," Grieves said. "And most of the crazier stuff is experimental. So they can use government money to play with it, but they don't have to disclose details. Not yet. And anyway, even with the X-40, AI control is just a feature. Agon markets it as a remote-controlled weapon. They kind of hide the AI."

"Why?" I said.

Grieves shook his head. "I don't know."

I looked to Brooke. She stared at Grieves, her mouth half open, something like disbelief and rage playing across her face. I understood the disbelief part. The technology sounded like science fiction. Within the realm of possibility, but too outrageous to really believe.

Even if it was true, though, did it really matter? Newton had discovered a planned coverup of a bad strike in Yemen. That alone was enough to shatter Agon's reputation and open the door for investigators to have a look at any other problematic programs. We needed to get back on target.

"Can you get inside the facility with this ID?" I said, tapping the Agon employee card.

Grieves's gaze dropped to the card, and he blanched.

"No," he said. "No, I'm not doing that. I can't help you."

He started to stand. I beat him to the punch, putting a

hand back on his shoulder and pressing him back into the chair.

"*Listen to me*," I said, speaking through my teeth. "You see those two guys in there? They came here to kill you. Okay? They came here because they think you're a weak link in the chain. A potential loose end. I'm guessing you sent an email at some point. Or raised your hand in a meeting. Voiced your concerns. Am I right?"

Grieves avoided my gaze, but he nodded.

"So you're on a list now," I said. "It's their job to manage that list, and like it or not, you're now at the top. They've got a whole army of guys like those, with nothing better to do than run you down."

Sweat popped across Grieves's face as I spoke. His breath came in little bursts, and he looked toward the parlor, where Meathead Two's right foot was barely visible.

"But you can protect me," he said. "Right? You were military? We can go to the police!"

I shook my head. "No. No, we can't. Newton already tried that, and so did Matthew Pearson. We can't go to the police until we have *evidence*. And you, my friend, are going to help us get it."

rieves required some convincing. I tried the altruistic angle first, reminding him of Agon's corruption and the concerns that had first brought him to raise his hand.

That didn't work, so I went old school. I dragged him into the living room to view the dead and unconscious duo of Meathead One and Meathead Two, and to remind him that next time meatheads came calling, we might not be around.

That pushed him over the edge. He ran into the bathroom, and moments later the convulsing sounds of projectile vomiting echoed down the hallway. I stood with my arms crossed, Brooke waiting at the table. Dufort raiding the fridge.

"That dude has the courage of a pigeon," Dufort growled. "He's useless."

"Be patient," I said. "He's our best shot."

Adam Grieves reappeared in the kitchen a few minutes later, pale-faced with bile still dripping down his chin. Bloodshot eyes darted between the three of us; then he made a beeline for the pill bottle resting on the counter. I stopped him, one hand on his arm. The other offering him a glass of water.

"Drink first."

Grieves guzzled water. I handed him the pills. He took two, then sat at the table, still shaking. I chose a seat while Dufort took a triple-decker sandwich to the porch and resumed his guard duty. Probably all for the better. His horror-movie face wouldn't calm Grieves.

"We need your help." I kept my voice calm, arms crossed. Shoulders loose. Not pushing too hard, but standing my ground. It was a tactic that had served me well while interrogating drug-addled witnesses plucked from the seedier edges of Phoenix society. Despite the nice house and stable job, Grieves felt like one of them.

"I...I can't help you," Grieves said, voice wavering. "Don't you see? I suffer from social anxiety dis-disorder. It's...ch-chronic."

No joke.

I thought it. I didn't say it.

Brooke laid a gentle hand on Grieves's arm. She smiled very softly. Just enough to expose her dimples. Grieves wouldn't meet her gaze.

"I understand," Brooke said. "More than you know."

Grieves blinked a lot. He drained the water glass and tapped one foot. He shook his head.

"I can't even help you. M-mission logs aren't my thing. I'm a programmer! I program. I have no idea what you're looking for."

"Evidence," I said simply. "Anything that would prove the bad strike in Yemen. Or a coverup of that strike."

Grieves didn't answer. He ran sweaty palms over his

jeans. The Xanax seemed to be working—kicking in quickly over a freshly emptied stomach. He calmed a little.

He still looked like a nervous wreck.

"I don't know where to find that," he said. "That's not my department. The Jacksonville facility—"

"They brought the drive *here*," I cut him off. "Not Jacksonville. Culpeper. There must be a reason."

More blinking and rubbing of his palms against his legs. Grieves began to cry.

"I don't know! I don't know! That's not what I do."

I closed my eyes and inhaled slowly. Brooke cooed, her voice little louder than a murmur.

"Take a breath...it's okay. You're okay. Do you have a safe place, Adam?"

I watched from the end of the table as Brooke scooted her chair around the corner and put her hand on his back. Rubbing gently. Earnest, caring eyes fixed on him.

Grieves nodded.

"Close your eyes," Brooke said. "Go to the safe place."

Grieves complied. Minutes crept by in slow motion. Brooke continued to coo. Slowly, his body calmed.

"We may not need mission logs," Brooke said. "Maybe there's another way. Can you think of another way, Adam? Maybe some other records?"

This time, Grieves didn't panic. He remained still. He breathed evenly. He kept his eyes closed. After nearly two minutes, he swallowed.

"There...might be something."

"Yes?" Brooke asked. "Like what?"

Grieves opened his eyes. "D-diagnostics. From the drones. We get them automatically. After every mission."

"Every mission?" I leaned forward. Brooke shot me a warning look.

"It helps us write new code," Grieves said.

"Would these records include dates and times?" Brooke asked. "Locations? Weapons launches?"

Grieves looked up, eyes still red. Now his body was calm. "They include everything."

"And you can get them?" I asked.

Another nod. "They...keep them on secure servers. Inside Culpeper."

"That'll work," I said. "All we need is the Yemen records. Whatever drones were in the air at the time. We can give you the dates."

Grieves began to shake again. Sweat ran down his face. He swallowed hard.

"They'll kill me," he whispered. "They'll catch me, and they'll kill me, I know it. People have gone missing before. One day working...the next...just gone."

Brooke returned to cooing. I sat at the table for a while, racing thoughts bouncing in my head like Ping-Pong balls. Again weighing the options in my head. Recalling the facility. There was zero chance I could get past the gate. Not without an ID. It had to be Grieves.

But maybe...

I stood. Returning to the living room with the ugly orange shag carpet now stained by blood. I inspected the larger of the two meatheads—Meathead One.

He was about my size. Maybe a little heavier, but too much room is better than too little. I found his wallet. Found his employee ID—Bridgewater, not Agon. It bore the same electric chip as Grieves's Agon ID. The man's name was Russel K. Gordon.

Behind me, Brooke was encouraging Grieves, reinforcing the necessity of this mission. Telling him that the only way out was through—that everyone has a hero inside him. That this was his moment.

"They'll kill me," Grieves said again.

"No, they won't," I said, returning to the table and tossing down Gordon's ID card. "I won't let them."

"How can you be sure?" Grieves objected.

"Because I'm gonna be there," I said. "I'm going with you."

44

We locked a naked and unconscious Gordon in one of Grieves's closets, alongside his fully clothed—and fully deceased—comrade, Michael T. O'Hare. Problems for another day. Then while Dufort made a run to a hardware store for "supplies"—heavy-duty wire cutters for the fence, water bottles for the team, and 9mm ammunition for the Glocks—I dressed in Gordon's sweat-stained and oversized suit and fit his Glock 19 to my belt. I took his Bridgewater ID also, and on impulse I grabbed his credit card as well. Captured credit cards had proven useful over the past few days, but I assumed Falk's and Moss's cards to be canceled by now. It couldn't hurt to refit.

When Dufort returned, he and Brooke loaded into the Ford, and Grieves and I loaded into his faded Subaru. Our plan was simple. It would be Grieves's job to get us inside the facility. A direct inspection of my face matched alongside Gordon's ID card was certain to fail. But if I sat in the passenger seat, my head rising near the ceiling while Grieves passed the gate guard both IDs, there was no reason to think the guard would ask me to exit the vehicle. Even if he knew Gordon personally, he wouldn't be able to see me. He would likely assume that Grieves—nervous and accompanied by Bridgewater personnel—had become a security concern and was being escorted in for official investigation.

If I was honest with myself, it was a lot of assumptions. But Grieves didn't need to know that. Without me by his side, there was zero chance he completed this mission. Pretending to be Gordon was my best shot of bolstering his paper-thin courage long enough to obtain whatever evidence he could find.

Dufort and Brooke trailed behind us in the Ford as we left Manassas—close enough to lend a hand in case things went sideways, but far enough away to identify any meatheads who turned up. I didn't really think O'Hare or Gordon had notified anybody of Grieve's pending betrayal on their way to his house. If they had, somebody probably would have turned up by now. But more than that, I knew something about the way egotistical meatheads think. They don't want to call the boss and risk being given orders to stand down and wait for backup. They wanted to rush right in and get to pounding somebody, then produce the bloodied prize at the end of the night like a deer carcass.

With any luck, nobody would miss O'Hare and Gordon until we already found what we needed and had vanished into the hills. And if our luck ran out, at least Brooke and Dufort would know where we were. Prior to leaving Grieves's house, the three of us had downloaded a find-a-friend app that allowed us to track each other's locations. It was Brooke's idea, and I thought it was a good one.

I liked the idea of an angry ex-SEAL and an Army-trained driver standing by as a quick response force. I could do a lot worse.

By the time we neared Agon, Grieves had descended into an edgy, sweating mess. He no longer argued the necessity of the mission or his part in it. He no longer spoke at all. He just shifted in the seat, driving like a grandmother, the sides of his button-down shirt turning dark beneath the armpits.

"Stay loose," I said. "Whatever happens, *you* are in control. Okay? You control you."

Grieves nodded a lot. He wiped one arm of his shirt over his forehead. We neared the bulky block guardhouse, and Grieves reached for the window switch as a single man dressed in black stepped out and raised a hand.

"You recognize him?" I asked.

Grieves shook his head. "He's night shift. I work during the day."

The window slid halfway down under a groaning motor. The Subaru's brakes squealed. The guard approached.

"How can I help you, sir?" His voice was gruff, but not overly alarmed. Maybe more bored.

"Just headed into the office," Grieves rasped, his voice turning suddenly dry.

"ID?"

The guard's flashlight clicked on, and the beam flicked across the parking pass pasted to the inside of Grieves's windshield. I couldn't see the guard's face—his head rose above the roofline. That meant he couldn't see me, either. At least for the moment.

Grieves passed the guy our pair of IDs. The flashlight beam flicked again. A soft grunt.

"Gordon?" he asked.

I hesitated, heart rate spiking. I couldn't tell whether his

voice was familiar or simply surprised. Did he know
Gordon? Would he recognize his voice?

Screw it.

"Right," I said.

A soft grunt. "Aren't you on Holder's team?"

"Yep." I thought quickly. "Broke down on my way in.
Alternator, I think. Skinny here gave me a lift."

Another flick of the flashlight. I still couldn't see the guy's
face. Ahead of us the heavy steel gates blocked our path.
Grieves's hand trembled against his thigh. His lips parted,
then closed.

Hold it together, man.

The flashlight clicked off. Two IDs passed through the
window.

"Do me a favor," the guard said. "Tell Holder to take
another look at my promotion application. I've done my
time in the guardhouse—I don't mind getting my hands
dirty." .

I thought of the army of black-suited goons Holder
commanded—Falk and Moss in Jacksonville, Gordon and
O'Hare in Manassas. Plenty of others, I was sure. Gun-toting
bullies, ready to murder and kidnap on command like some
kind of corrupt praetorian guard.

The gate guard's comment about dirty work only
cemented in my mind that there were classes at play here.
Bridgewater security...and Bridgewater elite.

"I'll let him know," I said.

The guard turned away. A buzzer buzzed. A chain
ground.

The heavy steel gate rolled slowly open. Grieves didn't
move.

"*Drive,*" I whispered.

Grieves's foot fell off the brake, and the Subaru rattled forward like a lawnmower, suspension groaning, engine clacking. I breathed a strained sigh and waited for what felt like ten minutes as we rolled slowly through the forest and toward the compound. Grieves kept the car fixed at a precise 10 mph, his pace measured by the regular flash of security lights passing the car on either side.

At last I saw the office tower rising out of the parking lot, a hundred yards ahead. The giant American flag illuminated by floodlights. The black glass of multiple office floors reflected the moonlight. Only about thirty POVs filled the parking lot—a light third shift, I figured. Mostly manufacturing and technical. Likely not many office workers.

Grieves chose a random parking spot in the middle of the lot, and I figured it wasn't random at all. It was probably his usual. He shifted into park and cut the engine. The clacking motor died, and he peered out at the six-story office tower. It stood like a giant over us, a single word glowing in subdued blue, just beneath the flag.

Agon.

45

"Everybody checks in," Grieves said. "You'll need the ID card."

We walked toward the main entrance, Grieves scrubbing hands against his sides like some kind of crackhead under withdrawals. I couldn't tell how much of his agitation was due to his recent near-death experience and current activities, and how much was normal behavior. He seemed like the kind of guy who was always a little jumpy.

"The diagnostics records will be in the computer lab," Grieves said. "It should be deserted this late at night. Just... be cool."

"Take your own advice," I said. "You're shaking like a pig in a barbecue shack."

Grieves wiped his face. He stopped outside the building and peered up at the glowing sign. Then his dark eyes darted across the lobby beyond, and he took a half step back.

"I...I can't do this."

I glanced around the parking lot, conscious of security

cameras mounted to the front of the compound, a pacing Bridgewater guy in black tactical pants and uniform shirt working the sidewalk eighty yards away. Another car rolled through the parking lot, LED headlamps spilling across the concrete.

I put a hand on Grieves's shoulder, stopping him in place and speaking through clenched teeth.

"Get yourself together. You're doing this."

"What if they catch us?" Grieves started to pant, stumbling backward. I caught him.

"Then you'll die," I said. "But if you back out now, they'll still come for you. You hear me? The only way to erase this problem is to face it."

I gave his shoulder a little shake. Grieves blinked a lot, sucking in air like a wind tunnel. I glanced left and saw the Bridgewater guy looking toward us, head tilted. Chin raised. Curious, but not yet concerned.

"Move now," I said, releasing his shoulder.

Grieves did move. He stumbled along like a drunk scarecrow, all skinny arms and legs, still gushing sweat. But he didn't stop as we reached the hissing automatic doors and crossed onto industrial tile beyond. The open lobby was ornate in a very cold kind of way, with fake trees and plush white leather couches. A sprawling front desk and directory spread across the back wall, with a panel of metal detectors and armed guards protecting doorways leading beyond.

"You control you," I whispered, keeping my back straight and my shoulders up. Walking like I owned the joint.

Grieves nodded, and we reached the metal detectors. I flashed a quick smile at the guard, then looked away as I removed the Glock in its holster and laid it on the conveyor belt. The guard was dressed like the gatehouse crew, clad in black pants and a black uniform shirt, with a sidearm held in a drop holster. Not the black suit of Holder and his crew—the praetorian guard.

This guy was just security.

The guy barely glanced at my handgun as it hit the conveyor. Grieves slid into the lane next to me, producing his ID. I flashed Gordon's ID and scanned it across the card reader, just the way Grieves had done. Both computers beeped, Grieves's just a split second ahead of mine. I held my breath, waiting.

The second spilled into two, the computers spinning. My guard lifted the Glock and placed it on top of the X-ray machine, twisting toward the computer screen. Ready to compare my face with that of the man displayed by the screen.

My stomach descended into a knot. I looked automatically left, tilting my face away from the guard as Gordon's ugly mug appeared on-screen, looking nothing like mine. The guy squinted.

Then Grieves moved. He stumbled through the metal detector, slamming into the conveyor belt as though he had tripped. The small plastic bowl containing his keys, wallet, and a bottle of medicine went spinning off the machine and cascading across the floor. Grieves lost his footing and fell, smacking the floor with a theatric cry.

Both guards looked toward the commotion, the first hurrying to help Grieves up while the second went after the keys.

I passed quickly through the metal detector, grabbing the Glock and replacing it beneath my jacket. I helped the second guy scoop up the fallen items as Grieves returned to his feet, panting and clutching his chest. His face streaked with sweat. He snatched the bottle I handed him, twisting the cap off and popping a small white pill.

More Xanax. At this point I wasn't sure that he was acting.

"I'm sorry," he mumbled. "Panic attack."

"You good, little man?" one of the guards said. Grieves nodded quickly, swabbing sweat off his face. He smoothed his shirt and crammed the personal effects back into his pockets.

"F-fine. Just a long day."

The guard smacked the enter key on his computer keyboard. Behind me, I heard my guard do the same. Grieves turned for the automatic doors beyond the security station, and I followed, whispering through the side of my mouth.

"Nice job."

"I c-control me," Grieves stuttered.

The automatic doors hissed open. We crossed the threshold.

Then we were in.

46

I followed Grieves from ten feet behind—far enough to distance myself quickly if necessary, but close enough to keep him in sight. Beyond the automatic doors stood a bank of elevators serving the blocky office tower above us. Left of those was a hallway leading out of the back of the office tower, through a corridor, and into the main compound.

"C-computer...lab..." Grieves breathed heavily and stopped halfway down the corridor. There were no windows, the space illuminated exclusively by harsh fluorescent bulbs. Like a hospital.

I closed the distance and put my hand on his arm. "You good?"

He shook and didn't answer. The sweat streaming down his arm was thick enough to glue the shirt to his skin—his face pale enough to qualify as deceased. He really *was* having a panic attack, maybe held at bay only by whatever strength the Xanax lent him.

"Take a breath," I said, softening my voice. "The hard

part is behind us. All we need now is the file, and then we're out of here. Okay?"

Grieves stared at his feet. I gave him time, smiling to acknowledge a passing guy in a tweed suit with a matching pocket protector. He avoided my gaze, quickening his pace as he made for the exit.

"Just get us to the lab," I said. "One more step."

Grieves started again, and I gave him space. We reached the end of the corridor, and he scanned his card to gain access to the building beyond—that sprawling megastructure I had observed from the hillside earlier that same day. There was no manual security here, only cameras and the card reader. The doors hissed open, and the corridor instantly split into an intersection, identical hallways shooting off in every direction. Everything was stark white—white floors, white walls, white metal doors secured by key card access. A bank of elevators stood ready, but Grieves bypassed them. He scanned us into a stairwell, and we climbed quickly to the second level. Another white hallway greeted us, and Grieves turned right.

He walked quickly now, cheap leather shoes slapping the floor. Shoulders rolling as he moved. Still breathing just a little too hard. But he kept moving.

We passed a number of personnel in the hallway, most dressed in stark white lab coats. I acknowledged some with a quick nod, but ignored most. Nobody accosted us, and nobody wore the cheap black suits of Holder and his goons. We made it a hundred yards down the hallway, someplace to the left of the office tower, and then the hallway made a ninety-degree turn to the right, the wall ahead housing a flat white door in a steel frame. A black sign next to the door read simply:

COMPUTER LAB – PROGRAM DEVELOPMENT.

Grieves stopped, card in hand, and wiped his lip.

"Okay. You...you stay here."

I shook my head. "I don't think so."

Sweat dropped off Grieves's nose and splashed on the floor. He reached for his pocket, and I caught his arm.

"You can't keep popping that stuff. You're gonna shut down. Open the door."

Grieves pulled his hand away. "You don't look like me!" he hissed.

"What?"

"Everybody in there looks like me! C-computer guys. Not quarterbacks!"

I looked quickly down the hallway in either direction. I saw no one, but that could change in a split second. Marooned out here by myself, I was a sitting duck.

"*Hurry*," I snapped.

Grieves slid the card. The door lock beeped. He pushed his way through.

I stood outside at the corner of the hallway and checked my watch. It was just past nine p.m., Wednesday. Two days since my whirlwind kidnap at the bank in Jacksonville.

Two days before...

I snatched my mind back to the present, unwilling to travel that mental path. I needed to focus now.

Drawing my phone, I shot a quick message off to Brooke.

Sitrep. Inside. G is in play.

I tapped the phone against my palm, looking left as a door opened a few yards away. A guy in a lab coat walked out, carrying a bottle of soda. He offered me a disinterested nod as he passed, not even slowing. My phone buzzed.

Is G holding up?

I texted back.

More or less. Keep the engine warm.

Brooke's response was almost immediate.

Wilco. Be advised, two black cars just made entry. Virginia plates. More of Holder's people, I think.

I looked down the hall. I couldn't see them, of course, but just knowing those cars were on-site amped my blood pressure by a few notches. I checked my watch again—only five minutes had passed since Grieves entered the lab. Suddenly, I wished he had left his Xanax behind.

Breathe, Sharpe.

I rolled my shoulders and twisted my neck until it crackled. Then I positioned myself in the corner, keeping the phone in my hand as a prop in case somebody else should appear. I figured I would look less conspicuous just standing there if I was pretending to text.

Brooke's messages were still open, and for the first time I noticed that the little bubble with her name beneath it contained a photograph—an automatic thing, I figured. Carried over when she shared her contact from her original phone.

I tapped the bubble, and the photograph expanded to fill the center of the screen. It was Brooke sitting on a porch swing, rolling green hills spilling out behind her. Kentucky, I figured. She wore shorts and a tank top, her tan arms propped against the swing as she tilted her head and smiled.

Both dimples flashing.

That rush of warmth I'd felt a half dozen times by now returned, and I thought suddenly of the kiss. That unexpected, prolonged moment seated on the couch as her lips pressed against mine, her tongue passing through for just a split second. I felt again that electric surge racing up my back. That rush of chemistry overtaking my mind.

Raw and unfettered. Somehow very natural. Looking at her photograph now, I felt a touch of it again, and my mind blurred. I fixated on those dimples, that wavy raven hair. Just looking at her, I felt like I could almost smell the clean water and faint flowers, and I suddenly wanted nothing more than to be near her. To hear her voice. To touch her skin.

A door clapped open, and my gaze snapped up. The guy with the soda and the lab coat was back, returning to his office, offering another disinterested nod. I pocketed the phone, my cheeks feeling suddenly very hot.

I ran a hand over my face and turned away from the hall. I checked my watch and saw that seven additional minutes had passed. I reached for my phone to shoot off a message to Grieves. A check-in. An irritated demand for him to hurry.

Then another door swung open, somewhere down the hall. My gaze snapped up to see four men in black suits appear from the same stairwell Grieves and I had taken, a hundred yards away.

Tall. Bulky. Square shoulders and square haircuts. All four of them pivoting straight toward me, relaxed but moving as a unit. Like military guys. Or ex-military guys.

More meatheads, and long before I could pocket the

phone, I knew I'd never move in time. As I stood frozen, the lead guy pivoted in my direction, black-suited pant legs swishing, a debonair face rotating toward me. We made eye contact at a hundred yards, and something flashed across his gaze.

Then he smiled.

Holder.

47

H older recognized me in the same instant I recognized him. Then two things happened almost in unison—Holder raised an arm and shouted to his men, and the door next to me exploded open as Grieves burst out. The little guy was still sweating, but the panicked uncertainty on his face was now replaced by a triumphant grin, a little red flash drive held up in one hand.

"I got it!"

Down the hall to my left, the smack of leather-soled shoes arrested Grieves's attention. He looked that way, and the terrified pallor returned. I grabbed him by the shoulder and yanked him left as Glock 19s appeared as a quartet. We both hit the floor and slid around the corner, gunshots popping and bullets slamming into the metal door Grieves had just exited. Skidding across waxed tile, I caught myself on the wall and dragged us both back to our feet.

"*Run!*" I shouted. "Another exit!"

Grieves flailed, almost falling again. I caught him and propelled us both forward. Down the hallway ahead, doors popped open as terrified yet curious faces appeared by the dozen. I aimed for the first door and shoved Grieves.

"*Move!*"

"No, not that one! Dead end!" Grieves found his footing and yanked us to the left. We slid around the first door, and he piloted for the third. Behind us, I marked Holder and his goons reaching the turn in the hallway by the boom of voices and the sliding shriek of rubber soles on waxed tile.

"Stop them!"

Nobody was stopping us. The Glock cleared my hip holster, and I rammed it into the face of the first person I saw —another guy in a lab coat. He stumbled backward, and I pivoted the gun to the key card reader on the wall. The pistol belched fire, and a 9mm slug obliterated the plastic housing. Then we were through the door, and I yanked it closed behind us. The lock slammed, and I rushed forward again, barely stopping myself as my waist slammed into a metal railing, the momentum of my hurtling body almost carrying me over the top.

We stood on a metal catwalk suspended twenty feet over a massive, open room. It stretched to my right and left, reaching all the way to either end of the gargantuan building and consuming most of the width. A concrete floor, illuminated by blazing white lights, *packed* with machinery.

It was a manufacturing floor, and it wasn't difficult to guess what was being manufactured. Drones. Dozens of them. Giant, expensive units with thirty-, fifty-, and eighty-foot wingspans, immense propellers built into their tops and tails. All painted gray and black, standing in various stages of completion with a couple of hundred line workers surrounding them in gloves and safety goggles.

I grabbed the rail and yanked myself back, my stomach

flipping as I regained my footing. Grieves was already hurtling down the catwalk to my left, racing for a switchback staircase that led to the factory floor.

"This way!"

Something heavy slammed into the door behind me. I looked through the reinforced glass panel to see Holder's face glowering back at me, his Glock clenched against the window. He wrestled the door, but the latch was caught and the electronic mechanism obliterated.

I didn't hang around to see what he would try next. Racing down the catwalk, I reached the stairwell only yards behind Grieves and took the steps two and three at a time. I hit the factory floor, and Grieves turned right, breaking into a run toward the front of the building.

"No!" I shouted. "Not that way!"

It was too late. A wide metal door built into the base of the wall fifty yards away hurtled open, and two Bridgewater guards in security uniforms appeared, guns drawn. Grieves ground to a stop, and I opened fire, aiming just above their heads and sending a trio of jacketed hollow points slamming into the concrete wall. The guards dove for cover, and Grieves and I turned in unison for the maze of production equipment. I slid beneath an assembly line, knees riding over smooth concrete as I passed beneath a fifty-foot attack drone, half assembled with electronic guts hanging from the bottom. I reached the far side as screams ripped through the massive building, and shouts rang from the catwalk. Holder had broken through. He was calling commands now, and his men were racing for the stairs.

"Back exit!" I called.

Grieves was on his feet again, pointing toward the northern face of the building. The back side, opposite the office tower. He ran like an Olympic sprinter, the physical panic drowned by a flood of adrenaline and the animal desire to *survive*. Whatever it took.

I fell in behind him, and we ducked and swung down the assembly line, leaping over pneumatic hoses and electrical lines, dodging chains trailing from ceiling-mounted cranes, and orbiting more half-assembled drones. It was like something out of a video game—all bright colors and scattered tools, Holder someplace overhead screaming at his men while time stood still. I could *feel* the meatheads on our heels, and I knew Grieves could feel them too. He stretched out and hurled himself forward, reaching a break in the assembly line to our right and swinging around it.

"D-d-door!" he gasped.

I saw the door, framed in the wall a hundred feet away, leading into a farther section of the building. I knew it couldn't be exterior access—there was no possible way. The building was too large, and we'd only run through half of it.

But maybe this door would *lead* to exterior access. Then open fields beyond. The forest...

I couldn't think that far ahead. I sprinted for the door as handgun fire erupted behind me. Bullets skipped across the concrete, and we both dove for cover, still short of the door. Peering beneath another half-completed attack drone as I saw one of the meatheads drawing a bead on me with a Glock.

I fired first, sending a round screaming into a coil of one-inch pneumatic hoses draped beneath it, guessing them to contain compressed air. My guess paid off as a shrieking white cloud exploded through the ruptured hose, obscuring my pursuer's view and sending him stumbling sideways. I slapped Grieves on the back.

"*Go!*"

We made it to the door, and I wrenched it open. The moment we passed through, my nostrils were assaulted with the thick stench of hydraulic fluid and dust. The floor beneath me switched from waxed industrial tiles to dirt-smeared unfinished concrete. All around us industrial metal shelves reached for the forty-foot ceiling, packed tight with plastic-wrapped pallets. Rank air blew from the ceiling, driven by a circulation fan, while more overpowered lights glared in my face.

"Where?" I said.

Grieves coughed, slouching against a shelf and heaving. He held his chest and racked again, like a smoker with bronchitis. I grabbed him by the shoulder and shook.

"*Which way?*"

Grieves staggered and shook his head. "I...I don't know."

I looked automatically to the north—to the back side of the industrial building, where the airstrip and the forest lay. From the manufacturing bay behind us, I could hear Holder's men shouting, boots pounding. I looked for a latch, but there wasn't one. I shoved Grieves ahead instead, rushing beneath a shelf and down a long aisle blackened by forklift tire marks. When the door behind us clanged open, I pushed Grieves to the right, behind a stack of pallets. The gunfire resumed, but this time I didn't hear handguns. A shotgun thundered, sending shock waves ripping through the room as buckshot obliterated one corner of the crate we were sheltering behind. Wood splinters rained down, and packing peanuts showered the floor. I looked toward the noise and saw the corner of a cardboard box protruding from the edge of the shattered crate. It was marked in black ink, the outline of a small drone joined by thick black letters:

AGON MODEL X-40. READY TO DEPLOY.

Before I could reposition deeper into cover, the shotgun thundered again, this time shattering the face of the crate across from us. More wood rained down, and another box was revealed, this one half-destroyed. The labeling was just as clear.

AGON MODEL X-40.

"What are you doing?" Holder bellowed from someplace behind us. "You trying to get us all fired? Those suckers are a hundred grand *apiece!*"

The gunfire ceased, but I could still hear their ragged breaths. Not far behind. Loud in the suddenly still confines of the warehouse.

I licked sweat off my lip. Held my breath and listened. Holder hissed orders now, muted enough so that I couldn't hear.

But I could guess. He would deploy his men to either side of us. Send them down the long lines of shelving units to circle in from either flank while he remained in position at the middle, ready to exterminate us if we tried to leave cover.

How far to the door?

There was no way to know. I could only guess, estimating the amount of ground the manufacturing facility consumed against the overall size of the building I had viewed through binoculars the day prior.

It couldn't be much farther to the exterior wall. Twenty or thirty yards, maybe.

"Get ready to run," I said. I raised the Glock, and Grieves reached for my arm.

"Don't!"

I shook him free and strained my neck to peer around the shattered crate. I caught a glimpse of Holder's legs, wrapped in cheap suit pants, standing alongside a twin just inside the door to the factory floor.

Tracing the wall upward, I looked beyond the rails and slats of the shelves to the ceiling far overhead. And the massive fluorescent fixture, five feet by ten, covered in plate glass.

I aimed for the core of the glowing orb. Held a breath, and fired twice. The clapping thunder of 9mm pounded through the warehouses, echoing off the walls as both rounds tore through the light fixture. Plate glass exploded, glistening for a split second before the lights snapped out.

Then raining in a razor-sharp hail directly over Holder.

"Go!"

48

Once we were back on our feet, I knew we couldn't stop again. We found a door in the exterior wall, and I slammed on the latch, ignoring the warning printed next to it that this was an emergency exit, and an alarm would sound.

The alarm did sound, shrieking loud and joined by red emergency lights. I didn't stop, sprinting and driving Grieves ahead of me. The space on the back side of the building was awash with security lights, manicured grass quickly fading to smooth tarmac as we hit the compound's airstrip. We raced between parked attack drones tied down to the runway like jets on the deck of an aircraft carrier. Directly ahead, I saw the lines of hangars I had noticed before, but this time two of them were open. More attack drones rested within—smaller ones, looking more like miniature Predator drones with twelve-foot wingspans.

What the hell is this place?

Behind us, the voices redoubled, and the gunshots commenced. Grieves began to falter as my own heart thundered, and I grabbed him by the belt to keep him from pitching face-first into the tarmac. Bullets whistled over my head, and I bent low to the tarmac, still racing. Suddenly no longer in rural Virginia, now someplace in the mountains of Afghanistan, running for my life with the Taliban riding my ass.

"Get to the trees!" I shouted.

Grieves couldn't have responded if he wanted to. I could tell he was ready to drop, his body pushed far beyond its own capacity. Ready to let the enemy take him.

I never gave him the chance. Ramming the Glock into my waistband, I hauled his hundred-pound body up and threw him over my shoulder. Then I hurtled past the hangars, across another narrow grass strip, and into the waiting tree line.

I almost tripped as my feet skittered across roots and the darkness closed around me. From someplace behind, Holder continued to shout. The sirens continued to wail. Horns blared, and an automated voice on a loudspeaker called for an emergency evacuation of the building.

It was full panic, but I wasn't home free yet. Not even close. I remembered the twelve-foot, razor-wire-topped fence stretching around the property, and knew I had to reach it before Holder and his men could enter the forest. I could never win a one-on-five match, stumbling around unfamiliar territory with nothing more than a partially loaded Glock 19 to fight with. I had to get out.

Immediately.

Another fifty yards into the trees, the ground began to elevate in gentle waves, like miniature terraces building slowly upward. My legs burned, and I heaved as I rolled Grieves onto the ground. He quivered, his little hands clenching and unclenching as panicked eyes swept the woods around him.

"You got the file?" I said.

Grieves didn't answer. I shook him by the shoulder.

"You got the file?" I snapped, keeping my voice low.

Grieves swallowed and nodded. "P-pocket."

I released him. Looking back toward the airstrip, I saw flashing lights and blurred vehicles racing the length of the main building. But I didn't see people. I didn't hear Holder charging toward the trees. Not yet, anyway.

I yanked my phone out and speed-dialed Brooke. She answered on the first ring.

"Mason! What the hell? The whole place is evacuating!"

"We hit a snag," I said. "Tell Dufort we're extracting on the north side. Find the nearest road. I'll come to you!"

I hung up before she could argue, navigating quickly to the find-a-friend app to ensure I could still track her location. Brooke and Dufort were both together in the Ford, a mile or so away along a county road.

I pocketed the phone and reached for Grieves. He was shaking again, and I thought he might pass out. The sight of his pale face sent a momentary flash of sympathy ripping through me. Some people, whether by nature or nurture or raw misfortune, are simply not built to handle life. That wasn't his fault.

Hauling him up, I tossed him over my shoulder and started into the trees, legs still burning. But running anyway.

"Hang in there," I said. "We're almost home fr—"

My voice was cut short by a low whirring sound. Far too fast and aggressive to be wind among the trees, yet still soft and distant. It was unmistakably unnatural, yet the first image that flashed across my mind was that of a hornet.

A giant hornet. Or a storm of hornets.

I froze, looking quickly over my shoulder.

And then I saw them. Not one, but two drones. Neither of them larger than a backpack, hovering just inside the tree line, quad propellers buzzing like the hornets I had imagined. I made them out by the dull glow of red lights, like little eyeballs staring into the forest.

It was somehow more terrifying than a dozen Taliban fighters. My heart skipped, and I stepped quickly to the left, behind a tree. The buzzing grew louder, and I fished for the Glock. Grieves wheezed but didn't move. He hung limp as I cradled him with my left arm, my right drawing the weapon.

But I didn't move. I stood frozen behind the tree, restraining my own oxygen-hungry gasps as the buzzing grew louder. I could hear the drones individually now, growing louder as they moved together, then gliding farther apart again. I lifted the Glock and twisted around the edge of the tree, peering backward toward the compound. It was still a mess of screaming sirens and honking horns, but I could hear the drones.

And then I saw the nearest one. It floated fifty yards away, sliding between the trees like hot butter gliding off a pancake. Perfectly balanced, perfectly coordinated. I recognized the outline of Agon's X-40—the killer drone that I had seen printed on the crates in the warehouse. Silhouetted by the airstrip lights, I could see something long and slender hanging just beneath its airframe. About eighteen inches end to end, black and cylindrical, with a banana shape protruding from the bottom.

Is that an MP5?

The thought hit me just as the face of the drone swept over

my position, scanning slowly right. I hadn't moved, hadn't made a sound, but a split second after the muzzle of the drone's weapon glided over my position, it snapped back like an Apache helicopter bringing its guns to bear on a new target. I jerked my head behind the tree as gunfire split the night air—a short, snarling burst of it. 9mm slugs bit the bark next to my head, shreds of wood exploding around my face. Grieves flopped, fully unconscious now as I hit the ground. Another pair of three-round bursts exploded to my left, and I rolled to see the drone circling in. It glided sideways amid the trees, rising and falling automatically to circumvent limbs and spidery branches, its weapons remaining fixed on my position.

I dropped Grieves and opened fire with the Glock, aiming for the sweeping red dot. I dumped the magazine in something approaching panic, brass casings showering the ground. My last shot made impact, and the steady whirring sound distorted into a hellish mechanical grind. The drone shook, twisted, and dove behind a tree.

And then its twin was on me. A storm of automatic fire from farther down the hill, bullets hissing overhead and striking another tree, debris showering me. I dropped the empty handgun and grabbed Grieves, snatching him behind the next tree. The buzzing continued, growing nearer now. I couldn't see the drone, but I knew it was close. Drawing nearer by the second.

I threw Grieves over my shoulder and rushed up the hill, ducking and weaving, ignoring my burning thighs and thundering chest. Leaves exploded around my feet while twin MP5s chattered from behind. I swerved and jumped a fallen log, rotting wood detonating just behind me. The whir of the drone buzzed and faded as the device struggled to navigate a tangle of trees, but I knew it was still closing. That it would still catch me, eventually.

It was simply too fast. Too agile.

And too heavily armed.

I focused all my remaining energy on my legs, driving them like they belonged to somebody else. Grieves's head and arms slapped against my back, and through the inky black shadows ahead, I saw the outline of the exterior fence ripping through the forest.

Twelve feet high. Topped with razor wire. An impossible obstacle.

I charged ahead anyway, still ducking and weaving. Changing my path erratically, remembering what Grieves had said about artificial intelligence playing chess.

It learns you.

From behind, the drone still hummed, but the gunfire came in much sparser and shorter bursts. The drone was conserving its ammunition. Calculating how best to use its remaining firepower to drive its prey into a corner.

Hunting me.

The fence closed in. I wheezed, Grieves's body on my shoulders dragging me down. Slowing me up. Raking branches whipped across my face, and I almost fell as my toes caught a fallen limb.

Twenty yards. Then ten. The fence appeared just out of reach. The drone buzzed closer, hissing as it swept over a thorn thicket. Hairs stood up on my neck, an instinct born out of years of combat experience screaming that the drone was about to fire.

I dove for cover, and the forest exploded with gunshots. Fast, snapping sounds, stacked so close on top of each other they sounded like automatic gunfire.

But they weren't. I tumbled through the leaves, dropping Grieves and rolling faceup at the base of the fence to see a Glock 19 jammed between the chain link, muzzle flash blazing.

Brass rained down around my face, and Clay Dufort delivered the kill shot.

I didn't move, heaving and gasping, heart thumping like a bass drum. Dufort holstered the Glock without comment and produced his brand-new pair of heavy-duty wire cutters from the ground next to him. In short order he snapped a hole through the fence and helped to drag Grieves through.

Then I was through. We both climbed one last rise, fighting through thicker forest overwhelmed by briars. Then Grieves's landed in the Ford's back seat. I fell in beside him. Dufort took shotgun. Brooke slammed on the gas.

We spun off into the night, engine racing, my heart still pounding. Dufort dropped his magazine and reloaded from a box in his lap. Brooke bit her lip and peered into the rearview mirror.

Grieves was still unconscious, but a quick inspection of his body confirmed that he was uninjured. I dug through his pockets and found the flash drive, slapping it onto the console as I leaned into the seat and continued to heave. For a moment everyone was silent.

Then Dufort's lip twitched, and he spoke in a growl. "What the *hell* was that?"

I closed my eyes, envisioning the drone again. That red eye hunting me through the forest.

"The future," I said. "Aren't you excited?"

Dufort didn't answer. Brooke shifted into gear and powered us away from the compound. As I slowly caught my breath and calmed a thundering heart, I detected a strange tension from inside the Ford. A nervous quiet. I realized Brooke hadn't spoken since picking us up, and when I caught her face in the rearview, I saw red-rimmed eyes and a tear glistening on her cheek.

"What happened?" I said. "What did I miss?"

Brooke looked away. Her shoulders shook softly.

Without a word Dufort passed me his burner phone. The screen was illuminated by a webpage. A news article, I thought.

When I read the headline, all thoughts of my brush with death melted from my mind.

Matthew Pearson, Army Ranger Turned Bank Robber, Succumbs to Prison Injuries. Pronounced Dead.

I looked up from the back seat. I met Brooke's gaze. She cried openly now, bottom lip trembling.

"They killed him," she whispered.

49

The mood inside the Ford felt like that of a hearse as Brooke piloted us away from Culpeper, headed north along the eastern borders of Shenandoah National Park. I knew because I saw a lot of signs, but the landscape beyond the highway was pitch black, and I didn't care how beautiful it might be.

Nobody talked. There was nothing to say. Brooke cried for a while, and at one point Dufort rested a gentle hand on her arm, but neither of us tried to soothe the gaping rift of grief cutting through her chest. It was a feeling I knew all too well, and I also knew that there's nothing you can say. No medication that can fill the void. Not for Brooke, anyway. She would bear these wounds until the slow passage of time eased their venom.

In the meantime, there was something to be done about the source of that venom. The snake that murdered Pearson had tried to murder Spraggins, and would lay us all in our graves if given his way. I saw Holder in the lab hallway, that sadistic smile stretched across his handsome face. The face of a rapist, a murderer, and an American traitor. A man who might have had my back overseas.

But back here, in the land of the free? He was little better than a viper. A cunning, conniving animal. An oath breaker.

A dead man.

"What's our play?" Brooke's voice was hoarse from the front seat. She'd stopped crying, but she still looked broken. The pain I saw in the mirror cut through me like a knife.

"Hotel," I said. "Something off the road, as grimy as you can find."

"Why grimy?"

"Because grimy places don't ask for ID."

I grimaced as I settled into the seat, my right leg throbbing a little. I must have pulled a muscle while dashing through the trees. I just hoped I hadn't torn something.

"You're welcome, by the way," Dufort grunted.

"For what?"

"For the part where I saved your ass."

"Oh, right. You mean when the drone saw you, and your ugly mug fried its computer circuits. Nice job."

Dufort didn't answer, but I saw half his face in the side-view mirror, and his eyes smiled. Just a little.

Brooke pulled off the road a few miles later at a roadside motel just outside the Virginia town of Gainesville. I-66 ran nearby, leaving us a handful of hotel options. She selected the grungiest—a two-floor establishment with exterior-access rooms. I directed her to park in the back, and she booked the room. Two beds, first floor, back side. Fifty bucks in cash.

I brought Grieves back to consciousness with a gentle nudge and a little cool water on his face. He gasped and blinked a lot, but he didn't panic. As soon as he recognized me, all the bad memories seemed to rush in, and he ran both hands over his chest and stomach.

"You're okay," I said. "I got you out safe."

He nodded a couple of times. Then his right hand plunged into his pocket, and this time he did panic.

"Relax," I said, holding up the drive. "We have it. Come inside."

I led the way into the hotel room, Dufort double-locking the door and standing with his freshly loaded Glock hanging by his side. While Brooke washed her face in the sink and Grieves wrinkled his nose at the sagging pair of beds, I opened Brooke's laptop and rested it on the refrigerator cabinet next to the desk.

"You'll need to explain this," I said, poking in the flash drive. Grieves joined me at the computer and scrubbed his eyes. He wasn't shaking anymore. Not even pale. But he looked ready to drop from exhaustion alone.

The drive generated a file window, and that file window displayed a folder. Grieves clicked through, his bony little fingers inputting keyboard shortcuts to access everything. A loading icon spun; then a PDF popped across the screen.

I leaned close, squinting in the dim light to examine the document. I started scrolling, sweeping right through a page. Then two. The document went on for nearly twenty full pages, each of them packed with tiny black text that looked like the transcript of a computer talking to itself. There were a lot of symbols, a lot of irregular spacing. A lot of numbers and not much readable English. It was a confusing mess.

"What is this?" I said.

"Performance analysis data—assembled and compiled," Grieves said. "PADAC."

I looked to Grieves, both eyebrows raised. He licked his

lips as though he were waiting for me to get it. I wasn't getting it. Grieves scrubbed his face with his sleeve again. His body had calmed considerably since sitting down in front of the computer—or maybe since popping more Xanax. His voice came as a soft, steady stream now. Free of any stutter.

"Look. It's like I told you before. Mission logs are written from the performance data collected in flight by the drone. It's like...the black box on an airplane. A flight log. Only much more detailed. Every computer decision, every flight control, every weapons launch. Recorded for diagnostics and improved future programing."

"That's this?" I asked, pointing to the screen.

"Right...the flight log."

I shook my head. "I can't freaking read that. How do you know it's what we need?"

Grieves sighed. He tapped *control* and *F* to call up a search box, then input a series of numbers before smacking the return key. The document flashed to the fifteenth page, halfway down. Grieves spoke evenly.

"January 8, 2015. Serial number alpha alpha one seven nine charlie tango alpha eight four eight. Flight time three hours fourteen minutes seventeen seconds. 15°01'14"N, 45°03'05"E. Auto target sequence triple-A. Strike authorization code Juliet seven nine tango. Weapon deploy AGM-114. Positive strike."

Grieves looked up. Brooke and I exchanged a glance. I waited for the punchline.

"That's the strike..." Grieves said, as though he were waiting for the slow kids in class to understand a basic math problem. "The *alpha alpha one* sequence of the serial number designates a Falcon series drone. Like, a small predator. You saw a few of them at the factory. All the nine-charlie-tango units were equipped with proactive target acquisition technology...which was code for AI targeting. Auto target sequence triple-A means the drone was preauthorized to acquire targets. Weapon deployed was an AGM-114. I think they call them Hellfires. And the location..."

Grieves copied the coordinates from the PDF and navigated to a web browser. He used the hotel Wi-Fi to pull up Google Earth, pasted the coordinates in, and slapped *return*.

The digital globe spun. The screen blurred as the satellite image magnified a hundred times over. Then it clarified, suddenly, outlining a small, roughly rectangular country with water on two sides. All tan, mostly mountains and desert. The screen continued to zoom, drawing in on a spot deep in the mountains, right in the southwest corner of the nation.

Yemen.

"Positive strike," Grieves said softly. "Target destroyed."

Brooke held a hand over her mouth, gasping a little. Her gaze fixed on the screen. Tears bubbled to her eyes, and she struggled to blink them away. My blood ran cold looking at the screen, but to me it was just another section of desert. I looked to Dufort, and I saw the truth in his bloodshot eyes as clearly as I felt it in Brooke's gentle sobs.

Dufort nodded once.

I turned back to Grieves. "You're telling me this *proves* that on that date, at that time, in *that specific place*...one of those drones dropped a Hellfire?"

"Beyond doubt," Grieves said. "The mission log would be glossier...easier to read, I guess. But this is the source material. The authorization codes prove it. We...we made that strike."

He swallowed hard. I stared at the screen. Brooke turned away and covered her face while Dufort just glared.

But long before any feelings of triumph could take hold in my chest, a colder reality was setting in. I denied it, twisting and turning it, manipulating the picture in my mind and struggling to believe that I was wrong.

But I knew I wasn't.

I shook my head, turning away from the computer to face the others. "This isn't enough."

50

"What do you mean *it's not enough?*"

Dufort was the first to explode, veins popping from the side of his face, white scars turning whiter, red skin darkening to maroon. Brooke turned also, ocean eyes torn by storm, mouth half open. Drying tears streaked her face.

I held up a hand. "Just think about it. Put yourself in Agon's shoes. You're a billion-dollar company with enough lawyers to bankrupt a small nation. You're up to your neck in government contracts, which means you've got the DOD on your side. And who is coming at you? A bunch of war-shaken vets, led by a bank-robbing West Pointer with crippling PTSD."

Brooke flinched. Her mouth parted, but she didn't speak. Dufort raised a chunky finger.

"Watch your mouth, you—"

"Shut up, Dufort. I've seen as much combat as anybody in this room. I'm not judging anyone, but I'm also not in denial. I mean, seriously. How is this going to play out? Hit me with it."

I gestured, open-handed. Dufort looked to Brooke. She swallowed.

"The reporter," Dufort said. "We give it to her."

"Okay," I said. "So you give it to Davis. Then what?"

"She breaks a story," Brooke said. "It goes viral. We're still riding the publicity wave from the bank robbery, just like we planned."

"You're right," I said. "But *then* what? People are angry. Agon makes a statement. What's the first thing they're gonna do?"

"Deny," Grieves said softly.

"You're damn right they're gonna deny. They're gonna lawyer up quicker than a CEO caught trading stock tips. They're gonna say we manufactured this document. That we obtained the serial number from one of their drones, leveraged a disgruntled former employee to write an authentic-looking log. They'll say we made the whole thing up. A publicity stunt. A cash grab. An anti-defense establishment hatchet job."

Grieves shook his head, pointing to the screen. "No. They can't say that. We've got the authorization codes."

"The what now?" I said, lifting my chin and miming the condescending stance of a million-dollar defense attorney. "Your Honor, these aren't our codes. This is gibberish!"

Grieves flushed. "I *know* the codes. They can't just erase—"

"But Mr. Grieves," I said, "isn't it true that you're struggling with a crippling mental illness? Don't you have a long history of abusing anxiety medication? And did you not assist in the *violent* break-in of Agon's facilities, risking the lives of *dozens* during a psychotic meltdown?"

Grieves half-stood. His mouth opened, then closed. His hands began to shake, and before he could stop himself, he was reaching into his pocket. Fishing for more Xanax.

I looked to Brooke and Dufort. "You see? We have nothing. The mission logs would have been worth something, because normal people could have *read them*. Understood them. Embraced the outrage and demanded a full investigation of Agon by the FBI. This stuff—" I pointed to the computer. "It might *be* the same data, but it's presented in a dramatically different way. Obscure and complex enough to read like Greek to the average American. Agon's lawyers will have a field day with it. They'll expose Pearson for his PTSD trauma. They'll frame you all as a bunch of jaded, disillusioned maniacs, starving for attention. They'll sweep it all under the rug."

I finished my spiel, and nobody spoke. Brooke sat on the end of a bed, face resting in one hand, still sobbing softly. Dufort's glare had darkened into something approaching blackened stone, but it was no longer directed at me. He looked at the computer now, and his jaw trembled.

Because he knew I was right.

I turned from the small group and walked to the window, peeling back the curtain a little to look out over the parking lot. Twisting my head instinctively to look into the sky. Thinking about Agon and their fleet of drones.

And understanding.

"It's worse than we thought," I said. "They're not just building AI targeting systems. They're building autonomous killing machines. And they're using them, too."

I turned around. "Remember how Holder kept finding us

in Jacksonville? We were switching cars and hotels, but he *kept* turning up. And then at the warehouse, where Ronald was shot, it was like his people knew exactly where we would be. They pinned us down from the moment they entered the building. Holder looked right at me on his way out."

"How?" Brooke whispered.

"Drones," I said, speaking through my teeth. "High-level surveillance drones. Small enough to avoid detection by the FAA, but high tech enough to trail us all across the city. To film us when we switched cars and hotels. To trail us to the airport."

"And the warehouse?" Brooke said. "You think they can see through sheet metal?"

"They could with infrared," I said, suddenly remembering my encounter with the first X-40 in the woods outside the Agon complex. How I hadn't moved, hadn't made a sound, yet it had trained its guns right on me. Almost as though it were drawn to my body heat.

I looked to Grieves, and he nodded slowly. "We've been programming smaller units to track targets with infrared. I... I didn't think it was field ready..."

"Oh, they're ready," I said. "No doubt. They're hunting machines, and apparently they're already in mass production. Those crates in the warehouse section of the compound? *Full* of X-40s. Hundreds of them. Ready to ship."

I crossed my arms, blood boiling just beneath the surface. I didn't have the personal connection to the Yemen strike that Dufort and Brooke did. I hadn't spent the last several years of my life on the inside, watching this monster grow the way Grieves had.

But after my mad dash through the woods, heart thundering, vision blurring, running for my life from that incessant whirring sound...I didn't need to. I'd come face-to-face with the dragon. I could see what it was capable of. But more than that, I could see what it would *become* capable of.

"This company is corrupt to its core," I said. "They're not only willing to murder US soldiers and sweep the incident under the rug, they're willing to deploy a private army inside our own borders. Deploy drones to track and then hunt innocent civilians. They're building these things by the dozens, and where are they going?"

The question was rhetorical, but all eyes were fixed on me. I clenched my teeth. "This isn't just about Yemen anymore. What happened in Yemen will happen again if this sort of reckless, cavalier development is left unchecked. We need them exposed. From the ground up."

"How?" Dufort gargled, rage boiling just beneath his voice.

I closed my eyes. Breathed deeply to clear my mind. And thought.

But it was Brooke who reached the conclusion first.

"The congressman," she said.

I opened my eyes.

"Who?" Dufort said.

"Matt's father," Brooke said. "He's got a lot of sway. More than Kelly Davis, even. He could launch an investigation."

Dufort sneered. "Greasy pig. He wouldn't believe his own son. Why should he believe us?"

"That was before we had *proof*," Brooke said, pointing to the screen. "And Matt...he wasn't on good terms with his father. Never has been. A lot of bad blood. I think, maybe... it was easier for the congressman to sweep his claims under the rug. Blame it on PTSD. But he can't deny raw facts."

Dufort still wasn't sold. "He's a congressman, not Batman. What's he supposed to do that a reporter couldn't?"

"The appropriations committee," I said, looking up abruptly.

"The what?" Dufort said.

"Congressman Pearson sits on the appropriations committee," I said. "I read about it on the drive up here. He's a senior member. They're reviewing a big defense spending bill as we speak. Agon is a defense contractor."

"What does that mean?" Dufort asked. "I'm not a lawyer."

"It means he has *access*." My heart rate spiked. I took a step forward. "You don't land nine-figure government contracts without undergoing a *lot* of internal review. Without having to turn over all kinds of documents to prove your legitimacy. There are laws concerning public spending. If Pearson is on that committee, he has a right to discovery. He could ask for any number of things."

"He could ask for damning proof," Brooke said, hope driving back the storm in her ocean eyes.

I nodded. "He could ask them for a noose, and they wouldn't even feel it until he kicked the chair out from under them."

Brooke licked her lips and looked to Dufort. His wrinkled lip twitched, and he hesitated. Then looked to me.

"You really think that could work?" he said.

"Only one way to find out."

51

There was no reaching Congressman Pearson that night. The House of Representatives was in session, which meant he should be in town, but after the loss of his son, that might easily change. We made plans to contact his office first thing in the morning, and in the meantime I emailed all of the files Grieves had taken from the programming facility to Jacquie for safekeeping, adding a brief explanation about what they were and how much they mattered. Then we checked out of the hotel.

After consideration, I didn't think Holder and his people would be able to track us that night. In Jacksonville they had managed it by establishing contact and maintaining it even as we switched cars. But that contact had been terminated once they recovered the drive, as proven by the fact that we had taken them by surprise at the Agon facility. They didn't know about the Ford Edge and had no way of guessing which way we would drive after leaving Culpeper.

Even so, I felt better moving to a new hotel. Dufort drove, conducting a surveillance detection route from Gainesville to Centreville to Arlington before finally selecting yet another hotel on the outskirts of town. It was after midnight by the time we checked in—Thursday. The hotel was as grimy as the last, and the clerk didn't ask for ID. We rented two rooms this time, adjoining, and paid in cash.

As the four of us stumbled inside, I felt ready to drop. Grieves was barely standing, now numbed again by Xanax, while Brooke did a lot of staring at the wall through hollow eyes. Grieves and Dufort migrated to the second room by default, and I was grateful. I didn't think I could endure a night of Dufort's diesel snoring.

"I'll take first watch," I said, extending my hand for Dufort's Glock—our last remaining weapon.

Dufort shook his head. "Sleep," he said. "I got it."

I almost protested, but the exhaustion pressing down on my shoulders was so absolute, I wasn't sure I could perform watch anyway. I nodded my acceptance, and Dufort shut the door between our rooms. A moment later I detected the faint odor of cigarette smoke from outside and knew he was seated on the walkway, the Glock in his lap, surveying the parking lot.

A committed warrior. One of America's absolute best.

I settled onto one of the two queen beds and pulled my shoes off. Everything ached—especially my right leg. I was sure I had pulled something now, probably during one of my slipping falls as I tumbled through the woods, running from that drone. The memory was as crisp in my mind as though it were happening in real time. The rushing heart rate—the dump of adrenaline. The instinct to survive, no matter what it took.

The animal fear.

All soldiers feel fear. I'm convinced of it. Warriors

manage it well, while cowards run for cover. But we all feel the fear. It's part of the horror of war. Maybe the part that keeps us from always *being* at war over the smallest provocation. What holds the planet back from complete self-destruction.

But the X-40 drone hadn't felt a *thing*. And somehow, that was more horrifying than almost any of the war terrors I had experienced overseas. A lifeless, methodical machine. Preprogrammed to hunt. Unmanned and unfettered by human empathy.

A complete evil.

"Are you okay, Sharpe?"

I looked up to see Brooke sitting on the bed across from me, hands cradled in her lap. Still fully dressed, vacant eyes meeting mine but not really connecting.

"Yeah," I said. "Just spent."

Brooke nodded her understanding, then walked to the bathroom to wash her face. I rolled onto my back, my stiff and sweat-stained shirt crinkling as it settled against the pillow. I would typically take it off, but that felt wrong with Brooke in the room.

The sink cut off as I stared at a water-stained ceiling. Brooke returned to her bed and flipped the light off. Clothes rustled, and something hit the floor. Then the bed creaked.

I closed my eyes, shutting out the room, the stale smell of grimy carpet, and memories of the red-eyed X-40. Pushing it all away. Retreating to my favorite place. That mental sanctuary I reserved for the end of the day, when darkness closed in. Mia and I, in the bed of that old K-10, staring up at the stars.

I remembered, but for the first time in three hundred sixty-four days...I couldn't see it. My eyes closed, and the blackness swirled in, but the images wouldn't come. The feeling wouldn't come.

All I could think about was Brooke lying in the bed next to me. Her pants on the floor. Her breathing soft in the stillness. I remembered the smell of clean water and sweet flowers, and all memory of the desert wind simply vanished. I strained, and it simply wouldn't return. It was gone, like mist in the morning.

Then I heard another sound. A very soft, very vague sob. Barely audible over the hum of the heater kicking in, but coming from Brooke's side of the room. It sent hot pain racing through my stomach worse than a three-round burst from the X-40.

I slumped into the bed, giving in to the emptiness. To the cavern in my chest. Just...accepting it, for a moment.

"It never goes away," I whispered. "But it does get easier."

The sobs softened, then died. The room went very quiet, and for a brief moment I wondered if I should have kept my mouth shut. Then Brooke spoke softly.

"It was a stupid thing. We were only together a few months. Like two years ago, right after I left the Army. I knew from day one it would never last, but...I felt like...like he..."

"Saw you," I finished.

"Yes..."

"I know."

Brooke sniffed. I just stared at the ceiling.

"Was it that way with your fiancée?"

"Yes," I said. "That way...and so much more."

"I'm sorry," Brooke whispered. "I...I read..."

"You read about the shooting," I said. It didn't surprise me. Everyone I had met in the past year who learned my name and ran a Google search had found stories of the school shooting. Of what had happened to Mia.

"I'm sorry," Brooke said again.

"It's okay."

Another long moment. Brooke rolled on the bed, mattress creaking.

"It was Matt who broke it off," she said. "I would have married him, probably. It was that kind of thing. But...the mental stuff. Everything that he was going through. All the PTSD and nightmares and trauma. He couldn't take it."

"I'm sorry," I said. And I meant it. I meant it as much as I'd ever meant anything in life, because when you've been through hell, you don't wish that pain on anyone.

"Do you think they see us?" Brooke whispered.

"You mean...from the other side?"

"Yeah."

I thought about it. Thought about my beautiful fiancée curled up on the couch, reading her Bible. Mia was a Christian, and a committed one. Not a religious person. A person of very deep faith who radiated love and kindness to all around her.

If heaven was real, Mia was in it. I never doubted that for a second.

"I hope not," I said. "You can't be in paradise so long as you can still see hell."

Brooke sniffed again. Then her breathing softened and became very slow. I felt her presence only a yard away, dominating the room like a very strong but gentle magnet. Pulling on me slowly. I wanted to get up and walk to her. I remembered her lips on mine, and I wanted that feeling again.

But I didn't move. I just lay there, staring at the ceiling, wishing I could feel the cold metal of my K-10 instead.

Then Brooke's mattress creaked. Small feet hit the floor, barely audible. My heart raced as those padding footsteps drew closer. Crossed the end of my bed. Reached the far side. The blanket shifted, and warmth flooded the sheets as Brooke slipped in. She drew near to me. I felt her soft cheek on my arm, her lips touching my chest and kissing once. Her smooth legs brushed up against mine as she pressed in close.

My heart accelerated. But Brooke didn't move. She nestled her raven hair against my shoulder, and her breathing calmed. My heart calmed with it, very slowly.

And then we both fell asleep.

52

I slept all night, which wasn't fair to Dufort. When I woke just after sunrise, I found him sitting outside on the concrete steps leading to the ground floor, a paper cup of coffee in one hand, a fresh cigarette in the other. He grunted as I approached, blowing smoke from his nose and slurping coffee. A trickle of it ran through his twisted lip and down his swollen chin. He didn't seem to notice.

"All quiet on the western front," he said.

I settled down next to him, and he passed me the coffee. I took a sip, and he offered a cigarette. I shook my head.

"I'm sorry," I said simply. "I should have relieved you."

Dufort dragged on the smoke, taking his time. Then his voice softened, like I'd not heard it before. Still gurgling, but lacking his typical aggression.

"You had other things to look after."

I met his gaze, and I thought I saw something deep behind his wild eyes. Some kind of understanding...or permission.

I sipped coffee. "You get this from the hotel?"

A grunt.

"It's terrible," I said. "Let's find breakfast."

WE FOUND ANOTHER WAFFLE HOUSE, where Brooke matched my and Dufort's consumption of an All Star Special. Grieves only picked at his food, shooting nervous glances out the greasy windows at every passing car.

He hadn't even voiced a desire to return to his own home, and we all knew why. Grieves was as good as dead if Holder and his people found him. For better or worse, he was a part of this now. Until the end.

We held a brief conference during breakfast, and it was decided that Brooke should call Pearson's office, posing as Matt's girlfriend. Once the congressman was on the phone, we could impress upon him the necessity of an in-person meeting, but actually reaching him would be the trick. Especially under present circumstances, with a family tragedy underway.

Brooke made the call from the Ford, and I stepped to the corner of the Waffle House to finish my coffee and phone Jacquie. She answered on the first ring.

"Mason, I got your email."

"You have a look at it?" I asked.

"Briefly. All Greek to me."

"I know. But it's critical. Keep it safe."

"I will. But..."

I waited. "But?"

"You're putting me in a difficult position, here."

"How so?"

"I'm going to assume this documentation wasn't obtained legally."

I didn't answer.

"I just wish you'd give me something to work with. I don't like being kept in the dark."

I swirled what remained of my coffee in the paper cup, thinking quickly. Then I decided the risk was worth the gamble. Telling Jacquie might not be necessary, but I liked the idea of another trusted investigative mind working the case. Especially a mind that was physically removed from the present field of battle.

"Agon Defense," I said. "They're the target. Internal corruption, murder. It's a laundry list."

"Got it," Jacquie said. "I'll see what I can find."

I thanked her, but she didn't hang up. I felt a tension on the call, as though there was something she wanted to say, but wasn't sure she could voice.

That wasn't like Jacquie. She was the boldest, most direct person I'd ever met.

"Are you okay?" she said at last. "I can read a calendar."

"I know," I said. "I'm okay."

Another long pause. "I'll check on Agon. Talk soon."

Jacquie hung up.

I stared at the phone a moment, running my thumb across the screen. The time was displayed, and beneath it, the date.

November 14.

I pocketed the phone and dumped the coffee cup in a trash can. Then I returned to the Ford. Brooke was just finishing a phone call, and hung up with a little sigh.

"I left a message with his staff," she said. "They wouldn't tell me whether he was in town."

I looked northeast, toward DC. With the sun now hanging high in the sky, it should have been warm. The weather had turned bitter during the night, and a dull chill ran up my spine.

"He'll call back," I said. "Let's head that way."

53

We spent the next few hours driving into DC, then found a shopping strip to purchase a change of clothes for me, cigarettes for Dufort, and some female things for Brooke. Sprays, and shampoo to manage her "stupid hair".

I wondered which product smelled like clean water and fresh flowers, but I said nothing as we checked out. Grieves hadn't spoken all day except to mumble that he was running short of Xanax. There was no way we were risking a visit to his house, so he called in a prescription refill at a nearby pharmacy, and we picked the medication up through the drive-through.

Dufort was hungry, so we went ahead and found lunch. And then waited. And waited some more. Brooke called Pearson's office again, urging his staff to push her message through. Then I called, posing as a reporter, interested in obtaining a statement about the congressman's loss. I was fed a default "bug off" statement and hung up on.

"He could be in Pennsylvania," Brooke said. "Or Florida. I mean...if Matt isn't...isn't home yet..."

I watched Washington traffic roll by on a nearby four-lane. There were an inordinate number of black cars. Black SUVs, black sedans, black limousines. I supposed the capital should feel very important to me, but it only felt self-important, as though the town were chock-full of pretenders.

Maybe it was.

"You ever meet the congressman?" I asked.

Brooke shook her head. "No. Never."

"Ever talk to him on the phone?"

"No. He and Matt...didn't really talk. At least not while I was around."

I nodded, tapping the armrest. "Have faith," I said. "He'll call back."

And he did. At four thirty-two in the afternoon, as Dufort slept in the back seat and Grieves chewed his nails. Brooke's phone rang with an angry buzz from her lap, and she snatched it up like a striking snake.

"Hello?"

"*Speaker*," I mouthed. She switched the phone to speaker, and the tail end of a sentence crackled through. Male voice. Very serious, probably older. Late fifties, I'd guess.

"—called my office?"

Brooke swallowed. I gave her an encouraging nod.

"Yes, sir. My name is Brooke Oswilder. I'm...I'm your son's girlfriend."

Long, deep pause. I wondered if Pearson would hang up. The emotion in Brooke's voice sounded real and probably was real. But a guy like Pearson had to deal with all sorts of pretenders and psychopaths. Hazards of the job.

"I didn't know Matt was seeing anybody," Pearson said, at

last. His voice was flat, but he spoke slowly, as though he were holding something in. I tried to put myself in his shoes and simulate the grief he must be suffering, but the best I could do was resurrect my own grief.

I wasn't sure if losing a son was anything like losing a fiancée.

"We met in the Army," Brooke said. "It was..."

She stopped, and I realized she had choked up. Tears bubbled into her eyes, and I put a gentle hand on her arm. Gave it a squeeze and nodded.

"You've got this," I whispered.

"I'm terribly sorry," Pearson said. "It's a tragic loss for all of us."

Brooke pulled herself together. Sat up.

"Are you in town, Congressman? I mean, in DC."

Long pause. When Pearson answered, his voice had changed. It now carried an undertone of suspicion. I couldn't blame him.

"Why do you ask?"

"I need to meet with you. Today. There's something you need to know...about Matty."

I'd never heard Brooke call him Matty before. It sounded very natural, like she used to call him that all the time.

"I'm headed home," Pearson said. "I'm sure you understand, there's a lot going on."

"I know," Brooke said. "This won't take long. Please, Congressman. It's very important."

A long silence. I held my breath, suddenly realizing that Dufort had stopped snoring, and even Grieves sat motionless.

"You're local?" Pearson said, at last.

"Yes, sir."

"Are you familiar with the Capital Social?"

Brooke looked to me. My fingers raced across my phone screen as I typed the name into a Google search. The result was almost instantaneous. It was a restaurant downtown. A nice place, I thought. With nice prices to match.

"I know where it is," Brooke said.

"Can you meet me there at six thirty?" Pearson said.

I nodded. Brooke said she could.

"Talk then." Pearson hung up.

Brooke relaxed against her seat. She closed her eyes and wiped her forehead. I shifted into gear and piloted toward the four-lane.

"Is this wrong?" Brooke said.

"How could it be wrong?"

"The man just lost his son. And we're...deceiving him."

"He would never have granted us a meeting if we had been honest," I said. "And we're fighting to finish the job his son sacrificed his life for. Nothing could be more honoring."

Brooke accepted that without comment. I hit *Go* on my phone's GPS. It routed us north, deep into the city.

Straight to the Capital Social.

54

We arrived at the restaurant over an hour early and waited forty minutes before I entered alone and got a table. The plan was very simple. I would be in position inside the restaurant, examining a menu and stalling the waiter until the congressman arrived. Brooke would meet him, and then I would engage.

Dufort would remain in the Ford on watch duty, looking out for Holder and his thugs. Grieves would sit quietly in the back seat and try not to have a heart attack. If all went according to plan, Brooke and I would sell the congressman our story and convince him to take the next steps while we found yet another place to lie low for a day or two to button things up.

A good plan. But in my experience, good plans shattered under the first gunshot.

Inside the polished glass and brass doors, I found a quiet, multilevel restaurant full of little round tables covered in white silk tablecloths. Everyone—except me—wore a suit or a tuxedo. I wore jeans, a T-shirt, and a jacket. The guy at the host stand—maybe he was a host, maybe he was a maître d'—raised an eyebrow at me, but he didn't refuse service when I requested a quiet table near the back of the restaurant. I was seated with a good view of the front door and most of the dining room. Along one wall, a row of quiet booths ran, separated by mahogany partitions, with smokey dim lights overhanging them. The carpet was maroon and worn, the fixtures all brass. The dishes all china.

A fancy place, yet it still carried a casual undertone, as though it did most of its business at lunch or late at night. I remembered a little gold script on the door advertising twenty-four-hour service.

I wondered how many deals were brokered in this place. Politicians from opposing sides of the aisle, meeting to get drunk and hammer out the fate of the nation. Maybe deciding whether to send boys and girls barely out of high school to their deaths overseas. Maybe weighing the merits of closing a military base in the middle-of-nowhere Kansas, putting two thousand people out of work.

All over steak and lobster. Because, hell, nobody *here* was in jeopardy of missing a paycheck.

The waiter came, and I ordered water. I told him I was waiting for somebody. He gave me the same semi-disgusted elevation of one eyebrow as the guy at the host stand, but he didn't object. The water was cold and tasted just like water at a burger joint, except it came in a fancy glass.

Pearson entered at exactly five minutes before six thirty. I knew it was him, even having never met the man. He was shorter than his son, maybe five ten or five eleven, with thinning gray hair and a very hard face. Dark eyes, and a small bulge beneath his shirt where his gut spilled over his waistline. He wore an expensive blue suit and a trench coat and was accompanied by a guy who couldn't have looked more like a bodyguard if he were wearing a neon ID badge.

It was the eyes that gave Pearson away. Not only did they remind me of Matt, they were bloodshot and strained. His cheeks gray and sagging, as though he'd been up all night, racked by grief.

I rotated my water glass and watched him out of the corner of my eye as he was escorted to a rear booth by the maître d'. His bodyguard took a seat on a bench near the door, unfolding a newspaper with an aggressive and needless snap, then burying his face in its pages.

A lot of good you are, I thought.

Brooke stepped through the door a minute later, and the maître d' seemed to be expecting her. He led her directly to the congressman's booth, where Pearson rose to greet her and offered an awkward handshake. I gave them a moment to exchange greetings or introductions or pained condolences.

Once Pearson and Brooke were both seated and I could feel the tempo of their interaction stalling out, I rose from the table, cradling my water glass in one hand. As I approached the table, Pearson looked up, and the pain in his eyes sent a red-hot spear through my gut.

It was total. Consuming. A raw, transparent grief I knew all too well.

"Good evening, Congressman. I'm so sorry for your loss."

Pearson's back stiffened. He looked quickly to Brooke, then the bodyguard. Brooke made room, and I slid in next to her. Pearson grabbed the edge of the table as though he were about to slide out, but then he stopped. His gaze narrowed.

"Who are you?"

"Mason Sharpe," I said. "United States Army, 75th Ranger Regiment. Retired."

A long, piercing stare. His gaze snapped to Brooke, and I saw a hint of anger. But he didn't leave.

"What is this?"

"Just what I told you it would be," Brooke said. "A conversation. We need to tell you something."

"We?" He looked back to me. Hesitated. Then sudden recognition dawned across his face. "Wait. I know you. I've seen your picture. You were one of the hostages in Florida."

I nodded. "Yes, sir."

Pearson scrambled toward the edge of the booth, shaking his head. "I'm not talking to you. Call my lawyers."

I reached out with my left hand and caught his wrist. My fingers closed around cold, dry skin, and momentary panic flooded his face. His lips parted, no doubt ready to call the bodyguard.

"It's not like that," I said. "We aren't here to cause trouble. We're here to help your son."

Pearson's lips froze, indecision or maybe fear melting the cry in his mouth. I released him. Brooke filled the silence.

"Congressman, please. This is very important. Just give us ten minutes, and we'll leave you alone. It's what Matty would have wanted."

Pearson's cheeks flushed. "You'd use my son—"

"I really was his girlfriend, Congressman," Brooke said. "And I was there. For the robbery."

I winced a little, wishing she hadn't said that. I knew she was gambling on raw honesty to forge a connection, but I figured a politician as seasoned as Pearson would default to lawyering up. Meeting with two people from the robbery his son had committed had to be a potential legal nightmare, or at least a public relations one.

Then again, we had to broach that subject eventually. Maybe Brooke's instincts were better than mine.

Pearson pursed his lips. Pondered for a second, the lines in his haggard face creasing a little deeper. Then he checked his watch.

"Ten minutes," he said.

Brooke led the way. She started at the beginning. Not with the bank robbery, but with Yemen. She told the story of the missile strike and the burning trucks and the scalded flesh. Of the bodies and the dry rocks and the chaos.

Of how Captain Matthew Pearson of the 75th Ranger Regiment did what Rangers are bred to do—he led his people out of the fire.

Pearson's face remained blank as Brooke spoke, his jaw locked. I could see in his eyes that he already knew about Yemen, but I expected that. Matt had told him. They'd already had this discussion, when Matt had approached him about Agon.

Brooke finished the account, and Pearson checked his watch. It hadn't been quite ten minutes, and he didn't get up.

"I'm very sorry, Corporal," he said. "The country is indebted to you for your sacrifice."

Brooke looked to me, mouth half open. Frozen on the next bit. I decided to step in.

"Congressman, a couple of months ago your son approached you about...a discrepancy. With the Yemen operation."

Pearson's gaze snapped toward me. Suddenly his face was ice cold. He reached for the end of the table. I held up a hand.

"Please. Just hear me out. I know Matt called you. I know he told you about a blue-on-blue strike from a Falcon-class Agon Defense attack drone. And how it was covered up."

"You can't be serious," Pearson snapped. He turned back to Brooke. "Is *this* what you wanted to talk about?"

"It's important," Brooke said. "I know you didn't believe Matty. I understand. But—"

"I didn't believe him because he was *sick*," Pearson said, lowering his voice. Leaning across the table. "If you actually dated my son, you should know that. Whatever happened to him over there...it broke him. Mentally. I sent a son to war and..." He broke off, tears bubbling into his eyes. Voice turning soft. He clenched the edge of the table and looked away. Took a deep breath. "And welcomed home a shell," he said, at last. "A ghost of my son."

"I know," Brooke said. She was crying also, but she held herself together. "I was with Matty when the trauma began."

Brooke choked up, and again I stepped in.

"I've seen combat, Congressman. As much as your son. I've seen a lot of good soldiers die, and dozens more come home broken. War hits us all in very different ways. What happened to your son wasn't his fault, and it's nothing to be ashamed of."

Pearson blinked, one large tear splashing on the table. "Ashamed? You think I'm ashamed?"

"No, sir. But I think your son was. Our society has a way of making you feel weak for...coping."

Pearson shook his head. Looked away and wiped one eye with his thumb. Sniffed hard.

"My son was not ashamed," he said. "My son was a hero. But he was very sick. He was on a lot of medications. He never forgave himself for what happened—for the soldiers he left behind. That was *his* column. His mission. His responsibility when that IED went off."

"It wasn't an IED," Brooke said.

Pearson snapped toward her. "How could you possibly know that? Because Matt told you?"

"No," I said. "Because we have proof."

55

B rooke told the story. She began with the whistleblower's death and the bank robbery. She explained how I had joined the hunt, and glossed over details of our encounters with Holder and his team, not mentioning Ronald or his death, but discussing the loss of the drive.

Then she explained that we had found something else. Secondary proof. She said it came thanks to a second whistleblower—an AI programmer from Agon, who claimed that the accidental launch of the AGM-114 Hellfire missile on Matthew Pearson and his column was not a human error, but an artificial one. An error Agon bore direct responsibility for.

Brooke said nothing of our breach into the Agon facility. I figured that would come up at some point as the FBI stepped in, but hopefully we could delay that inevitability a while longer.

Pearson listened in raptured silence, his jaw working a little, teeth clicking as Brooke explained each point. He never broke eye contact—not even when the waiter came by for the fourth time to ask for our order. I sent the man away, and Pearson drew a long breath.

"Are you telling me..."

I unlocked my phone, rotated it on the table, and pushed it to Pearson. "That your son's column was struck by an Agon missile, and that Agon covered it up. Yes."

Pearson studied the document on-screen—the document we had stolen from Agon. The Agon logo was affixed to the header of the page, tight and complex text spilling out beneath it. I figured it was as much Greek to Pearson as it had been to me, but he scrolled through it anyway and then looked up again.

"This isn't possible," he said.

"It happened," I said simply.

He shook his head. "You don't understand. There are *investigations* after tragedies like that. Interviews. After-action reports. Analysis of the crater—"

"The military never returned to the blast site," Brooke said. "Only weeks after the event, Al Anad Air Base was evacuated. We withdrew from Yemen. I remember the interviews and the investigations. There was no analysis of the blast residue on what trucks survived. The investigation was the shortest of any military function I've ever witnessed. It lasted less than two days. Then we were all shipping out of Yemen, and that was it. We were told it was an IED. We were told that, for security purposes, the KIA would be listed as training fatalities, and that we were barred by law from ever speaking of the event. The mission was classified. What happened happened."

Pearson looked to me. I simply shrugged. It sounded absurd, maybe, to a man of practice and procedure. A man who believed in the system and served as an integral part of it. But to a man like me—a man who had spent collective years in war zones and had personally witnessed how chaotic and corrupt they could be—it was all too believable. The survivors of Captain Matthew Pearson's column were likely eager to put that blast behind them. They weren't sitting around speculating about corruption or asking about blast analysis. That wasn't how soldiers managed tragedy, especially after so many bloody years of the war against terror.

"It happened," I said again. Pearson sat slowly back, folding his arms. He looked out across the restaurant and worked his jaw, like a child fighting back a temper tantrum. The blackened rage I'd seen in his face before was back, freshly invigorated. I could only imagine how hot it must burn in his gut.

How he must want to wrap his hands around the throats of these people.

"Who knows?" he asked.

I shrugged again. "Just our team. One whistleblower. We weren't sure who to trust."

"You need the FBI," he said.

"Probably," I said. "But we're concerned that Agon will bury the evidence if they sniff an investigation. This document was stolen, technically. I imagine that makes it inadmissible in court."

Pearson nodded slowly. Then he faced me. "I can launch a congressional audit. Agon is bidding on a substantial chunk of our current defense budget. That gives us pretext for internal review. We can request pretty much anything. They don't have to comply, but with nine billion dollars on the line, they will. If they covered up Yemen, they've covered up plenty of things. Once we obtain some legal proof of corruption, we can go to the FBI from there. It will be too late for them to hide, then."

"How long will that take?" Brooke asked.

"Not long. The spending bill is up for a vote later this month. Agon will be motivated to move quickly. I can put my people on it and keep it quiet."

"That would be ideal," I said. "In the meantime, we'd like to lie low. Agon has a little army of private contractors. Seems they have nothing better to do than run us down. They've got a lot to lose."

Pearson nodded. "I'll need you close. We'll need affidavits of what you witnessed. We'll likely need you to testify when this thing goes to court."

I pinched my lips together, thinking quickly. Brooke was already nodding, but I didn't want to testify any more than I wanted to sign an affidavit. I was happy to propel the investigation at my own risk of life and limb, but being asked to hang around DC for months on end and be dragged through the muck of a federal investigation felt like a bridge too far.

Then again...Brooke would be here. I glanced sideways at her. Saw the light of real hope in her eyes.

I decided to keep my mouth shut.

"Do you have a place to stay?" Pearson asked.

"We've been using hotels," Brooke said. "They seem to be good at finding them, though."

Pearson dug into his pocket and produced a pen. He flipped a thick business card over and wrote on the back in bold, blue ink.

"I've got a cabin near Sperryville, just north of Shenandoah National Park. In the mountains. I haven't been there in a while, but it should be ready for you. Key under the flowerpot to the right of the front steps. Use it as long as you need it."

He slid me the card. I scanned the address, then flipped it over. The face of the card was white, printed in professional black font with the congressional seal stamped in gold in one corner. Pearson's name was listed in the middle, above two addresses and two sets of phone numbers. One for his office in DC, one for his office in Pennsylvania.

I pocketed the card.

Pearson leaned across the table, lowering his voice to barely above a growl. "Don't let this leak. It's critical that we take them by surprise. That company won't have a pot to piss in by the time I'm finished with them."

All of the pain I'd seen before gleamed now like nuclear radiation. Pure, manifested rage. Pearson looked like a man ready to commit murder with his bare hands.

We departed through the front door, the bodyguard falling into step behind Pearson. His car waited at the curb—another black sedan. Stopping by the door, he flicked a cigarette out and lit up, sucking down a long draw while we waited on the sidewalk. Two puffs in, he finally looked up. Not to me, but to Brooke.

"Did you love my son?"

Brooke nodded. Her eyes watered, but she kept her chin up.

"I'm so sorry," Pearson said, his own eyes rimming with red. Then he ducked into the car, the bodyguard shut the door and took the driver's seat, and the black sedan raced away.

56

Pearson's cabin lay nearly two hours away from downtown DC. We stopped along the way to purchase groceries and bottled water. I wasn't sure how long I planned to stay in the area now that the case had been offloaded into federal hands, but I liked the idea of lying low in the meantime. Holder and his thugs were still out there, still hunting.

I still wanted to kill Holder—eventually. But in the short term spilling more Agon blood wouldn't help the case. We already had the one dead guy in Grieves's house to worry about, not to mention his companion, who should now be conscious and likely pissing himself. Problems for the morning.

Pearson's cabin sat at the end of a long, winding blacktop. The drive was dirt and felt just as long and winding. Spidery bare hardwoods crowded in on either side, their trailing limbs tracing the roof of the Ford as we rumbled through the darkness. It was nearly eight p.m. by the time we stepped out of the car, and a cold front was moving through.

The temperature had dropped fifteen degrees from the day before, and a quick inspection of my phone's weather app confirmed that it would only continue to drop.

The cabin was clad in dry pine siding, very old and dusty. Not at all the kind of place I expected a senior politician to own, but not every congressman is a millionaire. The front porch slouched, the windows were covered by wooden shutters, and dead leaves gathered against the door.

I found the key under the flowerpot, right where Pearson said it would be, and stepped into a dark and musty interior. Wood floor, wood panel walls. A low ceiling. There was no electricity, but Dufort brought a flashlight from the car, and we found a propane camping lantern in the closet.

The cabin was single-story, built at the edge of a hill that dropped off from the back porch to a burbling creek fifty yards away. There were two bedrooms, both dusty but each equipped with queen-sized beds. One bathroom, with cobwebs in the sink and tub. No hot water, but plenty of cold. The kitchen and living space were all built together, with a gas stove, dusty dishes, and a couple of couches.

Everything about the cabin felt very tired and somehow sad. As if it had once been a happy place, but had long lain forgotten.

"Matty told me about this place," Brooke said. "The congressman bought it right after he was elected. It was kind of a...sanctuary. Matty only visited a couple of times."

I walked to the sliding glass door built into the back wall, looking out over the creek and into the forest beyond. It was serene. In springtime, I imagined it was probably beautiful. I could see why a widowed congressman would enjoy it.

Brooke busied herself in the kitchen, unpacking canned goods and fighting the stove to get the igniter to work.

Grieves stood in the living room, fingers in his mouth, still biting his nails. I was surprised he had anything left to chew.

Dufort closed in next to me, his distorted face pinched in that permanent sneer. He tapped a cigarette out of its pack and placed it between his mutilated lips, but didn't light it.

"Got to do something about our prisoner," he muttered.

"I know," I said.

"Any ideas?"

I hesitated, considering whether two bodies would be easier to manage than one body and one naked guy hogtied in a closet.

But no. I wasn't a murderer. I had zero heartache over killing the enemy in combat, but shooting a helpless prisoner in cold blood was a line I wouldn't cross. I wasn't Holder.

"We'll figure it out tomorrow," I said.

Dufort stepped out onto the deck without further comment. A moment later I smelled nicotine as his lighter sparked. It was the only sound in an otherwise silent forest.

BROOKE HEATED CANNED RAVIOLI, and we ate out of freshly rinsed bowls. Then Dufort returned to the back porch, Glock in his lap, cigarette in his hand, and Grieves curled up on the couch. I wasn't sure how many Xanax the little guy was popping, but he was about as zoned out as a person could become while remaining conscious, and it wasn't long before even consciousness abandoned him.

I couldn't blame him for the medication, even if every overdose might be shortening his life by years at a time. If the last year had taught me anything, I had learned that we all have our demons.

I cleaned the kitchen while Brooke sipped tea at the little breakfast table, not talking. The vacancy had returned to her eyes, and I thought she was probably thinking of Matt. Maybe remembering that meeting in Atlanta, or their huddle right before the bank robbery. Whenever they had last spoken as friends. As former lovers.

Ironically, the last words he had said to her had been angry, hostile words. Spoken for my benefit, of course, as the witness to their crazed robbery. But still a bad memory for Brooke. I recalled how he threw her back into the van, the door slamming shut, me reeling over the metal floor. I remembered the panic in her eyes and suddenly wondered how much of Matt's performance had been an act. How deeply his trauma had changed him. How many medications he might have been on that numbed his emotions and left his temperament raw.

We all have our demons.

I put the last cup away and closed the cabinet. Then I settled against the counter and looked at the floor. Through the crack of the partially closed sliding glass door, I could smell Dufort's cigarettes. Somehow, it was a calming odor, but probably not because of the nicotine. Looking at the big man's shoulders and remembering the Glock in his lap somehow relaxed me. It made me think that, for just a moment, I could let somebody else be on guard.

"I'm going to sleep," I said. "Tell Dufort to wake me if he wants to switch."

Brooke nodded without a word, and our gazes met for just a moment. The saddest hint of a smile touched her lips, barely enough to expose the dimples. I returned it and found my way down the short hall to the back bedroom.

I closed the door before kicking my shoes off and pulling my shirt over my head. Part of me wanted a shower to wash away two days' worth of sweat and grime, but I knew the water was cold, and I was too tired to think about towels or soap. I settled onto the bed instead, lying back with my face pointed to a drywall ceiling marked by water stains. Outside, the soft rustle of wind rattled the trees, but I didn't hear Dufort smoking. I didn't hear Grieves's gentle breathing from the couch.

I could only hear my own heart beating slowly. My mind winding down. Thoughts of the day, and of the congressman, and of Matt Pearson, and of Agon, and all the other mess I was surrounded by faded slowly away. My watch read nine p.m., but the clock in my head said three hours.

Three hours left until the calendar switched. November fourteenth became November fifteenth. Exactly three hundred and sixty-five days since...

I closed my eyes. Tried to see the K-10 and the stars and to feel Mia's breath on my cheek. Tried to picture her curled up on the couch with her Bible, or posing alongside me for a selfie somewhere inside South Mountain Park.

Tried *not* to see the school. The flashing red lights. The crimson on the floor...

Outside my room, a floorboard creaked. The doorknob rattled, just a little, then clicked. I opened my eyes to see Brooke slip in. She looked just as she had twenty minutes prior—raven hair falling next to her face, eyes a little red, cheeks a little puffy. Blue jeans and a tank top and an unzipped cotton jacket.

She stood just inside the threshold, looking at me. Not blinking, not speaking. And then she gently closed the door.

I sat up, swinging my feet off the bed. Opening my mouth, but not knowing what to say. Brooke closed the distance between us in a sudden rush, one hand landing on my bare chest, the other running down my arm. Then her lips met mine, and the nuclear heat I had felt at Davis's house returned redoubled. It flooded my chest and ran down my arms as her tongue touched mine, her hand running up the back of my neck and into my hair. I felt my own hand sliding beneath her jacket and around to her lower back, almost as though I weren't in control. Brooke broke the kiss and stared deep into my eyes. The ocean I'd seen all week was still there, as deep and dark and mystifying as ever.

But it wasn't in turmoil the way I expected. It was now very calm.

Without a word she slid the jacket off, then slowly tugged the tank top over her head. Raven locks fell over bare shoulders and smooth curves. My heart rate quickened, one palm now resting on her bare back, our gazes not breaking.

Then we fell onto the bed, Brooke on top, her fingers in my hair and mine in hers. Lips touching, tongues pressing, bodies so close together I could feel her pounding heart and knew she could feel mine. My chest tightened as her hand dropped down my stomach and traced my chest. My fingers ran up her back and touched the buckle of her bra—the same bra I had used to snatch her back into the van during the robbery. Now a distant memory. Now lost in the heat and passion of the moment.

From my pocket my phone buzzed—a systemic chime that signaled an incoming call. I ignored it as Brooke's lips moved to my neck, pressing her body close to mine, all warmth and soft skin and enough chemical overload to send us both into autopilot. I was drenched in the sweet smell of clean water and flowers.

And then I felt something else. A low buzzing through the walls. A muted, gurgling cry from behind the cabin.

Then a chatter of automatic gunfire, matched by the buzzing whirr of a hornet's nest as Dufort's heavy body slammed into the deck.

57

I rolled left on instinct—away from the back of the house. Away from the rear deck. I carried Brooke with me, and we slammed into the hardwood just as the next burst of chattering gunfire blew out the bedroom window and sent hot lead smashing into the wood-paneled wall. I lay on top of Brooke, pressing down. Covering her body with my own as the hissing rattle continued.

Outside the cabin, the air buzzed with the whir of an X-40—somehow a very familiar sound. But the cadence and pitch of the gunfire didn't match that of a modified MP5 submachine gun. This thunderclap was both louder and slightly slower.

Rifle rounds. Fully automatic.

"Under the bed!" I hissed, tumbling off Brooke. She wiggled left on instinct, eyes wide with terror, chest heaving. I hit the floor on my stomach and army-crawled to the bedroom door. In the living room beyond, Grieves screamed —short, panicked bursts, mixed at times with my name. I pulled the door open and crawled into the hallway, staying low, my own heart thumping like a war drum.

Then the gunfire returned, and glass shattered. A lot of it, raining over hardwood in the room beyond. It was the sliding glass door. Grieves screamed again as I reached the terminus of the hallway and peered around the corner.

He lay behind the couch he had been sleeping on, bent over and covering his head like a nineteen-fifties schoolkid practicing a nuclear drill. Cubes of obliterated plate glass lay scattered across the living room floor, and just outside the room, hovering over the deck, was an Agon X-40 attack drone.

The aircraft was four-bladed, as before, looking not much more complex than a camera drone a teenager might buy from an electronics store. But four times larger, mounted with that blinking red dot of an eye...and carrying twin black barrels, jutting forward like buckteeth, ammunition drums hanging beneath.

The drone didn't move, and neither did I. Grieves lay huddled low, shaking behind the couch. His face rose slowly, mouth hanging open, jaw trembling. I waved a hand to draw his attention, then held a finger to my lips.

"*Don't move,*" I mouthed.

Grieves made no acknowledgment, and I twisted around the corner again. The drone remained motionless over the deck, the guns pointed through the shattered glass door, but not firing. I leaned out another inch to get a view beyond the second couch...and then I saw Dufort.

He was dead. No doubt about it. Spread-eagled across the deck in a puddle of blood, a checkerboard of bullet holes blasted through his tree-trunk body. Boiling heat returned to my chest in a flood, but this time it wasn't the roaring warmth of untethered lust. It was pure rage, let off the leash.

The drone twitched abruptly. Spinning right, the guns pivoting toward me. I yanked my head behind the wall, pressing myself into the floor again. But the drone didn't fire. Instead it buzzed louder, then withdrew from the house. I listened as the hornet rush of its rotors faded into the forest.

What?

Then I heard another sound. A low, whooshing, rushing noise. It was somehow familiar, but I couldn't place it before the second drone appeared over the deck, and hot red fire flashed across the blown-out door.

Flamethrower.

A jet stream of sticky wet fire shot across the deck, landing right in the center of Dufort's body. In an instant the flames multiplied. Fire licked across the deck and hit the house. Dufort's mutilated face vanished amid the inferno. The drone spun in midair, exposing a single black pipe and two thick tanks mounded beneath. The pipe pointed through the shattered door, and a spark flashed across its mouth.

"Grieves! *Move!*"

I screamed across the living room just a second before the next jet stream launched into the living room—fifteen feet long, reaching all the way to the kitchen. Dumping flammable fuel across the hardwood floor for a split second before that stream ignited into rushing hot flame.

An overwhelming wave of heat washed over me—like a bomb blast or a car fire. I scrambled by as Grieves shrieked, dropping to the floor.

"Move now!" I shouted.

Grieves didn't move, and the jet stream continued. The

drone pivoted, directing fire toward the cabin walls, then toward the living room furniture.

I leapt from the hallway, hurtling toward the spot behind the nearest couch. Waves of heat passed across my bare back, scalding my skin as I landed on top of Grieves. I grabbed him by the arm and yanked backwards, kicking with my feet and clawing toward the hallway.

The drone saw us. I knew it, because the flame stopped. The blades whirred. The mouth of the flamethrower flicked in our direction like the muzzle of a tank.

I rammed my bare foot against the end of the smoldering kitchen counter, blackened wood scalding my skin in an instant. I kicked out hard as flames crackled through the kitchen and the jet stream shot toward me.

We slid across polished wood, reaching the shelter of the hallway just as the flame sparked. A millisecond later the path behind us was flooded by flames. I couldn't even see the couch anymore. Smoke clogged the air, and fire consumed the walls. The entire right-hand side of the cabin was now consumed—wood crackling, embers flying, jet stream still pumping into the living room.

My foot burned hot enough to draw tears to my eyes. I flattened it against the hallway floor, smothering any fragments of burning wood. Then I rolled right as Brooke exploded from the bedroom, still dressed in nothing more than blue jeans and a bra.

"Take him!" I shouted.

Brooke didn't hesitate. She grabbed Grieves and hauled him up. I returned to my feet and slammed through the door into the second bedroom—the front one, facing toward the winding dirt drive. I'd glanced inside soon after we arrived and found photographs of the congressman's late wife. A master bedroom, now regulated to a mausoleum I initially avoided.

All thoughts of respecting the dead were gone now. I plummeted inside and hit my knees next to the bed. Dropping my shoulders, I ripped through the blankets and bedclothes folded beneath, fingers searching for anything hard. Anything plastic.

Anything that felt like a case.

I found nothing, and I rushed to the closet. Hanging clothes and towels fell aside. From the living room the flamethrower ignited again, and fire roared from across the hallway.

"Mason!" Brooke shouted. Her voice choked on thick smoke.

"Get in here!" I called back, ramming my hand into the back of the closet. Hoping—praying.

My fingers touched metal. Smooth, cold, and cylindrical. I dropped to my knees and ripped the jackets away to expose the weapon. It was a break-action shotgun—single shot, with rust gathering on the barrel. A hardwood stock battered by scratches and dents, a single box of shells resting on the floor next to it.

It was a .410. About the lightest, puniest shotgun money can buy, but way better than nothing.

I grabbed both shells and gun as Brooke dragged Grieves into the front bedroom. Behind her, the roar of the fire had doubled. The hallway looked like a window into hell. In the living room a timber creaked; then a deluge of something heavy cascaded across the floor—probably burning ceiling panels.

"It's coming around!" Brooke cried.

I hit the breach latch and snapped the shotgun open,

exposing a filthy and rust-rimmed chamber. Tearing the top off the box of shells, I found 2.5 inch birdshot housed within. A light load for an already light gun.

I rammed in a shell anyway and snapped the weapon closed as thick black smoke poured into the small room. Brooke closed the door, but it was little use. Smoke continued to billow through the crack. Brooke coughed, falling against the wall.

I turned for the window.

"Get behind the bed!"

A shadow passed across the window—obscured by a thin curtain. The buzzing whir of the drone returned, barely audible above the roar of the fire.

I cocked the shotgun. Raised the muzzle. Watched as the shadow rotated, the silhouette of the pipe visible for a split second before it turned to face me.

Then I fired.

A hail of pellets blew through the window and struck the drone—not center mass. Not at the core, where the plastic would be thick, the internal components sheltered by light armor. I aimed for the left-hand blades instead, blowing both of them into tiny shreds of plastic. The drone dropped left immediately, spinning and plummeting to the porch in a wreckage of plastic.

Flipping the shotgun around, I used the butt to smash away the remaining glass in the window, sending shards of splintered wood raining over the deck. Then I snapped the breach open, the spent shell ejecting automatically over my shoulder, quickly replaced by a fresh one.

"Come on!" I coughed amid the smoke. Brooke appeared from behind the bed, still dragging Grieves. The little guy was alive with terror now, eyes wide, face slick with sheets of sweat.

I met Brooke at the window, my mind flashing back to my last interaction with the X-40s. How they had tracked me.

"They're using infrared targeting," I said. "Get Grieves down to the creek and into the water, as low as you can. The cold will shield you."

Brooke's wide eyes blinked. I saw fear, but not panic. Not desperation.

Because everyone feels fear. But soldiers power through it.

I squeezed her shoulder once. Brooke nodded her understanding. Then we both grabbed Grieves and dove through the window.

58

The flamethrower drone lay twitching and grinding on the front porch as we landed beside it. I rammed the butt of the shotgun over the core of the aluminum housing, smashing electronic components and sending the device into a permanent robotic grave. Then the two of us sprinted for the trees, dragging Grieves between us.

The cabin was now consumed by flames. Tall columns of hot red and orange reached for the sky as the roof began to collapse. There was no saving that cabin, no stopping the blaze. But in a weird way, the rush of heat was a strange kind of blessing.

The drones couldn't detect our body heat so close to the inferno.

"Make for the creek!" I said. "Go underwater if they come for you."

"What about—"

"Don't worry about me. *Go!*"

Brooke went, propelling Grieves ahead of her down the

hill. I stepped away from the cabin, sweeping my gaze through the forest. Searching for the gun drone...or drones. Had I seen only one? Or two?

God save me if there were more than that.

I cradled the shotgun under one arm and slid behind a tree. Then I tore through the box of shells, placing three rounds between the fingers of my left hand, and three more in my right. The rest spilled over the leafy ground, and I left them. Directing the shotgun into the air, I cocked the hammer and pressed the trigger.

Thunder boomed over the roar of the fire, and the response from the autonomous enemy was instant. A buzz of blades erupted from someplace in the trees to my left, followed almost immediately by a roar of automatic gunfire. Hot slugs raced above my head and tore through the hardwoods. Bark and shreds of wood exploded over the ground, and I scrambled for cover at the base of the tree. The shotgun snapped open. A fresh round found its home in the chamber. I cocked the hammer and waited.

The buzzing grew louder. The gunshots subdued into short bursts—no longer suppressive fire. This was strategic fire. I focused on the whir of blades and thought I now detected separate sources. One lay directly behind me, deep in the trees, unleashing three-round bursts toward my position a few seconds apart.

But the second buzz of hornet blades was separate. I traced it to my left, breaking from its twin, circling slowly through the trees. Closing on my exposed flank while its partner held me in place.

The damn things were working in *tandem*. Like trained soldiers.

I squinted into the trees, flashing firelight breaking the

inky blackness into patches of deep shadow and mottled orange light. The whirr of the second drone was muffled by the blaze now. I couldn't see it amid the cover of low brush and hardwood trunks, but I knew it was someplace to my left, drawing near to my flank.

Another three-round burst from behind sent splinters raining into my lap. I waited until the hail subsided, then rolled quickly left and dove for a depression at the base of a hickory tree.

I wasn't a moment too soon. An instant after I moved, the second drone fired. A blast of chattering gunfire shredded my previous position of cover, leaves and dirt exploding into the air. But this time, the fire didn't stop. The hail just kept coming, louder and closer, pivoting toward my new position as the drone closed the distance.

I left cover and sprinted, risking exposure to the first drone as I wove between the trees. More gunfire broke the stillness. All around me trees shook and dead leaves rained down. Bark exploded, and hot lead whispered past my head. I slid into cover behind a rotten log and rolled immediately onto my stomach. The muzzle of the shotgun rose over the log. I drew back the hammer and pivoted on instinct toward the incoming second drone—the flanking soldier.

I saw muzzle flash. I fired. Rifle slugs tore into my rotten log, and the shotgun slammed into my shoulder. The drone twitched, dropping slightly to the left. Its guns went silent, and it whirred out of sight. I ducked behind the log and reloaded, listening intently.

It wasn't dead. But I had winged it.

Heart pounding, mind numb with adrenaline, I descended onto my stomach and wormed quickly to the next tree. The air was thick with smoke and drifting embers. Fifty yards from the crumbling cabin, a pile of dry leaves had ignited into a bonfire. The Ford was on fire also, columns of rubber smoke reaching for the sky as the vehicle was consumed by flames. My skin was black with the soot, my eyes burning with it. I saw a flash of black plastic reflecting the firelight from fifty yards distant but couldn't hear the drone's blades. I kept my back to the cabin, creeping as close to the blaze as I could. Blinding the drones to my body heat. Searching the trees.

The next surge of automatic fire caught me completely off guard. It came from my exposed right side, and I rolled to see one of the twin X-40s racing in like an attack helicopter. Nose dropping, guns blazing. Ripping through what had once been the cabin's front yard in a desperate roar of hot lead.

I rolled onto my back, cocked and fired. Plastic splintered, and a rotor blade exploded. The drone twitched and dropped, bullets spraying mindlessly into the trees as it fought to self-correct out of a free fall.

Open breach, spent shell spitting over my shoulder. A fresh round, a cocked hammer. I raised and fired.

The X-40 spun to the ground in a spray of aluminum and plastic, but there was no time to celebrate. Three-round bursts thundered from behind me, dirt exploding on all sides like a field of landmines. I rolled right, fumbling shells as I scrambled for cover. Dust clogged my face, and a dense cloud of smoke obscured my vision. I couldn't see the drone, but the gunfire just kept coming. I reached cover behind a tree and snapped the shotgun open. Looking to my hands, I saw that only one shell had survived my mad dash for cover.

I loaded, closed the breach, and breathed evenly. Every part of my body screamed for me to panic. Raw fear beat at the iron gates of my mind, desperate to flood in. My heart thundered. Adrenaline surged.

But calm remained. I closed my eyes and sucked down a long breath. I focused on the chatter of ceaseless gunfire still ripping toward me in three-round bursts. It was as though the drone had given up on hunting and was now content to simply obliterate anything that moved.

My skin tingled as washes of heat swept the forest from the hellscape of fires. I wiped soot from my lip and shouldered the gun. The drone drew closer, the hail of bullets rapidly narrowing on my position.

I kept my breathing even. Focused on the timing of the three-round bursts, measuring the pace like a metronome.

One...two...fire...four...five...fire...six...seven...fire...

It was as systematic as an assembly line pumping out toaster ovens. As consistent as the tick of a clock.

A thinking machine. But still a machine.

I flinched as bullets bit the back of my tree. Listened to the buzz of the blades, now only twenty yards away. Then ten. Orbiting slowly to my left, only seconds away from drawing even with my exposed flank and riddling my body with bullet holes.

...fifteen...sixteen...fire...

I cocked the shotgun.

...eighteen...nineteen...fire...

Three rounds zipped into the tree, the nearest cutting past the bark and missing my hip by no more than an inch. I spun around the trunk, shotgun rising. Fully exposed to the muzzles of the X-40 long before the weapon reached my shoulder. Standing only five yards away like the broad side of a barn. A blatant target. Moving at lightning speed for a man, but like syrup for a machine. Taking my life in my own hands as I counted in my head: *...twenty-one...twenty-two.*

The shotgun reached my shoulder. My finger dropped over the trigger. I aimed and pressed all at once. The shotgun belched fire a split second before the machine guns were due to belch muzzle flash.

They never got the chance. Light load or not, bird shot at five yards is a hell of a weapon. The core housing of the drone exploded in a hail of plastic and aluminum, and the drone plummeted to the ground like a rock.

Leaving me to stand in a swirl of gun smoke, heart still thundering.

59

———

I found Brooke and Grieves shivering in the creek, pressed low in the water, just the way I had instructed them. I helped them back up the hill, where they warmed next to the flames.

The cabin was gone. The Ford was gone. Dufort was gone. For a hundred yards on all sides, small fires burned amid the trees, sending smoldering embers drifting into the air to further spread the blaze. It wouldn't become a forest fire—the ground was too damp for that. But standing amid the wash of raw heat and endless smoke, the woods felt like hell itself.

And I saw red.

I checked my pocket for my phone, vaguely remembering an incoming call as Brooke and I tangled amid the sheets. The phone was present and undamaged, but the battery had died. The screen was now black.

Retrieving what remained of the shotgun shells from the forest floor, I gave Grieves and Brooke ten minutes to dry, then met them at the back of the house. Brooke stared at the spot where the back porch had existed only an hour prior. I knew Dufort's body lay somewhere amid the embers, but by the time the flames finally died, I would be surprised if any part of the big SEAL remained. In a disgusting twist of fate, the flames had claimed him in the end.

That irony only fueled the rage flooding my body. It surged in like a tidal wave, like a tsunami as the implications of the drones arriving at the cabin rushed in. No doubt Holder had sent them. No doubt Agon had provided them.

But Holder hadn't known where we were. He'd had all day in Washington to pounce on us while we waited for the congressman to call back, but he hadn't. Because we had evaded him.

Only one man knew we were here. Only one man knew all four of us had taken shelter in the cabin, waiting things out.

Congressman Glenn David Pearson. An American traitor.

A walking dead man.

"Come on." I spoke through clenched teeth before leading my battered team away from the battlefield. I avoided the winding driveway, choosing the open forest instead. My bare feet stung as I crunched over sticks and rocks, but I hardly noticed. Grieves was the only one of the three of us who escaped the cabin both fully clothed and wearing shoes, but he looked the most shell-shocked. Vacant eyes stared at the ground as he trailed along behind Brooke, and his mouth hung half open.

But he didn't speak. Part of me wondered if he would ever speak again.

I used my mental map of the wilderness surrounding the cabin to circle deep into the trees before drawing near to the road again—but not passing onto it. The landscape was rough. The ground beneath my bloody feet rolled gently, with a lot of fallen trees and low brush clogging the path ahead. Cold wind stung my smoke-blackened face and sent shivers up my scalded back.

But I pressed ahead. I didn't know whether Holder and his people might be nearby, ready to finish the job after their drones went down in flames. I wasn't going to wait around to find out. I cut a trail through the forest until we reached the gravel drive of another cabin, at least a mile removed from Pearson's. I followed that drive to a small log house, no bigger than our last, but a lot cleaner. There were cutesy little signs about vacations and bears staked in front of the porch, with clean pillows resting in Adirondack-style chairs.

But no car. No signs of people.

I drove the butt of the shotgun through the front window, smashing away glass and wood before ducking inside. I let Brooke and Grieves in through the front door and found a light switch. This cabin was served by electricity, and a flood of fluorescent washed over us.

For the first time, I paused to check on Grieves. And then Brooke.

The two of them looked like something out of a horror film. Brooke's skin was so blackened by smoke that it nearly matched her bra, streaks of white skin shining through where she had scrubbed her face. Her raven hair was a tangled mess, her jeans torn.

Grieves looked ready to simply drop.

I met Brooke's gaze, expecting to see terror or maybe crushing defeat. Instead, I saw hellfire. Raw, unbridled rage, boiling the ocean in her eyes.

"They *killed him*," she hissed, her voice hoarse.

It was the second time she had uttered those words in barely twenty-four hours. The pain in her voice wasn't lost on me, like the agony in a child's eyes as she steps on broken glass. Fear and betrayal.

I wanted to offer comfort—to wrap her in a hug and hold her while she cried. It felt like the right thing to do, but my soldier's brain wouldn't allow it. The enemy was still out there. The battle wasn't over.

I secured the door instead, then laid the shotgun on the counter. I dug through half a dozen kitchen drawers before I found a cell phone charger that would fit my phone. Five slow minutes crawled by while it was resurrected from the electronic abyss. When the screen finally flashed to life, I had two missed calls, one voicemail, and three texts.

All from area code 480.

I skipped the voicemail and went right to the texts, already suspecting what I would find.

> Mason, call me.

Five minutes later:

> Breakthrough on the Agon case. Need to talk.

And then the final message. The voice of the midnight watchman shouting the alarm. Just a little too late.

> Connection between Agon and Matthew Pearson's father. Congressman is DIRTY.

My shoulders slumped. I piloted back to my phone app and redialed Jacquie. Two rings—then a quick answer, the voice laced with nervous energy.

"Mason? Is that you?"

"It's me," I said.

"Are you okay? Did you get my message?"

"I got it," I said.

Stone silence. She must have detected the rasping in my voice. The raw hiss of smoke inhalation and desperation and the subsiding adrenaline of open combat.

"What do you need?" Jacquie said simply.

"Backup," I said. "I need you here."

60

There were clothes in one of the bedroom closets— two button-down shirts of the same size. A little too small for me, and much too big for Brooke, but we both put them on anyway. Hiking boots in the closet reflected a similar problem, but by doubling up her socks, Brooke was able to make them work. I would have to remain barefoot.

There were no firearms in the cabin, and no other cellular devices. We took flashlights from the kitchen, bottled water and crackers from the pantry; then we left the cabin and returned to the forest.

Jacquie was six hours out—a four-hour direct flight, followed by delays at the rental car desk, and then an hour-and-a-half drive to Sperryville. She didn't hesitate when I called for backup. Good cops never do. She simply promised text updates and hung up, leaving us to shelter in the woods for the remainder of the night.

We didn't talk. There was nothing to say. The clock ground slowly on, passing midnight. Passing into

November 15, and bringing rage with it. I cradled the shotgun and remained alert, my brain supercharged by adrenaline, daring another drone to whirr its way into the forest. Almost begging for it to happen. Ready to tear it apart with my bare hands. But as the hours dripped by, nothing happened. We endured a brisk breeze cutting amid the trees, flinching at every howling coyote or crunching footfall of a passing deer. Waiting it out. Embracing the suck.

I relocated us every half hour, remaining on constant alert as the night marched into sunrise. Jacquie texted at five a.m. and said she was in a car and on her way. Brooke remained awake the entire time, but didn't talk. She just sat, wrapped in a flannel button-down, eyes blazing at the darkness, one arm wrapped around Grieves as he stared wide-eyed into the dark. Shell-shocked.

At last the sky slipped from black to gray and gradually to orange. Then a maroon Jeep Cherokee appeared on the gravel road a hundred yards away, sliding to a gentle stop. The driver's door popped open, and a petite black woman dropped out. Thick, dark hair jammed under a Phoenix Suns baseball cap. Iron face staring into the trees.

Backup.

I led my shattered army up the hill and out of the forest. Brooke went straight for the back door of the Jeep, helping Grieves in before she herself piled into the seat. Jacquie just stood at the nose of the rental, hands at her sides, staring at me.

It was the first time I'd seen her since just before I left Phoenix. I had cut Jacquie off after landing in North Carolina. Cut her off as I wandered the southeast, living in the back of my truck, ignoring her emails. Drowning in the waves of grief that now blurred together into one steady monotone of pain.

I saw that pain reflected in her dark eyes, now turning moist. Jacquie blinked a few times, and her right hand closed into a fist. Her lip shook, and the fist tightened.

Then she marched quickly across the road, chin up, eyes blurred, and threw her arms around me.

I stood rock still, a little stunned by the aggressive hug. Jacquie pressed her face against my chest, sniffing once as she clamped down on me. I placed an arm awkwardly over her shoulder, unsure what to say. Too emotionally numb to know how to respond.

"I freaking hate you," Jacquie whispered.

She sniffed again, and just the flicker of a smile passed across my lips. I squeezed her once; then she abruptly released me and stepped back, wiping her nose and clearing her throat as though there were a frog in it.

"You all right?" she said.

"I'm fine."

Jacquie jabbed her thumb at the passenger seat. "Get in."

I climbed into the Jeep, and Jacquie took the wheel. The shifter ground, and she smashed the gas. Then we were off, rumbling through the trees, headed back toward civilization.

Jacquie looked into the mirror, inspecting Brooke and Grieves, but commented on neither. Instead, she tapped the console next to her. I looked down to see a small sheaf of printed documents stacked like a pile of magazines.

"This congressman of yours is a walking idiot," Jacquie said. "It took me all of an afternoon to trace six-figure contributions from Agon to super PACs that funded Pearson's campaigns. It's not even secret. Then there's the small matter of the charity Pearson runs—

public records of which report another half a million dollars of donations from Agon in the last eighteen months alone. That scumbag is sucking their tit so hard he might choke."

I flicked through the stack, scanning tight columns of financial figures and political disclosures, each highlighted and annotated in Jacquie's precise handwriting. I would have been impressed, but I expected nothing less from her. Jacquie was easily the finest investigator I had ever met.

"He's not stupid," I said. "Just mindlessly arrogant. And he's going to choke—you can bet the farm on that."

I dropped the documents into the glove box and settled into the seat, one finger tapping my thigh. Thinking. And planning.

Jacquie gave me time, hitting the highway and turning automatically toward DC. The Jeep's big engine surged, and we hurtled along like a police cruiser in hot pursuit. Ten miles closer to our target, I finally spoke.

"Drop us at the rental car place. Then you should probably get back to Phoenix. Make sure you scrub your call and text history."

Jacquie rocked her face toward me, lip curled. "Excuse me?"

"I don't want this coming back on you," I said. "Think of a reason why you had to fly out here. Tell the department you had a family emergency. Don't mention me."

Jacquie's mouth closed, and she looked ahead. For a long while she didn't say anything, and I glanced sideways. I saw tears in her eyes, her mouth clamped into a hard line. Suddenly, she yanked the Jeep to the right, cutting across two lanes of traffic as horns blared behind us. We hit the emergency lane in a hail of rocks, and she slid to a stop. The shifter slammed into park, and Jacquie threw her seat belt off.

"Get out."

"What?" I said.

"*Get out!*" She threw her door open, dropping onto the pavement. I unbuckled and found my way through the passenger door in time to meet Jacquie, barreling around the nose of the Jeep like a cannon ball, all rolling shoulders and clenched teeth. I shut the door, exposing her right side.

I saw the flashing hand, but I didn't have a prayer of dodging it. Jacquie's palm rocketed toward me like a Sidewinder missile, smacking across my face hard enough to rattle teeth and send a shock wave ripping down my spine. I stumbled back against the Jeep, hand snapping to my burning face as Jacquie squared her shoulders.

"What the—"

"*Shut up,*" Jacquie snapped. "Just shut the hell up."

I did shut up. Jacquie stood like a caged bull, face tilted up, brown eyes watering. Fists tightened until her knuckles paled. She raised a finger and spoke through her teeth.

"You *abandoned me.* You turned your back on the one thing you are *never* supposed to leave behind. Your *partner.*"

I opened my mouth. Jacquie cut me short.

"Save it! I don't want to hear it. You lost...so much." Jacquie's voice choked, and tears dripped down her face. "Your whole life was ripped out from under you. I can't begin to imagine what that feels like. But you didn't lose *me*, and nothing that happened to you gave you the right to push your family away. I swear, Mason, if you keep this up, I'm going to bury you myself. Do you hear me?"

I closed my mouth. My eyes blurred also, and I nodded once. Jacquie slowly lowered her shaking hand.

"We're partners, Mason. We have each other's back... always. You hear me?"

I swallowed. Nodded again. Jacquie scrubbed her face with the back of one hand, sniffed hard and looked away. Then she jabbed a thumb at the Jeep.

"All right, then. Let's go."

I returned to the passenger seat, face burning red, but not from the slap. Jacquie piled in and adjusted the mirror. I saw Brooke staring wide-eyed from the back seat. Jacquie caught her gaze.

"What are you looking at?"

Brooke looked away.

Jacquie grunted. "I thought so."

She buckled her belt and shifted into drive. Sat for a moment with her foot on the brake. Then cleared her throat.

"Okay. So where is this scumbag?"

61

J acquie drove hard while the three of us outlined next steps. Grieves was still silent—sitting slumped in his seat, staring at his hands—but Brooke joined the discussion tentatively, still a little gun-shy of Jacquie.

I couldn't blame her.

"We need to regroup and refit," I said. "And then I want to talk to the reporter."

I explained to Jacquie about Kelly Davis and what she knew. With the additional information we had gathered from Jacquie's research and our intrusion into Agon, Brooke was hopeful that Davis would finally launch an investigation. I nodded agreement, but in my gut I knew it still wasn't enough, for all the reasons Davis had outlined previously. The evidence could still be smothered by lawyers. Davis would need something more—fuel on the fire. Some kind of boost.

And in the next twenty-four hours, she would have it. Because I had other plans beyond investigative reporting.

Plans that would level the score with Agon, Holder, and Congressman Pearson—permanently.

I was done playing nice. Done working angles. It was time to go for the throat of this thing. To cut the head off the snake. I only had to sideline the others first. None of them deserved to be implicated if things went sideways.

"Is this Jeep rented under your name?" I asked.

Jacquie snorted. I raised an eyebrow. Jacquie shrugged innocently.

"Busted a druggie last week. Petite African American female. Early thirties. ID looks a lot like me."

"You crafty devil," I said.

"I prefer the term *conniving witch*, but flattery of any kind is acceptable."

"Is the druggie in lockup?" I asked.

Jacquie nodded. "She's got an alibi. Nothing will come back on her."

"Good. Next we need a hotel. Then we'll rendezvous with Davis."

WE MADE a pitstop at a Walmart prior to finding a hotel. I walked in barefoot and bought jeans, a shirt that fit, fresh socks and underwear, and a forty-dollar pair of hiking boots.

I like Walmart clothes.

Brooke purchased her own things, remaining quiet as we checked out and returned to the Jeep. Ever since the house fire, I detected a strange sort of wall between us. An awkwardness that I hadn't felt since Jacksonville. It was as though we were complete strangers again and didn't know how to talk to each other.

Maybe it was the loss of Dufort, or the violence in general. Maybe it was Jacquie.

We found another grimy hotel, and I rented a room with the last of Falk and Moss's cash. Jacquie parked in back without needing to be asked, and Brooke and I took turns showering and changing. She stepped out of the bathroom, glistening with steam, sopping raven hair held back in a ponytail, her face a little red from scrubbing. Our gazes met for a split second, and Brooke looked quickly away, busying herself with her socks and shoes.

I hit the shower.

Kelly Davis answered her phone on the third ring, but she couldn't meet. She was in New York on some portion of a business trip, and by the sound of it, she was still sick. I outlined what we had confirmed about Agon, the congressman, and the friendly-fire strike in Yemen, focusing on the documents themselves and not how we had acquired them.

Davis listened without comment, then simply instructed me on where to email the evidence. She hung up after that, but I knew she was on the hook.

At least, if she wasn't yet...she would be soon.

Hanging up the hotel phone, I turned to my withered team. Grieves still hadn't spoken since the cabin fire, and I hadn't seen him eat or drink anything, either. Brooke sat on the end of the bed, picking at her fingernails, still avoiding my gaze. Jacquie sat at the hotel desk, arms folded, just waiting.

Everyone looked exhausted. A little broken, also. It would be my job to build them back into a team.

Rangers lead the way.

"Okay," I said. "We're almost to the end. There are three tasks remaining, and I'll need something from each of you to get us over the hump. But I'm going to carry the weight. Okay? When this is all said and done, we're all walking away. No interviews. No courtrooms. And definitely no jail time. We're going to knock this thing in the throat, spit on its grave, and disappear. Fair enough?"

Nods from Jacquie and Brooke. Grieves didn't answer, but I trusted he had heard me. It might require a little finesse on my part to get what I needed out of him.

"Task number one. Jacquie, this is all you. I need to know where the congressman lives. Home addresses in both DC and Pennsylvania. Personal contact information. Vehicle registration. Whatever you can find—but find it without leaving fingerprints. That's very important."

"On it," Jacquie said, rotating the desk chair to face the laptop she had brought with her.

I turned to Brooke. "Task number two. That thing at Grieves's house."

Brooke stopped picking at her nails. She and Grieves exchanged a glance, and Grieves turned a little pale. By now O'Hare's body was probably starting to smell, and the naked and hogtied Gordon next to him would be swimming in his own urine. It was a wicked sort of catch-22. If we had two bodies, we could simply bury them. Walk away. Pretend it never happened.

If we had two hostages, we could simply release them. Walk away. Trust their own self-interest to prevent them from turning to the cops.

But with one body and one hostage, neither option was plausible. We couldn't bring the body back to life, and I still wasn't ready to murder Gordon in cold blood.

"You're not going to..." Brooke trailed off.

"No," I said. "I'm not. But we've got to deal with them,

and we've got to do it without anything coming back on Grieves."

"What did you have in mind?"

"Killing two birds with one stone. Taking care of tasks two and three at once."

Brooke nodded slowly. "And task three is...?"

"Agon," I said, reaching for the Jeep keys. "Task three is Agon. It's time to cut the head off the snake."

62

I took the Jeep and found the nearest electronics store, driving alone. Jacquie was still hard at work on her laptop, and I asked Brooke to work on Grieves. I needed him to start talking again. Ideally, I needed him back in action.

But I would settle for information.

At the electronics store I bought another burner cell phone, a clock radio, a small roll of copper wire, a roll of electrical tape, and a soldering kit. Then I drove to a sporting goods store and loaded out with black coveralls, camouflage face paint, a long hunting knife, and a small box of black powder used in muzzle-loading hunting rifles.

My last stop was another Walmart, where I picked up a single strand of standard incandescent Christmas lights from the already bustling holiday section, a cigarette lighter, a nine-volt battery for the clock radio, and a new pair of heavy-duty wire cutters. Then I pulled through a fast-food drive-through and ordered a sack of breakfast for the team before returning to the hotel. Jacquie passed me a sheet of notebook paper as I entered, filled out in immaculate handwriting with more about Congressman Glenn Pearson than you could find on his own driver's license.

Personal cell phone number. Email address. Pennsylvania residence. DC residence. Even the street address for the barbecued cabin in Sperryville.

I would have been impressed, but coming from Jacquie, it was par for the course. The best investigator I've ever known.

I folded the paper and pocketed it. We stood at the far end of the hotel room, apart from the others. Jacquie cast them a sidelong glance, then lowered her voice.

"I have a question."

I waited, my stomach growing tight. I had a pretty good idea what she wanted to know.

"My contractor?" Jacquie asked.

I thought of Ronald in the warehouse. The moment Holder shot him, a cruel sneer on his face, bloodlust in his eyes. The way he toppled backward, confused and afraid. Stone dead before he knew what happened.

"They killed him," I said.

Jacquie said nothing. She didn't so much as blink. She just nodded once, but something very cold appeared behind her calm gaze.

"You gonna make that right?" she asked.

"You'd better believe it."

Another slight nod. Her shoulders loosened. Jacquie's trademark calm returned.

"Okay then. What next?"

I glanced across the room to where Brooke was digging through the sack of food, unwrapping a sausage biscuit for Grieves. The little guy was still zoned out, but some color had returned to his cheeks. I tilted my head to the door, and Jacquie followed me outside.

"I need them out of the way," I said softly. "I need you to sideline them."

Jacquie frowned. "Excuse me?"

"Don't get butthurt, Jacquie. This is important."

"I'm not a babysitter."

"And they aren't babies. But what comes next is just for me. I need to know they'll be out of the way."

Jacquie looked back to the hotel room door, chewing her lip. Her dark eyes glinted, and she looked sideways at me.

"Is this about the chick?"

I flushed before I could stop myself, looking quickly away. "Of course not. Why would you say that?"

"Because you two have been playing eye-tag all morning. She looks when you're not looking. You look when she's not looking. It's like freaking high school all over again. And, dude, I *hated* high school."

I didn't answer. Jacquie cocked her head.

"Did you knock boots?"

Now I knew I was flushing. I muttered a curse, and Jacquie put a hand on my arm.

"Mason."

I said nothing.

"*Mason.*" Jacquie's voice turned sharp. "Look at me."

I avoided her gaze as a lump swelled in my throat. Three hundred sixty-five days of bottled grief, compressed and distorted, exercised and inflated, surged to the top all at once. It was all I could do to keep myself together. All I could do not to fall apart against that rail, right in front of the world.

I saw Mia. I saw the school. I saw my K-10 and the desert

stars and my fiancée curled up with her Bible. I saw the bodies in North Carolina and the drug den in Atlanta. The summer camp in Alabama and Ronald's head exploding in Jacksonville. I saw sunset in Florida with my violin leaned against a camping chair. Late nights lying beneath the stars in the bed of my pickup, not sleeping for hours.

Asking the same questions over and over again like any of them even mattered.

Why? Why me? What does any of it mean?

And then I saw Brooke. Shirt dropping to the floor. Soft lips pressed against mine. That smell of clean water and fresh flowers as the glow returned to my chest.

Three hundred sixty-five days. One long, blurry, confusing life.

"Look at me," Jacquie whispered. This time I complied, even though I knew she could see the tears in my eyes. To my surprise, there were tears in her eyes, also. But when Jacquie spoke, her voice was gentle. And she smiled, just a little.

"It's okay," she whispered. "All of it. It's gonna be okay."

63

We spent the next six hours inside the hotel room, running out the clock. While Jacquie slept upright in the corner chair like an absolute psychopath, I studied Google Earth images of the compound, and Brooke hyper-focused on Grieves. She had coaxed him into eating and by midafternoon even managed to get him talking again. I hadn't seen him pop any more Xanax, but even while he continued to tremble and fidget in his seat, he was starting to feel like his old self.

I wondered what it must be like to live with such a crippling level of constant anxiety, and part of me regretted ensnaring him in this mess. It wasn't his fault that his employers turned out to be mass-murdering, politically corrupt scum.

Maybe his next job would allow him to work from home. After tonight, he was going to need a new office.

"I need to ask you about Agon," I said, speaking softly as I crouched next to the bed.

Grieves licked his lips, nodding slowly. His eyes were

frozen open, fixed on the carpet, and I suddenly noticed that he had stopped blinking. It was bizarrely unsettling.

"W-what do you need to know?"

I laid a notepad on the table. Clicked a pen open. "I need to know about the evacuation systems. I want to know how to get everyone out."

Grieves looked up. "Get...everyone out?"

I didn't answer. He looked at Brooke, and she didn't comment either.

"What are you going to do?" Grieves said. Sudden calm enveloped his voice. Not confidence, but the closest thing I'd heard to stability since meeting him. I clicked the pen closed. Folded my arms and weighed my options. Then I decided to trust him, because I didn't have much of a choice.

"I'm going to burn it to the ground," I said.

"Everything?" The calm remained.

"Every scrap. Every drone. Every computer. It serves a dual purpose—it'll draw national attention, which will give Davis the fuel she needs to drive her investigation. And it also hits Agon right in the nuts. Hard."

Grieves nodded slowly. "And...nobody is going to get hurt?"

"Nobody innocent is going to be hurt," I said. "That's why I need to know how to evacuate the building."

Grieves kept his palms pressed to his kneecaps, and we all waited.

Finally: "There's an emergency system. For fires or... other emergencies, I guess. It's not difficult to trigger. I can draw you a map."

"That's perfect." I handed him the pad and pen. He rotated the pen in his hand, then looked up.

"How are you going to do it?" he asked.

"Do what?"

"Burn it down."

I chewed the inside of my cheek, and I didn't answer. Everybody else waited. I could feel the tension in the room. Uncertainty, but frustration also. I wasn't sure what to do with that.

Grieves laid the pen down. "L-look. I realize I'm not...you know. I'm not like you. I'm...whatever. But you can't do this without me. And at this point, I want to s-smoke these suckers as bad as anyone. Okay?"

"Me too," Brooke said softly.

"I want to smoke all bad guys," Jacquie said.

Grieves nodded, a little emboldened. His chin rose just a half inch. "Okay. So...we're all in this."

I looked to Brooke. Her shoulders squared. She didn't blink. Then I shot a glare at Jacquie. My old partner sat in the corner, arms folded, popping her gum. A dry smile crept across her lips, and I wanted to shin-kick her.

This wasn't what we had discussed.

"You didn't give me a choice when you joined this fight," Brooke said. "You didn't give Dufort a choice, either. You stepped up...because that's what soldiers do. You can't kick me out now."

"And you?" I said, raising both eyebrows at Grieves.

He shrugged. Swallowed. Flushed. "I...c-control me."

Wow. Way to throw that one in my face.

"You're not good at taking help, Mason," Jacquie said. "Even worse at knowing when you need it."

I glared at Jacquie again. She shot me a sly wink.

"Okay," I said. "If that's how it is."

"That's how it is," Brooke said. There was iron in the

ocean now. I knew there were thoughts there that would need to be expressed later. We didn't have time right now.

"Forget the map," Grieves said. "I should come with you. There may be secure access doors. Some of them are code operated. I can get us through."

All of the uncertainty was gone from his voice. I half-wondered what new kind of pill he had taken, then noted his white fingers clenched around his pants legs. He was holding himself together by a thread.

Not a great guy to have at my side while infiltrating a hostile environment, but to his point about secure access doors, I might not have a choice.

"Okay," I said. "That would be good."

"You'll need a distraction," Jacquie said, popping her gum again. "I'm pretty good at those."

"Did you get rental insurance on the Jeep?" I asked.

"Obviously."

I rearranged the plan in my mind, adding three members to my calculus. Four soldiers in total. Like a Ranger fire team.

I couldn't deny, all plans worked better with a team.

"What about me?" Brooke asked.

"Extraction," I said. "You'll drive the getaway car. Which means we need another rental."

Brooke nodded, reaching for her phone. "I'm on it."

"Again about the fire," Grieves said. "It's a mostly metal building. Lots of fire-retardant construction. I don't see how—"

"Remember what you told me about those drone engines?" I asked.

Grieves frowned. "They're not really engines. More like electric motors, powered by hydrogen fuel cells..."

He trailed off. Looked up.

"There are a lot of test aircraft at that airstrip," I said. "That's a lot of hydrogen to keep on hand. Where is it?"

Grieves pinched his eyebrows together. Then a light bulb clicked on. "In the warehouse, adjacent to the manufacturing facility. A couple of big tanks, I think."

I nodded. "Big tanks. Lots of hydrogen. Just like the *Hindenburg.*"

64

W hen the clock hit five p.m. and the shadows outside lengthened, I knew it was time. I stood next to the window overlooking the parking lot and dug through my pocket. The simple white business card was still there, printed in tight black text. Just a name, a vague title, and a phone number.

No company.

No logo.

I dialed the number into my burner while Jacquie, Grieves, and Brooke waited in silence. I placed the device on speaker and listened to it ring. Once. Twice. Three times.

Holder picked up on four, voice rasping with exhaustion and strain, barking his last name as his only form of greeting.

"Get much sleep last night?" I said.

The phone went dead quiet. For a split second, I thought I might have taken him off guard. Certainly the phone call was surprising, but the protracted silence that followed my voice was intentional and too perfect.

He'd placed me on mute. He was snapping frantic commands.

I just waited.

"That you, Sharpe?"

"Does it sound like me?"

"It sounds like a dead man talking."

There was bravado in his voice, and anger. But I knew the bland insult was calculated to buy him time more than rile me up. I was okay with that. He could have all the time he needed.

"I won't be the one fertilizing daisies when this is over," I said. "You screwed up, Holder. You pushed the wrong people. And you just kept pushing. You signed your death warrant the second you started killing civilians. You made this personal. Remember that when I'm choking you out with my bare hands."

It was a long, theatrical monologue, delivered more methodically than necessary. But I meant every word of it.

Holder didn't reply immediately. I imagined he'd put me on mute again. Maybe he was hissing at his team.

Hurry up. Trace this call!

"What do you want, Sharpe?" Holder demanded.

"A couple of things. We'll start with the most obvious. I've got two of your boys tied up in the closet of a house in Manassas. One of them is dead. The other will be soon if he isn't tended to."

"Good for you. Why are you telling me?"

"Because they're a problem for me. I need that problem erased."

Holder snorted. "And what, you think I'm gonna oblige?"

"Absolutely. Because they're a problem for you, also. You already knew they were missing. If the cops find them, there will be some explaining to do. An investigation. Questions to be answered, like why they were in that house in the first place, or who they work for. It would be much easier for you if you sent somebody to collect them."

The line went quiet again, but this time I thought Holder really was thinking. I could still hear his breath.

"Give me the address," he said, at last.

Grieves had already written his home address on the notepad. I read it off.

"Okay," Holder snapped. "So I mop up your mess. Then what?"

"Then you and I are going to finish this. Once and for all."

"Sounds like a date," Holder growled. "When and where?"

"When you least expect it," I said. "And where it hurts most."

Then I hung up and looked straight to Jacquie. She checked her watch.

"Three minutes, eighteen seconds."

"Long enough?" I asked.

Jacquie snorted. "I could do it in half that time. If he didn't have you on that call, he deserves to be choked with your bare hands."

She shot me a sarcastic look, and I ignored her.

"Are you sure this is a good idea?" Brooke said. "It seems smarter to lead him off. Take the phone someplace in the middle of nowhere."

I looked at the phone in my hand. Thought about Holder in the hallway. Pictured him in a US Army uniform with Ranger tabs on his sleeves.

It would certainly be smarter to lead Holder and his thugs on a wild-goose chase. Leave Culpeper unprotected.

But I'd already promised myself that Holder wasn't walking away. He'd defamed the uniform. Smarter or otherwise, that couldn't be forgiven.

"He's the enemy," I said simply. "We don't run from the enemy."

65

We left the hotel just before sunset, split between the two rentals. Jacquie drove alone in the Jeep while Brooke climbed behind the wheel of a gray Toyota Highlander—compliments of Gordon's credit card this time. He might have reported it stolen, but his hands were tied.

While Brooke drove, I sat in the back alongside Grieves. I had already changed into the black coveralls, and I applied the camo face paint as we hurtled south toward Culpeper.

To his credit, Grieves was managing the stress well. He sat next to me, popping and re-popping his knuckles, watching the cars flash by and saying nothing. I wondered how long that calm would last once the gunfire started, but I knew it wouldn't matter. By then I would already be inside. Grieves's portion of this mission would be concluded.

It would be all up to me.

Once my face was sufficiently mottled in gray and green, I dug into the grocery sack next to me and retrieved the modified clock radio. During our wait at the hotel, I had disassembled the radio and located the two wires that fed the primary speaker—the speaker that chimed when the alarm was triggered. Using copper wire and the soldering kit, I connected those wires to the leads of a single incandescent Christmas bulb.

The light was made of glass. A careful application of the cigarette lighter had turned that glass brittle, allowing me to snap off the tip of the bulb without compromising the delicate filament suspended inside. Now exposed to oxygen, that filament would flash and burn out the moment electricity was applied to the lead wires.

But I didn't need it to glow for long. I only needed it to glow long enough to ignite the thimble's worth of black powder I had packed inside the bulb before covering the hole with electrical tape. With a backup battery applied to the clock radio, the modified device was one alarm away from igniting that black powder in a flash of hot, orange fire.

"Is...that the bomb?" Grieves asked.

"It's a detonator," I said. "It's what makes a bomb go boom."

I checked each connection of the device, then repacked it in the plastic bag. It would ride in my backpack into the Agon facility. And stay there.

"Did the Army teach you that?" Grieves asked.

His voice still quivered, but much of the stuttering had evaporated. I appreciated his focused effort to remain calm. The soldier's way was rubbing off on him. He was controlling his fear now and facing the enemy.

"The Taliban taught me that," I said, tucking the grocery bag into the backpack and thinking briefly about how many American soldiers had died at the hands of devices this rudimentary. A few American soldiers might die at the hands of this one—or ex-soldiers, anyway. Sullied cowards.

It was a poetic fate.

I looked ahead into the rearview mirror and caught Brooke watching me. We still hadn't spoken since fleeing Pearson's cabin—not really. The wall between us remained, reminding me that a conversation was yet to be had.

But not yet.

It was after seven p.m. by the time we neared Culpeper, and full dark. As we took the exit from the interstate, I looked back to find Jacquie riding in the Jeep only twenty yards behind. She still wore sunglasses, her head a shadow behind the windshield.

I raised the first of my burner phones and shot her a quick text.

> Make the first call.

I waited thirty seconds; then the phone in my lap buzzed. The display signaled a forwarded call—originating in the car behind me, from my newest burner phone. Now channeled to mine.

I held the device to my ear and listened as it rang. Holder didn't keep me waiting.

"More favors to ask, asshole?"

"Just checking to see if my last one was completed."

"Oh, absolutely. No problem. I found one of my guys swimming in a pool of his own liquified feces. The other was beat beyond recognition. I torched the house on my way out —you know. *No loose ends.*"

Holder's voice crackled with barely suppressed rage. I

glanced sideways to see if Grieves had heard the bit about his house. If he had, he didn't acknowledge it.

"I'm going to find you, Sharpe," Holder snarled. "I'm going to break you in half. The girl, too. And that ratty little nerd who snuck you past my guys. If you had half a brain, you'd be running for the hills—"

I hung up and signaled Brooke to turn right at the next light. Jacquie turned left, and the Jeep's taillights faded over the next hill. Grieves wiped sweaty palms over his pants legs. I thought about the face paint I wore and was glad I hadn't offered him any. He would have smeared it all over the car by now.

"Five minutes out," Brooke whispered. Her voice was soft, but not weak. I just nodded.

In my mind I could see Holder and his men at the Agon facility, scrambling to trace my last call. Without a GPS link, they would be unable to determine my precise location, but triangulation was a lot better tool than it used to be, and Holder was a man with resources. There weren't that many roads out here, either. With a little guesswork, Holder would settle on a route of approach and deploy his men accordingly.

The rolling Virginia mountains and open fields dotted with livestock grew darker the deeper we drove into the countryside. By the GPS mounted in the Toyota's dash, I traced our route three miles north of Jacquie's path. Each of us circled slowly toward the Agon facility as Jacquie made another call to Holder. The call forwarded to my phone, and I hung up the moment Holder answered.

As though I'd called by mistake. As though I had no idea he was tracking me.

Her Jeep wound slowly closer to Agon's front entrance

while Brooke piloted the Toyota onto the same road Grieves and I had escaped on following our last visit to Agon. The road at the top of the hill, beyond the trees where I had fought the drones.

The name of the game tonight would be reaching my target before more of those drones were deployed.

Brooke stopped the Toyota near where she had picked Grieves, Dufort, and me up that night, but she didn't cut the engine. She just waited, and I looked out the window into the trees. I remembered the long path amid thick under-brush to the fence. The hole in the fence that would no doubt be patched by now. I'd need to cut a new one. Then I would reverse my progress across the open field, between the hangars, over the tarmac, and straight into the ware-house facility. All while keeping Grieves alive.

"You sure you're up for this?" I asked, not looking away from the window. Grieves knew I was talking to him. He swallowed audibly.

"You can't do it without me," he said weakly.

"Not easily." I faced him. "But easier than having you crap out on me."

Sweat glistened on his forehead. He nodded a couple of times. Scrubbed his hands over his pants again. Then he faced me for perhaps the first time since we met—truly eye to eye. Man to man.

"I control me," he said.

I smiled. "Hell yeah you do."

My phone buzzed, and I unlocked it to find a text from Jacquie. Two short words.

In position.

I texted back.

> Stand by.

Then Grieves and I piled out. The air outside the Toyota was crisp and cold. It stung my lungs a little and made me miss Florida. I stretched to loosen my muscles, and doubled-checked the knife tucked into my right pocket.

My only weapon. But if this thing went off according to plan, it would be more than enough.

I shot Grieves one last questioning look, and he simply nodded. He looked okay. At least as good as he'd looked the first time we'd tried this stunt. I turned back to shoot Brooke a thumbs-up, but she no longer sat behind the wheel. The driver's door was open, and Brooke stood at the tail of the Toyota, shifting her weight awkwardly from one foot to the other.

I met her there, leaving Grieves at the edge of the road. Brooke shivered a little in the light breeze. Her face was paler than it had looked in Florida. Her eyes a little wider, her raven hair a little frizzier.

But still so beautiful.

She opened her mouth, then stopped. I closed the distance between us and wrapped her in a hug. Her lips met mine, and when she drew her face away, there was black grease paint on her nose. I saw tears in the ocean eyes, and she kissed me again.

"We'll talk," I said. "Later."

I gave her body a squeeze; then she returned quickly to the Toyota. The driver's door shut, and the motor rumbled. I watched as Brooke faded around the corner, already engaged with the next leg of her mission.

Leaving Grieves and me standing in the cold, where I was surprised to see the hint of a smug smile hanging on his lips.

"Shut up," I muttered. "And fall in."

Then we both turned for the trees and embraced the darkness.

66

I jogged like a wraith through the forest. Moving silently. Rushing from tree to tree, headed straight for the Agon facility. Grieves tagged along a great deal less quietly, but followed directions without complaint.

Even as the road disappeared behind us and the cold black of night closed on every side, he didn't falter. He didn't hesitate as we moved deeper into the trees, ever closer to the inevitable reality ahead.

I didn't worry about drones. I didn't worry about the fence or any of Holder's goons. All of those were defensive measures, used in a reactionary capacity—a critical error that any true veteran shouldn't have been guilty of. The best defense is always a good offense.

But when you have a nine-figure facility packed with hundreds of millions of dollars' worth of next-gen technology, you can't afford to be racing around on the offensive. You have to dig in. You have to wait.

You have to pray that you don't get outsmarted.

We reached the northern line of the twelve-foot fence

and scanned both ways for cameras, drones, or pacing personnel. I was deep in the woods, about half a mile from where I had first dueled the X-40s while fleeing the compound. The ground was a little more level here, but the undergrowth impossibly dense. It grew right to the fence line, some vines and brambles actually tangled amongst the chain link.

Another sloppy mistake. With unlimited cover at the fence line, it was impossible to conduct complete surveillance. It didn't look like Bridgewater was even trying.

Meatheads, indeed.

I slid to my knees and worked the heavy wire cutters I'd bought at Walmart. Each galvanized segment of fencing required focused pressure to snap, but I only need a small window to squeeze through. I peeled away a two-by-two-foot section and replaced the cutters in my pack. Then reached for my phone. I dialed Jacquie directly this time. I kept my voice low.

"Anything?"

"They've passed me twice on patrol," Jacquie said. "More dark sedans. They're definitely out looking for you."

"They haven't seen you?"

Jacquie snorted. "This ain't my first stakeout."

"Right. Make the call."

I hung up and waited. Jacquie's forwarded call to Holder rang right through, and I picked up on my end. Holder was just as quick.

"Sweating yet?" I asked. "I'm close, Holder."

"You're disappointing me, Sharpe. I read someplace that you were a Ranger. But Rangers are better than this."

"You know I read something similar about you—and I thought the same."

Holder's teeth ground audibly. "Spare me the self-righteous drivel. You got something to say, come on out and say it."

"Don't mind if I do."

I hung up and texted Jacquie.

Now.

I couldn't hear the roar of the Jeep's motor from nearly two miles away—beyond the tarmac, the facility, the far side of the fence. Beyond the gate and up the road to the winding forest road. It was too far away for the chirp of tires and rumble of the big motor to carry over the wind. But I pictured it in my mind. I saw Jacquie hurtling out of cover. Hitting the road and steering for the front entrance of the facility. Crashing along altogether too fast—like a Taliban insurgent behind the wheel of a Toyota pickup, a fifty-cal swinging from a mount in the back.

I pictured Holder's roving patrols—deployed after he traced my series of calls to that side of the facility—responding like dogs let off a leash. A scent on the wind, blood in the air. Hurtling forward to protect the gate. A storm of radio traffic sending shock waves of alarm through the Bridgewater security force.

Threat, main gate. Respond, respond!

I didn't hear the engines, the tires, or the radios. But I knew I was right when I heard the alarm. Distant and vague, rising from the front of the facility over a mile away and carrying on the wind.

My phone buzzed. It was Jacquie.

"I'm clear! Go!"

I hung up and ducked through the hole. Grieves followed. Together we crashed through the forest, moving quickly now. Sticking to the shadows but not stressing about the dry leaves or brittle twigs. The siren continued. I knew Holder would be on his radio, deploying his forces to respond to the Jeep, and once they found it empty and nose-down in a ditch, ordering them to search the woods and the road in both directions.

To *find* Mason Sharpe.

We reached the edge of the tree line, and I looked across a damp field of grass, beyond the hangars full of test drones and across a tarmac blinking with red and green lights to the facility beyond. A night test was underway. A large, Predator-style drone was landing, another humming at idle in a taxi lane.

I caught my breath and looked quickly in both directions for signs of Bridgewater personnel. I saw only two, both dressed in full-black tactical gear, both rushing from a hangar to the main building. They entered through a back door near a loading dock, vanishing as the door closed.

"Ready?" I asked.

Grieves breathed hard. But he nodded.

"Remember," I said. "Once I'm inside and the alarm is triggered, you clear out. Back to the fence, back to the road. Signal Brooke and burn rubber. You got me? No matter what happens. You follow orders."

Nervous energy overtook the fear in Grieves's eyes. Adrenaline was working its magic. The anxiety that plagued his mind was beat back by biological programming that overrode fear and commanded him to *act*.

It was a good sign.

"Good copy," I said. "You say good copy."

Grieves drew a deep breath. "Good copy."

I checked the path ahead, marking a clear route to the back of the building—to the same door Holder's people had just entered through. Into the warehouse, adjacent to the hydrogen storage facility.

Straight into the heart of the structure.

Then I smacked Grieves on the shoulder, and we both sprinted out of the shadows.

67

G rieves ran hard, but I still had to slow a little to keep from leaving him behind. We reached the edge of the tarmac, and the whirring propeller of the nearby drone resting at idle brought memories flooding back—memories of Iraq. Of Air Force tarmacs filled with similar drones. Or smaller Army airfields stocked with Black Hawk and Chinook helicopters.

Much louder aircraft, with a similar cadence of thumping propellers. A war zone, more similar to this than it now appeared.

Holder and Agon had pushed too far.

"Keep moving," I hissed, dropping my hand into my pocket to retrieve the knife as my feet hit the tarmac. The darkness was thick at the end of the runway, broken only by dim runway lights blinking red every couple of seconds. I didn't see any personnel near the drones, or any Bridgewater security members protecting the back side of the facility ahead. I only saw the door, drawing yards nearer. Grieves heaving behind me. The drone whirring nearby.

We reached the grass again, and still nobody had stopped us. No alarms sounded. No floodlights flashed on. I pressed my back against the rear of the warehouse wall, knife held at the ready. Grieves was four seconds behind, lagging and staggering. He caught himself on the concrete steps leading up to the door. I noted his shaking knees and spoke calmly.

"Take five. Catch your breath. You're good."

Grieves braced himself on the concrete and heaved. I looked up the steps to the door. It was protected by a key card reader, but just as Grieves had said, there was also a keypad glistening beneath a very dim light. I pictured the warehouse interior. All those rows of metal shelves, lined by X-40 drones and God only knew what other methods of carnage. According to Grieves's map, the hydrogen storage lay at the far west end of the building—farther removed from the manufacturing facility than I would have liked, but given enough hydrogen, it wouldn't matter.

"You good?" I hissed.

Grieves straightened. He took the steps without waiting for me to urge him, wiping his brow, then inputting a code on the keypad.

A red light flashed. The door failed to unlock. Grieves gritted his teeth, looking more irritated than concerned. He input another code. Another red light.

"What's happening?" I demanded.

"They ch-changed the codes," Grieves said, a tremor carrying through his voice.

"Are we locked out?"

Grieves forced a very insincere smile. "P-please. There's a f-fire code used to render access to first responders. It will override the lock, but it also tr-triggers an alarm in the security center. It's your call."

I looked down the length of the building, measuring the distance to the hydrogen bays. Thinking about how many doors might block our path, and how many people we might encounter.

"How far to the evacuation alarm?"

"There's an emergency control panel just inside."

Screw it.

"Go," I said.

Grieves input the code. The red light was replaced by a green, and the door clicked. I didn't hear an alarm, but that didn't surprise me. It was likely silent.

Grieves yanked the door open, and I passed inside, ducking into a hallway paved with industrial concrete and lined by more metal doors. Grieves led the way, hands shaking, shoulders trembling. But not stopping. He marched quickly to the end of the hall, where a T-shaped intersection offered paths to the left and right. I heard voices someplace not far away. Grieves ignored them, proceeding directly to the far wall, where a large computer panel outlined by red plastic was built into the wall. There was a cabinet housing a fire hose and an ax. A red lever for triggering the fire alarm.

Grieves bypassed both and hit the computer panel. His fingers flew over the keys, his lips moving silently as he worked. The computer asked for a code, and he punched it in. The input was good this time. The voices grew louder, joined by thumping footfalls. Too fast to be casual. Too urgent to be business as usual.

"Hurry," I hissed.

Grieves didn't look up. He slapped the return key with the side of one hand. Then he waited.

A split second went by like a minute in slow motion. Then a blaring alarm ripped down the hallway, accompanied by flashing white and red lights. It was louder than loud —brighter than bright. I was momentarily disoriented as the recording of a male voice joined the cacophony.

"Attention all departments: Toxic gas leak detected in manufacturing. Evacuate the building immediately. Proceed to your vehicles and exit the parking lot in an orderly manner. Make way for first responders. Repeat: Toxic gas leak detected..."

I tuned the alarm out and grabbed Grieves by the arm, yanking him back down the hallway. The footsteps marching toward us were lost in the noise, but I was no longer worried about them. Anybody dumb enough to stand in my way now would get what was coming to them.

"Good work," I said, speaking close to Grieves's ear. "Now go!"

I smacked him on the arm, and to my surprise the little guy extended a trembling hand. I shook it once.

"Good luck," he mouthed.

Then he was gone—back out the exit door. Back across the tarmac and through the woods to Brooke and her Toyota.

I turned toward the blare of the alarm, the hunting knife clasped in one hand. Headed for the hydrogen.

68

I sprinted down the hall. White lights flashing, alarm blaring, recorded voice repeating the same message over and over. Most of the facility was empty, just as it had been the last time Grieves and I broke in. Office workers and layers of middle management don't work the third shift. Only essential staff for deadline manufacturing would be present, and the alarm was driving them out. I reached the next door and still hadn't seen anyone. The door was closed, but the lock opened automatically as I pressed on the latch —electronically disabled to aid in evacuation.

Grieves's little trick had worked. The facility was wide open, and I burst back into the warehouse section without meeting resistance. The same rows of boxed drones greeted me as before, but I now noted a pair of open rolling doors with trucks backed in to a loading dock. Two abandoned forklifts and a pallet jack sat in the middle of an open space between the shelves. An abandoned lunch box rested on a table next to a six-pack of soda.

But no people. The workers had fled.

I checked my watch. Eighteen minutes had passed since Jacquie ran the rental Jeep into the ditch in front of the facility. Holder and his crew would have reached the wreck by now and searched the surrounding forest. They wouldn't have found me. They wouldn't have found Jacquie, either. She would be long gone, melted into the darkness like a shadow, waiting for extraction from Brooke and the Highlander.

The Bridgewater thugs might have hunted for a while, but then the alarm would have gone off behind them. The evacuation alert. Holder would have put two and two together, realizing he'd been duped. Even now he would be fighting his way through the current of fleeing worker bees.

I was already running out of time.

I moved beyond the shelves and the open loading docks to the next door, nearly a hundred yards away. It was unlocked, just like the last one. The next segment of the facility was a supply bay full of all kinds of raw materials used in the manufacturing of drones. Steel, plastics, lots of wire. All organized on shelves with another forklift on standby. The alarm pounded from overhead. I quickened my step.

Then a door someplace to my left burst open, and heavy boots thumped the ground between blasts of the alarm. I swung instinctively into the shadows between two high shelves full of drone components. Through a gap in the shelves ahead, I noted two men marching into the room from my left—fifty yards out. I saw black tactical vests and MP5 submachine guns swinging from single-point slings. Rubber gas masks held in place by tight straps.

It was Holder's praetorian guard, farther ahead of the game than I estimated. Suspicious of a trick, but not completely convinced that the alarm from inside the facility wasn't actually a terrible coincidence. Hence the gas masks.

I checked my watch and wondered how long it would be before first responders arrived. I had to finish before then. I didn't have *time* for this.

I held the hunting knife next to my face. The two Bridgewater guys proceeded inward, hands wrapped around the grips of their MP5s, flashlights blazing from their muzzles. They moved in a tight tandem formation. One guy leading. The second guy covering. Sweeping the shelves with LED beams, quickly clearing one segment of the warehouse after another.

It was inevitable that they located me. Only a matter of time. My edged weapon would be no match for a pair of MP5s operated by trained professionals. They were forcing my hand.

I eased down the length of the shelf, remaining undercover. My Walmart hiking boots moved silently over the concrete as I danced sideways, riding the edge of a flashlight beam. Circling slowly to the left, back the way I came. I drew even with them, but they couldn't see me. Their peripheral vision was hampered by the heavy rubber gas masks. I started forward, feet soft on the concrete. Passing the knife off to my left hand, I rotated the blade until its single edge faced me.

Ready for combat. Because the enemy had arrived.

The two guys moved in tandem another five yards. The guy in the front swept left and right with his MP5 while the guy behind conducted broader, slower rotations. My foot thumped the concrete a little harder than I had intended. Both men froze.

It was too late for them. I reached the guy in back and

grabbed him by the straps of his gas mask, wrenching his head back. He choked in mad panic, flailing with the MP5. My knife hand swept up and slashed his throat, tearing through skin, muscle, and windpipe in one savage slash. The guy in front dove automatically for cover, sidestepping behind a shelf. Pivoting around. Raising the MP5.

Long before he brought it to bear on me, I released the gas mask and caught the dying guy's fallen MP5 as it dangled from its sling. The second guard opened fire. I found the MP5's trigger and returned fire. Bullets slammed into the chest plate of the throat-cut guard on top of me. I stumbled backward and started to fall. I clamped the trigger again.

The next three-round burst of the captured MP5 caught the second Bridgewater guy right in the gas mask, and we all hit the floor.

The throat-cut guy was still rasping for a last, desperate breath as I pushed his body off me. Death clouded his eyes as he hit the floor. I didn't wait to check for a pulse. After returning the knife to its belt sheath, I disconnected the MP5 from its quick-detach sling, flipped the weapon light off, and took an extra magazine from his plate carrier.

Then I was sprinting again, across the storage room. Straight for the giant rolling door with two massive signs bolted next to it. The first was black and red and printed with bold words:

DANGER: HYDROGEN.

The second was more nuanced. It included the illustration of an open flame with a circle and a cross over it. Tighter lines of text printed beneath barred the use of any spark or open flame.

The *Hindenburg* had left a legacy, it seemed. But not enough of one. They should have placed this stuff in a concrete bunker. Maybe Agon had decided to cut corners. It was a decision that would cost them.

I reached the door and tore off the plastic cover mounted over the electronic controls. I mashed the button to raise the door, and was met with a flashing red light and no movement. I mashed it again, checking for a safety switch.

There was none. The mechanism must have been disabled by the leaking gas alarm. Smart enough—you didn't want your hydrogen bay open during an emergency. But unless that door opened, this party was over before it began.

I searched the length of the wall and found a personnel access door—solid steel save for a reinforced glass panel about six inches wide. I tried the handle, but it wouldn't open. There was a keypad and a card reader, and both flashed red in cadence with the alarm still blaring overhead.

Disabled, like the rolling door next to them. I didn't have time for that.

Ramming the MP5 against the glass, I fired four times in a tight square, driving spiderweb cracks in every direction. Then I flipped the gun around and smacked the butt into the center of the square.

Glass shattered, exposing a tight mesh of the reinforcement wires. I went to work with the wire cutters, heart thumping, blood surging. I could feel the clock in my mind, counting up the seconds since Grieves had triggered the emergency alarm.

The building would be empty by now, but first responders would arrive soon. Culpeper wasn't that far away. Was there a standing fire department?

I rammed my hand through the hole and caught the latch on the inside. Unlike the exterior latch, this one succeeded in disabling the lock. No doubt designed that way to allow for escape in an emergency.

The door opened, and I dropped the cutters. The hydrogen bay beyond was dark, but illuminated every two seconds like clockwork by the flash of the emergency lights.

Looming in the shadows, twenty feet ahead, two massive cylinders rested on metal frames, each as large as a semi-truck trailer.

I was in.

69

I flicked the MP5's weapon light on and ran to the first cylinder. The front of it was fit with a mess of complex copper pipes and gauges, most of them leading toward the wall that faced the airfield. For refueling, no doubt. I had no idea how any of that worked—I only knew that hydrogen is typically stored as a compressed gas.

A gas that is very, very explosive.

I located a spot beneath a two-inch copper fitting and slid to my knees. The backpack came off, and the clock radio came out. I had taped the copper wires attached to the Christmas light on top of the clock, reducing the entire unit into a compact cube about the size of a softball. The LED numerals on the face of the clock glowed 3:38, which was radically incorrect, but that didn't matter. It only mattered what time I set the alarm for.

I checked my watch again and thought about incoming first responders. The countdown had to be fast enough to detonate before they arrived, but slow enough to allow time for my escape.

I picked eight minutes and set the alarm for 3:46. I switched my watch from stopwatch to timer and set the time for the same. Then I set the device beneath the tank, a few feet from the copper pipes. I returned to the door and found a fire locker mounted next to it, housing a fire hose, a fire extinguisher, and a red fire ax.

The first blow of the ax to the pipe bent it but failed to rupture it. The next blow opened a tiny crack. I smelled nothing—no thick, sweet odor like I was accustomed to detecting from the little propane bottles I camped with. But I heard a hiss, and when my hand passed over the crack, I felt cold air rushing by my hand.

I struck again. Twice more. Then the brass fixture nearest the tank tore away from the pipe, opening a two-inch portal of unlit hellfire.

Immediately the air left my lungs. My chest felt heavy, and I stumbled back, holding my breath as I dropped the ax and turned for the door. The pipe behind me sounded like a gushing fire hydrant—more of a roar than a hiss. I reached the door and checked my watch. Seven minutes, two seconds remained.

I ripped the door open and crunched over broken glass, stepping back into the storage room...and straight into a burst of automatic fire.

The door thumped shut behind me as I struck the concrete, bullets whistling overhead and smacking the concrete block wall. My captured MP5 was pinned beneath me as I thrashed away from the door and along the wall. I couldn't bring it to bear on the shooter from across the room, but I didn't want to, anyway. I was thinking about that surge of gas filling the hydrogen room and reaching the security window I had shattered.

I was thinking about muzzle flash.

The gunshots ceased as I passed behind one end of an industrial shelf. I could no longer detect the nuance of the footsteps between the blare of the alarm—my hearing was shot. My head pounded. The flash of LEDs and repeated warnings of the recorded voice filled my skull.

Ironically, those warnings were now legitimized.

"You'd better not shoot!" I shouted. "You smell that? That's hydrogen. One more trigger pull, and we all go up!"

The gunman couldn't smell anything—hydrogen is odorless. But it was the quickest way I could think of to communicate my point.

Get to the door. Get the hell out.

"Bullshit!" a macho male voice shouted back. I didn't recognize it, but other than Holder, I had spoken to very few of the Bridgewater goons.

"Try me and see!" I called back. "You'll be dead before you know what happened."

My chest felt heavy again, like it had in the hydrogen bay. I could feel the breathable air vacating the room, driven out by the surge of raw gas. I briefly wondered if the sparking Christmas light charged with black powder would ignite the hydrogen in the absence of plentiful oxygen.

I wasn't waiting to find out.

I made a quick dash to my right, across an open aisle between shelves. Farther from the hydrogen bay. To my left I saw the gunman, twenty yards down the aisle, MP5 raised. But he didn't fire. He staggered right as I ran past, his eyes flashing wide behind a gas mask.

He'd come prepared, just like his buddies. But gas masks are nothing more than fancy filters, and without breathable air to filter, he might as well have been wearing a ski mask.

The gunman moved instinctively right, circling to get behind me. A good tactic, minus the surge of hydrogen pouring into the room from that angle.

I abandoned him, sprinting directly to the wall and turning for the next door. The door back into the primary warehouse stacked with boxed X-40s.

The gunman hit the ground behind me, his body starved of oxygen, blackness closing around him. My own vision narrowed, and my heart thundered as I reached the door. I drove through without concern for what lay ahead, head thumping as my body sent louder and louder demands for oxygen to my brain. I was close to passing out. The flood of hydrogen was winning. I didn't even bother to check my watch as I barreled into the next room, gasping for air.

And then I stopped.

Holder stood twenty yards away, framed by thirty-foot-high industrial shelves stacked with boxed X-40s, blocking my path. His feet were spread apart. His shoulders squared toward me, braced in a fighting stance.

An MP5 already shouldered, the muzzle centered on my chest.

Holder wore a gas mask like his men, but his eyes were visible behind the curved face shield. Narrow and dark, glaring hellfire at me, his right index finger curled around the trigger.

But not firing. Not yet.

I didn't move. The heaviness was returning to my chest. The wave of gushing hydrogen had reached the warehouse. I imagined an invisible blanket of it surging over my head— lighter than air. Filling the ceiling first before inevitably descending over the floor.

Holder could fire, and we might both go up. Or we might not. It was a roll of the dice.

I smiled.

"What you gonna do, Holder?"

Holder didn't move the gun. He kept both hands wrapped around it in a perfect fighting stance. Then I saw his eyes glance upward. I followed them and noted a wavy distortion of fluorescent light from the overheads. Distorted by gas—the invisible rendered visible for a split second.

"Hydrogen," I said, still smiling. "I wouldn't pull that trigger if I were you."

Holder's gaze returned to me. His eyes hardened.

Then he slowly lowered the MP5. He reached up with his left hand and tore the gas mask free, exposing his handsome, leering face.

The *consultant*.

"First responders coming?" I said.

Holder spat. "I held them at the gate."

"I thought you might. Wanna hide the bodies first, right?"

Holder looked over his shoulder, back toward the ceiling, as if he could check the volume of gas. Gauge his time. Then he threw down the MP5 and drew a long black combat knife from his belt. The silver edge glistened as it rotated in his palm, then pointed toward me.

"Just one," he snarled.

I took a step forward. Drew the knife from my belt. Glanced down at my watch.

Five minutes remaining. I could run now—sprint past him and reach the door. Get outside and stall for time. Deal with Holder later. Maybe appear at his house, late one night, and slip up from behind.

But no. Not a chance. I wasn't a murderer, I was a soldier. This was a field of battle, and the pig standing in front of me had sworn an oath and then broken it to the tenth degree. He'd betrayed his country. Betrayed the Army. Betrayed the brotherhood.

He'd become the enemy.

I clenched my fingers around the knife and started toward him.

70

Holder met me halfway, his long legs eating up the space between us with the MP5 abandoned on the ground behind him. He rolled the knife as he walked, bold jaw clenching, dark eyes blazing hatred. He was bigger than me—not by a lot, but enough to notice. Slightly larger arms, slightly broader chest.

I didn't care. That only made him a bigger target. He might be a badass in a tactical vest with a list of martial arts titles as long as his arm, but I'd been a scrapper since I was four years old. And, perhaps more importantly...I wasn't afraid of being cut.

"You know what I hated most about the Army?" Holder snarled as the gap between us shrank to four feet, and we automatically began to circle.

"Feeling like a fake all day?"

Holder's lip curled. He spat again. "Ha. Exhibit A. It was the self-righteous, stuck-up pricks like you, Sharpe. All the rah-rah, chest-thumping, patriot horseshit."

"I wouldn't expect you to understand any of the above,

Holder. It's a big army. Throw enough life-forms in the mix, and you're bound to end up with a few bottom-feeding dogs."

Holder's teeth clinched. I knew he was going to lunge even before his shoulders tightened. The knife rose, and he spun sideways. I swung easily to my right, missing the blade by half an inch, and swiping down with my own. Metal met flesh, just skimming his arm, but biting deep enough to draw blood.

Holder flinched and withdrew. Again we circled as the oppressive weight returned to my chest. Not bad, yet. Just like the weight you feel when you're driving into the mountains and the air begins to thin.

You know you're running out of oxygen.

Holder remained tense, muscles bunched, jaw trembling. I could see the bloodlust in his eyes like a hungry hound—the very dog I had described. It wasn't the first time I'd seen it. What had I hated most about the Army?

The scum like Holder who defiled the uniform.

"You should have shot me, Holder. By the time the firemen get here, there won't be enough left of you to identify."

Holder lunged again, aiming for my chest this time. Depending on my inability to dodge the weapon. Counting on me to stumble back and flail with my arms. Maybe drop my knife.

I counter-lunged instead, slashing for his face. I was out of range, but the biological instincts buried deep in his psyche didn't allow him time to calculate for range. The emergency signal was the same, regardless.

Protect face!

He ducked his head, staggering sideways. His knife hand

sliced past my ribcage, tearing through my shirt and ripping through skin. I kept pressing, slamming into him full force. Now I was within range, and while his knife arm was extended and trapped against my ribcage by my elbow, my knife arm was wide open.

My next slash sliced right through his face, ripping into his mouth and shredding flesh on its way out. Blood sprayed across my forehead, and Holder shrieked. I jerked left, snatching the knife out and bending his arm backwards at the elbow, all at once. The force of the movement was sudden and overwhelming. His weapon clattered to the floor, but he wasn't out of the fight. He ripped his right arm free and swung a left hook toward my jaw.

It was a natural instinct—to go for my face the way I'd gone for his. But now my knife was beneath his arm. My head twisted left, my right ear catching the edge of his fist as it ripped past. I flipped the knife in my hand and drove it down—hard. Beneath the body armor. Above his belt. Right into that fleshy part of unprotected abdomen just north of his pelvis.

The knife sank all the way to the hilt, and Holder howled. He staggered back, and I let him go, giving him a little shove with my left palm and releasing the knife. Leaving it up to the hilt in his side.

Holder's shoulder blades struck a shelf, and two boxed X-40s hit the ground. His face washed white with pain, and his left hand found the knife in his side. I wiped my lip and checked my watch.

Three minutes, twenty-two seconds.

I knelt and retrieved his fallen blade.

"Come on, Holder. You done already?"

Holder's jaw shook. His fingers closed around the knife

in his side, and his eyes bulged as he ripped it free. Another guttural cry burst from his throat. I thought he might fall. The air was thin, and his face had turned blue. My own vision darkened around the edges.

But I wasn't going anywhere.

"I will always keep myself mentally alert," I shouted over the screeching alarm. "Physically strong, morally straight."

Holder's arm shook as the blade rose. He clamped his free hand over the gushing wound even as my own blood streamed down my ribcage. I ignored it. Holder lunged, and I sidestepped him, driving my left elbow into his ear hard enough to bust a melon. Holder screamed.

"I will shoulder more than my share of the task, whatever it may be," I snapped, pivoting around him and driving my boot into his lower back. Holder slammed face-first into another line of X-40s. The blinking red and white lights gleamed across his left leg where crimson blood had saturated the black fabric.

"One hundred percent," I boomed. "And then some!"

Holder whirled, releasing his wounded side and clenching both hands around the knife. He charged me. I didn't move. I kept my blade at my side. Shoulders squared. Jaw clenched. Speaking through my teeth.

"Gallantly will I show the world that I am a specially selected and well-trained soldier."

Holder reached me. The bloody blade plummeted toward my throat. His bulky body crushed ahead like a charging Mack truck, all muscled mass and wild eyes.

I moved at the last second, slamming my left forearm against his hands and driving them to the side. Sending the blade over my left shoulder and into a box behind. His own momentum carried him on, right into my chest. Right into my open arms.

My left arm clamped around his back and pulled him in. Our chests crashed together with a meaty thud. The breath left my lungs. His spit and blood sprayed across my face as the breath left his lungs.

I raised the knife and drove the tip over his shoulder blades and straight into the base of his unprotected neck. Just an inch, sharp and sudden enough to send his eyes bulging out of his head, more blood spraying from his lips. He choked.

I kept him in the bear hug. Pulling him close. Snarling through my teeth.

"*Never* shall I fail my comrades. Under no circumstances will I ever embarrass my country."

Holder's gaze turned very cold—flooded by raw, unbridled hate. His teeth clenched. He began to fall.

I held him up, one hand still wrapped around my knife. Then I spoke the final words. I finished the oath.

"*Rangers lead the way!*"

I rammed the weapon up to the hilt, straight through his spinal column. Holder's eyes rolled back in his head, and his body went limp. I let the knife drop with his body, gasping a little as the polluted air in my lungs further thinned. I blinked, and my eyes stung, but it wasn't from tears.

I felt zero remorse as I kicked my feet clear of the body and spat blood from my mouth. My watch read ninety seconds. I gave Holder a final, disgusted glare; then I started toward the door in a fast walk.

I didn't bother with the little side door Grieves and I had used. I went for the open loading dock instead, my most direct access to fresh air. Dropping off the loading dock, I broke into a run for the tree line.

I made it halfway up the hill before the blast ripped through the Virginia countryside, louder than a JDAM bomb striking a Taliban stronghold. I hurtled to my knees as a sizzling-hot shock wave slammed against my back, shoving me forward. As I turned and looked toward the facility, I saw nothing but fire. The entire building was gone, shreds of sheet metal, industrial supplies and a few hundred AI-operated drones glistening in the sky like fireworks.

Only half the office building remained. None of the manufacturing facility. Even the hangars next to the airfield were on fire. Agon and their billion-dollar war machine was little more than a basin of embers and ashes.

I pulled myself upright against a tree and just enjoyed the warmth on my face. One arm clamped against my side helped to stem some of the blood flow from my wound, but as my heart thumped, I could feel more sticky hot wetness creeping down my leg.

I wiped my jaw. Straightened my back. Thought about Matthew Pearson and Tyler Spraggins. About Ronald the contractor, and Clay Dufort the Navy SEAL. About all those bodies left in Yemen. Abandoned and forgotten. Sold out by their own country.

I cast a sharp salute toward the inferno—for all of them.

Then I turned up the hillside and fought toward the fence. One more target left to engage.

71

Congressman Glenn Pearson's Pennsylvania home was nothing short of a mansion. It sat behind a broad metal gate, surrounded by an immense rolling golf course and a host of similar houses, all stone-faced with circular driveways. Four- and five-car garages. Multilevel pools. In-home spas.

Luxuries reserved for the rich and generally earned by years of hard work and success.

But not in the case of one Glenn Pearson. For the congressman, these luxuries were the spoils of war—literal war. Blood money, stained by the sacrifice of men and women who would never taste such opulence.

I parked the rented Toyota at a grocery store a mile away from the gated neighborhood and started through the woods in the general direction of the golf course, walking easily and enjoying the crisp morning air. Ironically enough, it was warmer in Pennsylvania than it had been in Virginia. It occurred to me that this was the first time I'd ever visited the Keystone State, and I wished I had time to swing through

Philadelphia and eat a cheesesteak. I wondered if they were really as good as people claimed, or if the Liberty Bell was worth seeing.

There was something to be said for the symbolism of cracked liberty. Even in the purest of intentions, voids always emerge. Little grimy creatures crawl through them, hiding from the light. Gathering in the grit and feeding off the deterioration of a once flawless symbol.

Or maybe I was reading too far into the metaphor.

I reached a pathetic little six-foot chain-link fence and flipped over it with ease, landing in more dry leaves and reaching the edge of the golf course. I used my phone's built-in GPS to track a path around the perimeter of the elite property, all the way to the back where Pearson's eight-thousand-square-foot mansion sat, a sprawling rear deck overlooking a rolling field and a rippling creek.

The view of country living, without any of the inconvenience. More poetry of corruption.

Pausing at the edge of the property, I snapped on a pair of surgical gloves before circling away from the street and the driveway. I tacked toward the massive back deck overlooking that countryside view instead. I heard Pearson's voice long before I saw him. Barking and angry, carrying the tone of a man speaking into a phone. It rang from atop the deck. As I neared, I smelled the fresh water of the babbling creek, clean and somehow sweet.

It reminded me of Brooke.

By the time I left the trees, I could see Pearson standing on the deck, his back turned to me as he jabbed a coffee cup at the creek and barked into a cell phone. There was no security nearby, but I didn't expect any. Housed behind his iron gate and his six-foot chain-link fence, Pearson felt safe.

This was his home, after all. The headquarters where he felt most comfortable in conducting his filthiest business. He didn't want security around. He didn't want anyone to overhear the call.

I overheard it, and I knew what it was about. The smoked Agon facility. The dead Bridgewater thugs, cooked to a crisp inside. The complete lack of clues as to who, or *what*, had made the attack.

An accident, the fire department thought. A problem with the hydrogen bays. A leak that had triggered the evacuation alarm, followed by some manner of ignition that resulted in the blast. They couldn't be certain, of course. The fire had consumed the security cameras. Immediate footage from inside the facility had been lost.

Pearson wasn't buying it. He wanted answers. He wanted *blood*.

I stepped silently up the stairs and onto the deck. I glanced sideways through a sprawling panel of thick glass into the living room and open kitchen of the mansion. I saw a dog. Dirty dishes in the sink, dirty clothes on the couch.

No other people. And no security.

Pearson hung up with a curse and flung his coffee cup into the yard. Black coffee sprayed across the grass before the mug broke on the ground. He turned for the back door, face flushed, jaw clenched.

Then he saw me, and his face paled. He stopped, eyes wide, and dropped the phone.

I didn't move. I just stood at the far end of the deck, hands in my pockets, shoulders relaxed.

"Hello, Congressman."

Pearson looked behind me, as though he expected there to be others.

"I'm alone," I said. "And unarmed."

It was mostly true. I hadn't brought any weapons. Then again...I didn't need any.

Pearson closed his mouth. Then the flush of red-hot anger returned. He lifted a fat finger.

"You—"

"Have a seat, Congressman."

I cut him off. Pearson made no move to select a plush patio chair. His jaw worked, almost as though he were chewing gum. I could see the wheels turning in his mind. Estimating what I might know, and whom I might have told. What I might have heard as he finished the call.

The fact that I was here at all should tell him something.

"Well," I said, "I'm going to sit."

I took a patio chair, spinning it to face him. The cushion was thick and comfortable. I interlaced my gloved fingers.

"I don't know what you think you're doing, but I'm a United States—"

"Traitor," I finished. "You're a United States traitor. And to save us both a lot of time, I'm going to tell you exactly what I'm doing—exactly why I'm here, and exactly what I know. Now *sit down.*"

Another brief moment of calculation. Then Pearson did sit down. Maybe because he wanted to hear me out, but probably because he didn't have a choice. He shot me a "*Well?*" look. I went straight for the throat.

"I know you knew about Yemen," I said. "I know you participated in the coverup. I know you've been pocketing Agon's dirty money while funneling billions of taxpayer dollars into their defense contracts. I know you sold us out at the cabin, and while you may not be directly complicit in the death of your own son, we both know Bridgewater made it happen. For reasons beyond my worst estimations of humanity, you're somehow okay with that."

Pearson's lip twitched. His mouth opened, but he didn't speak. I kept going.

"Everything I know has been documented, or is being documented. As we speak, my associates are busy transmitting that evidence to the FBI. To CNN. To investigative reporters at every major news outlet. You may be aware that last night Agon experienced a little...disturbance at their Culpeper facility. That disturbance is drawing a lot of attention. More attention than you can sweep under the rug this time. So whatever you're about to say, and whoever you think you can call...it won't matter. You're done. Agon is done. All your secrets are about to rise from the grave. You can take that to the bank."

I hadn't meant for the conclusion of my speech to contain a pun, but I didn't mind. I watched Pearson swallow hard despite himself. He placed both hands around the arms of his chair. His fingers bit into the metal.

"You're bluffing."

"There's two things I never do, Congressman. I don't bluff, and I don't violate my oaths. You've already managed the latter, several times. So don't waste time with the former."

He blinked. Ran his tongue over tight lips and glanced at my shirt collar.

"I'm not wearing a wire," I said. "I don't need one."

Another very long moment of stillness. At last Pearson seemed to collect himself. Then he leaned back in his chair.

"Okay," he said. "Cards on the table, then. Why are you here?"

His dark eyes glanced down to the surgical gloves encasing my hands. "You gonna kill me?"

"I don't know," I said slowly. "I came here prepared to. I would certainly like to. But I'm not a murderer, and I'm not interested in becoming one. I guess whatever happens next depends on your answer to a very simple question."

Another swallow by Pearson.

"I'm not a perfect man, Congressman," I continued. "I've done a lot of very ugly things, and I'm not above getting my hands dirty when good causes are at stake. I do my best to hold no man to a higher standard than I hold myself. I've already dealt with the murderous scum on the front lines of this thing. Their sins are first degree. Your part in this mess is second degree. Indirect, possibly. So I'm willing to give you the benefit of the doubt. I'm willing to believe this wasn't just about the money. That there was some greater good at stake. That you didn't know just how rotten the bones were."

Hope kindled in Pearson's eyes. A stray trail of sweat ran down his forehead. But he didn't relax. He knew the punchline was coming.

"But?" he prompted.

"But you have to *sell me*." My tone dropped to barely above a growl. "You were elected to lead this country. To do justice. To act with integrity. To tell the truth. You swore an oath. So..."

I raised a finger. "As an American who swore an oath to defend this country against enemies foreign *and* domestic...I want you to *sell me*."

Pearson didn't answer. I saw the calculation behind his eyes again—the question of whether or not I was bluffing. Of whether or not I was fishing for an admission, with an FBI van full of listening devices parked down the street.

I didn't care what he decided. I would sleep well that night either way. But if he was smart, he would feel the corner I had backed him into, and he would take the exit.

He was smart.

"Do you know how many American soldiers have died fighting terror since 9/11?" he asked.

"Over seven thousand," I spat the number out. He didn't seem surprised.

"Plus contractors," he said, "and civilians. The body count is endless, and people are *still* dying."

"Like your son?" I couldn't resist.

"My son died a long time ago, Mr. Sharpe. I sent a bright, brilliant warrior into the Army and got back a shell. A broken ghost of a man..."

Pearson's voice cracked. His gaze dropped.

I wasn't sold.

"It's called PTSD, Congressman. It's a cost of war."

Pearson nodded. "Yes. Yes, it is. Just like the blood and the bodies. You're too young to remember, but my generation was raised fatherless. Vietnam claimed nearly sixty thousand lives. Before that, it was Korea. Forty thousand lives. Then the Second World War—half a *million* Americans."

"Freedom isn't free," I said.

"No." Pearson's gaze turned hard. "It isn't. And it never will be. But it doesn't have to be so damn expensive. We aren't fighting with spears and sticks anymore. The technology Agon is developing will change the world. Soldiers will put on their uniforms and report for duty in offices, not battlefields. They'll push buttons, not triggers. Men like my son will never again be robbed of their youth by the horrors of war."

I raised an eyebrow. "Seriously? That's your sales pitch?"

"Don't get coy with me, boy," Pearson snapped. "People like you are so far down the food chain you don't even know what's best for you. Matty was just like that. All virtue and bravado—blind to the price you're paying. America is drunk on war. We're so intoxicated by it, we don't even realize what we're doing. My work with Agon will change everything. You should *see* what they can do with artificial intelligence. The targeting is *flawless*. You can take out a combatant in his living room. It's revolutionary. It will take the human off the battlefield—the life out of the casualty list."

"Only half of it," I corrected.

Pearson looked confused.

"Those drones aren't built to shoot other drones, Congressman. They're made to kill *people*, and the farther we remove our soldiers from the battlefield, the easier it will be to end those lives without a second thought. Take it from somebody who's actually pulled a trigger in combat—it's hell on earth. It's the worst possible thing we can do as a species, and the only thing that keeps us from doing it over the slightest provocation is the *reality* of it. What you're talking about would make death a video game controlled by greasy-fingered bureaucrats who will never smell the stench of that death. You're a fool if you think that story has a happy ending."

"So you'd send more young Americans to die?" Pearson barked.

"Not for a second—but I was never the one sending them to die in the first place. *You were.* You and your soulless friends. Half the wars you just rattled off could have been avoided under proper leadership. The other half could have at least been shortened. But that's not how the military-industrial complex works, is it? The machine that pays for mansions in Pennsylvania."

Pearson's teeth ground. A fat, red finger shook as it jabbed at me. "You can spew your self-righteous poison, boy, but at the end of the day somebody's got to get the job done. These wars are going to happen whether you like it or not. The inbred animals who hate our freedom will never stop attacking us. So what if we kill a few more than we intended? I'd kill a hundred—no, a *thousand* rag-headed rats to save the life of a single American. That's patriotism, Sharpe! That's leadership!"

His voice boomed over the deck. Spittle landed on my face while his own turned crimson red. A crazy light had overtaken his eyes.

Not just rage. This was lust. Be it for blood or money or something else entirely...it didn't even matter.

I stood up slowly.

"No," I said. "That's insanity. And it's also the wrong answer."

Pearson blinked. His mouth closed. I turned my back, moving across the deck. I heard Pearson stand.

"You'd better consider who you're messing with, son! It's not just a United States congressman—the people I work with are ruthless. You don't want to be their next target. You hear me?"

I stopped near the steps. Looking out over the beautiful rolling countryside, I thought about how peaceful it appeared. About what protected that peace...and what threatened it. I turned around slowly.

"What?" he snapped. "*Now* you're going to kill me?"

My fingers tightened into fists. My heart rate quickened. I inhaled...then slowly shook my head.

"No. I'm still not a murderer. But the thing is, Congressman, I don't think I have to be. Like you said yourself, the people you've climbed into bed with are ruthless. I've set them back, certainly. Upset their apple cart. But I'm just a guy. Once this story breaks, they won't be worried about people like me anymore. They'll be worried about the Department of Justice. About witnesses. About weak links and loose ends."

I gently pulled the gloves off, replacing them in my pockets. I sampled the Pennsylvania air again, and for the first time all week...I relaxed.

"I guess what I'm trying to say is...if I were you, Congressman, I'd *run* to the FBI."

Pearson blanched. His mouth closed. He took a half step forward. I simply turned back to the steps and started toward the forest.

"You're wrong, Sharpe!" Pearson called after me. "You don't know what you're doing—people will *die* because of you!"

I ignored him. By the time I reached the tree line, Pearson's phone was ringing again. He continued to shout, hurling threats and pleas. Deals and compromises.

But I never looked back. I just kept walking.

72

Kelly Davis was like a bloodhound—she might have taken some convincing to begin the hunt, but once she caught the scent, she was unstoppable. Three days after my visit to Pearson's mansion in Pennsylvania, Davis's first investigative report hit the *Washington Signal*—front page.

*WAR MACHINE: DIRTY SECRETS, DEADLY TECHNOLOGY,
AND BETRAYED SOLDIERS.*

Most of the piece was superficial, barely scraping the surface of the details to come. Davis summarized the blue-on-blue strike in Yemen before diving into the deeper story of the Agon machine. There were quotes from Tyler Spraggins and a number of former Agon employees. There were references to an ongoing FBI investigation and deeper corruption that might link back to congress.

There was no direct connection between Davis's piece and a brief column on page three that outlined the unfortunate demise of one Congressman Glenn Pearson, who had been discovered at his Pennsylvania estate stone cold, apparently overdosed on heroin. Whatever connections would be discovered between Agon and the congressman would unfold over time, I was sure. Davis's piece was only the beginning—the first blast of wind in a hurricane that would slowly sweep across the country over the course of months, not hours.

The damage it would wreak would be absolute. I could already envision the protests. The outrage. The congressional hearings. The presidential statements.

I wasn't yet sure if I could envision actual reform. Only time would tell.

I spat a wad of chewing gum over the printed picture of the slain congressman, wadded the paper into a ball, and tossed it into the trash can at the end of my park bench. Glenn Pearson's death wasn't the only one the *Washington Signal* had yet to connect to Agon. The murder of Ronald Jenkins, my encryption specialist, wasn't even on the radar of Davis and her staff, but I had already made certain that his family in Atlanta had recovered the body, assuring him a proper funeral. In the eyes of the law, that case might never be closed. There was little to be done about that.

But the enemy had been destroyed.

Cradling a paper cup of coffee, I surveyed the landscape of American icons spread out before me. Reaching west to east lay the Reflection Pool, encased in a dead grass beltway of the National Mall. To my right sat the bulk of the World War Two monument. Directly ahead, across the Pool, I could see the Vietnam Veterans Memorial. Behind me, the Korean War Veterans Memorial.

More than half a million American casualties, lost in the

endless war against tyranny. Sitting amid them all, slumped on a bench, just trying to keep my hands warm, I couldn't help but wonder.

I wondered if those half-million ghosts would be proud. If they would be honored. If they would respect the decisions I had made.

I didn't doubt they would at least understand. Good soldiers had that in common—none of us are perfect. But we're doing our best. At the end of the day, that's all you can really ask for.

The rustle of dead leaves on the sidewalk caught my attention. Brooke approached from beneath the trees, wrapped in a winter coat, cradling a coffee of her own with a small brown package tucked under one arm. She kept her head down as she reached the bench, offering a nod but not speaking as she sat. She sipped her own coffee, and her gaze darted across the pool to the Vietnam wall. Then the World War Two building.

"I wondered why you picked this spot," she whispered.

"Do you think they have any clue?" I asked. I didn't need to specify whom I was talking about. Our gazes were both drawn naturally to the crowds of civilians drifting past the wall—schoolchildren and tourists with baby strollers. International groups of travelers from Asia and Europe, all laughing and jostling each other as they stumbled along the sidewalk. A few dozen of each.

"No," Brooke whispered.

"I used to resent that," I said.

"You don't anymore?"

I leaned away from the bench, resting my elbows on my knees. I sighed. Sipped coffee. Enjoyed the burn on its way to my stomach.

"War shouldn't exist, Brooke. People like us...we shouldn't exist. I'm not sure if I'll ever understand why we do, but that...*that's* the way humans are meant to live." I gestured with the cup to the tourists. "Innocent. Untarnished. Happy. Some may call it disrespectful...maybe it is. But the way I see it, that's part of what we fought for. We bled so that they never have to know blood. We took the war to the enemy so that the war would never stain our own people. They're able to laugh because they don't know. There's some beauty in that, don't you think?"

Brooke blinked slowly. I glanced sideways and saw a cold edge creep into her ocean eyes.

"I wish I were big enough to see it that way," she said.

I laughed. "If it makes you feel any better, I still want to jack slap the lot of them."

That brought the flicker of a smile to her face. Just a flicker. She rotated the cup and blinked again. Now that cold edge melted, and it turned to a trace of tears instead. She swallowed.

"You brought me here to leave, didn't you?"

I looked at my coffee cup. My own throat grew thick. The rehearsed speech, the practiced explanation, all the words I had planned froze over in my chest. I didn't know what to say. I didn't know where to start. I thought about the wall between Brooke and me that had so quickly developed following that impassioned moment in the cabin.

I'd blamed it on the trauma then. On Dufort's death. On the stress of the mission.

It wasn't until the smoke cleared that I knew in my gut what had really built it. An empty feeling following a moment of would-be passion. A cold reality I had yet to face.

"It's Jacquie, isn't it?" Brooke asked.

I looked up very suddenly. "What? No."

Brooke smiled. "Have you told her that?"

"We're just friends. Old partners."

I could see in her eyes that Brooke didn't believe me, but I knew better than to press the point. I was caught off guard just enough by her question to jar my thoughts back into motion. I breathed deeply. Back traced my thoughts to the root and decided to start there.

"When I...when I lost my fiancée..." I stopped. Brooke didn't pressure. I set the cup down and faced her because she deserved it.

"I thought I'd lost the world. I thought I'd lost the very meaning of life. I could tell when you talked about Matthew that you felt the same about him...that there was something special there, robbed before its time."

Brooke blinked hard, but she didn't look away. I offered a weak smile.

"I've had a lot of flings in my day, Brooke. A lot of one-night stands and misunderstandings. I don't judge myself for that, but...when you've had the real thing—the thing that brings you to life. The thing that grounds you and makes you want to change. The thing that makes you want to give another person the world. When you've found love like that...you don't want anything less. I don't know if I'll ever be able to offer somebody the real thing again, but I know I'm not there yet, and in the meantime I don't want to be the guy who tangles in the sheets and leaves a broken heart. You deserve the real thing."

I held her ocean eyes and waited. Brooke's lip trembled, and a giant tear ran down her cheek. For a moment I thought she might break down, and I questioned everything

I had just said. A hot knife sank into my gut, and I wondered if I should have lied.

But then Brooke smiled. Sad but sincere. She ducked her head.

"Wow. She was a lucky woman."

I flushed. Brooke put a hand on my hand and slid down the bench. Her neck bent. Her lips found mine. She kissed me. Not a passionate kiss. Not the pretext of something hot and wild like I felt in the cabin. Just soft and sweet and as sincere as the sunrise in her eyes.

I kissed back. Brooke squeezed my hand again, then she lifted the package off her lap and extended it toward me. "I got you something."

"Oh?" I cocked an eyebrow. She gestured for me to open it, and I tore through the paper. A black nylon belt was housed within. Very thick and sturdy, with a black metal buckle. It looked to be my size. I squinted, a little confused.

"It's a belt..." I said.

"Yep. But check the back side." She pointed, and I traced the underside of the fabric, touching nothing save stiff nylon until I reached the very back, right where a person's spine would be. Then I felt the pocket. It was invisible, closed by Velcro. When I tore it open, a small metal object fell out.

It was a handcuff key. I laughed.

"In case you ever get kidnapped again," Brooke said.

I rolled the key in my hand and kept smiling. Brooke stood and breathed a slow lungful of the crisp air.

She looked good. She looked like she was going to be okay.

"If you're ever in Kentucky, Mason Sharpe..."

I stood also. I wrapped her in a warm hug. "I'll give you a call, Corporal."

73

J acquie drove me to the airport in the latest of our rental car fleet—nearly sixty minutes of crawling through DC traffic while she kicked back behind the wheel with dark sunglasses slid halfway down her nose and chattered like a teenage girl on crack.

Congressman Pearson. And the investigation. And probable political backlash. And how Matthew's memory would be honored. And how Spraggins would get out of jail. And how the Phoenix Suns just might do it this year. She was starting to believe!

I wanted to throat punch her. I just closed my eyes and smiled instead.

As we neared the airport, she finally slowed down. I opened an eye and noted her blinking a lot, fiddling with the rearview mirror, muttering about the idiot who cut her off. Griping about how much she hated the East Coast.

She caught me looking and muttered a clipped, "What?" then pushed the glasses up her nose.

Jacquie pulled alongside the curb at the drop-off and

turned her face toward the window. She shifted into park but didn't reach for the door. She grew very still.

This was the moment I'd dreaded. The moment I still wasn't sure how to manage. I half expected her to drop out of the car, march her little body around and slap the daylights out of me. Again.

Instead I heard a sniff, and my stomach tightened. I suddenly remembered what Brooke had said and wondered if I'd missed something all these years. Misread something. Possibly even misled, by accident.

I opened my mouth, and Jacquie put up a hand. "Just... give me a second."

I did. She kept her face turned away and scrubbed her cheeks with the back of one thumb. Inhaled slowly and turned.

To my surprise, she had removed her glasses. Red-rimmed eyes were streaked with tears, but she didn't cry now. She set the glasses down.

"I won't drag this out. There's only two things you need to know."

"Okay." I waited.

"The first is...Mia was incredible. One of the best people I've ever known. Better than you deserved, frankly."

I smiled. Jacquie laughed a little.

"You didn't deserve to lose her," Jacquie continued. "But you did. And it sucks. And you have the right to work through it your own way. So...yeah. Just accept that."

"And the second thing?"

Jacquie lifted her chin. "The second thing is...you're a pretty special guy yourself. And you've got a lot of life left to live, and a lot of love left to give. And I just hope that one day...Mia's memory can be a happy one."

I sat very still, unblinking. Unsure what to say.

Jacquie nodded a couple of times, sniffing once. Then somebody blared a horn from behind us, and she rolled her eyes to the ceiling.

"Ugh. Freaking East Coasters, I swear. *I hear you, asshole!*"

She dropped out of the rental in a little ball of piss and vinegar, waving a middle finger at the car behind us. It was a taxi. The driver shouted back in something other than English, then his engine surged, and he raced around as Jacquie shouted profanities after him.

I followed her to the back of the SUV, where she popped the hatch before remembering that I didn't have any luggage —my backpack already rode my right shoulder. Jacquie shut it and stood awkwardly, shifting from one foot to another. Then she seemed to reach a *screw it* point, and threw her arms around me. I hugged back, squeezing her little frame close and blinking back an unexpected blur in my vision.

"Thank you, Jacquie," I whispered.

She released me abruptly, running the back of one hand across her nose and waving the other dismissively.

"What are partners for?"

I pocketed my hands, fingers closing over my thinning wallet and nothing else. I'd already scrapped the second of my two burner phones, smashing it the way I'd smashed the phone at Pearson's house.

No trail left behind.

"Well," Jacquie said, "fly safe, big guy."

She shot me what she must have intended to be a salute. Coming from a woman who'd only ever worn blue uniforms, it didn't look right, but it made me smile. I saluted back and turned for the airport entrance.

"Oh!" Jacquie shouted. "Third thing."

I met her at the front of the SUV, looking over the hood. "Yeah?"

"Freaking *call me*, or I swear I'll do worse than jack slap you."

I laughed. "I will," I said.

And this time, I meant it.

74

My flight to Florida was nonstop. I used the last of my cash to purchase a taxi ride from the Jacksonville airport to the south bank of the Saint Johns River, leaving myself literally penniless. We crossed the river using the blue drawbridge, and I thought of Matthew Pearson one more time.

Spraggins was already out of jail on bail, making arrangements for his buddy's memorial. I might give him a call when I settled back into my truck and found another phone. I felt confident that once Kelly Davis was finished with her investigations, Spraggins would be finished with jail time. Sure, he'd still committed a crime.

But no judge in his right mind would sentence him to any significant incarceration.

The taxi dropped me off at the front entrance of the bank towering alongside the river. I stretched in Florida sunshine and removed my coat, grateful to be back in a temperate climate again. The crime scene tape was gone from the front of the building, and business seemed to be proceeding as usual.

I found my way inside and waited in a stiff lobby chair until a guy in a suit finally approached me. I didn't recognize him. I didn't recognize any of the staff. Maybe the bank had given all the regular people some time off to recover.

Civilians aren't used to automatic gunfire, after all.

"Can I help you, sir?"

I motioned to the guy's office—the same office I'd sat in when Spraggins and Pearson had barreled in, guns blazing—and he closed the door as we settled inside. I dug out my Arizona driver's license and slid it across the table.

"I was here before," I said. "Talking to another guy. I don't see him."

"Oh, right. He's on leave. We had a little...incident last week."

The guy looked all conspiratorial. I raised an eyebrow. "Really?"

He leaned across the desk. Lowered his voice. "Bank robbery. Hostages and automatic weapons. They're still patching the holes."

He pointed through the glass wall of the office to the lobby ceiling. I noted white spots of spackle smeared by dust. Whatever the marks were, they didn't cover bullet holes.

"I hope everybody is okay," I said.

The guy sat back in his chair, rotating my driver's license in one hand. "Oh, yeah. I mean, people are a little rattled. Who wouldn't be? I'm a volunteer sheriff's deputy, so I've seen this stuff before. They'll be okay."

A confident nod.

He rattled a password into the keyboard, then went to work typing my details into the machine.

"I actually saw a news story this morning," he continued. "Seems some hotshot reporter up in DC thinks the robbers weren't after money. Can you believe that?" He laughed.

"What were they after?"

He snorted. "Something in a safety-deposit box. Some hard drive or something. But I don't buy it. It's always about the money, man. Always."

I thought of Pearson—not the soldier. The congressman. His blazing face and curled lips. The hundreds of thousands flowing into his personal accounts.

And I said nothing.

"So what can I do for you, Mr. Sharpe? Did you want to open an account?"

"Actually...I'm here for something else."

"Oh?"

"Your bank sent me an email a few weeks back. About an IRA...in my late fiancée's name. Apparently, I'm the beneficiary."

"Right..." He clicked and scrolled. Scrolled and clicked. I just waited. Then his eyes widened a little.

"Here we are. Ms. Mia Hayes, Phoenix, Arizona?"

"That's right." My voice softened a little. He shifted awkwardly, like he wanted to say something, but didn't know what to say, and wasn't sure if he should simply let the moment slide.

He was a volunteer sheriff's deputy. He'd seen this before, but never learned how to handle it. I understood.

"I'm very sorry," he said, at last.

The words hit me in the chest, just the way they had six dozen times since that gut-wrenching morning three hundred and seventy-two days prior. I braced myself for the pain. For the anger. For the emptiness. For the cloud of nothing.

But none of it came. I felt the sadness, but I didn't fight it. I just nodded.

"Thank you," I said.

The guy clicked a pen and conducted some meaningless maneuvers with the mouse. Then he cleared his throat.

"Well, Mr. Sharpe, I have good news for you. Your fiancée was a good saver. She left you a nice chunk. We can transfer it into an IRA in your name, if you'd like. That would probably be the best thing. Save you some taxes. I can tell you about some investment options..."

His voice faded away, and the suit and bobbing head in front of me followed it. I thought once more of Mia. My Mia. The good saver. The shameless laugher. The life of the party.

The real thing.

And for the first time, I felt the hole, but the pain faded.

"Mr. Sharpe?"

I blinked again. The banker cocked his head. There was a brochure spread across the desk. Little white letters on a field of blue, all about interest rates and retirement programs.

"Can I introduce you to a retirement specialist?" he pressed.

I looked at the brochure. Pictured Mia squirreling that money away for God only knew how many years. For her family. For her future. I hadn't even known about the account, but thinking of her made me smile.

The family had evaded her. But the love lived on.

"I think I'll take it in cash," I said.

"In...cash?" It was as though I spoke Greek.

"Right."

"Uhm...okay. I have to advise you, Mr. Sharpe. That isn't the most responsible conversion of this account. There would be fees. If I could—"

"Take the fees," I said. "Bring me the cash."

The banker didn't argue any further. He had to get a manager. There were documents to sign. A visit to the vault. A lot of counting and formality.

And then I was handed a cash bag with a zippered top—forty-two thousand dollars in large bills housed within. The full balance of the account, minus the fees.

I put it in my cargo pocket and walked out of the bank. Warm Florida sunshine spilled across my face, and I breathed in salt air from the river. I walked the one mile along the south bank to the long-term parking garage where I'd left my truck.

It was dusty and smelled a little like gasoline as I heaved my way in. I sat facing the river from the third floor of the garage. Thoughts of Brooke and Dufort and Grieves and Spraggins and Matthew Pearson all faded away. Even thoughts of Jacquie faded away.

I thought about the cash envelope and how many months it would carry me through campsites and cheap hotels. At least a year, with a little frugality. If I picked up some odd jobs, a lot longer.

I could keep living this way indefinitely. Just breathing. Just meeting people and reading books and playing the old violin on the floorboard next to me.

For three hundred seventy-two days, it had felt like a coping mechanism. But somehow, it now felt different. It now felt like recovery.

I started the truck and found the road. I rumbled

through town, then turned south because south was a left-hand turn, and my right-hand blinker was blown.

It seemed like as good a direction as any. With open road and no place to be, I was ready to enjoy the quiet again. It would never bring Mia back, and I might never again be ready for the real thing. But for the first time since I watched her slip away, I was ready to let go.

I was ready to heal.

ABOUT THE AUTHOR

Logan Ryles was born in small town USA and knew from an early age he wanted to be a writer. After working as a pizza delivery driver, sawmill operator, and banker, he finally embraced the dream and has been writing ever since. With a passion for action-packed and mystery-laced stories, Logan's work has ranged from global-scale political thrillers to small town vigilante hero fiction.

Beyond writing, Logan enjoys saltwater fishing, road trips, sports, and fast cars. He lives with his wife and three fun-loving dogs in Alabama.

Did you enjoy *Fire Team?* Please consider leaving a review on Amazon to help other readers discover the book.

www.loganryles.com

ALSO BY LOGAN RYLES

Mason Sharpe Thriller Series

Point Blank

Take Down

End Game

Fire Team

Made in the USA
Monee, IL
16 December 2023

49491781R00268